The Karthagans have regained their ancient powers of manipulating nature, but at the price of madness. In their lust for control, they've destroyed their island and most of their race. They come now to Belega, where one of them, Camron, seeks domination over the known world. The Mage has come from the northern continent of Sennia to bring peace, but finding his strength no match for the coming struggle, he passes his abilities on to Natan, who only desires a simple life.

Now only Natan has the ability to stop Camron, but the personal cost is more than he imagines. It is only with the combined strength of his friends, his Karthagan lover, Kavi, and his deep desire to bring lasting peace to the earth, that he finds the courage to overcome Camron and restore balance to the world.

BELEGA

The Karthagans, Book One

Dianne Hartsock

A NineStar Press Publication
www.ninestarpress.com

Belega

© 2024 Dianne Hartsock

Cover Art © 2024 Melody Pond

First Edition, March 2024

ISBN: 978-1-64890-746-3

Also available in eBook, ISBN: 978-1-64890-745-6

CONTENT WARNING:

This book contains sexually explicit content, which may only be suitable for mature readers. Depictions of some violence, kidnapping, off-page rape, and death of secondary characters.

Chapter One

"I HAVE YOU."

Natan rose into a low crouch from the scrub brush, careful not to scrape his cloak against the foliage, and searched his memory for the trick Kavi had taught him. Oh, yes. He took a deep breath and let it out slowly, releasing all worries. His expectations. Letting go. The clip of the horse's hooves echoed in his mind, and he concentrated on that, the smell of the horse, the feel of its hide, the oats on its breath. He became aware of a vague fear in the animal's mind.

But the tenuous connection broke without time to try again as the soldier leading the roan brought him to a stop, his gaze sweeping the path ahead, alert. Gathering his scattered wits as best he could, Natan lunged to his feet and dove for the soldier's legs. They went down hard, Natan gasping at the whoosh of air against his cheek as the horse reared, hooves barely missing him. Knowing he was no match for the soldier physically, he scrambled to jab a knee into the man's back, then drew his thin knife and pressed it against the pulse at his throat, feeling him stiffen.

"Hold very still," he warned. The soldier didn't move as the keen blade inadvertently nicked his skin. Recalling Kavi's imprisonment in an Amara prison, Natan gritted his teeth and swung his arm back, then brought the hilt of the knife down sharply on his vulnerable skull. With a grunt, the man went limp. Natan climbed to his feet, cursing under his breath as the horse disappeared up the trail. He rolled the man over so his face wouldn't be in the dirt, making sure he could breathe without difficulty.

Frowning at the thick trees crowding them, he left his captive a moment to scout the vicinity, at last coming upon a small clearing off the trail. It took some effort to drag the unconscious soldier to the spot, and a relief to roll the heavy body down the last few feet. He retrieved leather strips from his pack, bound the man's hands and feet to a small sapling, then examined the soldier's head once again. Although the purplish welt had swollen, the bleeding had stopped.

Natan watched the soldier a moment and shook his head in disgust when he didn't waken. "Hit him too hard," he muttered, angry with himself. He built a small fire as the air grew chilly and sat with his back to a tree while he waited for the soldier to regain consciousness. Darkness descended on the forest, and he chewed his lips in growing anxiety. His dear friend, Captain Bryon of Amara, along with Lieutenant Jaden, had gone to Nagal to petition the Mage to help them recover Kavi. Had they reached the city yet? If so, Natan would need to be at the Lake of Glass to meet with them in a few short days. A lifetime, as long as Kavi remained captive.

He sharpened his knife on a whetstone to pass the time while the soldier remained unconscious. As the stars came out, an ache crept into his chest as he thought of Kavi and how they used to lie awake, watching for falling stars. Natan would make them tea in a little pot over the fire; then they'd wrap in warm blankets and talk quietly while the sky wheeled overhead. Sometimes they made love, Kavi's warm sleek body pliant as Natan searched out new ways to draw those sweet breathy moans from his lips.

And then it had all ended. Natan closed his eyes at the jab of pain in his heart. The Nagal soldiers had come to their camp and dragged Kavi away, laughing when Natan struggled, and methodically beat him senseless. That had been two weeks ago, and every attempt he'd made to find his lover had failed. The last time he'd been in Amara he'd been threatened with imprisonment himself.

He would do Kavi no good behind iron bars, he reminded himself.

Natan opened his eyes to find the captive staring at him from where he'd slumped against the tree. Natan went over and helped him to a sitting position.

"What's your name?" he asked with ice in his voice. The man continued to stare at him, insolent.

Natan looked him over carefully. "Let me guess. You're dressed as a Nagal soldier, though you're obviously not one. Maybe a deserter? Maybe a Barkuit spy?" He watched the soldier's face as he named the rival country, then leaned closer to whisper, "What of Kavi?"

"That trash?" the man asked in surprise, then yelped when Natan lunged at him, knife slipping into his hand.

"Say that again and I'll slit your throat. Now, what is your name?"

"Captain Syros Reed."

Natan sat back on his heels, fury hot in his chest. "Speak."

"I could tell you where they mean to bury him," Syros drawled, holding Natan's gaze, and smiled slightly at his sharply indrawn breath. "That is, once Landlan has drawn the secret to the Karthagans' power over nature out of him. The power the Barkuit army would kill to use in our coming conflict. Kavi was alive the last time I saw him, but I heard they mean to bury him soon. If you hurry, he may still be breathing. I don't know."

"And you didn't help him?" With a sudden enraged cry Natan drove his knife into the sapling inches from Syros's face. "He'd better be alive, for your sake."

He left his water skin for Syros, should the man succeed in freeing himself, then gave the soldier no more thought as he snatched up his pack and settled into the long run ahead, determined to be at the Lake of Glass on time.

KAVI CAME AWAKE with the echo of Natan's desperate cries ringing in his ears, and he opened his eyes to blackness and cold stone. His head throbbed as he sat up, and he put his shackled hands to his forehead, wincing when his fingers came away sticky with blood. Then he remembered the well-placed kick that had earned him the blow from Landlan and grinned. If he hadn't lost consciousness, he might have been able to find a way to escape while the man dealt with his pain.

Almost blind in the darkness, Kavi crawled along the floor, the chains binding his ankles clinking, until he reached a wall and sat with his back to its damp surface, wrinkling his nose at the smell of decay. His wrists and ankles burned where the skin had been scraped raw from the rusting shackles. Damn, he didn't want to be there anymore. Had it been a week? More?

Too long.

The clang of a bolt being drawn on the door startled him, and Kavi climbed stiffly to his feet. Light from the wall sconces in the hallway spilled into the room, making him cry out as it struck his eyes. It didn't hurt but appearing weak always served him well.

"You're still alive. Excellent. Shall we burn you today?"

Landlan seemed to savor every word he spoke, and Kavi willed his pounding heart to slow.

"Let's not rush things," he replied flippantly, then bit his tongue. For once, he should keep his mouth shut. His blood chilled as cold brown eyes looked him over. He swayed on his feet, frozen, exhausted, and Landlan leaned forward to flick his smooth cheek with a hard nail.

"Let's try this one last time. Tell me why you're here," Landlan demanded, and took Kavi's chin in a firm grip when he would have flinched away. "Your people were exiled from this continent years ago. Why break the treaty?" Landlan leaned closer and Kavi saw the glitter in his eyes. "What do you hope to find? Power? Wealth?" He suddenly made a sign against evil. "Do you hope to raise the dead? Rebuild the Karthagan army?"

The questions caught Kavi by surprise, and he laughed, too late realizing his mistake. Giving an outraged cry, Landlan viciously backhanded him, cutting his lip. The man struck several more times, his ornate silver ring slicing the delicate skin of Kavi's cheeks.

Landlan grabbed Kavi's tunic, pulling him close. "You listen, bastard. Thirty years ago, we drove your filthy race from our shores, you with your bright eyes and depraved magic. Your people should have stayed in their own country. We never wanted you here. So many of our people died, caught in your bloody civil war on our land. We're still healing from the destruction wrought by your people's perversion of the natural world. We won't let that happen again. I was young, but I remember the Barkuit soldiers routing your kind from every corner of Belega. It was either death or the sea for you. You should have chosen death. You'll soon wish you had."

Grabbing Kavi by his dark hair, Landlan wrenched him toward the door. Kavi stumbled, his legs numb, and he winced at the bite of metal from the shackles on his ankles. Landlan shoved him through the open doorway, Kavi cursing when he almost fell.

Twisting upright, he saw a leer spring on Landlan's face and his patience snapped. He charged forward, driving his head into Landlan's chin. Damn! The man was made of stone. With a cry of rage, Landlan grabbed his hair again and slammed Kavi against the doorjamb until his head rang. With a brutal jab in the stomach for good measure, Landlan slung Kavi effortlessly over a shoulder then made his way down the hallway. Kavi retched, sick and dizzy as he swung from side to side, bouncing hard against Landlan's back. In a moment they were outside, Kavi fighting the bile rising in his throat.

He felt too weak to struggle and let his mind drift into a gray haze, pulse roaring in his ears as they crossed the yard, gravel crunching under Landlan's boots. But even that small reprieve was denied him, as all too soon he was dropped with a thud to the ground. Kavi blinked and tried to focus on his surroundings, but the night was pitch dark except for the torchlight coming from the stone building behind them. Jumping at the harsh sound of metal over rock, he watched with blurry eyes as Landlan dragged a large grate from an opening in the ground behind the prison.

"Come, my dear." Landlan helped him to his feet and hauled him toward the hole. Kavi felt sick and confused, not sure what was happening.

Not until he stood at the edge of the pit did he understand, so he drew back in horror.

"No, you don't." Landlan grabbed his shoulders. "Goodbye, my sweet," he whispered in Kavi's ear, then gave a quick shove. Kavi screamed as he went over the edge, dropping quickly, his breath driven from him as he struck the hard dirt at the bottom. He rolled to his back with a groan and stared at the circle of stars that slowly disappeared as the iron lid slid into place. Once again, blackness surrounded him. And something else was with him, smooth and hard, with bits of cloth attached. Also, the stench…

He cried out in recognition and struggled to his knees, but with his hands and feet still shackled, there was no way out of the well.

"Natan, I need you!" he cried into the darkness, desperate and alone, then cringed as echoes clanged around him. There was no reply.

Chapter Two

BASAL CROUCHED BEHIND the wooden barrier they'd desperately erected during the night, nerves stretched taut. The Barkuit army had attacked Nagal at dawn, a minor skirmish to test their defenses. They'd learned a hard lesson and backed off, but Basal could hear them reassembling out of bow range.

He wiped impatiently at the blood and sweat that dripped into his eyes from a gash on his forehead. He'd ducked in time to save his head, dispatching the enemy soldier with a quick thrust of his short blade, but others of his men had lost their lives before the Barkuits had fallen back. Scouts now reported that the city was nearly encircled by the enemy. Basal grinned wolfishly, knowing Nagal had a few surprises set for them. And the Mage was with them.

A slight shudder ran over him as he crouched lower behind the barrier. The Mage. He'd heard rumors of the man last fall, and now the sorcerer came from the north, days ahead of the Barkuit army. Friend or foe? He wasn't sure, though he was quickly coming to trust him.

A shout went up as the sun rose, and the Barkuit soldiers began to stride across the clearing before the city walls. Light glinted on their curved swords and the bits of metal worked into their leather jerkins. Basal and his men remained in the shadow of the gates and waited for the army to come within sword's reach.

Governor Basal looked over the dozen or so men with him, young and fearless. There hadn't been a war since their grandfather's time, so the battle seemed more a game and adventure to them. Basal knew that would soon change as he watched the more experienced Barkuit soldiers draw near, grim-faced and confident. And why not? They'd already proven their prowess.

He gripped his sword as the enemy drew near, rising smoothly to his feet. "Ready, men?" The opposing army jeered and brandished their swords, and Basal heard their cry taken up around the city walls as the battle once again resumed on all sides. The heat of battle entered him then, and he closed his mind to the butchery he had to do. He felled his first two men easily, others falling back from the fierceness of his attack. They must have thought him mad as he recklessly charged their ranks, but he wanted this to end swiftly.

A sudden movement to his right caught his eye, and he watched as a stocky figure dashed from behind a screen of rocks on the hillside to slip down behind the enemy. Another, taller figure followed. He saw them jump a man, then lost sight of them as they went down in a heap. Fools. How did they think two could stand against the whole Barkuit army? Without a clear plan, he yelled and rushed the enemy in their direction.

"To the governor!" a soldier yelled and the men took up the call. Basal found himself suddenly with an army at his back. The Barkuit soldiers gave way at the brutal assault, the heart driven from them as they lost man after man. At last a single clear note of a horn was heard over the battlefield, and the Barkuit army slowly retreated. Bells rang from the city walls, calling the Nagal soldiers back.

Basal drew rein and his soldiers came to a stop around him. They were still some distance from the two figures he'd seen, but they stood alone now amidst the fallen, the Barkuit soldiers having deserted the area. Basal waved his sword, and the taller person lifted a hand. Nagal soldiers, by their uniforms. Probably on their way to the city. He'd see them soon enough. For the moment, his army needed food and rest while the respite lasted.

Turning his horse, he motioned, and his weary soldiers started for the city gates and what ease they'd find within its walls before the battle commenced once more.

"NOT THE BEST plan, Jaden," Captain Bryon said dryly, but a grim laugh escaped him as he cleaned the blade taken from the soldier they'd overwhelmed. A good thing Governor Basal had driven back the Barkuit army or their quest to retrieve the Mage for Natan would have been short-lived.

"We needed to get to the city. Shall we make our way there now?" Lieutenant Jaden returned Bryon's brief grin as he slipped a long knife into his belt, then waved toward the gates.

Bryon shook his head. "In a moment." He liked Jaden, but the soldier could sometimes be headstrong. He stretched stiff muscles and sighed. Becoming involved in the political wars of Belega was something he hadn't foreseen, preferring the more peaceful existence in the garrison at Amara. But when Natan had asked for his aide… Well, be couldn't deny him.

Bryon drew a troubled breath. The area around them was strangely silent. With the battle over, there should at least have been birdsong in the trees. Something was off… He sheathed the blade and walked beneath the copse of pines close by. The sun was hot, so he reached for the water flask at his side, drank, and passed it to Jaden. A flutter through the trees caught his eye, and his blood became frozen.

"They have captives?"

Jaden's gaze shot to his face, then he looked to where Bryon pointed through the trees. A ragged tent stood in a clearing, unguarded, with several drooping figures bound to trees by the entrance. The quiet in the glen was unnerving.

"Probably from the surrounding farms," Jaden confirmed, dismayed.

Fury blazed through Bryon. The innocent were always the first to suffer in war. "Come on," he murmured, expecting a trap. Unless…there was no one left to guard. He approached the tent with a heavy heart. The men bound to the trees were obviously dead, throats cut. Trusting Jaden to watch his back, Bryon cautiously parted the tent flaps, restive as his eyes adjusted to the dimness. There seemed to be many objects, but so oddly shaped it took a moment for him to realize what they were.

"It can't be!"

Jaden joined him and lost his breath in a sharp hiss; he turned his head to retch violently.

Bryon swiveled and strode quickly into the forest toward the city. Appalled, he pushed the palms of his hands against his eyes to escape the horror he'd seen. They were dead, all dead, tied together in bunches, women, children, and even a few odd animals.

Jaden caught up, but as they stepped back onto the battlefield, the clear notes of a trumpet rang through the air. They watched as Lord Basal rode from the city on his large bay, the counselors Garrett and Emile were on either side, the Mage riding behind. Soldiers marched in the rear with the flag of parley held high.

The company silently crossed the field and halted at the sparse tree line, close to them, then waited while the Barkuits assembled. A small group of soldiers marched toward them, led by a tall, broad-shouldered man in black leather and velvet. Basal dismounted, as did the Mage.

"My lord Basal Naguth." The broad man opened his arms as he approached, his voice booming across the field.

"My lord Franz Gargary," Basal replied with a curt bow.

Gargary stopped and placed his hands on his hips with a leer for the horsemen.

"Mage," he acknowledged at last with an insolent nod. Gregor merely stared placidly at him until Gargary turned away with a scowl. "We accept your surrender," he exclaimed magnanimously.

The Nagal soldiers sputtered in outrage, and Basal raised his hand for silence. "Don't be absurd, Gargary. I want to know what it will take for you to leave our land. I think you've misjudged our strength and need a way to depart but still save face. We've come to offer you that."

"Ha!" Gargary glanced sideways at his men. "Come, let's talk."

He motioned away from the others and the two men walked out of hearing. The Mage watched them thoughtfully a moment, then made himself comfortable on the grass, pulling his robes, dark as his skin, around him. The opposing soldiers remained tense and glared across the short distance at each other. Gregor ignored them and closed his eyes.

Bryon made his way to his side, hand loose on the sword at his belt. The very air vibrated with the passions and fears of the men. "Gregor?" he hesitated as the tension thrummed in his ears. "What's happening?"

"The lords are negotiating peace." Gregor let go of a long-held breath and opened his eyes. "I should like to say it's good to see you, but you've chosen a very dangerous time to make an appearance. Basal fears treachery. What is so important?"

"Natan sent us," Jaden put in urgently. The Mage sat up straight, face going grim.

"Kavi was taken by the Amara council for questioning several weeks ago," Bryon explained. "We haven't seen anything of him since, and Natan has grown concerned. He seeks your help."

"And naturally a captain of the guard and his lieutenant act as his messengers," Gregor observed, curious.

Bryon's face heated. "He is like my own son, Gregor, as you are well aware. Jaden is his cousin. We would not fail to help him. And sending us should tell you how grave he finds the matter." Anger sparked in Bryon's chest. "And you brought the Karthagan, Kavi, to Belega, from the isle where his people have been banished. Why, his presence threatens the very peace Belega strives for, while our enemies will stop at nothing to learn the secret of his powers. Do you not have some responsibility to him?"

A sliver of fear traveled Bryon's spine when the Mage pressed his lips together, but then Gregor let out a slow breath. "Very well. I will return to Amara as soon as may be—" he broke off and rose to his feet as the governors of the two provinces shook hands and walked back to the waiting companies.

"It's done. Back to camp." Lord Gargary waved a lofty hand at his men. "I'll take my leave, Lord Basal. Long peace to both our peoples."

"Long peace, Gargary. As soon as our captives are returned."

"Of course, of course," Gargary was already turning away. "The prisoners will be released in the same condition in which we took them, let me assure you."

"My lord!" Bryon shouted, appalled, and the Nagal men tensed. Basal looked keenly at his face, then turned sharply to Jaden who held the same horrible truth in his anguished features. He swiveled in rage to the Barkuit lord, who merely laughed. A glittering blade suddenly appeared in his hand, and he made a quick jab at Basal.

Basal dodged, but with a roar, the armies converged. The clash of their weapons rang in Bryon's ears. He saw Councilman Garrett go down and Emile stand over his body, sword flashing. Harsh cries from the forest announced the arrival of more Barkuit soldiers. Bryon rallied the horsemen around the governor until Basal and the Mage had mounted.

They took off for the gates and Bryon grabbed Jaden's arm. "Let's go!" They ran across the open field and saw the horsemen enter the city. The bells clamored along the walls. Basal turned at the gates to check their progress. A Nagal soldier went down beside Jaden with an arrow in his leg. Bryon flung an arm around him to rush him forward. At last, they cleared the archway and the gates were slammed against the full force of the Barkuit army.

BASAL STOOD ON the parapet of the tower and looked over his city, his face utterly weary. So many losses that day. His people had been incensed by the Barkuit treachery. They'd fought the larger army with a ferocity that surprised and then frightened them. Nagal had won the day, and even as Basal stood on the wall, he could see the Barkuit army routed. He'd had trouble recalling his men from the battlegrounds, but they needed to rest. Tomorrow would be time enough to regroup, bury their dead, and ensure the Barkuits had left their lands. He knew the war was far from over; Gargary would never give up so easily. But at least they had a little breathing space.

He rubbed his face, then sighed in deep frustration. This was a war he had never wanted. How was he to convince Gargary of the same? He stepped from the parapet and strode restlessly along the balcony. The sun was low in the sky, so he moved out of the shadows of the tower and into sunlight. The Mage sat there against the warm stones, his black robes wrapped tightly about his thin body as he watched the setting sun. The sadness in his eyes touched Basal's heart, so he sat beside him in quiet sympathy.

"Things didn't go well today, Gregor," he said simply, and the sorcerer nodded. Basal rested his head back against the stones and closed his tired eyes. He'd sat up there with the Mage a few evenings ago, the sun already setting. They'd laughed in the easy comradeship that had sprung up between them. Gregor had described himself as a teacher and explorer, and Basal couldn't help but be fascinated by his stories of faraway nations and cultures.

The Mage was returning to his homeland of Sennia across the Belegan Sea after wandering in neighboring countries. As soon as his apprentice, Kavi, joined him, they'd leave to study the lands between Nagal and the sea as they made their way to the northern coast. But now Kavi had been taken…

"I cannot express my concern and sorrow at Kavi's disappearance," Basal said haltingly, and winced at the swift pain that crossed Gregor's face.

"I shouldn't have left him," Gregor confessed. His next words startled Basal. "Mostly I had hoped to help his people. There is a wrongness on the Isle of Wind that eludes me, hard as I sought to uncover its source while I was there. Almost a wrongness in nature itself. Kavi is a man of keen intelligence, gifted in his control and manipulation of the natural world. With his aid, I had hoped to find the root of the malady, and then send him home to repair the damage. But I have underestimated the greed and lust for the Karthagan power many still hold in this country. I can only hope to find him safe now."

Gregor stirred and drew a deep breath to continue. "The information I've gathered is still relevant. Lord Gargary's wife, Sara, gave birth to a healthy boy three months ago and is not yet recovered. We know Gargary would give a great deal to be with them in the northern city of Siagan, where Sara is staying with her family. Hence the parley. What I hadn't perceived is that, in his enormous greed, he would allow his young wife to suffer alone rather than give up the chance to win the Southern Territories for his son." Gregor hung his head. "This war is my responsibility alone, as is all the deaths that have occurred this day because of my short-sightedness."

"No, my lord Mage," Basal protested, his voice steel. "Gargary alone is responsible, and he will be held accountable, one way or another."

Quick steps sounded on the stonework, and Bryon appeared around the corner. "My lords—" He gave a short bow, hesitated, then continued. "—may I speak with you?"

Basal motioned for him to join them, but the soldier chose to pace. After a moment, Gregor cleared his throat. "You wish us to leave for Amara?"

"Yes!" Bryon stopped, visibly fighting to rein in his temper. "Forgive me. But you know Natan, Mage. He would not ask for help unless utterly certain. He…senses things. Kavi is in danger, and Natan begs for your help."

With an inward sigh, Basal rose to his feet, hating what he had to say as Gregor climbed to his feet as well. "You cannot go, Gregor. We need you here. You know as well as I that Gargary will return, and your presence gives the soldiers confidence. And if Gargary proves the stronger, we will have need of your magic."

Basal held his breath. He had no claim on the sorcerer. Gregor could come and go as he chose. That he had sided with Nagal had been a blessing. Basal silently urged him to choose them once again. "Surely the guessed-at peril to the Karthagan shouldn't supersede the very real danger here?"

"If Natan says Kavi is in jeopardy, there can be no doubt," Bryon put in. "And Landlan, the council leader in Amara, holds a special hatred for the Karthagan people since the war. Would you have Kavi's death on your conscience?" He spoke to Gregor, but Basal knew the words were directed to him as well.

Gregor stood in contemplative silence, head bowed. Watching him, Basal caught the slight shake of his head as he came to a decision, and keen disappointment swept him.

"The Karthagans are a unique people," Gregor observed, looking at him. "Bright and quick to learn, living close to the natural world. One can't help but feel drawn to them. And Kavi has proven to be the most gifted of them all. I know you are in peril here, Basal. I do not leave you lightly. But the world is in danger, and Kavi has a part to play. I must ensure he is here to see it through."

Basal held up his hands. "Do what you must, Gregor, but please, return swiftly. We will need you with us these coming days."

"My lord," Gregor bowed, then hesitated and startled Basal by pulling him into a rough embrace. "Hold fast. I will return," he promised.

Bryon shifted restlessly on his feet, so Gregor gave him a decisive nod. "Let us go," he said, an almost desperate note in his voice.

Bryon hesitated. "Lieutenant Jaden—"

"Stays with the governor," Gregor said adamantly. His gaze slid to Basal. "I shan't deprive Basal of both his best soldiers."

Bryon snorted but followed Gregor as he turned away. Basal watched them hurry into the tower, to emerge a few moments later into the courtyard below. The Mage's cloak billowed behind him as they made their way to the stables, Bryon shifting a pack on his shoulder: meager supplies for their journey.

"Peace," Basal murmured as they departed the gates. His gaze traveled to the tree line and Gargary's camp in the distance. A heaviness settled on his heart. "Peace to us all."

Chapter Three

NATAN LOPED ALONG paths and barely discernible deer trails through the forest he'd spent his life in. The moonlight helped but he would have done well enough without it. How many seasons had he and Bryon hunted these same pathways? He frowned, regretting the knife he'd left with the captive soldier, a gift from Bryon. There was another strapped to his ankle, small but deadly, but he wasn't as practiced with it as he was with the larger blade. Too late to exchange them. His temper always did get the better part of wisdom.

He dropped to a walk as he approached the lake, fighting to catch his breath. He was already a day late meeting with Bryon and his instinct told him to hurry. Or maybe it was the Mage reaching out to him. How was he to know? Coming to a sudden break in the forest, he paused, awe sweeping through him. The water stretched out before him, glowing as if frozen in the moonlight.

"So lovely," he whispered.

A sound broke the stillness and he raised his head, listening. Hooves clomped on a nearby trail, drawing closer. Natan chewed his lips. There was enough time to hide, but if this was the help he'd been expecting, he didn't want them to pass him by. He held his ground but pulled the small knife from its holder, palming it in his left hand. He'd surprised more than one attacker with the hidden blade.

Two horses emerged onto the sandy bank of the lake and Natan's shoulders slumped in relief. Bryon. He sheathed the knife and trotted over to him, calling out as he approached. The horses were brought to a stop and the soldier slid from the saddle, meeting him with open arms.

"Natan, I was hoping we wouldn't miss you in the dark."

"I have some news—" Natan's throat tightened on a knot of pain, and Bryon pulled him into a rough embrace. Natan sighed, pressing his hot eyes to his shoulder. Bryon's uniform smelled of sweat and dust and horse, familiar, comforting. Natan had been orphaned when fever took his parents, Bryon the only man who'd given a damn about the lonely child surviving in the shack by the river, making sure Natan didn't starve or freeze during the long winters.

Bryon nudged him back to search his face. "What is it?"

Natan swallowed. "They plan to kill him. They may already have done so." His voice broke while he blinked back tears.

The man with Bryon shifted in his saddle. "No. I still feel his spark."

Natan's gaze jumped to him, a dark figure with a sheen of moonlight on his ebony skin. He stepped closer and made an awkward bow. "Mage. Thank you for coming."

The man seemed not to hear him, his gaze on the bright lake. "There is a great energy here. What is this place?"

Bryon smiled slightly. "I call it the Lake of Glass, but what's its true name is, I couldn't say. Not many people come this way. The main road to Amara is farther east."

"It should be called the Lake of Wonder."

The enchanter swung from the saddle and knelt beside the luminous water, reverently touching the still surface. He watched, seeming mesmerized, as circles spread out from the contact.

Natan shifted on his feet, looking from the water to the trees standing over them, then at the nearly full moon overhead. Pushing aside his awe of the sorcerer, he shot Bryon a worried glance, skin twitching. It was all he could do not to grab a horse and race to Amara, where Kavi was being held, the danger be damned. "We should go."

"We will," Bryon assured him. "Forgive me for being late to return. The city of Nagal is besieged by the Barkuit army, so it took me some time to retrieve the Mage. Governor Basal was reluctant to let Gregor go." They watched the sorcerer stir the water again. "Give him a moment."

"No, Natan is right." Gregor reluctantly left the shoreline. "But I'd like to return here when the chance is available."

He mounted his horse and guided the animal into the trees. Quickly, Bryon swung into his own saddle, then lifted Natan up behind him. They followed the sorcerer, crouching low in the saddle as the trees closed in around them. The Mage set a quick pace, seeming sure of their path. Natan clung to Bryon a little tighter, knowing the danger of a misstep in the darkness.

"Gregor will keep us safe."

Natan wished he shared Bryon's confidence in the magic user. The

Mage's reputation was widespread, both as a teacher and as a man of strange talents. He claimed to have come from an Isle off Belega's northern coast. Perhaps he had. Those waters were strange. The Karthagans also claimed they came from the north, a race of people with incomprehensible powers, dangerous. It was only through great loss of life that the Barkuit army had driven them from Belega onto the Isle of Wind to the west.

The Mage had spent some time with the Karthagans, though Natan had trouble believing he'd returned to Belega only a short two months before, bringing Kavi with him. So much of Natan's life had changed since then. He wondered again why Gregor had taken a Karthagan as his apprentice. Heat gathered in his gut when he pictured Kavi's flawless olive skin and dark soulful eyes. Then pain stabbed at him. Kavi had permitted Natan to touch his body. Had he ever reached his heart?

He sighed and rested his head on Bryon's strong back, giving himself over to the motion of the horse. Belega was unsettled, the country divided in two, Nagal in the south, Barkuit to the north. Barkuit had long been threatening the border and now brought the war to Nagal's capital city. Did Nagal have the strength to drive them back?

He rubbed his tired eyes. His first concern was to rescue Kavi. Best leave the politics to the soldiers.

They reached Amara by first light, but where Natan and Bryon both urged caution, the Mage jumped from his horse and strode headlong into the council building. They hastened to follow, Natan noting that all who saw Gregor's grim face stepped quickly to the side. Crossing the room, they descended to the prison rooms below. Natan's heart stumbled when they found them empty.

"You're too late," a voice sneered.

The Mage turned, pinning the speaker to the wall with his brilliant gaze. "What do you mean?"

Councilman Landlan tried to look away, but Gregor gripped his chin and made him meet his stare. "Speak!"

Landlan narrowed his eyes, jerking his chin out of his grasp. "Find your own answers, witch."

Disgust swept Gregor's face. "Get out of my sight," he said and turned his back, surveying the empty rooms along the corridor. Natan shivered at Landlan's soft laughter as he left them, but the Mage entered one of the cells. A little fearful, Natan followed, then stood in the doorway, Bryon at his shoulder, as the sorcerer paused in the center of the stone floor. There were no windows, only the flickering light from the wall sconces in the hallway illuminating his dark figure.

The Mage opened wide his arms and Natan heard his quickly indrawn breath. "So many voices…" Gregor's own voice was tinged with wonder, but Natan saw pain flicker over his features as if he listened to words they couldn't hear. Horror appeared on Gregor's face, and he brought his hands sharply together. "Enough!"

The released energy swept outward through the room and crashed into the cell walls. Natan ducked, covering his head with his arms as the stone walls shattered as if made of glass. The shards slid to the floor in a waterfall, leaving bare earth and a pile of rubble behind.

Natan met Bryon's wide-eyed stare, but the Mage strode past them on his way out, snagging their attention. "I've learned where Kavi is. Come."

They followed him, Natan's heart beating wildly. He longed to ask the Mage what he'd seen. Did Kavi still live? But Gregor's expression was set, cold, and Natan kept his questions to himself.

They left the building and Natan's anxiety worsened when Gregor led them around to the back of the structure. The dry grass crunched under their boots, the sun growing hot on Natan's neck as they crossed the short distance to a covered well in the middle of the clearing.

"No," Natan said with horror and dropped to his knees. The Mage made no comment, his face etched with grief. Natan's blood chilled; he was thankful for the numbness that spread from his heart, blanketing his fear. Bryon knelt beside him, and they carefully dragged the heavy lid off the well, watching closely for a cave-in.

The Mage leaned over the gaping hole and peered into the darkness. "Kavi?" he called brokenly, the plea of a father to a lost child. There was no reply and Gregor clenched his hands.

Bryon stood. "We need my rope."

"I'll get it," Natan offered, setting his lips in a firm line. He needed to know. He got up and ran for the horses nibbling grass in front of the building. Fetching the rope coiled under Bryon's pack, he trotted back and tied off one end to a nearby tree, ignoring the fact that his hands were shaking and there were tears on his face.

Tying a few knots at the other end, he stood on the edge of the pit and began his descent, the two men braced to help lower him. It wasn't a long climb, but heaviness fell on his heart as the earth and darkness closed around him. The smell of decay soon made it difficult to breathe. He shouted to the men when he reached a pliant surface, and he carefully tested his footing until he found solid ground.

Gingerly taking a knee, he felt in the darkness for Kavi and touched bare bone, so jerked his hand away with a cry of disbelief. Gods! How many victims were down there? With great effort he shut his mind to the horror of it and fumbled around. Rot and death, bodies mostly decomposed. No one recent…

Natan shuddered reflexively when his hand landed on a solid shoulder. Kavi's skin was icy to his touch. *Please be Kavi! Please be alive.* He pressed shaky fingers to the cold neck. Finding a faint pulse, he didn't waste time. He tied the rope under the person's arms, though grief swept him and he pressed kisses to their cold face. "I'm here now," he said brokenly. "I'm so sorry."

He secured the rope, then tugged, and the men above lifted the limp body with care. The rope was lowered back to him, and Natan scrambled to follow, heart pounding with hope. Kavi looked ashen in the sunlight and Natan knelt beside him where they'd laid him on the ground. He touched his face, feeling warmth returning. "Wake up, please," he whispered. He could hear Kavi's struggle with each shallow breath he drew, his spirit far away on some journey of its own.

He looked up at the Mage hovering over them. "Can you help him?"

Gregor nodded, dropping to sit on the dry earth. He put a hand on Kavi's forehead, the other on the iron shackles at his wrists. Bending, he placed his forehead against his hand on the manacles. Natan saw sweat burst on his brow. "Help me," he whispered. A chill ran through Natan. Who were the gods he called to? Gregor shook with extreme effort, and the hair prickled on the back of Natan's neck. What…

"Please!" Gregor gasped, and suddenly the structure of the iron shackles crumpled and fell to nothing. Quickly, the Mage moved his hand to Kavi's bound ankles, and the iron shattered under his touch.

Natan lurched back with a surprised shout, but then reached for

Gregor when he swooned, catching him before he slumped to the ground.

"I need a moment," the Mage panted, then fell unconscious. Natan shot Bryon a panicked look. The soldier had been standing guard over them and now shifted on his feet, looking uncertain. Bryon settled his lips in a grim line.

"Make Gregor comfortable while I get water to clean Kavi's wounds," Bryon suggested.

Natan was grateful for something to do. He eased Gregor onto the ground, then turned to Kavi and caressed his face. "Kavi?" he called, wishing he'd wake. Kavi's breaths came quickly, like Gregor's, but though his lids fluttered, he remained unconscious. His wrists and ankles were raw and bleeding, some of the sores festering. Bryon returned with his pack and waterskin, so Natan tenderly cleaned Kavi's wounds, then dressed them with strips of cloth.

"Why doesn't he wake?" he asked as he tied off the last bandage. Placing a kiss on Kavi's cold forehead, he sat back on his heels.

Bryon shook his head. "I don't know, lad. We've done all we can, for both of them. We simply have to wait."

Natan nodded and settled on the dry grass. After a moment he took Kavi's hand. He'd wait forever, if he had to.

Chapter Four

GREGOR SUDDENLY RETURNED to himself, taking a moment to collect his scattered thoughts before opening his eyes. He blinked in the harsh sunlight, his gaze going immediately to Kavi lying still beside him. "Any change?"

Bryon shook his head as Gregor sat up stiffly, Gregor keeping his eyes on Kavi's sallow face. Gregor touched Kavi's forehead with the back of his hand. "He's burning up, but I can do nothing for him in this foul place."

Natan drew a harsh breath and Gregor flicked him a glance. The young man genuinely cared, but more than that, Gregor sensed the stirring of a deep passion in him for the Karthagan. Dangerous in these times. "Let's take him to that wondrous lake we passed," he said. "But first there's something I must do before we leave." He reached out a hand to Natan. "Help me up, please."

Natan took his arm, and Gregor had to mask his start of surprise. There was power in the lad, much more than in any other person he'd encountered in Belega so far. Interesting. Rising, he stood over the open well. Natan and Bryon exchanged a worried look, then stepped to either side of him.

Gregor drew in a deep breath of the heated air, scented with dust and pine, and exhaled his doubt. Kneeling, he opened his hands over the darkness. Inhaling, calming the quick beat of his heart, gathering his strength, he began to chant a low, melodious song that brought tears to the eyes of his listeners by its pathos, a song of goodbye.

He stretched his arms in an embrace as a gray mist rose from the well. Unmindful of the tears blurring his vision, he raised his face to the sky and watched the wisp of souls dissipate into the bright sunlight. His heart in tatters, he crossed his arms on his chest and took a deep breath. "Be at peace," he murmured.

Natan's tortured moan caught his attention. "Bryon?" The young man's voice sounded ragged. "Kavi was down there. Thrown in that hole with the dead."

Bryon moved to Natan's side and slid an arm across his shoulders when a low sob broke from him. "It's all right, lad. Let it go. He's safe now. How could we have known he was there?"

Gregor watched them a moment and suddenly his restraint broke. All the fear and pain and torture inflicted by the leaders of Amara on their prisoners, guilty or not, all the sorrow they'd caused, swelled into a violent rage within him. He lifted his arms and his deep voice boomed across the air. "Enough!"

The silence of a held breath descended on the earth, but then a deep rumble was felt underfoot. The ground vibrated, and with a sudden lurch began to roll in a low wave toward the well. Natan and Bryon stepped back in fright, but Gregor stood immobile until the last second. He retreated as the ground swept by his feet and slid into the hole until only a slight depression remained where the well had been. The shaking grew less, and with a fading growl, the earth fell still once more.

Gregor stood as if turned to stone as the violence of nature burned within him. He gloried in that energy, knowing it was but a gift to be returned.

At that moment, Landlan strode from the council rooms behind them, shouting at Gregor as he crossed the field. "How dare you! Several of our buildings have—"

Gregor held up his hand and the man's voice faltered. Gregor knew in that moment he could easily take his life. Landlan's face grew ghastly as if he guessed his thoughts.

Gregor gave him a cool look. "I shan't kill you." He bent toward him. "I'll take you to Governor Basal instead. He'll be very interested in the atrocities you've done here. I don't think he'll be as lenient as I, do you?

"Bryon," he continued as the energy dissipated into nothing within him. "See that he's bound tightly and brought with us."

"My lord." Bryon gave him a quick bow and pulled a few strips of leather from his pocket.

Landlan backed up a step, then paused with a quick glance at Gregor. "You're making a mistake," he threatened. "As council leader, I was well within my rights here."

Bryon merely shrugged and tied his hands at his back.

Gregor went back to Kavi, his body trembling as reaction set in. He stumbled and Natan leaped to his side.

"I'm all but spent," he confessed. "Will you please gather the horses? We must leave here as quickly as possible."

"Of course." Natan made his low bow, then hurried to the front of the building. Gregor ran a shaky hand over his eyes, relieved when Natan returned in short order, riding the roan and leading two others behind him. He dismounted and aided Gregor onto the horse's back. Bryon tied Landlan to the saddle of the spare mount Natan had retrieved with their own, not questioning where he'd gotten it, then swung up behind their prisoner.

Natan knelt by Kavi and lifted him gently, handing him up to Gregor, then jumped onto the remaining horse.

"Guide us to the Lake," Gregor requested, then set heels to his mount as Natan sprang forward.

The ride became a nightmare to Gregor as his arms grew numb from holding Kavi, yet he couldn't give him up when Natan asked. He kept him alive by shear strength of will, praying he'd have enough energy at the end of the journey for the task ahead. Hours flowed one into another until they came at last to the Lake of Glass in the twilight.

"Permit me." Bryon reached for Kavi, and Gregor drew a ragged breath as he let him go. He all but fell from the saddle, then turned blindly toward the lake, every movement a torture.

"Lean on me, Mage," a kind voice said, and Gregor found Natan at his side. He smiled when the lad put a strong arm around his waist and helped him to the edge of the water. He sat cross-legged on the sand and Bryon laid Kavi beside him.

"Give me a moment." Gregor hung his head, sick with fatigue, and closed his eyes.

"Lend me your strength," he pleaded silently to the earth. The world grew quiet around them with only an occasional sound from Bryon as he tied the prisoner to a tree, then helped Natan set up camp. Gregor let the peace of the lake fill him. He could feel the very essence of life thrumming in the air and vibrating in the water. A few stars appeared in the sapphire sky, promising a clear crisp night.

He breathed deeply, knowing the time had come. He rose to his knees, placed a hand on the still water of the lake, and watched with delight as tiny ripples spread out from the contact in glittering rings. He cupped a little of the water to bathe Kavi's hot forehead.

"Mage?" Natan said tentatively as he and Bryon joined them. He knelt and carefully turned Kavi's head to show the trickle of blood from his ear. Gregor met his gaze and gave a slight nod, confirming Natan's fear.

"What is it?" Bryon looked from one to the other of them.

Gregor shook his head. "I'm not sure. Pressure is building inside his head. I won't know how serious the injury is until that pressure is released."

He closed his eyes and emptied his mind of all thought and concern. Sharp agony and fear struck him from the others. He threw a wall up between them. So much pain, but that was also part of life, so he gathered that force as well.

A sudden smile lit his face. He felt alive! Power tingled through him. He held Kavi's pale face in his dark hands and searched his features. Flawless olive skin washed almost white with pain, lids closed tight on almond eyes, his dark hair was matted with sweat, grime, and streaks of blood.

Gregor closed his eyes once again to look deeper. The bones of Kavi's face were fine and thin, and he trailed fingers along the thickness of his temple. He bent his will and could feel the structure of the bone, its smoothness beneath his touch. He walked his fingers gently over Kavi's scalp, feather-light on the swelling at the back of his head. Skin gave way to blood and swollen tissue. There, the tiniest of fractures in the bone. And beyond that…

His mind screamed at a pressure that would burst his skull. No, not his skull, Kavi's, the swollen matter pushing against the bone and out the tiny crack that had bruised it. Gregor concentrated on that small fissure and then he was inside, his thoughts touching Kavi's mind, healing the tiny wounds.

All at once, the pressure that stopped Kavi's ears and pounded in his temples eased. Gregor withdrew, his spirit crashing back into his own body in a rush. He blinked several times but couldn't focus. With a deep sigh, he toppled beside Kavi as his strength gave out.

He floated, weightless, for a long while, but awoke sometime in the night. Taking a deep breath, he let it out slowly, felt the hard earth beneath his body and a warm blanket over him. The soft breathing of the others floated on the air. He felt weary to his very bones, his thoughts sluggish. He couldn't remember when he'd last experienced such utter exhaustion.

Reluctantly, he opened his eyes. Kavi lay sleeping on his back close by, and he knew he should check on him to make sure he was healing properly. But he couldn't bring himself to do it, not yet. He turned on his back and looked in misery at the tree branches and moonlit sky overhead. He didn't know why circumstances had brought him to Belega in the middle of a war. Why wasn't he allowed to go home?

He closed his eyes and tears slipped down cheeks grown hollow in the last few weeks. He'd already given so much of himself, and he could feel the suffering of those nearby who needed more of him.

He wondered if his mother still lit a candle in the small front window at home for him. Had Elsa forgiven him? What of his children? His heart twisted at the thought of his beautiful ones. But he'd been unable to stay in Sennia, even for them. The people like him, the ones with power, were being hunted. But all he longed to do was return home.

He took a deep breath and willed himself back into forgetful sleep, knowing the pain of the world would still be there when he awoke.

NATAN WOKE IN the early morning to wipe the tears off his face. He'd dreamed of Kavi and the horror of the pit he'd been thrown into. He'd suffered. Natan should have protected him better. When he'd grown ill and the Mage had left him in Natan's care, he'd sworn to protect the Karthagan. Bitter regret dripped into his heart. He'd failed.

He rose and stoked the fire, setting a pot of water on a few stones to heat for tea. Glancing in Kavi's direction, he saw that both he and the Mage still slept, so he rested back on his heels. The Mage. Gregor said the name meant "teacher" in his own land. Natan wondered what magics he'd taught Kavi in their time together. He knew Gregor had spent some months on the Isle of Wind. But Natan was still surprised he'd come back with a Karthagan as his apprentice. That people had been forbidden to return to Belega.

Natan called to mind the first time he'd seen Kavi, and his blood heated. When Gregor had stopped in Amara on his way to the Isle of Wind, Bryon had brought him to stay with Natan for several days in his home on the coast. Natan wasn't sure why the Mage had chosen him or what the magic user could learn from him. But Gregor had seemed content to walk in the forest or tarry by the river, speaking or sitting in companionable silence. Natan had readily promised him a bed when he returned from his sojourn, even though his shack on the river was tiny, with room for only two: Gregor on the bed and Natan sleeping on the rug by the hearth.

When he'd come back, Gregor had ridden into Natan's yard with the beautiful Karthagan sitting at his back, and Natan's heart had thudded strangely. His first dazed thought had been to wonder where the man would sleep. Maybe he and Gregor shared a bed? Natan found he didn't like that image at all, especially after the man slid off the horse and walked up to him, virile, lithe. The warmth in his dark eyes and smile enveloped Natan, though the man stopped short of touching him.

"I'm Kavi. Thank you for opening your home to a stranger," he said in low, musical tones, holding out his hand. Natan blinked, losing his voice in a tide of yearning. He'd never seen a Karthagan before. Kavi was breathtaking—slim, strong, his olive complexion flawless, black hair falling like silk to his shoulders. He had dark gems for eyes, intelligent, questioning. Natan's lonely heart reached for him, wanting the man for his own.

The Mage's soft cough recalled him, and he stammered through his greeting, blood rushing at the strength in Kavi's fingers. His heart pounded. Natan felt awkward, callow, embarrassed by his poverty. He wished they hadn't come. His solitary life had left him ill-equipped for the longing that swept him. Kavi's full lips lifted in a knowing smile, and Natan dropped his gaze, mortified by emotions he didn't know how to control.

As if sensing his distress, Gregor pulled him into a quick embrace. "It's good to see you again, Natan. I hope you don't mind that I brought a guest. We won't stay long. A few days, and with the weather this delightful, we'll sleep under the stars."

"Stay as long as you need," Natan countered and felt the hot blood in his face at Kavi's low chuckle.

"Damn the man," Natan said now, poking at the fire. He couldn't help looking again at the men slumbering close by. Bryon slept a little apart, near the prisoner, but Kavi had rolled against the Mage, a hand on his hip. Natan bit his lip, turning back to the fire and the simmering pot. He knew it meant nothing. Kavi was an affectionate man. But his body ached, re-membering their glorious nights together and the bright smile on his lover's face. He hadn't known then that Kavi liked to play at love, giving freely of his body but allowing no one near his heart.

"Good morning."

Natan started, unaware anyone had woken until Kavi squatted across the fire from him. He sounded tired. Natan searched his face. Exhaustion and pain were evident, yet his eyes were clear. "How are you?" he asked gently.

"I'm well. The Mage took the horror from me…" Kavi trailed off as the water boiled over its pot. They watched it a moment, then Kavi laughed, easing the tension between them. "Making tea, Nattie?" he asked, arching a brow. "Remember the time you let the water boil over until it put the fire out?"

"That happened one time, and it was your fault for distracting me."

Natan could have bitten his tongue but Kavi only laughed merrily. "You're the one who kissed me, remember."

"Well, you *are* a nice diversion," Natan pointed out and used a stout stick to remove the pot from the stones while Kavi retrieved the tin of tea from their supplies. They sipped the hot brew in companionable silence. They had always been a good match, comfortable in their silences as well as shared conversation. Especially after they had…

Natan swiveled, reaching for another stick for the fire to hide his face. On their second day staying with him, Kavi had come down with a fever. Nothing serious. But when Bryon brought the news of fighting in Nagal, the Mage had left, entrusting Natan with his apprentice's safety, much to Natan's alarm.

Kavi's fever broke on the fifth day. Natan had given him what medicines he knew and tried to cool his burning skin with cold water from the river, keeping tight control on his straying thoughts as he bathed Kavi's body. But this morning was different. Kavi's skin no longer scorched his fingers. In fact, it was warm, soft as silk. Natan trailed the cool cloth down Kavi's chest, his olive-toned skin unblemished, muscles defined, a few dark curls circling the dusky nipples. Natan passed the cloth over one tight bud and watched in awe as it hardened further. His mouth went dry. Natan licked his lips, his cock growing heavy when he thought of touching his tongue to it, taking it into his mouth.

He slid the cloth lower on Kavi's body to where the curls grew thicker under his naval, above the loose blanket. *Oh gods.* Until then he'd been able to stay detached. The man had been sick, after all. But now…

He yelped when his wrist was grabbed, instinctively dropping the cloth to reach for a weapon. But then he caught Kavi's rich, brown gaze on him and froze.

"Feel free," Kavi drawled. Natan flushed hotly and would have fled except for the fire smoldering in the Kavi's dark eyes. Held captive, Natan trembled, aching. Kavi's slow smile made his heart flutter, then surge when Kavi threaded their fingers together and deliberately slid their hands under the blanket to his thickening member…

"Nattie?"

Natan jumped slightly, dropping the wood into the fire when Kavi's questioning voice brought him back to the present. He glanced up into his quizzical gaze. "Distracted, Nattie? Thinking of me?"

He shrugged. "Maybe a little," he confessed, knowing it was useless to deny it with the hot blood stinging his cheeks. Kavi's piercing gaze softened, and he touched Natan's arm, withdrawing his fingers quickly at a snort and grumble from Bryon as he came awake. Natan muttered a curse, not sure if he was relieved or disappointed by the interruption, and scowled when Kavi grinned at him.

Without thought, he lurched forward to seize Kavi's mocking lips in a hard kiss. "We're not done," he muttered.

A flame smoldered in Kavi's dark eyes. "I concur," he murmured, running his tongue slowly over his bottom lip as if savoring Natan's flavor.

Heart pounding, Natan rose to his feet as the camp stirred, and took the Mage a cup of tea. They packed in short order, deciding to eat as they traveled. It was a three day journey to Nagal, with the Mage restless to be off. Bryon took the prisoner in front of him on his horse, Landlan quiet and docile. No one was fooled; Bryon loosened the knife at his belt.

Natan took a moment to stomp out the fire, looking up when Kavi rode over to him. He frowned. Kavi had taken his horse as if he owned it. But Kavi smiled down at him, warmth in his eyes as he put a hand out to help Natan mount, so Natan's anger dissipated. He gave Kavi a wry smile and swung up behind him, resting his hands on Kavi's hips.

They followed the Mage into the forest at a fast trot, and in a few moments, Natan gave in to the urge to lean against Kavi's back, pain and joy mingling as the man's warmth seeped into him. He ignored Bryon's exaggerated snort from the horse behind them, used to the soldier's acerbic humor.

The journey proved uneventful—long hours in the saddle, short stops to rest the horses and eat sparingly. Each night Natan rolled in his blankets, kissed an equally exhausted Kavi, and fell into dreamless sleep until roused for his turn at watch.

They approached Nagal in the late afternoon of the third day, with the restlessness Natan had been feeling all morning growing as they drew near the city.

"What is it?" he asked the others as they rode through the thinning trees.

"I don't know." Gregor looked at the sky in concern. "The air seems thick, and I think I smell smoke. We should hurry."

They quickened their pace and soon broke through the tree line, before bringing the horses to a halt in dismay. The fields outside of Nagal were littered with bodies, most of them Nagal soldiers, and the gates had been torn down. Smoke curled up from several areas within the city walls. An unnatural quiet lay over the land.

Bryon stared at the scene in disbelief. "How can this be?"

He laid heels to his horse while the others followed more cautiously. Natan watched in apprehension as Bryon sprang through the gates unchallenged. The battle was recent, perhaps only last night, and Natan noticed that the bodies of the opposing force of Barkuit soldiers grew more numerous as they neared the walls. It had been a bitter fight.

They walked their horses through the fallen timbers and spotted Bryon just inside the walls talking with Captain Emile, who was apparently in command of the city. Repairs to the gates had already been started.

Landlan sat up, alert, on the horse Bryon had abandoned, and Kavi nudged their horse closer. Natan leaned over to pick up the dangling reins, glancing away from Landlan's scowl.

"The Barkuit army broke through last evening, but we routed them," Emile explained as he approached Gregor. "Lord Basal took the army after them as soon as the city was secured, but by then the Barkuits had several hours head start." He clenched his hands in barely controlled rage. "Gargary advanced to the gates under parley, then predictably attacked when the emissary rode out to him. We expected another trap, of course, but Governor Basal saw no alternative other than to meet with him. We'd hoped Gargary had had enough of death. As it was, Basal was almost killed in the initial skirmish, but we managed to pull him back to safety."

Gregor swore darkly. "I should have been here."

Natan felt Kavi stiffen and put a hand on his shoulder. He still wasn't sure of their relationship, but knew Kavi was very protective of the Mage. Gregor sighed. "Can we help with the wounded, Emile?"

"There's no need. Our doctors have seen to them."

Gregor nodded. "Then we'll eat and start immediately after Basal. I should be with the governor."

They dismounted, but Gregor stopped Natan while Emile led the others up the cobbled street. "Can I speak with you a moment?"

Kavi glanced back at them, but at a slight shake of Gregor's head, instantly planted himself at Bryon's side, talking animatedly. Natan grinned when the soldier scowled at Kavi. Though Bryon had a soft spot for Kavi, he wouldn't tolerate his flirting. Which left Kavi no choice but to tease him every chance he could, Kavi had explained to Natan with an impish wink. Natan laughed softly when Kavi flung an arm around him and the soldier shoved him away, but sobered when the Mage took a troubled breath. "How can I serve you, lord?"

Gregor's smile held a hint of sadness. "I fear the coming days will be dark, my lad, so I'll need someone by my side to watch for the treachery I might otherwise miss." His thick brows drew together. "I don't always understand motivations."

Natan's heart lurched, and he searched the Mage's lined face. "There's something more, isn't there?"

Gregor headed up the street after the others, and Natan fell into step beside him. "There's a wrongness on the Isle of Wind which eludes me," Gregor began, "hard as I sought to uncover its source while I was there. Almost a perversion in nature itself." He touched Natan's arm to halt him, his eyes staring into the distance. "I fear the malady is spreading. I can feel it here, in Belega, like a taint in the air. This battle is only the beginning." He ran a shaky hand over his face. "It's taking its toll on me. I've used nature's energies all my life, but recently it's been growing harder to do. Like a poison inside me, eating from the inside out. There will come a time…"

He shook his head as if throwing off the dark mood and gave Natan an apologetic smile. "Don't worry. There's still a lot of life in me, but I could use your help."

"There has to be someone more worthy?" Natan faltered, out of his depth. "Kavi…"

Gregor searched his face. "I don't think so," he said quietly, and nodded to emphasize the words. "No, I think you're the one. Kavi has talent and strength, but I see a wisdom in your eyes that will be needed."

Humbled, Natan took a knee. "I will do the best I can, Mage," he stammered, not knowing how to pledge his loyalty so feeling foolish.

Gregor helped him to his feet and gave him a kind smile. "I know you will."

They made their way through the quiet streets. Men and woman went about their work with bowed heads, shocked beyond speech at the savagery of the Barkuit soldiers. Many of the graves to be dug that day would be for children. The company stabled their horses and proceeded to the castle.

They entered the ancient structure, where they were offered a simple meal at a long table. Landlan's hands were untied so he could eat, though Bryon kept a sharp eye on him. Gregor took the chair opposite, thoughtful. Natan sat a little apart and watched a brightly colored bird hopping on the stone windowsill while repairs continued in the courtyard below. Kavi joined him, sitting close enough their thighs touched. Warmth spread through Natan's core, driving the cold from around his heart.

"Did the Mage say something to trouble you?" Kavi asked after a moment when Natan continued to stare out the window. Natan looked at him and lost his breath at his beauty, the olive skin almost translucent in the soft light, the dark liquid eyes that kindled under Natan's gaze. Natan was intensely conscious of their last fierce kiss and moistened his lips without thought.

Kavi's breath caught and he gave Natan a smile full of promise, leaning close to whisper, "The next time we're alone, my love, we'll do much more than kiss."

Hot blood stung Natan's cheeks while his pulse thundered. He could so easily lose himself in Kavi. He dropped his gaze to Kavi's full, slightly parted lips, and longing swept him. He still felt awkward and clumsy against Kavi's confidence and carefree nature. What did the handsome man see in him? Did he sense his painful loneliness? Was it pity? He quickly swallowed a sigh.

"Gregor fears he is too trusting," Natan confided, tearing his attention from Kavi back to the sunshine outside. "He senses a wrongness in the world, things out of place, and wishes me to look for deceit in those around him he might not catch."

He saw Kavi's thoughtful nod from the corner of his eye. "That might be wise. Gregor perceives only the good in others." Kavi touched Natan's hand, drawing his gaze once again. "And this will give us more time together," he said and purposefully bit his bottom lip, sending Natan's pulse surging.

They gazed at each other a long moment, Natan swaying toward him, when commotion in the room made him draw back. Kavi's soft, satisfied laugh left him confused, unsure, and he rose to his feet to follow the others. Did Kavi mean to play with him? A distraction from the boredom of travel? He wasn't sure he wanted to know the answer.

Chapter Five

THE COMPANY RETRIEVED their horses from the stable, thanked Emile, and started on the trail after Basal and the Nagal army. With the loan of several extra horses, they made swift progress over the rolling hills of Nagal's farmlands, despite the hindrance of the prisoner tied to his saddle. Near the close of the afternoon, Natan brought his horse up to Bryon's mount.

"Lord Fredrik's hall isn't far from here. Should we rest there for the night?"

Bryon frowned, his gaze going to Landlan's slumped figure on the horse he led by its reins. "Basal doesn't trust Fredrik, suspecting ties with Barkuit. Safer if we push on and join the army."

Natan nodded, shifting to a more comfortable position in the saddle as an ache settled into his bones from the long ride. Kavi gave him a commiserating look and rode closer, placing a hand on Natan's thigh. Instantly, his pain lessened, and he looked at Kavi with wonder. Kavi laughed, leaning in to give him a quick kiss, the brush of lips, leaving Natan breathless and wanting while Kavi trotted his horse up to join Gregor at the head of their small party.

Evening of the second day of hard riding brought them to the edge of the Dakon Forest.

Gregor drew rein. "The main body of the army is still several leagues to the north of us. They should be making camp soon and we'll rendezvous with them in time for a hot meal. However," he continued as if noticing their tired faces for the first time, "let's stop a moment to rest the horses."

"You're too kind," Kavi muttered and swung down from the saddle.

Natan slid from his horse and hurried to lend a hand to the Mage as he dismounted, then paced to loosen muscles grown stiff. The company shared dried fruit and jerky as the horses grazed. A small stream trickled nearby, and when he finished eating, Natan washed his face, grinning when Kavi knelt beside him to plunge his dark head into the cold water. Quickly raising his head, Kavi flung his hair back, and Natan jumped to his feet with a shout as water sprayed over him.

Kavi laughed, his face bright. He stood and stepped closer to Natan, water clinging to his skin, droplets decorating his thick lashes. Natan's heart pounded, but Kavi moved suddenly and wiped his face on Natan's tunic, smirking up at him when he protested. Without thought, Natan bent to press his lips against Kavi's chilly ones, dipping his tongue in to taste his sweetness. They drew apart, Kavi's eyes wide, but the others crowded around the stream to fill their water skins, and Natan ground his teeth when Kavi stepped away without a word. Couldn't they have even a few moments?

Natan turned toward the horses, to see Landlan sitting on a small boulder, eying him. His brown gaze flicked to Kavi and a calculating look creased his handsome face. Natan tightened a fist. He'd kept away from the prisoner, unable to control his fury at Kavi's treatment. It flared to life now, and he took a step toward him, wanting to smash the slight sneer from his countenance.

Gregor's voice halted him. "Natan?"

"Sir?" Natan held himself in check with great effort.

"Come and help me, please."

Damn. The Mage was perfectly capable of mounting his horse without Natan's assistance. He glared at Landlan, who laughed openly, inflaming his anger. Seeing red, the fear and anguish of Kavi's capture roiling inside, he strode over to him. Bound or not, Natan was going to beat him bloody.

Bryon stepped into his path. "Hold on, lad."

Natan stepped around him, his attention all on Landlan's smug expression. "I'm going to kill you," he promised as he marched up, set on kicking him in the head, but Bryon shoved him to the side. Natan stumbled, then swirled, lunging toward Landlan again.

"Natan, stop!" Bryon shouted and grabbed his arm. Natan shook him off. Landlan had struggled up, face white. Natan wanted to batter his head in. He clenched his hands into fists, but Kavi appeared between them.

Natan halted, breathing hard, and Kavi gave him a tender look. "Come with me," he coaxed, sliding an arm around him. Natan let himself be led away, though he shot Landlan a look of hate, exalting when the man paled further. Kavi took him to their horses, turning Natan to face him, keeping his arms loose around his waist.

A smile quirked Kavi's lips. "My hero," he murmured and kissed the corner of Natan's mouth. "Come on. He's not worth your attention."

"I could kill him…"

"No, my sweet, gentle man." Kavi shook him slightly. "Don't let him stain your beautiful soul. He is nothing."

"But—" Natan stopped as he noticed Gregor's thoughtful gaze on him from where he still stood by his mount. Suddenly, deeply ashamed, Natan walked over to him.

"Sir." Natan swallowed against a tightness in his throat.

Gregor gave him a faint, sorrowful smile, then cupped Natan's cheek with a gentle hand. "Anger is a natural response, my boy," he began, holding Natan's gaze. "But it is also a poison. You must learn to let it go."

"But he put Kavi in that well," Natan protested. "What am I to do with that?"

"Acknowledge it, then put it aside and do what needs to be done. At the moment, it's to take Landlan to Governor Basal. Harming him in anger is revenge, and revenge is never the right answer."

Natan hung his head, feeling he had disappointed the Mage, something he never wanted to do again. "I'll try my best," he promised in a quiet tone.

"I know you will. Now, help me on my horse."

Natan helped him mount, then turned in surprise when Kavi led his horse over, Natan's horse trailing.

"Ride with me, Nattie," Kavi said kindly. Heartsore, Natan nodded. Kavi urged him onto the horse and swung up behind him, gathering Natan in his arms.

Bryon secured the prisoner once more to his mount, climbed on his own horse, and they continued through the growing darkness.

After another few hours of travel, Bryon motioned for them to stop, and they waited in listening silence, Natan unaccountably uneasy. A sharp whistle sounded nearby, and Bryon nudged his horse forward. The Nagal army had spread tents out in a clearing, fires lit for individual meals. Most of the soldiers hailed Bryon as they rode through camp, but Natan began to hear an unfriendly murmur as the men caught sight of Kavi.

Seeing Kavi's set face when he glanced over his shoulder, he called softly to Bryon. "I think Kavi and I will find a spot under the trees to sleep." He motioned outside the army's circle of tents.

"Very well," Bryon acknowledged. "I believe me and our dear Landlan here will join you. The men seem unusually tense. They may kill Landlan out of hand."

Landlan threw him a murderous look, but Bryon merely laughed.

"I want you with me, Natan," Gregor interrupted, his voice brooking no argument.

Kavi slipped from the saddle and gave him a cool look. "Go on, Nattie. You'll find me when you're done playing soldier."

Natan winced at the jibe and chewed his lip as he followed the Mage to where Governor Basal's tent had been pitched. Kavi had little use for soldiers, and sometimes his sharp tongue could sting. Was he jealous of Natan's time with Gregor? They dismounted with a word of gratitude as a man came up to take their horses. Basal appeared in the doorway of the tent and Natan drew a steadying breath. He'd met Basal once before, when the governor had visited Amara, but that had been years ago. The man's strong, vital presence was just as intimidating as he remembered. Heart hammering, he followed the Mage into Basal's shelter when he beckoned.

Basal stared at a map of Belega on a low table in the center of the tent as they joined him.

"What next, Mage?" he asked in a hard voice. "I understand that you had an obligation to aide your apprentice, but I lost many men because of your absence and almost lost the city as well. I need you with me, your wisdom, and…talents. The Barkuit army is close. And you say there has been treachery in Amara? I'll speak with your prisoner in the morning. What is your advice on our present situation?"

"There is always my original idea," Gregor said quietly.

Basal frowned, walking away from the table to pace the small area. "You still want me to try for Willum, Gargary's child?"

"It would work, my lord," Gregor said firmly. "Gargary will never stop now. He's gotten into your city. And though you forced him out, he's tasted victory, and he's unbalanced enough to drive his men to death to obtain it again."

Basal came back to the table with its maps. "But to take his son!" He swore bitterly, exposing a frustration he never showed to others.

"And how many of Nagal's sons has he taken the life of, Basal?"

The governor started at the harsh words. He looked away and took several deep breaths. "What is your counsel?"

"I'll take Natan with me to Siagan and bring back the child," Gregor said, holding up a hand when the governor began to protest. "I know a way inside the city. I was a guest of Council Leader Mandel for many days, and the ineffectual man gave me free rein of Siagan. There's a large stone marker…" He proceeded to outline his strategy.

Basal gave a nod when he'd finished. "Very well," he said heatedly, clearly at odds with Gregor's plan. He started to leave the tent, then paused to look back at the Mage, returning to take a knee.

"Forgive me," he whispered. "I am a fool."

Gregor helped him rise. "No. Just a man who's given his heart to his people."

Natan continued to stare at the map after the governor had gone, not sure what to do next. The Mage's hand dropped on his shoulder, startling him, and he looked into his kind eyes. "Go to your friends, Natan. We'll speak more in the morning."

Natan shifted on his feet. "Why me, my lord? I have no special gifts. I'm not a warrior—"

Gregor held up a hand to stop him. "I trust you at my back. Get some sleep, Natan."

The Nagal soldiers were settling into their blankets for the night as Natan wound his way through the tents to where Bryon and Kavi had set up camp. They'd both stretched out on the ground, Landlan tied by his hands to a nearby tree with enough slack he could lie comfortably. Natan found his pack and blankets and picked a spot close to the fire.

Bryon opened an eye. "Any news? Just a moment." He stood, glowered at Landlan, then tugged on Natan's arm. "Come on."

They moved out of earshot, Kavi joining them with a blanket over his head and wrapped around his shoulders for warmth.

Natan leaned in and said quietly, "Apparently we've caught up to the Barkuit army. Basal intends to attack tomorrow while Gregor goes to Siagan for Gargary's child."

"The child? And why isn't the Mage sending one of us?" Kavi murmured.

Natan smiled impulsively at the sweet face peering from under the blanket, stepping closer to him. "Gregor believes he has the best chance at retrieving the child. Lord Gargary has tasted victory, and the Mage thinks holding his child ransom is the only way to stop the war."

"The Barkuits had victory because Gregor went after me instead of staying to defend Nagal."

"You can't know that," Natan hastily put in, not liking the edge in Kavi's lowered voice.

"Maybe not," Kavi replied, his tone stubborn. "But I am responsible, nonetheless."

Bryon took an impatient breath. "Let's get some rest," he muttered. "We'll deal with Gargary and the Mage's plans tomorrow."

They moved back to the fire, and Natan climbed under his blankets, aching to be close to Kavi in the darkness illuminated solely by the soft glow of the campfire and the brilliant stars overhead. The forest had grown quiet with only an occasional sound from the army camp to break the peace. He felt eyes on him, met Kavi's gaze, and his heart leaped at the secret smile that stole over his face.

Swallowing his nervousness, he beckoned to Kavi. They slipped from their blankets, Kavi gathering a few and following him deeper into the trees without a word. He knew Landlan watched them leave but put it from his mind. At a particularly secluded spot, he stopped and drew Kavi into his arms. Stars glittered through the tree limbs overhead, Kavi's body warm against the cold night air. He breathed in his scent—leather and horse and Kavi's own delicious skin. He ran his fingers through Kavi's silky hair, touched his cheek. "Are you well?"

"I am," Kavi assured him, turning his head to kiss Natan's knuckles.

Natan searched his face, sensing his weariness. He spread the blankets on the moss-covered ground, eased him down, and Kavi nestled in his arms. Natan thrilled at the feel of his body against him. He leaned his head back and looked at the stars, grateful for the peace Kavi's presence always lent him.

"I'm sorry about the well," he said softly, regretting his words instantly when Kavi drew a sharp breath. He hurried to finish. "I should have protected you better. I can't begin to imagine your horror in that place."

"I try not to remember." Kavi's voice shook, and Natan tightened his arms around him when he continued, "I've done nothing to your people. Why do they hate me?"

Natan didn't have an answer. A soft radiance touched the treetops as the moon rose, and he rolled to his side to meet Kavi's bewildered gaze, his face pinched by an inner fear. Natan bent and gently kissed him, a gesture of assurance and comfort. He drew away, but with a cry of pain, Kavi pulled him tightly against him. The scent and heat of Kavi's skin shattered Natan's restraint as he fumbled for buttons. Sweet madness. Surrender. Kavi laughed against his neck, licked his skin, and Natan's blood caught fire.

He rolled, pinning Kavi under him. While the sky wheeled overhead, their bodies twined, hands and lips roaming. Natan wanted to taste Kavi everywhere, search for the sweet, sensitive places that made his lover gasp his pleasure. But not here, vulnerable as they were with the Nagal army so close. Instead, he slipped his hand into the warmth of Kavi's breeches. Kavi moaned, biting Natan's shoulder, muffling the delicious sounds as Natan gripped him.

He looked up and tears stung his eyes at the beauty of Kavi's face in the moonlight, lost in bliss. Kavi arched, drawing a knee up between them, and swallowed Natan's groan in a deep kiss. Gods! This wasn't enough. Natan ground against Kavi's thigh, needing to be inside him, buried deep in the heat of the man. Instead, he tightened his grip on Kavi's swollen member, wondering if he dared take it in his mouth.

The thought drew another groan from him. His hand squeezed involuntarily, and he heard Kavi's breathing hitch. Kavi's strangled moan vibrated through Natan, then warmth spilled into his hand, tipping him over the edge. He shoved against Kavi, hard enough to bruise, his own ecstasy sweeping from him, his mind reeling with the pleasure of it and the knowledge it was his lovely Kavi who sent him there.

Chapter Six

SYROS TURNED AWAY in disgust from the couple he'd stumbled upon in the dark, so immersed in each other they hadn't been aware of him. The Karthagan had obviously set out to seduce the young man, bewitching him with his exotic beauty and magic. The sooner he found a way to kill him…

He pulled the long knife from his belt, the same one Natan had left with him after tying him to that tree. It would be easy to walk over there and kill them both, engrossed as they were in each other. Syros frowned as moonlight glinted off the blade. No, he had no quarrel with Natan. The youth had shown him mercy when he could easily have left him to die.

"My debt is paid," he said softly, giving them a mocking solute. He moved away to approach their camp with caution. Bryon slept, but the man was a keen soldier and worth keeping an eye on. Landlan lay on his side, sleeping, arms bound to a tree. Syros nudged him with a boot. "Are you ready?"

Landlan hissed, lurching toward him, then settled against the tree when he saw who it was. "Yes. And impatient. I was ready to leave an hour ago."

"That fool Natan is still awake but distracted enough at the present." Syros cut Landlan's bindings. "Let's go."

Landlan rubbed the red abrasions on his wrists. "In a moment. I want to pay my respects to Bryon. Bastard enjoyed binding me a little too much."

Syros scowled. "Don't be a fool. One shout would have the whole Nagal camp down on us."

A leer marred Landlan's handsome face. "And since you're wearing one of their uniforms, Syros, they'd stretch your pretty neck in a heartbeat."

"Perhaps." Syros looked down at the rich green of his attire, missing the more muted grays of the Barkuit soldier. He hated this game of pretense. Someone else could spy for Gargary next time. He wanted to go home.

"Hurry," he said.

Landlan gave him a cool look and took a step toward Bryon's sleeping form. Suddenly impatient, Syros moved to press the knife against Landlan's side. "I've had enough of this. We're going to the horses. Now."

"Losing your nerve, Syros?"

"Tired of your stupidity. I was sickened by your actions in Amara. I'm disgusted you'd murder a good soldier in cold blood now. If it wasn't for Gargary sending me specifically to retrieve you, I'd leave you here to Bryon's tender mercies."

Landlan's eyes widened, showing his surprise. Then, anger flashed in the dark depths, and he turned on his heel, stalking into the forest. Syros swore under his breath and trotted after him, gesturing toward the horses he'd hidden. He'd need to watch his back with the man.

NATAN SCRUBBED A hand over his sleepy face while Bryon stood with his hands planted on his hips in the morning light, surveying the slashed ropes once holding his prisoner. He jabbed fingers through his hair, understandably frustrated. "How much of a head start do they have?"

Natan lifted a shoulder. "It's hard to say. We've both suspected Landlan of having Barkuit ties. The man's ambition is boundless. This seems to corroborate that. I don't believe anyone from Nagal would have aided him."

Bryon made a noncommittal sound, and Natan shifted uneasily on his feet. Landlan was gone, freed by an unknown person, and to his horror, Kavi had vanished as well. They'd tracked the men to the spot where horses had been kept, then trailed them far enough to determine they were heading toward the Barkuit camp to the north, while Kavi's tracks, made later, trailed east.

"Looks like your Karthagan friend has fled," Bryon said over his shoulder as he gathered his pack.

Hot anger flashed through Natan. "Don't be absurd. Kavi must have a plan to somehow help us."

"Easy, lad. I know you have a fondness for him. As do I. But Kavi's a Karthagan. What do we really know about them?"

Natan pressed his lips together on a bitter retort. Bryon and he had been friends a long time. The only family he'd known, actually, besides his cousin, Jaden, a lieutenant in the Nagal army. But still…

"Kavi's not like that," he muttered as he pushed by the soldier, gathering his blankets and pack in angry silence. Bryon met him at their horses staked nearby; it took only moments to saddle and bridle the animals. Natan trotted his mount into the trees, leaving Bryon to follow or not as he would.

He tried to ignore the ache in his heart. He'd woken in the early morning, stretched, and smiled at a delicious languidness in his body. Rolling to his side, he'd reached for Kavi to pull him back into his arms but instead sat up, disappointed to find himself alone in their haven. But then, Kavi never did stay with him. Natan had chewed his lip on a flicker of concern and climbed to his feet, dressing quickly. The Nagal soldiers had done little to mask their suspicion of the Karthagan. Had something happened to Kavi while Natan slept?

He'd reined in his fear. The sky had lightened, moments away from sunrise, and only his and Kavi's tracks showed in the surrounding moss. He'd followed the faint trail back to camp to discover Kavi had taken a blanket, a packet of food, and one of the horses.

"I would have gone with you," he muttered now, leaning low in the saddle to mark Kavi's passing. He had little doubt where the man was heading.

Bryon snorted, trotting up beside him. "By the direction he's taking, I assume he's going after Gargary's child."

Natan nodded curtly. "He blames himself that Gregor wasn't there to help defend Nagal, even though I was the one who sent for the Mage."

"Little fool," Basal grumbled, though his face showed a deep concern. "Come on, we have a hard ride ahead of us to reach Siagan, more than a day, and I fear there is no safety for a Karthagan traveling alone in these parts."

Natan settled into the saddle and urged his horse after Bryon, the two men racing their mounts through the thinning forest. Long hours passed with grudging stops to rest the horses. Natan's anxiety grew with each delay, not lessening until the city of Siagan and the tall stone marker Gregor had described to Basal came into view early the following morning.

He slowed his horse. "There should be an entrance to the city concealed near the stone, an escape for its rulers long ago. Hopefully the council leader here, Mandel, hasn't had it filled with dirt."

Bryon rose in his stirrups, casting his gaze over the landscape, high desert pine and granite boulders leading up to the cleared land before the city walls. "Does Kavi know about it?"

"Stands to reason. Siagan once belonged to his people, before the Barkuits drove them out of Belega."

Coming to the large stone, they jumped from the lathered horses and hastily removed saddle and bridle.

As Bryon tethered the horses, Natan climbed through the brush to the roughly hewn rock shaped into the image of a seabird with folded wings. He cast about and found a wide hole in the ground between nearby boulders, noted the rope trailing into darkness. "He's here."

Sitting on the crumbling edge of the opening, he swung his feet over. Bryon came up, though he remained silent, and Natan glanced at him, surprised to see the anger in his face. "What is it?"

Bryon glowered at the dark hole. "The question is, why did he come here alone?"

Natan tested the soundness of the rope. "Maybe he didn't want us to try to stop him. All Karthagans are resolute. We learned that lesson long ago."

Bryon sucked in his breath. "That's what gets them killed."

Panic stabbed at Natan's breast, hot as fire. Is that what would happen to Kavi? Would he rush into danger without Natan there to protect him? It was a moment before he found his voice. "It's why we love them," he countered, then slid into the earth, climbing hand over hand down the rope into darkness.

When he reached the bottom, he discovered a tunnel leading into the hillside. After taking a last look at the sky far above, he entered the passageway. The blackness in the tunnel was complete. The wall sconces at the entranceway were empty of their torches, and he stumbled over the uneven ground, releasing a pungent odor as he trailed fingers along the wall for guidance.

At last his hand brushed against another sconce and he lifted down the torch he felt there. Fumbling in a pocket, he removed the flint he carried, knelt, then pulled out his knife. It took several attempts to ignite the fabric wrapping one end of the stake, and he thankfully watched the small flame when it caught.

He could travel more swiftly through the narrow passageway after, though it was still some time before he came to a fork in the tunnel. He looked curiously down the dark corridor on the right. Cold air breathed out, and he turned away, his face paling as he shivered. A waiting horror lingered down there. He hurried forward and ran straight into someone coming the other way.

"Kavi!" He caught the man as he stumbled back.

Kavi thrust a wailing bundle into his arms. "Here, take the child."

"What?" He heard the angry shouts following Kavi. Natan dropped his hand to his knife hilt, but Kavi pushed at him.

"Mandel spotted me. Take him!" He shoved again. "I can delay them. Go!"

Desperation tightened his face as he turned toward the right-hand tunnel. Natan took a shuddering breath. Kavi had to feel the wrongness in the air in that black passage. He took a step forward, fearing for Kavi's safety, but it was as if a wall had suddenly been thrust between them. Pain pierced his mind, and he heard a command, shouted in Kavi's voice, "Go!"

The cries of soldiers rang in the darkness, almost upon him, and he bolted back the way he'd come. The child grew quiet as the earth closed in around them. Natan panicked slightly, feeling entombed. His breathing grew ragged, painful, as he pushed on. It seemed an eternity before he reached the well and the opening to the sky.

"Bryon," he hissed skyward. The soldier's face instantly appeared in the circle of light overhead. "I have the child. Help me up."

He looped the rope under his arms, and Bryon pulled as he climbed, the child, Willum, clutched to his chest. On reaching the top, he used his feet as leverage to scramble out of the pit. Lurching to his feet, he ran for the horses, ignoring the tears streaming down his face.

Bryon caught his stirrup as he swung into the saddle. "What of Kavi?"

"He's still in the tunnel. Bryon, I have to go!" Natan pulled free and laid heels to the horse, springing into the night. Every instinct screamed at him to go back for his lover, but he closed his mind to those thoughts. Getting the child to Lord Basal and stopping the war became his only goal. Nothing else mattered.

KAVI STOOD AT the mouth of the tunnel and stared into the blackness of the cavern, stalling to let his pursuers catch up.

They were down there, all those bodies lying in the lake. Impressions of horror and pain and black despair swirled in the freezing air on the lake's surface.

He dropped to his knees, covering his face with shaking hands. "I'm afraid, Gregor."

His broken whisper echoed through the chamber. A low wail rose from the water in reply. Kavi searched for Gregor's presence in his mind. The Mage wasn't there, though their connection had been strong outside this terrible place. He was alone. The wail rose to a shrieking wind, and Kavi opened his arms to gather it in. Pain struck him first, confusion and a dawning horror as memories that weren't his crashed into his mind…

Bodies lay beneath him, his limbs growing numb where they lay in the icy water of the lake. A heavy weight struck his back, and another, driving the wind from his lungs. Wait! He was still alive! But voices and gruff laughter drowned out his thoughts. Another body splashed in front of him, and he found himself staring into the unseeing eyes of Grahm, his dear friend, his broken body lying at an unnatural angle. Another weight fell on him, crushing his face against the body beneath him. He could no longer breathe, and his last gasp became a wail of despair…

The drowning man's cry rose into the air and became part of the others in the shrieking wind around Kavi. It gathered force, then roared toward him. The small part of Kavi's mind still lucid in the swirling chaos became aware of swift footsteps approaching down the passageway. It was time. He threw himself to the damp earth. The furious wind roared over his head and swept into the tunnel.

The pursuing men were plunged at once into the nightmare of

decaying bodies and screaming wraiths. Some went mad and slew them-selves. Others fled into the tunnels, babbling of dead faces trapped in their minds.

Kavi sobbed into his hands. Not all the grief was his. Anguished voices had ridden that wind, full of anger and sadness. But the voices had changed. A cry of such hope-filled gladness went up as the wind burst into the tunnels, and he found himself weeping in joy without knowing why. He rose shakily to his feet to mourn anew as the wisp of a lonely wail floated from the darkness over the lake. That of a soul left behind.

He sent a tentative thought out, searching, but exhaustion claimed him. "I'm sorry," he whispered to the loneliness and turned away. He'd taken only a few hesitant steps up the tunnel when a flicker of light ap-peared. Kavi waited, having little strength to defend himself. Footsteps ap-proached, and he sagged in relief on recognizing Bryon's stocky figure. Bryon's face looked wild in the torchlight, eyes wide with fear.

"The wind—"

"I heard it." Kavi motioned to the still lake. "They're released now."

Bryon came close, awe in his voice when he spoke. "I ducked into a side tunnel and the wind swept passed me. Who were they?"

"My kin, killed by the Barkuit army long ago."

Gregor gave him a searching look, his keen gaze softening. "If that is so, I'm glad they're free."

Kavi raised his brows in surprise. Did the rough soldier actually have a heart? He inclined his head. "Thank you."

They started up the passageway, but of a sudden Bryon stopped and turned back, taking several stumbling steps.

Kavi gripped his arm. "What is it?"

The soldier halted in confusion. "Funny." He laughed uncomfortably. "I felt compelled to go back to the lake as if something had called me."

Kavi looked gravely into the darkness and shuddered. "I don't have the strength to go back."

They continued, Kavi staggering with exhaustion when they at last reached the opening. They climbed out into the sunlight, gathered the horses, and rode into the trees without a backward glance.

NATAN EYED THE coming night with concern. The child had slept fitfully, cradled in his arm during the day, Natan feeding him water and the juice from a few berries when he'd cried. But what would he do with it when it woke again? It would surely be hungry and wail loudly for its meal. He could only hope the Barkuit army remained far to the northeast. He'd calculated that by heading straight for the city of Barkuit he might intercept Lord Basal just outside its gates.

The long night passed with brief stops to rest the horse and walk the crying child. The infant would take sips of water mixed with juice now and then, but Natan realized his stomach wouldn't be content with that much longer. He put the child on his shoulder, rubbed his tiny back, and wrinkled his nose.

Kavi owed him another shirt, he thought as he cut a final spare garment into more swaddling for the boy. After seeing to the child's needs, he swung back into the saddle, tucking the baby against his chest for warmth as the night drew to a close.

Fear that Kavi might still be trapped in the tunnels under Siagan spurred him on. Morning found him entering the plains just outside the

Dakon Forest. He pushed on during the day, driven by Kavi's command lingering in the back of his thoughts, stopping only to rest the horse and, once, to feed the child a thin broth he made from wild carrots and the jerky in his pack. When night came again, he slept, the baby tucked against his shoulder, but a few hours later found him back in the saddle.

The following day was an agony for both him and the tiny boy in his care, with snatches of sleep as he clutched the saddle horn. His mind wandered as exhaustion overcame him, and he dreamed of walking with Kavi on the shores of the Lake of Glass.

He jolted awake as his horse stumbled up a slight rise in the terrain late that afternoon. After sliding from the saddle, careful of the sleeping child, he staggered to the lip of the hill. Relief flooded his heart at the sight of the Nagal camp in the field below. Small moans escaped him as he spent the last of his strength struggling down the gradual incline. He needed to get back to Kavi…

Gregor and Governor Basal met him halfway. Drawing the child from his numbed arms, Gregor handed the infant boy to Basal; then Natan found himself enveloped in Gregor's embrace. He sobbed against his shoulder, his body trembling, spent.

"I didn't think I'd make it here," he said brokenly, tears of exhaustion and grief streaming down his face. "It took so long, and I left Kavi…"

Natan broke off as Gregor's thoughts pushed into his mind. He could sense him there, a fierce presence, searching. The Mage's bittersweet triumph took him by surprise, and he shook with sudden fear.

Gregor's grip tightened as Natan tried to pull away. "No, Mage!"

"Yes. I've been waiting for you. It's time. This is right."

A shock of energy and strength crashed into Natan's body, and for an instant, he felt powerful beyond imagining. The Mage sighed, then dropped heavily. Natan went to his knees with him to cradle the limp body in his arms.

"Why?" Tears made it difficult to see. He brushed impatiently at them and caught Gregor's final sweet smile.

"I was mistaken, Natan. I wasn't drawn to Belega to aid the governor, nor to help the Karthagans. It was you all along. I never guessed…"

"No, Mage. No!" Natan choked on his words. "I'm nothing. You can't do this. There has to be someone else—"

"Hush, my boy," Gregor admonished. "We all have paths to follow in this life. Mine led to you. There's a terrible imbalance in the world. I can't see my way… I don't have the strength." He took a hard breath. "I've had a pleasant life, did some good in the world. But this new danger is beyond me. It's your turn to set things right. At least teach them to be careful. Let me go. There's too much for you to do to waste time here."

"Gregor." Natan pressed a kiss to his dark cheek. His tears flowed freely.

"Natan."

He looked into the Mage's eyes and found them full of a deep sadness. "Tell my mother and my darling wife and children that I'm sorry. I truly did want to make it home."

Natan nodded, his heart breaking as he watched the spark of life fade from the beautiful eyes, heard the last breath he took. He laid Gregor with all gentleness on the ground, then rose to his feet.

"I have to go," he said hoarsely, dazed, unable to take in what had just occurred. "I left Kavi…"

"I'll take the child. He'll be safe," Basal assured him. "Do what you need to do." The governor whistled and his horse trotted up. "Take my mount. I'll see to Gregor."

Natan looked at him helplessly, before turning to the Mage lying so still on the earth.

Basal touched his arm. "I don't understand what just happened either, but Gregor believed in you. Believe in yourself." He stepped back and bowed suddenly. "Take care, Mage."

Natan watched open-mouthed as the governor strode toward the soldiers waiting on the hillside. Wiping his tears, he bent to give Gregor one last embrace, then leaped into the saddle on Basal's tall horse and began the journey back for Kavi and Bryon.

He tried unsuccessfully not to think of Gregor's actions. Why him? Why had the Mage sacrificed himself? Why now? A more frightening thought—what exactly had Gregor done to him?

Natan hung his head. He'd achieved nothing great in his life. Lived in solitude in the mountains, a lonely child until Bryon had stumbled on him one summer. The soldier had taken pity on him, given him friendship, taught him his letters, how to read. Natan had often thought of him as his father, replacing the one he'd lost. When he was older, he'd occasionally scout for the Nagal soldiers stationed in Amara. A simple life.

Until Bryon had brought the Mage to Natan's home last spring, asking Natan to keep him safe the few days before Gregor sailed to the Isle of Wind. The man had been kind to him, and Natan would sit at his feet in the evenings in front of the fireplace to listen to his stories of the great cities of Belega: Barkuit and Nagal, Karthag and Siagan. Fairy stories to Natan's wondering ears.

Natan had missed Gregor's company when he'd gone, his hut

seeming lonelier than ever. He grimaced. That had left his heart wide open, making it easy for Kavi to slip inside and lodge there when the Mage had returned with him.

The hours passed into evening. Natan decided to rest his horse again when the flicker of a cook fire caught his eye. His heart thumped as he eased from the saddle. Was this his friends or an enemy? After looping the reins on a bush, he crept silently through the trees, crouching in the ferns to peer over a fallen log. Sure enough, Bryon poked at the fire while Kavi stirred something in a pot. Both men looked grim faced, Kavi's beautiful complexion almost white with exhaustion.

Natan stood and tossed a pinecone near Bryon's foot. Both men instantly rose, hands dropping to the knife sheaths on their belts.

Bryon squinted in the growing darkness. "A fine pair we are, Kavi, being caught off guard," he said, and strode toward him. Natan hastened through the fern to meet him.

"Natan," Bryon gripped his arm. He bent to look into his eyes. "Something's happened. Did the child not arrive on time?"

"I don't know. I think so," Natan's voice trailed into bewilderment, confusion and exhaustion enveloping him.

Bryon put an arm across his shoulders. "Come sit for a moment." He led him to the fire. Natan shook, disoriented. Why was he falling apart now? He tried to rise, but Bryon pushed him back to the ground. He hung his head, panting.

"Easy, lad," Bryon cautioned.

Kavi grabbed a blanket and wrapped it around Natan's shoulders, then quickly threw more wood on the fire. Bryon sat beside Natan to talk of the weather and how the early crops should be ready to harvest back home. He rambled on, giving Natan time to work out the panic that had assailed him. Listening to Bryon's comforting tones, Natan recovered by the time Kavi had some strong tea made.

He took the hot cup with a grateful smile. "Sorry." He sipped the comforting brew. "I don't know what came over me. It suddenly seemed too much." He paused and set the cup down. "Sit with us, Kavi. I have something to tell you. I don't know how to begin."

"Nattie?" Kavi sat and unexpectedly took his hand.

Natan played with his slender fingers, grief choking his breath. "The Mage is dead," he whispered.

"How?" Kavi managed in a strangled tone, eyes going wide with shock.

Natan moved restlessly, unable to keep the distress from his voice. "He did it for me! I arrived with the child, on the point of collapse, and he wrapped his arms around me and spilled the energy of his life into me. I tried to pull away, but he only clung tighter." Agony thickened his voice. "Why would he do this?" Overcome, he hid his face with the blanket.

An arm went around his shoulders. Bryon. "I don't know, lad. But the Mage always has a reason for his actions. We need to trust him in this."

Natan leaned into him, and Kavi put a hand on his shoulder while they grieved.

Bryon stirred all too soon. "I'm sorry, Natan. We need to go. The governor may be facing the Barkuit army even now."

They packed their few provisions in silence, and after putting out the fire, rode into the coming night. They traveled swiftly, but even so, it neared dawn before they spied the fires of the Nagal soldiers' encampment just outside Barkuit. Natan let out a breath of relief, his strength completely spent. Finding a spot on the edge of the army, the three dropped from the saddle, rubbed the horses down, and fell asleep by a communal fire, dead to the world.

Chapter Seven

THE USUAL DISARRAY of maps was missing from the governor's table the next morning. Instead, the evidence of a hastily eaten meal took their place. Natan swallowed convulsively as he and Kavi watched from the tent opening as Basal scraped the last spoonful of broth from his bowl. He couldn't remember the last time he'd eaten. Seeing them at the entrance, the governor motioned to the pot and bowls on the table. "Please, help yourselves."

Natan blushed. They probably *did* look half-starved. Kavi and he dished up, then shared a camp chair. There was a thinness in Kavi's cheeks Natan hadn't seen before. He glanced quickly away, hoping no one had seen his stare, to catch Basal's eyes on him. The man had taken advantage of their arrival to help himself to another serving. They finished, and Natan put his bowl on the ground.

"My lord," he said, then cleared his throat, feeling the glitter of tears on his cheeks. He'd woken to the thrum of unwanted power moving in his blood, a terrible reminder of all they'd lost. "You can never know how sorry I am about the Mage. I know he was your friend, and if I could, I'd undo what has happened."

Basal swore, sounding frustrated. "Damn the man. But there's nothing to forgive. Gregor always chose his own path."

Natan stood and moved to his side. Basal rose quickly as he took a knee before him.

"I pledged myself to Gregor," Natan said quietly, his heart thudding. "I now make that same pledge to you. The Mage would want me to stand by you in his stead, if you are willing."

Basal studied his face. Something flickered in his eyes. Anger? Fear? It was gone and he lifted Natan to his feet. "I accept your help. Thank you."

Natan sighed internally, feeling the weight of responsibility settle on his shoulders, then raised his head, alert, at a sudden shout from the sentries south of the camp.

Basal glanced at the camp through the open tent. "Good. That must be Jaden."

In moments, the young lieutenant strode into the tent along with Bryon. Natan hid a grin at his awkward bow. His cousin wasn't any more comfortable around the stern governor than he was himself. "Gargary has accepted your offer of treaty, my lord," Jaden said in clipped tones.

"Very good." Basal rubbed a hand over his face. "I hate using a child like this."

"As do I," Bryon stated forcefully. "But the Mage's plan is sound. Gargary would never stop fighting otherwise. Only the fear of losing his heir has brought the war to a close."

"Gargary's sent a nursemaid to look after Willum, as you requested," Jaden put in.

"Excellent. At least he'll do that much for his son. Shall we join the others?" Basal motioned them from the tent.

Jaden flashed Natan a smile over his shoulder, and Natan gave him a nod. Though they were similar in appearance, his cousin had a joyous, friendly nature, while Natan was far more reserved. They'd only learned of each other's existence a few years previously, their families being estranged, the others fearing the subtle powers Natan's mother had wielded, not un-derstanding. But Natan's heart had warmed to him, knowing he wasn't alone in the world.

Kavi had risen to his feet with them, and Natan glanced back when he didn't accompany them from the tent, then stopped abruptly at the lost look on his face.

Letting Bryon know he'd join them shortly, he returned to Kavi's side. A million emotions chased around inside him when Kavi chewed a lip.

"What do I do now, Nattie? Without Gregor?" Kavi asked softly.

Natan's heart jolted. "Stay with us," he urged.

"For what purpose? I was the Mage's apprentice. He was going to teach me how to use my gifts the way he did. Who can teach me now?"

Natan opened his mouth to speak, but no words came. He looked at Kavi helplessly, then grabbed up his hands and kissed them. When Kavi remained stone-still, he dropped them immediately. "I'm sorry. Just, please stay," he whispered. "Wait for me."

He strode through the bustling camp, cursing vehemently. He knew the danger of pushing Kavi, but he'd been unable to stop himself. The Karthagan had seemed lost, standing there alone. Natan bit off another oath. All he could do was help Basal with the treaty to end the useless war. Then maybe he could convince Kavi to stay.

He met the others on the front line, where Basal outlined his plans. They were simple: move the army within sight of the Barkuit walls, well out of bow range, and set up in standard ranks. He'd keep horsemen on the perimeters to watch for any furtive movements from the enemy. A small party would enter Barkuit to sign the treaty. When they returned safely, the child would be sent in. The army would then pull back to the Dakon Forest and wait to see if the treaty held.

"Keep your men alert," Basal warned his captains. "The Barkuits are a treacherous people in war, as we've all witnessed. We can only hope that all goes as planned today."

They dispersed. Natan looked over the empty fields laid out before the Barkuit gates and sent up a silent plea to whatever gods would listen that all went well that day. He'd never crossed paths with Gargary, but a cold chill ran through him at the thought of their coming meeting. He started a little when a firm hand slipped into his and he looked with surprise at Kavi's set face.

"Be very careful today, Nattie. My heart is heavy."

Before he could answer, Basal returned, taking his place before the army. A sense of foreboding seemed to come over the soldiers and a strange quiet fell.

Basal frowned across the silent fields to the gates of the city.

"Come with me," he bade Jaden, who unfurled the blue flag of Nagal. The governor rode up and down the ranks of soldiers, giving an encouraging word here, simple praise there, while the falcon of Nagal waved proudly overhead.

Basal returned to the front where Bryon waited. "Are we ready, Captain?"

"Yes, my lord."

Basal glanced at Natan, who gave a quick nod, then mounted his horse.

Kavi put a hand on Natan's calf, gazing up at him. "Remember what I said. Be safe."

Basal gave the Karthagan a curious look but said nothing. The four men from Bryon's company who were to ride with them came up now, so Basal touched heel to his horse. They trotted toward the city gates with Jaden carrying the flag before them.

KAVI WAITED ON the front line on a borrowed horse, keeping an eye on the nursemaid Gargary had sent. She was a young woman, obviously nervous, probably worried for her own child Kavi had heard waited at home for her. Kavi gave her a kind look, and Marda shyly returned his smile, hushing the baby in her arms.

He looked across the fields. Lord Basal and his men had already disappeared behind the city's gates. Kavi settled comfortably into his saddle. From what he understood, Lord Gargary was a braggart, so it might be a while before they actually signed the treaty.

Time passed slowly while they waited. Kavi wondered again what he was doing there. The Mage was gone and the people of Belega had little love for him. He could turn his mount around, ride to Amara, borrow or buy a boat, and return to his isle home. But he still felt Natan's passionate kisses on his hands, saw the desperate light in his eyes. Natan's loneliness tugged at his heart, not with pity but admiration for the life Natan had built for himself from nothing. No, he wouldn't leave him quite yet.

The baby slept, but Marda shifted uncomfortably as the sun grew hotter. At one-point Kavi caught himself drowsing in the saddle. He yawned and sat up, blinking the sleep from his eyes. While he was thus distracted, Marda suddenly laid heels to her horse and darted onto the field.

With a whoop Kavi gave chase, Nagal soldiers close behind him. The girl rode with surprising skill toward the two men now racing from Barkuit, but Kavi had almost caught her when his horse went down with an arrow through its foreleg. He hit the ground hard, the breath driven from his lungs.

The approaching horses stopped. He heard the thud of boots; then rough arms went around him. Dazed, he struggled, but was easily lifted and slung across a saddle, the rider mounting behind him. An iron clasp kept him from falling, but the jolting of the horse as it ran made him nauseous. They came to a sudden stop, and he glimpsed the city walls as the man dismounted and pulled him down, tossing him over a broad shoulder. He tried to fight, but the pounding in his head made every movement a nightmare.

"Why did you bring that thing?" a familiar voice snarled. "Landlan, I swear, if you mess this up…"

"Be calm, Syros. I need something to amuse myself while you play your little political games."

"Just keep him out of my way." The captain pushed open a side door in the city's wall. Kavi saw Marda enter with the child; then Landlan threw a blanket over his head, and he had to make the journey to the castle in darkness. They wound their way down several long passageways. At last,

Landlan dumped him onto a stone floor, jolting his bones, then pulled the blanket from his head, not bothering to bind his hands.

"Keep still and you may live a little longer," Landlan whispered and laughed quietly at his involuntary shudder. Landlan grabbed his shoulder to drag him to an archway. Kavi realized they were in the antechamber off the courtyard of the castle. Landlan leaned on the wall and calmly cleaned his nails with the long knife he'd taken from Kavi as he listened to the voices outside. Marda stood behind them, huddled over the child.

"It'll be over soon," Landlan commented to the room.

Kavi stared, wide-eyed, at the scene before him. Natan stood in the courtyard beside Lord Basal, looking completely out of place amidst the soldiers gathered around the two governors. Bryon and Jaden stood on either side of them. Landlan choked on a laugh when Basal handed Natan the treaty.

"The boy can barely read," he said nastily.

Kavi wished he still had his knife.

Natan perused the document, then nervously cleared his throat. "It's all here, my lord: the end of hostilities, with the new border being drawn at the Dakon Forest between the respective territories. And the trade agreement is covered as well."

"My expansion into your territory was a mistake," Gargary confessed. "I want my son to grow up knowing peace. If he then chooses to expand his domain… Well, that's for the future."

Kavi watched intently as Natan searched the man's face, then gave the parchment back to him with a nod.

"I accept the treaty, Lord Gargary," Basal said with formality, and the men shook hands. Gargary pulled the bottle of ink and a quill to himself.

Landlan chuckled. "You know, sweetheart, I think Gargary has completely taken in your Governor Basal." He turned to Kavi when he made no answer, but suddenly the clash of weapons arose from the courtyard. Landlan hissed, "There's that fool Syros. What's he trying to achieve now?"

"Wait, my lord," Syros yelled as he raced across the courtyard. "Treachery! The child is dead."

Kavi let out a cry of warning when Basal rose at Syros's words, only to see Basal stagger when Syros hurtled into him, plunging a knife into his side. Basal managed a sharp blow to his assailant's unprotected head, and Syros dropped to his knees. Bryon unsheathed his sword with an oath, facing the four Nagal men who'd come with them and traitorously drawn swords against him.

A soldier fell with Jaden's arrow through his throat. Then Natan had his knife out and, ducking under the wide arc of a flashing sword, dropped his attacker with a wicked slice across the abdomen. He stepped back as blood gushed over his hand and stumbled into Gargary, who'd pushed forward with a roar.

At that moment, Landlan sprang from hiding, and Gargary's cry broke off into a horrible gurgle as Landlan's knife slid across his throat. Kavi saw him topple, eyes wide with surprise as blood poured from the gaping wound. Landlan wiped his knife on Gargary's tunic. Rising to his feet, his voice boomed over the walls. "To arms! The Governor has been murdered!"

Picking up their own wounded governor, Bryon and Jaden ran for their horses. Natan was quick to follow, and they escaped, unknowingly leaving Kavi behind, even as soldiers came running from all sides.

It had all happened so quickly. Landlan strolled over to Kavi, sheathing his knife. He looked him up and down. "Well, not what I had planned, but still to my advantage." His expression settled into a leer. "And now I have all the time I need to wheedle your secrets from you. Something I will enjoy doing immensely. Come with me." He jerked Kavi by the arm, then shoved him, stumbling, into the courtyard.

"Girl, come here," Landlan commanded over his shoulder. Marda shuffled over to him, holding the child as if he were a safeguard.

"Follow me," he muttered impatiently. Marda stayed close on his heels as he grabbed Kavi's arm and shouldered his way through the milling crowd.

He gave an exaggerated bow to Syros, who stood with hands on hips over the dead governor. "My lord Syros."

Syros flashed him an irritated glance. "We weren't going to kill him."

Landlan raised his brows. "My lord, I disagree. This is perfect. We'll let it be known you thwarted Nagal's plans to kill both Gargary and his child. We'll declare you Regent of Barkuit." He glanced at the soldiers surrounding them, who instantly nodded their support, surprising Kavi. Barkuit was a strange land.

Landlan's smile chilled him. "The governorship passes directly from father to son. Keep the child close to you, be his councilor and adviser, and one day tell him how the Nagal governor betrayed and murdered his father. You'll control Barkuit, and in due course, all of Belega, all in the name of Gargary's son. And all without the danger of estranging the council."

Syros looked at him in wonder. "And what will you get out of this?"

"Oh, merely the pleasure of serving Lord Willum and Barkuit's Regent. And, oh yes, a place on the council would be nice."

Syros looked him over again. "Done." He shook Landlan's hand.

"Woman," Syros turned to the trembling figure still clutching the child. "Take our new governor inside. It'll be your responsibility to care for him, and mind you, do it well if you value your family's lives."

"Yes, lord. I'll tell my husband." Marda curtseyed, then hurried to find the groundskeeper and impart the news to him.

Kavi's gaze darted between the two men. Neither had anything to gain by letting him live. The soldiers around them shifted, making room for men with a litter to carry Gargary's body out. Separated from Landlan for an instant, he dodged into the milling soldiers. Landlan shouted but Kavi managed to slip inside the castle and sprint down a passageway leading deeper into the structure. The Barkuit army was in disarray after their governor's murder, soldiers watching him pass in surprise but making no move to stop him. Kavi ran until his breath gave out, then sank into a dark corner to rest. In due course he made his way outside.

KAVI CROUCHED IN the darkness between two buildings and stared at the barred gates of Barkuit from the inside. Fifty paces without cover lay between him and the barrier, the distance running the enclosing length of the walls, so no getting nearer without being seen. Guards swarmed like ants in the city. Rumors of treachery within the walls had circulated, and no one would sleep easy that night.

He sat cross-legged on the ground and tiredly rubbed his face, wrapping the blanket he'd found in an empty room around his slim body. The soldiers should tire during the night. No one seemed to be sleeping now to take a watch later, and he might be able to slip out then.

As night crept on, Kavi tried to rest in the narrow alley, but instead of becoming sleepier, he grew more awake as the night progressed. There was a prickling in his scalp as if lightning approached, and he stood up to peer at the gates. Soldiers still patrolled the walls and walked the streets, but they now wore bored expressions. The power didn't emanate from them.

A thrumming began in his ears. The Mage? No, but he could feel Natan in the bright place in his mind Kavi kept only for him. He was doing something. Kavi closed his eyes. Yes, he called on the strength Gregor had left him, drawing on the energies of the natural world. Kavi also sensed his uncertainty, the doubts he held. He needed to believe.

Kavi strove to send Natan what strength he could, but he was at too great a distance. Why did his Nattie have need of such power? The answer came to him in a sudden slash of warning in his heart. Basal must be dying. If that happened, there would be no stopping the Nagal soldiers from attacking the city. Hundreds would die. The slaughter would be ghastly, on both sides. It came to him that Natan would die.

"No!" Kavi took a step out of the shadows without a thought of where he was. The men around him stopped in shocked surprise.

"Intruder!" One of the soldiers recovered enough to shout, lunging for him. Kavi broke his arm with a quick sidestep and a twist of the man's arm around his back. Snatching the soldier's knife from his belt, he laughed as men came at him with their clumsy swords and fumbling knives. He'd sparred every day since childhood with better warriors than these. He shoved the wounded soldier from him, then silently cleared a wide field around himself with three soldiers dead and several missing their fingers.

Kavi strode toward the gates, drawing on the energy of the earth that came so easily to his people as horsemen rode up to block his way. A powerfully built man jumped from his mount to confront him. Landlan. "You cannot leave, my dear. You're to be held for aiding in the murder of Lord Gargary."

Kavi heard his words, but power flowed in him and he made to walk around the man. Landlan reached out to restrain him, jumping back at the glitter of the knife in his hand. Landlan beckoned another horseman forward. This one trained an arrow on Kavi's heart. Kavi looked at the soldiers. The thrumming of power in his ears made it difficult to think, and he couldn't focus his eyes. He stepped back to widen the space around him.

"Let me through," he said, his voice sounding strange to his own ears.

Landlan shivered, and then anger swept over his face. "No. I think I'll kill you instead." He motioned to the bowman with a jerk of his head.

Kavi laughed, a wild high-pitched note that set men's teeth on edge. He opened his arms. "People of Belega." He'd raised his voice and all within hearing stopped in their tracks at the throb of power in the air. "You've hated and feared me since I first stepped on your shores. You fear my people because of our gifts. I'll show you that you were right to fear."

He stooped to pick up a handful of dirt. A tiny part of his mind pleaded for reason, but he'd gone beyond that point. Power flowed into him from the earth and from the air he breathed so deeply. He opened his hand and blew lightly on the dust he held. It began to swirl, slowly at first, then with increasing speed, until a tiny whirlwind formed in his open palm. With a sound of delight, he tossed the swirling mass into the night sky.

The cyclone hit Barkuit with a roar of wind and blinding dirt. Men and horses became drawn into the swirling chaos as it touched down. Kavi stood at its calm center with Landlan. The man fell on his knees, unnerved by the terror of the wind. He begged Kavi to stop as the bowman, along with every man within reach, continued to be swept from the walls and streets. Kavi had become part of the storm in all its glory and ignored him.

But someone urgently called his name. As his consciousness slammed back into his body, he recognized Natan's voice and knew safety lay close by, just out of reach. He flung his arms toward the gates, and Landlan screamed, the cyclone nearly taking him as it burst through the oak and stone of the wall, leaving a large gap in its wake.

Kavi folded his arms on his chest, the whirlwind dying to nothing. Dust settled on the silent world. A quarter of the city lay in ruins at his feet. Broken buildings and crushed men tangled in heaps of mortar and stone and blood around him.

He walked unseeing through the shattered gates. Power still pulsed in his body and held him in its sway. On impulse, Kavi moved toward the voice that softly called his name in the night.

NATAN FALTERED, WEAK from holding the energy surging inside him. He covered his eyes and concentrated on the soul adrift in the flow of power.

"Go after him," he panted.

Bryon stooped closer, tilting his head as if to hear him better.

"Kavi's lost," he urged. "Bring him to me, please."

"Yes, lad."

Natan sat on a campstool beside Basal in the large tent, waiting, his head bowed as he gathered his thoughts and strength. He could see Kavi in his mind, a solitary figure in the dark, who walked unharmed out of the wrecked gates of the city. In a few moments, he watched Bryon and his soldiers approach him.

They stopped a few paces away and Bryon called Kavi's name. Kavi's skin resembled pale marble in the moonlight, his eyes glittering at some inner vision. He let Bryon take his arm to lead him toward the Nagal camp. A murmur of fear and growing anger rose from the newly awakened soldiers as they approached.

"Peace," Bryon growled. The men gave back grudgingly to their captain, only to close in again behind the Karthagan. Bryon kept his head down, hiding the anger glittering in his eyes.

Natan climbed painfully to his feet as they brought Kavi to him. He took his hands, shaken to his depths at having him safe. He placed Kavi's hands on Basal's chest. Moving closer, so their bodies touched, he set his own hands over them and cleared his mind.

"Kavi?" he called, searching for his spark in the recesses of his thoughts. He could no longer feel him. He asked for strength in humble supplication. The essence of life stirred in answer. Yet even as he felt the power inside him, doubts flooded his mind, and he cried out, anguished, pulling his hands from Kavi's.

"What is it, Mage?" Bryon touched Natan but Natan jerked away.

"I'm not him!"

"You're not Gregor. I know that. But you are our Mage now. Our teacher. Gregor believed in you. Believe in yourself. Trust him."

Natan frantically searched his face. Bryon steadily returned his look, nodding encouragement. Taking a breath, he turned back to the wounded men and started again. Where could Kavi's spirit be?

He let his own spirit go into the whirling tide of life to seek for the one special soul that belonged to his friend. "Kavi?" he called. He found him, walking on a white beach. He slowly approached him, arms outstretched.

Kavi turned to him with a smile and embraced him. "Hello."

Natan held him as they shared a moment of peace together on the lovely shoreline.

"You need to come back," he said gently. A frown touched Kavi's face, but he made no reply. "We need you," Natan pressed. "Basal needs you."

Kavi started at the governor's name as if awakening. "Basal? He needs me?"

"He's lost, my dear, and I can't find him without you. He won't hear me. I need to add your strength to mine."

"How can I help?"

"Come with me. Perhaps together we can find him. He hasn't much time left. He'll soon be beyond recall, and if we lose him, war will follow."

Kavi looked at his face, then nodded at whatever he saw there. The sand seemed to shift under their feet, and Natan gasped, momentarily dizzy, as he found himself back at the tent with Kavi standing over Basal's still form.

"Call to him, dear. Find him for me," he murmured in Kavi's ear.

Kavi closed his eyes. "Basal?" he whispered hesitantly, and then after a moment said firmly, as if speaking to a stubborn child, "Come back with me."

Natan gasped as Basal's chest rose on a deep breath, then firmed his lips and sent his own spirit to flow through Kavi's hands into Basal's weakened body. Natan didn't have the ability to heal him, but the strength he and Kavi had together allowed Basal to heal himself. Natan shied away from Basal's sharp mind, having no wish to see his private thoughts.

A shudder ran through Kavi and he made a sound of pain. Basal's fever suddenly broke, and they both staggered back, the connection snapping. Disoriented, he needed Bryon to help him to a nearby cot where he dropped, exhausted. Kavi swayed where he stood, so Bryon settled him into another bed, tucking a blanket around his shivering body. Natan turned his head and blinked dazedly at Kavi's drawn face on the pillow.

"Are you well?" he asked, hoping Kavi had made it all the way back to him.

"Yes. Natan, thank you. I lost my way…"

"I'll always find you," Natan promised, hoping to the gods he spoke the truth. He blinked his heavy eyelids, sleep creeping up on him. The gift of power from the Mage frightened him even more than the morning he'd buried his parents and returned alone to his empty shack. He'd drawn energy from the earth, the air, from life itself, until it surged through a body barely able to contain it. His soaring spirit had held it in check by sheer will.

"But will I always be strong enough to control it?" Doubt ate at him. Kavi had touched that power and been lost to it, a Karthagan born with the gift. How could Natan hope to do better?

He sighed, curling up on the cot to sleep. His mind wandered into strange dreams of a world torn apart by war and madness, the people using their gifts of power to destroy what they couldn't possess. He woke several times, heart pounding, sweat stinging his eyes, so nearly sobbed with relief when he finally opened his eyes to daylight, the long night over.

Rubbing his gritty eyes, he sat up, his gaze going immediately to the nearby cot. Kavi still slept, his dark hair half hiding his sweet face. Natan allowed his gaze to caress a soft cheek, the stubborn chin. He touched his lips with a finger, aching to feel the press of Kavi's full lips against them, the wicked slide of his tongue into Natan's mouth. Gods!

Dragging his gaze away, he looked desperately to where the governor still slept. There were many things to attend to. He climbed stiffly to his feet and crossed the room. Basal's forehead felt cool to the touch. A good sign.

"My lord, it's time to wake," he said, voice soft. Basal's face wrinkled into a frown and Natan sighed, knowing he was rousing the man to an unpleasant day. He heard horses approaching in the distance so put a hand on Basal's shoulder, shaking gently. "Basal, they've come. Wake up."

Basal's lids fluttered against his pale skin, then opened on dark brown eyes. The curious, sleepy gaze quickly turned sharp and the governor pushed up on an elbow. "Natan? What is it?"

Bryon entered the tent at that moment flanked by two soldiers. He gave the governor a quick bow. "My lord, Barkuit is here. They still wish to sign the treaty."

Basal shot Natan a glance, but Natan kept his expression neutral. This was for the governor to decide. He'd not interfere. His senses had heightened immeasurably with the power the Mage had passed to him. He caught the echo of emotions and turmoil in the minds around him, but he didn't trust his interpretation of them yet. The sharp cut of truth and the insidious tendrils of deceit were an intricate dance, hard to separate.

Basal climbed stiffly to his feet, drawing on the clothes Bryon handed him. "What can you tell me?"

"After the assassination of Governor Gargary, Captain Syros was proclaimed Regent of Barkuit, standing in for the baby, Willum, until he comes of age. At least that's how it's been explained to me. He's here now with several soldiers and that bastard, Landlan."

Basal sat back on the cot, pulling on his boots. "They have the treaty with them?"

"Yes, sir."

Natan straightened his clothes and ran fingers through the tangles in his shoulder-length hair. He dearly wanted to find a river soon to wash away the grime and sweat of the last few days. Basal rose to his feet, lifted a brow, and Natan nodded. Hearing his name called softly, he looked behind him, felt his heart stumble as he met Kavi's intent gaze. Was that pride in his bright eyes? For him? Damn, Kavi confused him, left him in knots of longing and elation.

Bryon put a hand on his arm. "Time to go, lad."

Natan followed the soldiers outside the tent, wincing when Kavi's quiet chuckle trailed after him. Would he ever understand him? He seemed to delight in teasing him, keeping Natan off-balance. Sometimes he wished he'd never met the Karthagan.

"Liar," he muttered. He hadn't been alive until Kavi touched him. The group wound their way through the waking army camp, soldiers bowing to the governor, then watching them pass with speculative eyes. They knew Basal had come in bloody and wounded the night before, yet here he walked, strong as ever. Natan avoided their gaze. He'd scouted for some of these men, but most were strangers to him. He sensed their suspicion of anyone this close to Basal who wasn't one of their own. And the betrayal by some of their fellow soldiers hadn't lessened their mistrust.

The Barkuit contingent was seated at a makeshift table on the outskirts of camp, their crimson-and-silver banner waving overhead. Landlan rose as they approached, a grin spreading on his face at their cold bearing. "Well met, Bryon," he called, then laughed outright when Bryon spat several profanities and dropped a hand to his knife. "Now, now. That language is no way to greet a fellow townsman. And Basal. Tell me"—he leaned toward them—"feeling better?"

"Enough, Landlan."

Natan spoke softly, but Landlan's mouth closed with a snap. He seemed confused when he met Natan's gaze, and he shivered, lowering his eyes.

Syros rose from the table. "Governor Basal, welcome. I regret to inform you that Gargary has died of his wound. I'm here as acting Regent for Governor Willum, who is much too young at present to rule. Shall we see to the treaty?"

Basal nodded and took the indicated chair opposite Syros. "Mage, please be my witness," he requested.

Landlan shook his head as if waking from a daze and reached into the saddlebag beside the table, removing the treaty along with quill and ink. He unrolled the parchment with a flourish, then showed it to Basal, who took it gingerly in his hands. Natan read over his shoulder.

"It seems in order, my lord," he said, thanking the gods the treaty had been scripted in simple words. He could read, and though some terms were still outside his grasp of understanding, he was somehow aware of the intent behind the words. He caught Landlan's smirk and felt the sting of blood in his cheeks. *Damn the man.*

Basal smoothed the parchment on the table to sign his name on the bottom. The others looked on curiously as he handed the quill to Natan to sign as witness. Natan's face heated again at Landlan's mocking laugh when he carefully added his name. Syros scowled as he took the pen and scribbled his signature across the bottom. With a cry of triumph, Landlan signed the document as his witness. With that done, the men stood and shook hands.

"Peace," Syros said, sounding sincere. Their horses were brought, and Syros and his men mounted.

"A pleasure, Basal." Landlan gave a mocking bow. He swung effort-lessly into the saddle. "And Captain." He turned to Bryon with a wolfish grin. "Your soldiers, the ones who turned to our side? I paid them very well. There may be others. I don't remember." His grin widened. "In any case, I'll be seeing you soon."

He laughed at Bryon's startled look. With a jaunty wave, he laid heels to his horse and followed the others across the field to Barkuit's broken gates. Natan watched them enter the city, hoping they'd done the right thing that day.

Chapter Eight

NATAN FOLLOWED BASAL into the center of the army camp, shoulders tensed, hunched against the stares of the soldiers. He had to will his muscles to relax, longing to return to the days before the war. But there was no going back, for any of them. In signing the treaty, he'd reinforced his claim as the Mage, Basal's teacher and counselor. At that moment, he wished he'd never left his simple shack on the river.

Basal stopped when they came upon his group of commanders. "The treaty is signed," he informed them. "Break camp. Let's go home."

The news traveled the ranks, and the men cheered at the sudden end of hostilities. The camp became a flurry of activity as fires were doused and forgotten packs retrieved. With a bow, Natan excused himself to hurry to the tent he'd shared with the others the night before. It worried him to find it empty. Where had Kavi gone? Picking up his pack from against a canvas wall, he stepped into the bustling army to look for him. For the most part the soldiers ignored him, going about their business. But there were enough black looks and muttered words after he passed that it was a relief to find Kavi sitting on a boulder outside of camp talking quietly with Bryon while they shared a meal.

He wrinkled his brow. Something about the scene troubled him. The two appeared to be isolated, the soldiers keeping away from them, and though occasionally someone would glance their way, it was with a dark scowl. The animosity burned his heart.

"Kavi, gather your things and find a horse. We're going."

Kavi looked up, his protest dying on his lips at whatever he saw in Natan's face. "Yes, Mage," he said, jumping from the rock and disappearing into the camp.

"You're going, then?" Bryon asked, watching him closely.

Natan gave a sharp nod. "At once."

Bryon slid to the ground. "As you wish, my lord." He bowed formally. "Of course, I'm coming with you."

Natan studied the leaves under his feet. "I've been a blind fool, Bryon. I thought our people would accept Kavi, given time. Or at least let him live in peace. I see now that I've been mistaken. Old fears are hard to put aside. And without Gregor to protect him…"

"Don't condemn the soldiers, Natan. They've seen Kavi's power, and it scares them. He destroyed the Barkuit gates, don't forget. You scare them as well. It's going to take time for them to grow accustomed to you."

"Perhaps. In the meantime, I want to see Kavi safely to Amara and then on a ship to the Isle of Wind. I fear for his life in Belega."

Kavi came up, leading the horses, Governor Basal at his side.

"You are welcome to ride with us, Mage," Basal urged. "I will guarantee Kavi's safety."

Natan smiled despite his troubled heart. "Thank you, my lord. But there are many soldiers here, and the nights are dark. You can't watch them all. We'll travel alone and swiftly. Besides—" He gave Basal a crooked grin. "—if I can't protect him, who can?"

Bryon shifted on his feet, eyeing the soldiers gathering close. "Natan, we'd better go."

Natan looked questioningly at Kavi, who lifted a brow. "Do I have any say in this?"

Chewing a lip, filled with doubts, Natan hoped he wouldn't argue. "Please, Kavi. We need to do this. Trust me."

Something flickered in Kavi's eyes, too quick to read clearly, but Natan could have sworn it was admiration. He kept the thought close to his heart when Kavi's face settled into its usual mocking smile. "For now, my dear Mage." He swept Natan a bow and climbed into his saddle.

Natan picked up the reins of his own mount, but the governor put a hand on his shoulder. "Be safe, my friend," Basal said warmly. "I am not done with your wise counsel as yet. I believe our beloved Mage knew what he was about in choosing you for his successor."

Natan swallowed a hard lump in his throat. "Thank you, lord," he said, grateful for the confidence in him, then swung into the saddle. Bryon mounted his own horse, and they left at a trot, Natan breathing easier as they left the Nagal camp behind.

Late evening had fallen by the time they reached the Dakon Forest. Natan slid from the saddle thankfully, ready for some hot tea and sleep. Kavi joined him, and they looked curiously at Bryon, who remained in the saddle.

"Bryon?" Natan asked when the man continued to stare into the darkening forest.

The soldier stirred and met his gaze, eyes wide. Natan's heart jumped at the fear lingering in their brown depths. "We have to keep going. Something calls…"

"Bryon!" Natan made his voice purposely sharp. "What do you mean?"

Bryon shook his head, confusion sweeping his face. "I'm not sure. A voice calls to me, lost, so lonely." His eyes widened further with surprise. "Someone in Siagan. I have to go—"

"No, you don't." Kavi's angry tone startled them. "It's a ghost from the caves under Siagan. I hear her too. Leave it be, Bryon."

"I can't…"

Kavi shrugged, a cold mask settling over his features. "Suit yourself. I, for one, still have nightmares of that foul place. I won't return."

Natan chewed the inside of his bottom lip, feeling torn. "I have to stay with Kavi," he said at last, hating to choose between them.

Bryon nodded. "That's your only option, Mage. Stop by my cabin on your way through Amara. There's fresh supplies put away in the pantry, and you can rest there safely until you start your journey."

Natan reached out his hand to grip Bryon's. "Thank you. You've always been good to me." He frowned, adding, "Stay out of Council Leader Mandel's way. He's known for his cruelty—"

"And I hold too many secrets," Bryon finished for him.

"Be safe."

Bryon nodded but glanced aside, hiding his expression. Natan sighed, but he saw no alternative. For good or ill, he had to go where his heart decreed, and it seemed Bryon's fate lay elsewhere. Apprehension touched his heart, but he put it aside. Bryon had to find his own way.

He waited until Bryon rode into the trees then staked the horses, rubbing down their coats while Kavi built a fire. Natan's thoughts raced. The Karthagan had been unusually quiet, not meeting his eyes when they shared water and some dried fruit as they traveled. They hadn't had a chance to speak about what had happened in Barkuit. Natan let out a weary breath, braiding his horse's mane while he fought to control his disappointment. Would Kavi never open his heart to him?

Once he'd settled his turbulent emotions, he joined Kavi at the fire. Again, Kavi ignored him, poking at the burning wood with a stick. Natan's mind raced as he tried to find something, anything, to say to nudge through the barrier Kavi had put between them.

He almost missed Kavi's whispered, "I'm afraid."

Natan blinked in surprise. "Of what?"

Loathing crossed Kavi's face. "Of myself," he said in despair. "I stood in that courtyard in Barkuit and simply let the power fill me. I didn't think of the men there. I didn't know if friends were close by. I only knew that I was trapped and needed to be free. I had the power to be, and I used that power with no regard for anything in my path. I gloried in that power, and men died." Kavi hung his head.

Natan had no answer for him. He'd felt that same energy pulsing through himself, luring him with its promise of power and glory. He wasn't sure how he'd resisted…

Shuddering with the memory, he pulled Kavi against him. Slowly Kavi's tense body calmed, and he settled into Natan's arms with a sigh. Natan held him close, holding his breath in the rare, intimate moment.

"I think that's why my people were so drawn to the Mage when he came to our isle," Kavi began, voice muffled by Natan's coat. He moved, resting his head against Natan's shoulder. "He claimed to simply be a traveling scholar, but we could sense the power in him, greater than our own. Yet, despite the power at his command, there was a deep peace within him, at the very core of his strength. We hoped he'd teach us to use the energies of life as he did, to remain in control through that same sense of oneness he felt with the world. But now Gregor is dead and with him perhaps the last hope for my people."

"There's always hope." Natan stared into the red-and-blue flames dancing across the burning wood. Doubt ate at him again. He wanted to finish Gregor's task, to bring peace to the Karthagan people, if only for Kavi's sake. But he held none of Gregor's serenity in his heart, only the fear of failure and the very real danger of losing control.

He remained silent, so Kavi tilted his head to look at him, his beautiful eyes dark with misery and uncertainty. Natan impulsively leaned down and kissed him, nudging his tongue against those soft as silk lips. Kavi opened to him so Natan, heart pounding, slid his tongue into the warmth of his lover's mouth. Kavi gripped the back of his head, holding him down, taking control.

Natan let him, going willingly when Kavi pushed him onto his back. Kavi tightened his hold in his hair while he deepened his kisses, demanding Natan's response. Pain and pleasure. For a brief instant Natan panicked. What if enemies were close by? But Kavi suckled his lips, then shifted and licked along Natan's throat, pulling at the hem of his shirt. Natan sank into the grass. All his life he'd needed to be careful, alert to danger in order to survive. Kavi stripped him of this, taking Natan's body however he chose, and Natan surrendered.

He gasped when Kavi nibbled across his stomach, cool air striking his skin as his shirt was pushed upward. Kavi nipped one of his nipples, tugged on it, and pleasure exploded through him, the cry strangled in his throat. A rough tongue licked at the sensitive bud while Natan hardened under the assault. He threaded fingers through Kavi's dark hair and dared to push downward, rewarded by Kavi's chuckle and that wicked tongue slipping along his body.

Kavi made short work of the knot at Natan's pants, undoing the strings, then moved to kneel between his legs. Natan raised up on an elbow, drinking in the sight of Kavi hovering over him. After Kavi removed his own shirt, Natan devoured his flawless, olive skin, the sleek, toned muscles of his chest and abdomen. Kavi captured his gaze and deliberately looked downward. Natan followed suit, his breath hitching on a surge of hunger and lust as Kavi undid his own pants, spilling his gorgeous cock.

Natan impatiently brushed at the tears in his eyes, aching with need for this elusive man. Kavi's keen gaze softened, warmth replacing the bright glitter of desire. He lowered himself over Natan and took them both in hand.

"Darling," Kavi breathed against his lips and kissed him. Natan scrambled to reinforce the wall protecting his heart. Kavi in this gentle mood devastated him, his loneliness filling with Kavi's scent, the heat of his skin, the pleasure pounding through his body. Kavi's sweet tongue plunged into his mouth, breaking him. Natan whimpered his surrender, Kavi stoking the flame in his heart while his skillful hand drove them into ecstasy.

BRYON DREW HIS horse to a halt, frustrated, confused. What was going on? He'd planned to travel due south, skirting the northern cities after deciding it was safer to take Kavi's advice and ignore the voice calling to him. But as the day progressed, he somehow kept turning east despite his best efforts, until he found himself outside of Siagan. Bewildered, he slid from his horse's back and staked the animal. He couldn't understand how he'd gotten there, the one place he wanted to avoid at all costs.

He stared at the carved stone marker of the hole he and Natan had entered on their last visit, a shiver running through him. Something lingered down there that he had no desire to face. And yet it nagged at his mind, drawing him with a Siren's call he couldn't resist nor ignore.

"Well, let's go," he muttered under his breath, putting aside the warning from Natan about the council leader, Mandel. He'd make sure not to get caught. Although his skin crawled, he lowered himself into the darkness of the earth. When he reached the floor, he gave one last look at the sky far above and took a shuddering breath. Gathering his courage, he plunged into the tunnel in the mountainside, calling himself every black name he could think of. Fool, mostly.

As he made his way deeper into the tunnel, he became hyperaware of the earth around him, heavier than life. The thin air stole his breath as he groped through yet another narrow passageway to the right, fear knotting his stomach. He'd been unable to find a spare torch in any of the wall sconces and fumbled in blind darkness toward the horror waiting for him.

He could sense the creature ahead, bearing a loneliness as deep as a black well, despairing. It called to him and he went, although his courage shriveled to nothing in the darkness. But that other will grew stronger, pulling him to the foul water below. He wondered vaguely if the water of the underground lake remained as cold as Kavi had described.

The walls of the tunnel opened again, giving him the feeling of a vast space, and he straightened his spine in relief, though the damp air made his bones ache. He blinked as his eyes swam with speckles of color while they struggled to adjust to the darkness. Bryon began to resent the power that lured him against his will, his temper rising.

"What do you want?" he called into the darkness and opened his arms, daring it to do its worse. Pain struck him suddenly, doubling him over, driving him to his knees. His tongue swelled. His lips cracked and blackened. There was no water to ease his thirst…

No! This was not his pain. He experienced *her* thirst…

She sat in the dark room, full of fear, weeping. They had forgotten her. How many hours had it been? Or was it days? She swallowed, her throat on fire, thirst an overwhelming need. She'd quickly lost track of time, her senses going in the numbing blackness around her. She feared her mind would go as well.

Then they'd come, the others, the spirits in the lake. They called to her, pleading for release, until her mind slipped and she fled into a black forgetfulness of her own design…

Bryon drew a sharp breath, and the pain eased as quickly as it had come. He sat back on his heels, blinking away the terrible vision. The urgency remained however, quivering in the air, a plea that became an ache in his heart. He stood and reached out, touched the wall again and began to follow it to the right around the lake. Nausea hit him in a glinting swirl of colors, and he leaned against the wall, retching violently.

"Enough!" he begged, but the pull of the creature was relentless, and he stumbled along the uneven shoreline. At last he reached the rotten frame of a door. Placing his palms on the wood, he pushed, and the soft boards yielded. Suddenly desperate, he slammed his fist into the wood until it split beneath his blows. His hands became bruised, then lacerated on jagged splinters as he continued to batter at it, but a frenzy took control of him and he couldn't stop.

Bryon finally drove a shoulder into the weakened frame. With a loud crack it gave way, and he fell through to the room beyond. He lay panting on the dirt floor as pain struck him in waves that left him sobbing into his hands, praying that it would end.

Cold fingers brushed against his face in the darkness. He cried out in terror and tried to draw away, but the touch had frozen him to the earth.

A voice dry as dust whispered in the black room, "Thirst."

Bryon's tongue turned to ashes.

"Loneliness," it breathed, and he stood suddenly on a grassy hillside with his heart pounding as he leaned on the shovel, looking at the open graves of his parents and sister, lost to illness.

"Despair," the voice commanded, and Bryon cried out as his memories rushed to a bleak day and the well Kavi had been thrown into.

"Death," the voice commanded in the darkness, so Bryon went gratefully into the pit.

Pain, and the coldness of the ground where he lay prone on his stomach, brought him back to the lake. He raised his head. Colors swirled, screaming in the icy blackness.

"Why are you doing this to me?" It was an effort to speak. Thirst became an agony he couldn't ignore, and he tasted blood where his lips had split open.

Someone grabbed his hair, jerking his head back. He felt cold fingers on his throat. "It's no more than you did to me and my people. But know this." He felt a warm breath on his cheek. "Barkuit will never triumph over us."

"I'm not from Barkuit," he managed as she pulled harder on his hair, making breathing difficult.

"You lie."

She slammed his face against the ground while sharp nails dug into his scalp. He screamed as his skull seemed to rip open, and then she walked into his mind. The crawling sensation came close to driving him mad.

She released him suddenly, and he heard her back away, her own breath coming in sharp gasps in the darkness. "I don't understand."

She sounded lost, bewildered. Bryon found he could move and dragged his protesting muscles to sit cross-legged on the ground. The blinding pain began to ease in his head, so he took several deep breaths until the dizziness passed.

"Who are you?" he asked carefully. Since she called to mind an animal half wild with fear, he tried not to frighten her further. He could sense her hesitation. Slowly she came and sat opposite him, and they contemplated each other without sight in the darkness.

"Well, girl, you've hurt me, believing me an enemy. What do you intend to do with me now?"

He heard her indrawn breath and quick movement and steeled himself, but instead of pain, he felt awe as a tiny flame appeared in the blackness. It seemed to float above a delicate hand and grew until it illuminated a face of such beauty it stole his breath. Karthagan, to be sure, no older than Kavi. But while Kavi's eyes were dark, hers were a piercing amber. Her fair hair framed a complexion of the lightest olive.

She studied him with equal intensity. "You're not Barkuit," she acknowledged with a tilt of her head, curious. "Where do you come from? Are you also a prisoner?"

"I'm from Amara on the western shoreline. And no, I'm not a prisoner." A frightening thought sprang into his mind, and he recoiled from the young woman before he could stop himself.

She startled, clearly alarmed by his reaction. Then she looked at herself, at the clothes that had become tattered rags and her hands that were now thin claws. She sent him a pleading look but lowered her gaze instantly.

"Forgive me for offending you." She gave a painful laugh. "I've been here a long time." The light in her hand dimmed as if to hide herself.

Bryon cursed softly, stirred to pity. He gently touched her face and felt warm skin. He took her hand, finding the pulse of life. However she had come to be there, she seemed real enough now, and that sufficed for the moment.

"Come with me out of this horrible place," he told her.

She nodded and let him help her up. The flame in her hand brightened, so they could see their way clearly out of the tiny cell. The young woman stopped at the edge of the lake. Bryon heard her soft cry of pain.

"He called to us," she whispered in growing panic. "He called and my people rose from the lake at his bidding. But I couldn't follow. I couldn't get past the door." She covered her face with a shaking hand. "I don't understand. What's happened to me?"

"Hush, girl." Bryon gently put an arm around her to turn her from the water. "Come away." He took her hand, and she followed as one asleep. Often the flame in her hand would go dim, and they would stumble on the path. But then the darkness would frighten her, so the spark would flare up brilliantly again. At last they came to the rope and the way out. The woman looked at the blue sky shining in the opening above them, her incredulous smile breaking Bryon's heart.

"Up you go, lass," he said huskily and helped her climb the rope.

They found the horse where Bryon had picketed it, mounted, and he turned them toward the sunset. They remained silent as they traveled, Bryon listening for the sound of approaching hooves, but a few hours of riding brought them safely into the Southern Territory. As the sun lowered, he drew to a halt. It was time to ask some questions. He dismounted and turned to help the young woman, but she'd already jumped from the saddle to begin stripping the horse. He gave her an approving nod and set about making a fire. A small stream flowed nearby, so he filled the largest cooking pot in his saddlebag and set it over the fire to heat.

"Dinner?" the woman asked as she watched him.

"No." He smiled at her and pulled his pack close, taking out a strip of cloth and ripping it in two pieces. He also removed a soft shirt and britches. He looked at the pants and then at the woman and frowned before cutting a string of leather from a coil at the bottom of his pack. Rummaging further, he found a small packet of soap. He bundled everything together and handed it to her.

"I'm going to find something to eat." He nodded toward the trees. "While I'm gone, I'd like you to wash and put on these clothes. Not much to look at, I'm afraid, but they're clean and warm." He turned away, then hesitated. "My dear, I don't even know your name."

The young woman scrambled to her feet. "I'm Lady Kirstin, my lord." She gave him a deep curtsy.

Dull color flooded Bryon's face. "No need for that, lass. I'm no lord. Merely a lowly soldier."

She made no comment, but he saw the subtle altar of her expression, a cooling of her friendship. He gave her a stiff bow and stalked off. If the lady thought he was going to fumble over himself to please her, she was doomed to disappointment.

He returned sometime later with a few fish to find the fire built up and tea brewing. Kirstin's silken hair was tied in a loose braid, and she wore his clothing, making him smile. She looked like a child. He gutted the fish and they cooked them on spits.

"This is like camping with my father and my brother, Kayden," Kirstin said. An impish smile stole over her face. "Of course, we'd be eating venison from the hunt and drinking red wine."

Bryon rose and gave her an exaggerated obeisance. "Your pardon, my lady. I'll try to do better the next time I rescue you."

He grinned as she laughed, peace restored. Bryon watched her in the firelight, questions springing to his lips. He swallowed them down, admitting that he feared the answers. She'd been imprisoned by unnatural means, he had no doubt, but those questions were best left to someone with more wisdom than he.

"Well, girl, get some sleep," he said presently, omitting her title to put her at ease, and tossed her one of the saddle blankets. He rolled himself in the other, closing his eyes.

Morning found them traveling west, Kirstin wearing his cloak and Bryon wrapped in blankets against the chill. At noon they turned sharply south. He hoped that by doing so they would skirt Lord Fredrik's land. He didn't like the rumors coming out of there, though they could use fresh supplies. He didn't care for himself, but Kirstin deserved more than a handful of nuts and dried fruit for breakfast.

He swore and pulled the horse to a stop, hearing voices on the trail ahead. As horsemen rode out of the forest, Bryon looked over his shoulder, a challenge in his eyes. Kirstin answered with a fierce look of her own and they were off, the horse rearing as Bryon turned him sharply. An arrow whistled over Bryon's shoulder as he tucked into the saddle and raced back down the trail the way they'd come.

He veered south as soon as the trees opened, hoping he didn't lame the horse on the uneven terrain. A horn began to sound behind them as the horse labored under the strain of two riders. He gave a great shout of excitement, never having been a fugitive before. His heart raced as adrenaline pumped through him, blood roaring in his ears. He glanced back and caught Kirstin's look of utter glee as they sped along, and he grinned wickedly. She'd do.

They traveled in that manner as far as the horse could endure; then Bryon slowed to guide him west again. They needed a safe place to hide, and he knew the perfect spot, fate willing.

Chapter Nine

KAVI STRUGGLED TO wake against a terrifying sense of drowning. In his dreams, the energies of life swirled around a woman in a bewildering kaleidoscope of color. She turned her face to him, and Kavi cried out as rich amber eyes pierced him from across the sandy beach.

"No!" he cried as he finally woke. The water of the Lake of Glass remained smooth and still. Moonlight shimmered on its surface. Kavi dropped his head back on the blanket to stare at the few remaining stars in the morning sky.

Natan shifted in the blankets, pulling Kavi closer in his sleep. Kavi smiled. Natan had been very attentive while they traveled, making sure he ate and caring for the horses. They hadn't made love again, though Natan did a poor job hiding his longing. But Natan needed more from a lover than Kavi could willingly give, and despite himself, Kavi had grown fond of him.

Which only made what he needed to do that much harder. He

carefully untangled their limbs and climbed to his feet. A frown crossed Natan's pretty face, but he didn't wake. Kavi studied him, recalling the pleasure of that strong body moving against his own. Warmth gathered in his heart, surprising him. Definitely time to be going.

He threw his pack together in a burst of impatience, intending to reach Bryon's cabin that day, gather some supplies, and go on to the sea. Natan had told him where his small boat lay hidden. Kavi rubbed the sleep from his eyes as he saddled his horse, then swung onto its back, riding at an easy pace into the dense forest.

Following Bryon's directions, he found the cabin by midmorning, only to stop on the trail in surprise. Bryon described his home as being a dilapidated shack set amongst weeds. The reality took Kavi's breath for a moment. A gentle green slope rose out of the surrounding pines with the white pine cabin at its crown. Wildflowers bloomed profusely around a wide porch, and a vegetable garden and stone well took up the yard on the right.

After walking the horse to the back of the dwelling, he dismounted, then climbed the rear porch, finding the door unlatched as promised. Taking a breath, he stepped directly into the kitchen. With a slightly guilty conscience, he rifled through Bryon's stores and packed enough for several days. He knew Bryon had offered the provisions to Natan, but he did what was necessary. He needed to get to the sea before Natan caught up to him.

The thought brought him little cheer as he reluctantly left Bryon's cabin. As much as he dreaded it, he knew he would have to travel past Amara to reach the stream that would lead him to the sea. As he drew near the village, a cold dread crept over him, a lingering nightmare of the well he'd been shoved into, his despair. He made a wide detour around the place.

At last he came to the stream Natan had described. Thick growth hung over the swift flowing water, and it took some time to find the path hidden in the brambles, little more than a game trail. Kavi thoughtfully chewed his lips. If he walked slowly, would Natan catch up? Or had he already started for his own home, leaving Kavi to make his way to the Isle of Wind alone? That would be best. Natan would no more be welcomed on the Isle than Kavi had been in Belega. Thoroughly out of sorts, Kavi plodded along the trail, listening to the cheery murmur of the stream until he eventually came to the sea.

Wearily stripping the saddle and bridle from the horse, he let him go with a whispered word to find its way back to Nagal, then studied the waves hitting the shoreline. The tide flowed against him. Discouraged, he threw a saddle blanket onto the sand and lay back against a clump of driftwood, gloomily watching the waves come in.

The sound of the ocean soothed his taught nerves. Kavi closed his eyes, thinking of the white beaches on the Isle of Wind. Would Natan like his home? He began to drift off, picturing Natan's pale skin growing bronze in the bright sunlight. Suddenly he sat up, hand slipping to his knife. Footsteps padded on the forest trail behind him, and he unexpectedly heard whistling. Kavi rose into a crouch, but fell back on his heels in part dismay, part gladness, as a slim figure emerged from the trees.

"Hello, darling. Don't bother to get up." Natan gave a mocking bow and made himself comfortable on the blanket beside him.

Kavi opened his mouth several times to speak, then exasperation washed through him, swamping his sudden joy. "What are you doing here?"

Natan studied the tips of his boots. "I'm coming with you."

Kavi snorted. "My father might have something to say about that.

Gavin Herran won't suffer a Belegan on the Isle of Wind."

Natan shrugged. "Nevertheless, I'm going. The Mage said the Karthagans will need my help. I plan to offer it to them."

"No. You're not—"

Natan claimed his mouth. The kiss began almost mockingly, but as it deepened, Kavi gave in to Natan's yearning and growing passion. Natan stopped all of a sudden and leaned his forehead against Kavi's.

"The tide's changing. Perhaps we should go," Natan suggested in a broken voice, his hands gentle on Kavi's arms. But Kavi could hear his quick breathing and feel the tremble in his body. He tried to catch Natan's gaze, but Natan turned his face away.

"Nattie?" he asked, but Natan wouldn't look at him. Kavi touched his face, but he jerked away as if struck. Biting his lip, Kavi cupped Natan's face with his hands, turning Natan toward him. A terrible longing was etched in his face, and deep in his eyes, Kavi could see the beginnings of despair.

With a soft cry, Kavi went into his arms, seeking his lips. Natan took his mouth hungrily, desperately, but all too soon broke off their kiss.

He stood, putting a hand out to Kavi. "The boat is farther up the beach. Let's go."

Kavi stared at his hand a moment, bemused, then rose without his aid. He followed Natan along the tree line and helped pull the skiff from the tall grass. They pushed it into the surf, and in a moment caught the swell of the tide, then rode the waves far out to sea. Natan stared at the receding shoreline until Kavi put a hand on his shoulder. "You can still go back."

Natan threw him a furious look, then moved to the far side of the skiff and tied off the sail. Kavi shrugged, then set about making the boat comfortable for the journey. It would take several days to reach the Isle of Wind. In a few short words, they decided to sail by turns, and soon enough, Natan found a spot on the planking and pulled the blankets over his head to sleep. Kavi scowled at him. He hadn't lied to Natan, never promised his heart. If the man chose to be hurt, that was his own affair. Kavi looked out at the broad expanse of water, setting his teeth for a couple of uncomfortable days while they sailed for the isle.

Kavi was surprised at how easily they worked together during the voyage, Natan seeming to get over his heartache in short order. But on their second day at sea, Kavi felt Natan's eyes on him from where he lay in the bottom of the skiff, and Kavi frowned at him. Natan should be sleeping. He'd been up most of the night, until early morning, while Kavi slept, and he needed to be alert for whatever lay ahead.

"We'll reach the isle soon enough," he said impatiently. "Get some sleep."

Natan obediently dropped his head back on a coil of rope, closing his eyes.

Kavi turned his attention to the tiller, his hair loose, streaming in the wind. A smile strayed to his lips as he kept an eye on the sails and the smudge of land in the distance, loving the freedom of the sea, the salty breeze in his face. And he'd see his father, Lord Herran, and his kinsmen soon.

Then a shadow seemed to pass in front of the sun, and his sudden cry of alarm startled Natan awake. He scrambled up to join Kavi as they rounded the headland. Black smoke billowed from the tree line of pine and oak. Kavi gave Natan a panicked look, heart pounding.

"Run her ashore," Natan said grimly, and Kavi turned the bow sharply into the wind. He held the tiller steady as waves washed them aground; then, as soon as they touched land, Kavi grabbed his pack and leaped over the side of the vessel, Natan following suit. Taking a moment to drag the skiff beyond the tide, they then raced up the beach.

Dodging into the trees, they found the smoldering remains of the manor house. Kavi stared at the fallen timbers in stunned disbelief. "Father?"

Natan gripped his shoulder. "We don't know anything yet. Don't despair."

Kavi dashed tears from his eyes, and they made a hasty search of the surrounding grounds, discovering the stone walls of the structure crushed to rubble on one side and blown outward on the opposing side, as if caught in the swing of some giant pendulum.

Closing his eyes, Kavi carefully stirred the energies of the earth, searching. "Father?"

He let out a shaky breath in sudden relief. "I feel him somewhere to the southwest. Come." He pushed into the forest and Natan followed his hasty steps without question.

LORD GAVIN HERRAN stood on an outcrop of rock on the western shore and looked at the forested valley below him. His cousin Kayden's people hid in the trees. He could feel them. They'd come to his home two nights ago, and the Red Twins, Kayden's sons, had called a firestorm down from the skies that tore through the hall with a suddenness that left the few survivors stunned. Gavin still didn't understand how they'd managed to get so close to the manor without being detected. He didn't want to know what had befallen his guardsmen.

Only he and a few members of his wife's household had survived and fled this far, but it wouldn't be long before their enemies discovered them. His army was scattered somewhere to the east with no hope of arriving in time to help.

Gavin climbed from the rocks. Stepping into the ocean, he waded through the high tide to the cave where his small group took refuge for the night. His wife's sister, Johana, and her husband huddled close to the fire with their servant Wenda, all that had survived the brutal attack. His wife, Sylva, had died long ago in another such attack.

Gavin's heart grew hot as he thought of the friends and kinsmen who'd perished in those few seconds when the house burst to flames and collapsed around them. Oh yes, the Red Twins were in for an unpleasant surprise if they thought they'd go unpunished for that deed. He squatted by the fire to share in the mussels the servant girl had gathered for their supper.

After the cold, miserly meal, exhausted and scared, the family stretched out on the damp sand to get what rest they could. Gavin turned his eyes away as Johanna pulled her husband into her arms. A falling beam had struck Logan, a glancing blow on his temple. The resulting concussion had left him dazed and confused, childlike in his dependence on them for safety. Gavin grimaced, missing the man's not inconsiderable talents in the manipulation of nature.

It took some time before he fell into a restless sleep, only to awake in the night from an evil dream. What had roused him? He listened to the pounding waves, then his heart thumped, and he scrambled to his feet in the darkness, seeing them there in the cave's mouth, the Red Twins.

"Hello, cousin," they said in one voice. Their cold disdain dripped ice into Gavin's blood. A sudden, wild screech beside him made them all jump, and Wenda's small form darted across the stones toward the boys.

"No!" Gavin shouted and watched helplessly as the girl stopped in midstride, clutching at her throat, her eyes bulging as she slowly strangled without the boys even lifting a finger.

Gavin took the moment of distraction to act. Calling up the sea with a thought and sweep of his arm, he brought a thunderous wave crashing into the cave that swept the boys off their feet.

"Come!" he yelled to the others and darted through the high water to the cave entrance. The older couple followed, but not before Gavin saw the boys regain their footing. They laughed gleefully as their quarry floundered through the waves to the shore. Closing their glittering golden eyes, they clasped hands. A large form glided past Gavin, and he gave a cry of warning. Too late. Johana screamed as the shark dragged her under. Gavin reached the beach and turned to help Logan.

The man had stopped in the shallow water and faced the outcrop of rocks that hid the cave. The Red Twins walked without concern through the turbulent water toward them. Gavin saw Logan lift his hands to the sky. Clouds gathered in a rumble of thunder.

The children sneered at the stricken man's efforts. Without a motion from them, a waterspout formed around Logan and lifted him off his feet, sweeping him far out to sea. The spout dissipated and Gavin watched in disbelief as he disappeared under the rolling waves.

Gavin raced up the beach, then dodged into the trees, cursing the Red Twins under his breath. His stride faltered when he heard his name cried out in his thoughts. Who? His gaze raked the surrounding trees, unexpectedly spotting his son and a stranger in the nearby brush.

"Kavi?" He looked back at the twins wading ashore and moved quickly to Kavi's side. "Come with me." He took Kavi's hand with a sharp glance at the outsider.

They followed his quick stride, which became a run as he tried to put distance between them and the boys. They continued at that pace for nearly an hour until all three were stumbling with exhaustion.

"Father, I need to stop," Kavi panted and Gavin nodded, giving in to his own fatigue. They halted in the midst of some huge boulders, and the stranger flung himself on a low ledge, where he hung his head as he fought for breath. Kavi touched his face, the attractive Belegan giving him a rueful smile.

Gavin leaned heavily against a rock, watching them. Kavi asked over his shoulder, "What happened?"

"It was the Red Twins," he said grimly. "They came in the night without warning. Kayden has been raiding our outlying posts all week, but we never imagined he could reach the hall undetected. Kavi, everyone from the household is gone."

"Father," Kavi faltered, then straightened and looked him in the eye. "Our beloved Mage is gone as well, killed in the war taking place on Belega."

They remained silent a moment while Gavin digested the news. The Mage had promised to help them learn to control their powers. What would happen to them now?

At last Kavi drew a steadying breath. "Father, this is Natan, from the village of Amara."

Natan climbed from the rock and gave him a low bow, but Gavin ignored him, his anger simmering. Why had Kavi brought a stranger, a

Belegan, to their home?

"Seems to me it was the small-minded people of Belega who killed our Mage," he stated after a moment. "Men such as this." He looked at Natan with dislike.

"No, Father," Kavi said urgently. "They are not all like that." But there was doubt in his voice.

Natan again bowed awkwardly to Gavin. "I'm sorry for your tragic loss. The Mage imparted some of his abilities to me, and I offer you my service, such as it is, if you care to make use of it."

Gavin gave him a scornful glance, feeling little power in him. "There is nothing you can offer us," he said, dismissing the man. What had Kavi been thinking?

A withdrawn look came over Natan's face, and he climbed back on the ledge of rock and closed his eyes. After a brief hesitation, Kavi climbed up beside him. Gavin saw the stranger open his eyes in surprise, then pull him gently against his shoulder. He snorted in disgust. He'd need to do something about that. His plans for Kavi didn't include the Belegan.

He sank down and put his back to the boulder, his mind running in circles. He'd spy out his enemy's camp tomorrow, find out what Kayden planned next. Kayden had destroyed most of Gavin's supporters, but he'd be damned if he'd let his cousin seize control of the isle. Gavin's side of the family, his father in particular, had fought too hard to keep the leadership of the Karthagan people out of their cousins' hands. He wasn't about to give up his authority now. He'd sink the isle to the bottom of the sea first.

Gavin's sleep was interrupted by dreams of blood and ashes, so it was with relief when he finally opened his eyes to the morning sunlight. He sat up and rubbed his face, stretching painful muscles. Catching the faint murmur of voices above him, he narrowed his eyes. The sooner he separated the two men the better.

"Time to go," he called over his shoulder and walked to the edge of the boulder field, looking to the trees beyond. His lips curled with a satisfied smile when they came up behind him, but he didn't spare them a glance, trotting into the dense forest.

He led them cautiously from tree to tree in a roughly eastern direction, stopping often to concentrate, trying to avoid the Red Twins. He wouldn't hazard a guess where they were. Kayden seemed to have lost control of his children, the fool. They showed no concern for the lives they took.

At midmorning Gavin called a halt beside a quickly moving stream. Tall pines grew to the sandy banks, boulders in the stream sending the white water thundering toward the falls around the bend. The Belegan tossed his pack on a rotted tree stump and removed a packet of fine string and hooks. Climbing onto an outcrop of rock, he then dropped the line into the water, ignoring Gavin's snort of derision.

Kavi watched him as well until a sly smile stole to his lips. He moved to the riverbank downstream of the Belegan and placed his hand in the water. Wiggling his fingers, he began to chant in a singsong voice. Of a sudden, a dark flicker in the water swam up to him, and he scooped the fish quickly onto the sand. Natan gave him the flash of a smile, which quickly changed to dismay at the power-lust evident on his face. Kavi caught several more in like manner and carried them up the bank to clean.

Gavin laughed unpleasantly at the Belegan's concern. "He only called an animal. Nothing to be frightened of."

A strange expression crossed Natan's face, and Gavin suddenly shot a tendril of thought toward him, trying to pierce the barrier of his mind. But then a burst of pain blinded Gavin, and he let out a sharp, surprised breath. He pulled his thoughts back, and the ache abruptly ceased. Through a blur of involuntary tears, he saw Natan shake his head, looking slightly confused.

"Interesting," Gavin muttered as he walked up the bank to help Kavi with the fish while the Belegan slowly wound up the string and hook and replaced it in his pack. Kavi cooked the fish on spits over a small fire, and Gavin ate his portion in reflective silence. There had been strength in the Belegan's mind. Enough to block him. Was he as strong as the Mage? Perhaps, though he managed to hide his strength from Gavin's delving.

Gavin suddenly glanced up and stood, scanning the trees around them. Fear slithered up his back. "The Red Twins are close. We have to go," he warned and stomped out the fire.

Chapter Ten

BRYON ROLLED OVER and swore as he came up against a rock. Opening blurry eyes, he grimaced at the sunlight playing in the tree limbs overhead. He'd ridden all day and most of the night with the woman he'd rescued, and all he asked now was a few hours of uninterrupted sleep.

He heard the voices again and peered at the city below. Filthy, tired, and the few days' growth of beard on his face itched like mad. Also, he'd lost the string to tie his hair back. Someone was going to pay. A small cavalcade rode into the valley directly below him, sunlight glinting off their armor.

He edged back. After the Karthagans had been forced to leave Belega, their city of Karthag had been left mostly deserted, with only a skeletal troupe of soldiers and a few civilians living in the beautiful city. But it seemed Regent Syros was reinforcing the army's presence there. Bryon chewed a lip, reviewing his options. Where should he take Kirstin? He'd hoped to find refuge in one of the empty houses below until he could think of what to do with her. But would it be safe?

Kirstin stirred next to him, and Bryon took a deep breath. "It's time to wake."

She smiled sleepily. "Morning already?"

Bryon grunted and Kirstin sat up, a frown crossing her face as her eyes fell on the city below.

"You say that's the city of Karthag down there?" she asked, voice deceptively quiet.

"Yes," he answered. Her frown deepened and Bryon pressed his lips together.

"My uncle rules there. Why are you taking me to my enemies? Are you angry with me?" Kirstin's voice had dropped, low and dangerous. Bryon groaned in frustration. He'd hoped to avoid this conversation. Someone else should explain the passage of time to her. He would certainly make a muddle of it.

"Kirstin," he began slowly. "I need to tell you something that may confuse or frighten you, but I need you to promise me something first."

"What?"

Bryon stared at his boots and felt like a fool.

"Well?" she asked impatiently.

"You have to promise not to hurt me like you did at the lake." Bryon winced at remembered pain. "I can't take that again, Kirstin. I shall have to leave you if you do."

Kirstin looked as if she wanted to argue, and then a flush of shame touched her face. "Very well." She shrugged as if it was of no consequence. Bryon saw that it was as close to a promise as he would get.

"Now, I'll ask you again, sir," she pressed. "Why are you taking me to a city full of my enemies? Do you hate me that much?"

"Kirstin, how long do you think you were in that cell?" he countered.

Kirstin looked puzzled. "I don't know," she admitted. "A few days? A week?" A longing for reassurance laced her words and Bryon took her hand.

"My dear, prepare yourself." He looked into her eyes as they widened. "The Karthagan war ended almost thirty years ago. Your people were driven across the ocean to an isle in the Black Sea. There are no Karthagans living in Belega anymore."

Kirstin looked at him blankly. "Thirty years?" She stared at her slender white hands. Bryon gave her time. He saw with dismay the slow dawning of horror on her face. Her sudden wild laugh startled him.

"Father did this." A fierce light sprang into her eyes as she scrambled to her feet. "He did this to me!"

Her laughter took on a strange note, and Bryon had a sudden fear for her sanity. "Kirstin!

He reached for her, but she pulled away in anger. "Don't touch me. Why, what a monstrosity I am! I should be dead. Or so many years older."

It was Bryon's turn to be angry and frightened. He climbed to his feet as she continued her manic laughter, clearly in shock from his words. He struck her hard across her lovely face. She only laughed all the more frantically. He struck her again and pinned her against a tree with his strong hands.

"Look at me!" he shouted at her. She thrashed against him but couldn't loosen his hold. "Kirstin," he called her name softly, and she grew suddenly still. "Look at me."

Kirstin shook her head.

He leaned forward to whisper gruffly in her ear. "This is not your doing. There is no evil in you. You are not a monster. Please, Kirstin. Look at me."

She raised eyes wet with tears, but the crisis had passed, and they were once again clear. Bryon closed his own eyes in silent thanksgiving.

"Well," he said, releasing her. "That went well."

Kirstin giggled through her tears. Bryon smiled reluctantly in return while they resumed their seats on the outcrop of rock and watched the city awaken.

"I know what happened," Kirstin confessed in a tired voice. Bryon looked at her closely but saw only sadness in her face. He regretted the bruises already showing on her clear skin, but he hadn't known what else to do.

He listened with compassion, as she continued, "Father kept a special cell for what he called his 'dangerous' enemies. Men of great power. He sealed them in with all the strength at his disposal, and they could never be released except by his command. That was the cell I was imprisoned in, for my own safety, he'd said. And such was my faith in my father that I truly believed I couldn't be freed without his word. Ever. But I was wrong, wasn't I? It was another voice that called to me, and I awoke at his bidding. And it was you who freed me."

She turned on him suddenly. "You knew!" she accused him. "You knew I'd been there for an unnaturally long time. Why didn't you tell me? Was it to be kept a secret forever?"

Bryon shrugged. "I'm only a simple man, Kirstin, as you're so fond of reminding me. I had no idea how you'd come to be there. I only knew that you *were* there, and that you were in need, and that I am very glad I found you. Although it has been a mixed blessing," he couldn't help but add, a slow grin lifting his lips.

She dimpled at him. "Of that I have no doubt."

She grew pensive as they watched the few merchants open their shops and townsmen enter the streets of Karthag. Bryon heard her sigh several times, and he glanced at her. "What is it?"

Kirstin opened her mouth, then bit her lip, turning away. He clasped her shoulders and turned her back to him.

"Do we really have to go down there?"

Bryon blinked. "Well, no," he said slowly. "But I thought, well…" he trailed off, uncomfortable.

"Yes?" she encouraged.

He scowled. "I thought perhaps you would like a place with hot water to wash in and have a real meal for a change. And…and, blast it, girl! Aren't you bothered you've been traveling alone in the wilderness with me?"

Her peal of laughter sent the hot blood to his face. "Traveling alone with you! Really, Bryon?" She tousled his dark hair with its splashes of gray. "You're like an uncle or something. No one could possibly be uneasy."

Her laughter floated back to him as she went to pack their things, and he slowly followed, feeling he'd just been put quite soundly in his place. He wondered fleetingly if Natan was having any better luck with his Karthagan.

He needed to decide where to take the girl. To his home? Maybe. It was a place to recoup anyway. They headed south, crossing out of the Northern Territory by noon. Bryon urged haste, not stopping until the sun was long set and he couldn't see the trail in front of them.

BRYON WOKE IN the early morning after several hard days of travel, stifling the cry on his lips. He'd dreamed of Kavi, his dark hair streaming in a wild wind as he gathered all the forces of nature to him. He took them in, and the madness within him spread out to Belega and Sennia and on, until all the world was engulfed in chaos, war, and death. Even in the bright morning sunlight he felt sick with dread.

He glanced to his left and found Kirstin close by, wrapped in blankets. She had grown distant these past days, her thoughts turning inward, and occasionally he caught a strange gleam in her eyes. He didn't know what went on behind that amber gaze. Did she have terrible dreams of her own? She looked very much alone in that moment. Bryon sat beside her, leaning his head back and closing his eyes to let the sun warm him.

In time, she stirred and sat up, beautiful and wild, giving him a cool look. "Why are you still here?"

Bryon stayed silent, his own bitter words best kept unsaid.

"Are you going to trot after me forever? You needn't bother," Kirstin went on acidly. "I can very well take care of myself."

Bryon fumed. "The servant's being dismissed?"

He was unprepared for the pain that slammed into him, piercing his eyes, tearing his mind apart. Kirstin leaned closer to watch and laughed as she entered his mind.

He sat on the porch steps of his home and smiled at the laughter of the children playing in the sunshine.

"Watch me, Father," a small girl cried and tried a handspring.

"Me, me!" cried the little fairy of a girl following her sister, and she put her head down and rolled over. Bryon laughed and clapped his hands for the children, his very

own. A woman came up behind him and put her arms around him, placing her cheek against his. Her light hair hid her face…

Kirstin pressed closer. "You can't hide her from me."

"No!" Bryon shoved Kirstin from him and lurched to his feet, only to fall on his knees, retching violently as pulsing light and sound sent his mind into chaos. Slowly the pain receded, and he fell back against a tree, resting his aching eyes against his knees, exhausted.

Kirstin watched him and the satisfied smile on her face faded. "Bryon?"

He couldn't move. *Leave me be.*

"Bryon, I'm very sorry." Her voice broke, and the tears came.

Bryon looked bleakly at her. "I'm sorry, girl," he said in a hollow voice. "You've taken everything from me now, even my dreams. I have nothing left to give you. Not even forgiveness." He struggled to his feet with no thought but to get away from her.

Kirstin rose with him, gripping his arms, slight panic in her voice when she spoke, "No! Bryon, they're not gone. I've borrowed them, is all. They'll return on their own. I promise. Bryon?"

Bryon drew a shuddering breath, the pain receding under the weight of the sorrow and deep regret in the pleading amber eyes.

"I said I would leave if—"

"No! Bryon, please…"

Bryon saw her struggle against pride, felt the easing of her grip as she surrendered and began to slide to her knees. *Gods!* He refused to watch her beg.

"Enough, girl," he said hastily, holding her upright.

"I *am* sorry." Kirstin clutched his shirtfront. Emotion tightened Bryon's chest. This was intolerable. He put her from him and gave her a stern look, though his lips twitched with a wry smile he couldn't control. "We're good, but you now get to cook dinner the next two weeks."

Kirstin gave a small, watery laugh in relief. "Thank you."

Bryon nodded curtly, fighting an intense urge to pull her to him. Did she recognize herself as the one who featured in his dreams of home and family? Kirstin watched him, a new light in her eyes. Her lips parted—

The soft clop of hooves disturbed them. He glanced through the trees to see a figure approaching, then dropped a hand to his knife sheath. He smiled faintly when he recognized the soldier as he rode up. "Jaden."

Jaden jumped to the ground. "Captain. I didn't expect to find you here."

Bryon's senses heightened at his grim tone. "Is there danger?"

"Perhaps." Jaden's gaze went to Kirstin. "Basal has me on patrol, watching for any hostilities from Barkuit. It will be a while before they're trusted. But you travel with a Karthagan. I thought Kavi was the only one on our shores?"

"This is Lady Kirstin. I rescued her from a Siagan prison, right out from under that fool Mandel's nose." He hurried on at Jaden's surprised expression. "I'll explain in a moment. What danger do you think we're in?"

"Lord Fredrik's men are everywhere. He's offered a bounty for any Karthagan brought to him. He must have learned of Kavi, but I believe any Karthagan will do. You need to get her to a safe place."

"Why is Fredrik so bent on capturing a Karthagan?"

"They say for revenge. Apparently, his parents and a brother were killed in the Karthagan war. Personally, I think he wants to gain knowledge of their powers. Twist them to his own use. A very dangerous ambition, meaning trouble for the rest of us anyway."

Kirstin drew a sharp breath and clenched her hands till her knuckles whitened.

"I'm afraid," she whispered, seemingly unable to meet Bryon's gaze. "I'm afraid to the very heart of me. I've had terrible dreams lately. Premonition, of our powers being contorted in this way by a single entity. Also, there is some force pulling me toward this person, driving me beyond reason to seek him out, whether to stop or join him, I do not know. I think he's on the Isle of Wind with my people."

Bryon shivered, his own nightmares playing over in his mind. "Kavi?" Images flooded his mind, and he heard the cry of a soul in torment, caught in madness and despair as the world was torn apart around him.

Kirstin caught his hands. "We must stop him," she said fiercely.

Bryon gave a sharp nod, but he had caught a glitter in Kirstin's eyes he didn't like. To his knowledge, the Karthagans had always sought power. Did she crave the terrifying force that Kavi wielded? He hesitated. There was madness waiting below the surface for her if she chose that path.

Jaden spoke from a few paces away. "If there's trouble on the Isle of Wind, shouldn't we go?"

Bryon thinned his lips, fear tightening his chest. "We'll make for Amara and the shoreline with all haste to catch the tide. You needn't come with us, Jaden."

"I will. Basal would have me stand at your side in this, captain. And Natan could be in danger. I won't abandon my cousin when he might finally need me."

"Very well." Bryon drew a troubled breath. "We'll go to the Isle of

Wind and see what the Karthagans are up to. And the sooner the Mage is with us again the better I'll sleep."

Chapter Eleven

NATAN WOKE UP alone again. The three of them had traveled in a winding easterly direction yesterday, spending the night in a hollow formed by the roots of towering redwood trees. He heard Kavi's voice somewhere close by and Gavin's deeper tones in reply and pulled on his boots. He scratched his chin. What he wouldn't give for some hot water and a shave. And Kavi's friendship.

The dim light of morning was growing brighter as he joined father and son. "Good morning."

Gavin nodded as he walked up. The Karthagan leader appeared alert, but nervous, and seemed relieved by Natan's presence. Or at least by the presence of his abilities, such as they were. Natan smiled ruefully as Kavi stood quietly by. Kavi had lain against him during the night but may as well have been a thousand leagues away for all the warmth he'd given.

"We should reach Alek and the rest of my people by noon," Gavin said in a low voice and rocked on his heels as if anxious to be off.

"Alek?"

"Alek is my cousin," Kavi put in as he looked carefully from tree to tree as his father had done. "His parents were the ones killed in the sea yesterday."

"He is also second in command now, after me," Gavin added. "Though it breaks my heart to have to tell him his parents couldn't be saved." He swore in sudden frustration. "Something's wrong here."

Natan stiffened, every nerve alert. "My lord?"

Gavin gave him a sharp glance. "It's the Red Twins. They were trailing us throughout the day yesterday. However, I can't feel them at all today. But worse, I can't even detect Kavi, although he's right here."

"You feel it's a trap, that they're somehow deadening your senses?"

"Yes, except that I've never heard of it being done before. We can always feel when the energies of the earth are being used. Now we can't. I don't know what to think."

"Well, if it is a trap, do we have any way of stopping them?"

Gavin gave him a hard look, assessing. "No," he answered slowly. "Our only hope is to reach the others before they spring their net. Even then I can't be sure."

Natan nodded, glancing over at Kavi, who continued to search the treetops, and shook his head, not sure he could keep him safe.

"We should go," Gavin insisted, so they moved into the forest.

Natan watched Gavin's anxiety grow as they moved through the trees and frowned. This would never do, this running and hiding, then running again. They needed to find a defendable place behind which to gather their strength. He could feel the jaws of the trap closing so decided to call a halt when Gavin raised a fist. They stopped instantly. Natan looked into the trees and saw archers at the ready.

"It's Gavin Herran," Gavin cried, opening his arms, weaponless. The bows stayed trained on them as one of the soldiers climbed down.

"My lord, forgive me." The man bowed low, but a cold light remained in his eyes. "Hold out your palm, please."

Gavin blinked in surprise but quickly offered his hand. The soldier pressed his fingertips against the rough skin.

Gavin drew a quick breath. "What do you mean by this, Jarod?" he asked, his voice dangerous.

The soldier hastened to reassure him. "We've been tricked before by our enemies, my lord. I was charged by Alek to check any trespassers in this manner."

"Very well," Gavin said. "But, Jarod, be gentle with my companions. Touch their minds as lightly as may be, or I promise, you'll answer for it."

"Of course, lord." The man bowed again. He took Kavi's hand and nodded after a brief moment.

Natan tensed as the Karthagan soldier touched his hand. He felt an unpleasant crawling in his mind as if the man tried to enter his thoughts. Jarod looked puzzled, while Natan felt a sudden push inward and stifled a cry as pain burst behind his eyes.

Jarod ceased immediately. "I'm sorry, Gavin. This man's spirit is buried deep. I can't reach it without causing pain."

"Then let us through on my authority. We'll let Alek sort it out when we reach camp."

"Very well. Stay close to me, if you will. The men are nervous."

It was half a league to the camp. Natan counted a good five-score men and women as they entered. There were few children. An eerie silence fell on the company as they passed through and they eyed Natan with suspicion.

"Uncle!" A tall, intense young man strode up to grip Gavin's arm. "I feared the worst."

"We're safe, Alek." Gavin tried a smile, and then his face fell.

Alek drew a sharp breath. "My parents?"

Gavin shook his head and a spasm of pain crossed Alek's face before he went on in a shaky voice, "Please, come to the fire."

"Commander, wait," Jarod said with a quick look around. Alek paused questioningly. "This man," the soldier motioned to Natan. "I couldn't touch his spirit."

"I don't see that it's necessary," Gavin put in unexpectedly, surprising Natan. "He came with Kavi from Belega. They keep their spirits buried."

"But the others may object if he's not proven safe," Jarod argued, and they knew he included himself.

Alek looked gravely at Natan. "Of course," he said regretfully. "Please, come with me."

They moved to a small pavilion, where Alek motioned Natan to one of the camp stools. He pulled a chair opposite.

"We of Karthag live closely with the energies of the world," Alek began. "And so, the power that makes up our individual spirits is easy to sense. We can tell a friend or foe by how this energy responds to our touch. I realize that things are different on Belega, and I apologize now for any discomfort I may cause you."

He placed a hand on Natan's forehead. Natan drew a steadying breath as a tingling began in his head. The tingle grew rapidly to sharp pricks.

Pressure increased, and he gasped at the pain that throbbed suddenly in his temple.

"Let me try," a familiar voice spoke. Kavi? Natan tried to open his eyes, but flashes of light made him wince away.

"There," the softest of voices murmured in triumph as Natan's pain receded, leaving a calmness behind. He was startled to suddenly find himself back at his home. The sun was shining through the windows of his shack on the river, where he stood in a bright warm ray. There was a step beside him, and he turned to Kavi.

"My love," he breathed as he took him into his arms. Kavi smiled at him and all the loneliness of his life swelled in his heart. He hungrily kissed him…

"No!" He swatted at the hand pressed on his forehead, rising to his feet in fury. With a muttered oath, he strode to the edge of the pavilion and stared blindly into the forest. Kavi had no right to do that! He rocked on his heels and fought to catch his breath at the pain in his chest.

"Natan?" Kavi placed a hand on his arm. Natan turned roughly on him.

"My dreams are my own," he ground out through clenched teeth. "How dare you take them from me?"

"Take them?"

"Yes!" He turned away at the sight of Kavi's disbelief and swore darkly. He continued more softly, "I loved the sunlight in my home, its warmth, but now as I try to call up the memory, it feels like a wisp of a dream I can't quite grasp. You stole the images from me when you forced your way into my mind." He fell silent, the anger melting away. He only felt tired.

"So," he asked after a moment, with distaste, "did you find my spirit?"

"Yes," Kavi whispered with awe. Natan laughed harshly and walked away to join the others who'd gathered at a communal fire. Alek offered him a place beside him with a kind look.

After eating his fill of a shared meal, Natan sat at the fire with a cup of hot coffee and a full stomach, neither of which he'd had in days. He grew drowsy as the others talked around him and wondered if he'd be allowed to sleep for a while. He'd decided to just lie down where he was when he felt a strange sensation in his head. He rubbed a hand over his face and hair.

Alek noted his sudden grimace. "Are you in pain?"

"No, not markedly." Natan hesitated, then scrubbed vigorously at his scalp. "It's as if something's crawling over my mind but not finding a way in. Is someone here doing this?" he asked, glancing at the circle of faces around him.

Alek jumped to his feet in concern and placed a hand on Natan's forehead, ignoring his instinctive jerk away. He stepped back from Natan as if burned. "The Red Twins! This way."

The others surged to their feet, and the cry went up as Alek raced through the camp. Natan followed on his heels, drawing his dagger as he ran. Others fell into step behind them. Alek slid to a stop as a roar and the crashing of timber shook the air.

"Down!" he yelled. Natan and those following dropped instantly. Branches snapped and twisted overhead as a gale raged from one end of the camp to the other. Men were burned as campfires roared into the sky. It was over in seconds, leaving them stunned on the ground.

A heavy limb had fallen on Natan, and he heaved it off in panic.

Where was Kavi? He didn't remember him coming with them. He hurried back through the devastated camp, climbing over fallen trees and limbs, dodging the scattered fires, blind to all but the need to find him.

"Kavi!" he called as he came to where Alek's camp had stood. The tent and pavilion burned, causing Natan to choke on the black smoke. A soft cry drew him to a small hollow formed by the exposed roots of a fallen oak. Bright eyes looked up at him, and he scrambled swiftly to Kavi's side.

"Are you injured?" he asked anxiously, afraid to touch him. Mud streaked Kavi's clothing and face, but he climbed to his feet to stand steadily enough.

"I'm not hurt," Kavi said in amazement. "And you?"

"Kavi!" Natan breathed his name. Kavi's eyes were clear, for the first time in days seeming to see him.

"What?" Kavi appeared puzzled, but Natan drew him close and, despite the mud, kissed his cheeks and eyes. What would he have done if he'd lost him just then? When voices approached, Natan could have wished them all in the sea.

He leaned back and looked in Kavi's face. "Will you kiss me?"

He was thrilled to his very core at the blush that rose in Kavi's cheeks, the fond smile that lifted his lips. Kavi nodded and drew Natan's head down, giving him a fierce kiss. Natan groaned and crushed his slim body to him.

"Darling," he said brokenly, kissing him once more before letting him go. Voices called them and they climbed out of the hollow to offer what aid they could to the wounded. It was gruesome work, bodies torn, sometimes shredded almost beyond recognition. Natan's horror grew as they passed from one nightmare scene to the next, but it was long hours before he could finally curl up in a blanket and sleep.

THE NIGHT PROVED too short, and Natan winced as he burned his mouth on his coffee the next morning, though the pain was welcome after the numbing emptiness he'd felt since the events of the previous evening. They'd lost fifteen men and women to fire or fallen limbs, and three more seemed to have disappeared entirely. It had taken all of Alek's strength of will and persuasion to keep the survivors from hunting the Red Twins then and there.

"The boys are too strong when united," Gavin had shouted over the angry cries of the group as they challenged Alek. "We must come at them unawares. Let's tend to our wounded, and tonight we'll plan our revenge."

Natan had felt Gavin's eyes on him as he sat outside the circle. Alek had wanted him at the meeting so the people could see he was no threat. But as he listened to their plans and suggestions, a sense of unreality came over him. They spoke of air and water and earth as weapons to be hurled at their enemy. Each proposal became more horrendous as their hate built in a rising crescendo that had Natan on his feet in dismay. Icy silence met his intrusion.

"You wish to speak?" Alek asked him quietly, but the glitter in his black eyes showed him as incensed as the others.

"Your plans are tantamount to suicide," he answered with passion.

"Do you mean we should just sleep and let the Red Twins destroy us?" Gavin asked coldly.

"No, my lord, quite the opposite." He ignored the sneer that settled on Gavin's face. "Wouldn't it be better to send a few scouts out to see where the Red Twins have gone? In the meantime, move your camp to a more defendable location, and perhaps lay plans for an ambush."

The Karthagans muttered impatiently, but then Alek nodded. "I see the wisdom in that and will choose the scouts in the morning," he proposed, sounding tired suddenly. "Let us sleep now. We'll meet again at first light." The lieutenants nodded and went to their various tents to sleep.

Natan lay by Alek's fire that night, the nightmares proposed as possible attacks by the Karthagans playing over in his mind, visions of an earth torn apart by war. He sat now with a scalded mouth and a dead heart in the dim morning light. Alek took a seat opposite him and reached for the coffee over the fire.

"Did you rest?" the commander asked politely, the lines on his face betraying his own sleepless night. Jarod's arrival forestalled Natan's reply.

"Commander, you'd better come with me," the man said urgently, sending Natan a dark look. Alek rose and motioned Natan to follow as if afraid to leave him alone in the increasingly hostile atmosphere of the camp. They hadn't far to go. About a quarter of a league south they found two guards buried to their chests in the ground, dead. It appeared as if a quicksand had opened at their feet and then hardened again to slowly crush the life from them. Their expressions were horrible to see.

"Keep the men away," Alek said in stifled tones. "I'll leave at once to track the Red Twins, probably leading to where their father, Kayden, has set up camp. Natan, I should like you to come with me, if you would. A clear head may be needed," he added with a strange light in his eyes.

"Of course." Natan followed him back to the camp. They saddled and packed horses, leading them by the reins as they searched out Gavin, finding him on a small hill watching the sunrise with Kavi.

"We've picked up the Red Twins' trail, and I'm leaving immediately with Natan," Alek informed the Karthagan lord.

"Very good." Gavin gave Natan a speculative look. "I'll move the men to the Black Irons. The caves there should be easy enough to defend. Alek, use care."

"Always." Alek gripped Gavin's arm. "Goodbye, Uncle."

Natan studied Kavi's face during the exchange. He sat a few paces away and listened indifferently, as if what they did was of little interest to him. Natan had watched that look creep slowly back into his eyes yesterday evening. He seemed to be turning inward, neither speaking to him nor welcoming Natan's intrusion into his thoughts.

Alek noted Natan's troubled expression and suddenly clapped him on the back. "Never mind him. It's this place and these times. I think we shall all be mad before the end." With a sudden wild cry, he threw himself into the saddle, then raced from the camp. Natan quickly followed, Alek's shrill laughter echoing in his mind.

They rode at a mad pace for what seemed hours. Natan grew worried for the horses, hides slick with sweat, when Alek pulled his horse to a walk in the dense woods.

"Let me show you something," he said and nudged his suddenly skittish mount forward. They came abruptly to the edge of the forest, where Natan caught his breath. There was nothing beyond but a wide expanse of sea and sky, as if the ground had been sheered away, then dropped into the sea, laying thousands of paces below. Alek dismounted and sat at the edge of the abyss. Natan joined him, numb with shock.

"My people have been at war a long time," Alek stated in a tired voice. "My grandfather and great uncle began it, fighting for leadership on Belega.

When they were at last driven from the continent to this isle, only a few hundred of our people remained. And the fighting has never stopped, back and forth, until it's become life to us.

"Last fall Kayden came over the Silver Mountains and attacked us once again. This was Gavin's answer. He and the Red Twins did this, our men against theirs until the very earth was ripped asunder. So many deaths that day."

Alek turned glittering eyes to Natan. "There must be a madness in our blood. Perhaps nature's revenge for the way we've abused her. I don't know, but the few of us left keep fighting and dying. When will it end?" He buried his face in his hands.

Natan had no answer to give him. Maybe something in the abilities passed to him by the Mage would be a way to help them. But seeing Alek's wild eyes, he wondered if it wasn't already too late.

Alek rose to his feet and drew a deep breath. "When we reach Kayden's camp, we'll need to create a diversion, keep them off balance to give Gavin time to reach the Black Iron Hills."

"Do you have something in mind?"

Alek gave him a sly smile as he swung onto his horse. "Several ideas, in fact," he said, his voice frighteningly gleeful.

THE RED TWINS ran swift as deer through the forest, springing over fallen logs and underbrush, up and down hollows, laughing and calling aloud until they erupted into their father's camp. Kayden heard them coming, and although he frowned at the noise, he let it pass, as he did everything else. As it was, the twins were barely in his control. He couldn't risk their alienation.

"Boys," he acknowledged as they tumbled at his feet.

"Hi, Father," they exclaimed as one and sat cross-legged in the soft dirt. Long black hair glinted almost blue in the sunlight around their thin faces. Their unique eyes, of so light a brown they seemed golden, rested unblinking on him.

Kayden studied them. "What did you find out?" he asked when the boys offered nothing further.

"We saw cousin Gavin," Aiden answered and picked up a pebble. "Kavi was with him and a strange man. We followed them to Alek's camp." Aiden began to toss the pebble back and forth between his hands. Ethan watched curiously, then made a motion with his hand, and the pebble stopped in midair.

"Hey, let it go." Aiden slapped at his brother, who merely laughed. Then a light came into the boy's eyes that made Aiden sit back. The pebble began to rotate swiftly. Aiden closed his eyes tightly and screeched as the pebble whizzed by his ear.

"Ethan!" he hollered, shoving the boy over. Ethan lay in the dirt and laughed to himself.

Kayden watched him uneasily. Ethan was a few heartbeats younger than his brother and rarely spoke but was given to bouts of frenzy that seized him without warning. Then there was no knowing what he would do. Aiden claimed that it had been Ethan who'd killed their mother as they were born. There were times when Kayden believed it. He sighed, remembering Cinda, wild and beautiful, whom he'd loved and feared in equal measure.

"What happened at Alek's camp?" he prompted the boys.

Aiden's face broke into a wide grin. "We destroyed it!" He giggled.

"Children," Kayden chided softly. "You were only supposed to find it for me. Never mind," he hastened to add as their faces clouded. "How many would you say were left?"

"I don't know. What did Camron make for lunch?" The boys jumped up and ran for the mess tent. Kayden swore bitterly as he followed. The children were out of control, with their grown cousin Camron just as dangerous. They'd prove the death of their people yet.

Chapter Twelve

GAVIN STOOD AT the entrance to the extensive caves of the Black Irons in the afternoon sunlight and smiled grimly. It had come at last. Eight long months of strike and miss, touch and run. This day would put an end to all that. His scouts had informed him of Alek's success in his dangerous game of diversion, keeping the enemy unbalanced by sudden attacks and retreats, drawing them slowly toward the noose. Now, after four days, they were prepared, and the enemy had drawn into sight.

He turned to the young man sitting on a boulder overlooking the valley. "Kavi, I need your help with something."

Kavi seemed not to hear him and Gavin shrugged indulgently. Probably off looking for the Red Twins again. Gavin was anxious to pit Kavi's strength against theirs. Not alone, of course, but with his added powers, they might…

"Kavi," he raised his voice and the man started.

"Yes, Father?" he murmured as if awakening. "They draw near," he added in a dead voice.

"I know that, son. I need you to come with me now."

"Of course." Kavi slid from the rock and followed him into the forest. Their people were ranged along the top of the slope, weapons sharp, bows at the ready.

"I want to show you something," Gavin said when they reached the bottom of the incline where the land flattened into the valley. They scrambled over the rocky terrain, coming to a stop in the middle of a wide gully. Searching the ground, Gavin dropped to his knees with a satisfied grunt. Kavi knelt beside him and curiously stared at the rocky soil.

"You see," Gavin said, pointing to where patches of black tar had risen to the surface. He laid his hand beside a patch. Sweat broke out on his face, and he began to shake with the effort it cost him, but slowly the tar oozed and spread along the sand.

"What do you think?" he panted as he sat back. Kavi looked at the trail of tar as a cold smile touched his lips. Sitting on his heels, he opened his arms. A sudden shout from a sentry in the valley warned them of the approaching enemy, and with a fey laugh Kavi struck his hands on the sandy earth. Kayden's people clamored into the gully from the valley and the land cracked open at their feet. Tar boiled out of the fissure, swallowing their screaming, writhing bodies.

Gavin had to strike Kavi's face to break his focus. "We have to go!" he shouted as more figures appeared along the edge of the gully. An arrow skipped across the sand beside them as Kavi rose to his feet, and they raced up the slope.

The Red Twins appeared behind them. Anger mottled their faces on seeing the pit, and calling the wind, they toppled trees over the expanse. With wild cries, Kayden's people swarmed across.

As the enemy approached, Gavin turned, drawing the long knife from his belt. Kavi did the same and crouched behind a tree. *Now.* Gavin leaped upon the closest man, thrusting his blade deep into his abdomen. Then he had the man's knife as well and turned on the others. Thrust and duck, razor edges cutting through skin and bone. He hissed as someone's blade skimmed across his forearm. A quick slice from Kavi's knife brought Gavin's attacker down. Gavin heard Kavi's excited pants as the woman's life blood pumped into the ground beside them.

The battle was short and bitter, with Kayden calling his men back in disgust as the Red Twins set fires indiscriminately, burning friends and foe alike. Kayden drew his company to the far side of the valley, and Gavin knew better than to follow. The boys, in that mood, were likely to burn them all to the ground. Instead, he recalled his men to the caves.

NATAN STRODE ACROSS the slope, anxious to find Kavi. Alek and he had arrived during the battle, skirting Kayden's army to the east. Casualties had been great on both sides and fear began to beat in his heart. He needed to see Kavi, immediately.

"Natan!" Kavi's cheery cry stopped him; then Kavi was in his arms. Natan held him loosely while his body shook, overwhelmed by the relief that flooded through him. He gathered the beloved body closer and let his tears flow into Kavi's hair. There was no response from Kavi, but he saved that pain for later. For the moment it was enough to hold him and know that he still lived.

Natan reluctantly released him. He knew better than to look at Kavi's face but did it anyway. Kavi smiled at him with disdain, the expression in his eyes calling him a fool. Natan gave him a curt bow and turned into the forest, Kavi's soft laughter following him. He stopped on the edge of the slope and stared with unseeing eyes at the beauty of the mountains rising on either side of the valley. Then he saw the Red Twins.

"Hello," they greeted him in one voice. "Do you want to play?"

His skin caught fire, but though there were no flames to be seen, he screamed as pain seared along his nerves, burning him from within. The boys watched him writhe on the ground.

"Come on." He heard one of the boys urge through his agony. "Father's calling us."

The other ignored his comment. "Remember the squirrel I burned? It pulled its own fur off to escape the flames. Do you think this one will do the same?"

"Ethan!" Aiden shook his arm. "Father's really mad."

Ethan shrugged and turned away, disappointed. Aiden hesitated. "You better release him. If he dies, we can't play with him anymore."

"Oh, very well."

Natan no longer felt the flames on his body as he watched the boys disappear into the forest. He lay on the hard earth a long time, the haze of pain slow to leave him. The sound of moving water finally penetrated his shocked senses. Gathering his strength, he crawled to the nearby stream and slipped his tortured body into the cold water, and cried out as it flowed over his skin. Then blessed numbness took over. After a while he managed to pull himself to the bank, collapse into the mud, and let the blackness of unconsciousness take him.

The cold air woke him during the night. Natan sat up and hugged his knees, shivering in his wet garments. He hadn't been physically hurt, but his skin felt incredibly sensitive, the rub of his clothing keeping him from clear thought.

It dawned on him that he needed to get warm or he wouldn't last the night. Dragging his aching body to his feet, he headed toward the dim glow of a fire within the caves. It seemed a hundred leagues away, but he took one step toward it and then another. A dogged stubbornness took over as he struggled up the slope with no other thought than reaching the heat of the fire at the end.

Gavin looked up as he stumbled into the cave and dropped across the fire from him. Drawing up his knees, he buried his head on his arms. With a grunt of disgust, Gavin pressed a cup of hot tea on him. He took it gratefully, though his chattering teeth made speech impossible.

Alek peered through the darkness at them from where he lay wrapped in a blanket, the others sleeping nearby. He rose with a yawn, and Gavin made room for him as he squatted by the fire.

"Can't sleep?" Gavin inquired and Alek shook his head. He raised a brow at Natan's damp clothing but refrained from questioning him.

"We'll gather our forces and attack again at first light," Gavin informed the commander. "Perhaps with some fire of our own…"

"Yes, or maybe send an avalanche into the valley," Alek countered, his eyes kindling at the idea.

"No."

The men looked at Natan in surprise with a touch of hostility. He gave them a bland look in return. "I have an idea, but whether you choose to listen or not is your affair."

Gavin studied him. "Go on."

"If you attack now, Kayden will merely trap you in the caves, and more than likely the Red Twins will bury you alive here. I believe the wiser move would be to draw them out of the forest. We should retreat to the coast and set up a defensive position, one where we can see them coming and have room to maneuver. This cave is a death trap."

Gavin and Alek looked at each other.

"We'll give it some thought," Gavin taunted.

Natan shrugged, then dropped his head to his knees again. Soon he slipped to the ground as close to the fire as he could get. Unexpectedly, Gavin rose and gathered a few blankets to throw over his huddled body.

Natan began to drift toward dreams when he was startled awake. He scrambled to his feet as the ground rolled under him and the cavern walls groaned.

"Earthquake!" he cried and ran toward the entrance.

Gavin caught his arm. "Too late! The mountain's falling. We need to go deeper into the caves."

The ground rumbled and lurched beneath their feet, and the ceiling began to fall in huge slabs of granite. Despite this, the Karthagans made their exodus farther into the black tunnels in utter silence. Light flickered ahead, making the going easier as they tread the uneven pathways.

Natan anxiously scanned the nearby faces, letting out a held breath when he spied Kavi with Gavin farther ahead. It was some time before the rumbling stopped and the group came to a wide cavern where Gavin called a halt. Natan climbed out on a jut of rock and sat quietly in the shadows.

He blinked at a flare of light, then reminded himself that nothing should surprise him anymore. Several members of the company stood close to Gavin with their hands outstretched, cupping bright flames of fire that sent shadows darting about the cavern. Natan counted quickly and shook his head. Less than threescore of Gavin's people remained. How many were left of Kayden's side he couldn't hope to guess. Not many, he felt sure.

"It seems we've been caught in our own trap." Alek spoke from somewhere to Natan's left.

"We should have struck first," Gavin shot back, clearly incensed.

Natan smiled grimly, knowing sooner or later Gavin would make Natan pay for opposing his plans.

"Let's return to the cave's entrance at once," Gavin pressed. "The earthquake has stopped. I'm confident that if we unite our strength we can break through the fallen rock and come at Kayden's people in the confusion."

"I don't agree." Alek moved toward Gavin. "That's insane. The Red Twins would have us writhing in our death throes in the blink of an eye."

"Insane?" There was a cold intensity in Gavin's voice that prickled the skin. He advanced on Alek until he stood eye to eye with his nephew, intimidating in his fury. Natan could sense a strange energy gathering itself around the company as they watched the confrontation.

Alek took an insolent step back. "Yes, mad. You'd bring the cavern down on us if it would gain you sole control of the isle."

A knife appeared in Gavin's hand, but before he could strike, a fey laugh shattered the silence.

"It's too late, Father," Kavi called gaily. He stood on a rock behind the crowd and looked at them with unfocused eyes, a wild manic beauty in his face. "Kayden's gone. They've left the valley. But Kayden… I don't know. Something terrible, something exciting is happening. I can't see what." He slipped on the rock and caught himself, laughing the harder. Gavin sheathed his knife and went to him.

"Come down," he murmured with an outstretched hand.

"As you wish." Kavi leaped from the rock. Natan jumped to his feet as Kavi fell hard on his knees, but his face was wreathed in bright smiles as he scrambled to his feet and took his father's hand.

"Shall we go?" he asked. "It's a long way to the other entrance."

Gavin inclined his head, and the company resumed their trek.

Chapter Thirteen

THE RED TWINS gleefully surveyed the collapsed opening to the cave. Aiden had thought up the earthquake and was very pleased with himself.

"I could have done better," Ethan bragged. Aiden punched him on the arm, so Ethan jumped on him.

Kayden watched them wrestle with a sour expression. "We should go," he told them.

"Not yet, Father." Aiden threw Ethan off so he could stand. "I want to see if they'll come back out."

"Me too," Ethan piped up and stood beside him.

"We have a lot of wounded to care for," Kayden reminded them. "And they won't come out this way. They'll make for the northern entrance near the coast. We can rest and catch them up in a few days when they emerge.

"Camron," Kayden turned to his nephew, and his lips thinned. Aiden looked curiously at his cousin. The young man had been caught in the fire on the hillside, his face and hands scorched and blistered. He had also breathed in the searing heat from the flames and his voice had been burned from him.

"Will you please have the camp ready to move?" Kayden asked, his voice sounding gruff.

Camron pulled his speculative, brown-eyed gaze from Aiden. "As you wish," he whispered.

"I want to stay here," Ethan pouted as their cousin slipped into the forest.

"No, son. The ground is unstable. We need to move camp to a safer area," Kayden repeated.

"No, Father, we need to stay," Aiden added his voice to Ethan's, his temper rising.

"We're leaving, boys. Now." Kayden's tone was harsh, and he took a step back, fear on his face as Ethan narrowed his golden eyes. Sweat sprang out on his body, but his screams were strangled in his throat as his body convulsed grotesquely, then burst into sudden flame. Aiden watched with interest as he was quickly consumed.

"I didn't know he would do that," Ethan commented.

"I'm hungry," Aiden said, and the boys ran back to camp. They stopped in surprise, finding the place deserted.

"Where did they go?" Aiden asked curiously.

Ethan screwed up his face. "Shall we go hunting?"

Aiden thought a moment. "Not now. I want to find the foreign man again. He was fun to play with."

"I wonder if he'll burst like Father did?"

"Maybe," Aiden replied. "Come on!"

The boys snatched up their packs and jogged into the forest.

"Won't the foreign man be surprised to see us," Ethan giggled as they ran.

NATAN FOLLOWED BEHIND the company, often losing sight of the flames of light, only to have them reappear as he rounded a dark corner. They'd been three days in the darkness, and he'd begun to doubt if he could endure it much longer. His food had run out yesterday, with apparently no one thinking to offer him a share of theirs. Indeed, he was ignored. Water had become a growing concern for them, and even Gavin began to speak of their need for it.

He stumbled in his weariness and almost fell as the floor dropped into a smooth chamber. He could see that water had been there at one time. The air filled with an intense eagerness from the thirsting company as Gavin knelt in the center of the basin and placed his hands on the smooth granite.

"There's moisture here, deep in the rock," he informed them. A low rumble echoed in the room and down the dark passages as he concentrated.

Kavi knelt beside him and placed his hands over his father's. Water began to seep to the surface of the stone until they had to scramble to their feet as the ground opened and water gushed into the basin. The people stood back, Natan fearing the water would fill the tunnels, but it stopped at a hand's breath deep. They cried out in relief and some even laughed as they drank their fill.

Gavin stood behind Alek as he bent over the water, and Natan watched in disbelief as he lifted a heavy rock. He shouted a warning as Gavin brought it down on the back of his nephew's head. Gavin was on Alek instantly, pushing his head under the water.

"No!" Natan shoved his way through the silent crowd that seemed to revel in the violent act and dove at Gavin's knees, knocking him aside. Natan scrambled to his feet, then hurriedly dragged Alek's unconscious body out of the water. Relief flooded through him as Alek drew a sputtering breath.

A blow to the side of his head smashed Natan to a knee, but he sprang up with a snarl, pulling his knife. He pressed the blade hard against Gavin's chest.

Gavin glanced at it. "Do you mean to kill me?" He stepped into the knife so that it cut through his tunic into flesh. "Kill me."

For a second Gavin's eyes were clear of madness, and Natan saw the tortured soul begging for release. He stood back, shuddering at the sudden desire that heated his blood, wanting to feel his blade slice open the man's chest, see the dark blood on the floor, hear the death rattle of Gavin's last breath. He sheathed his knife with a shaking hand.

Gavin stepped up to him. "Defy me again, and I'll kill you." He turned his back and surveyed the onlookers. "We'll camp here," he said abruptly.

Natan staggered out of the flickering light and fell into a dark corner. He couldn't stop shaking, couldn't halt the excitement that raced through his blood at the thought of causing another's death. His breath became ragged sobs as he strove to cling to his sanity when all was madness around him.

Kavi knelt beside him, but he drew back, bewildered by his presence.

Kavi's eyes were luminous in the soft glow of the flame he held. The beauty of his face stabbed Natan's heart. Kavi touched his face with infinite gentleness and ran his fingers over Natan's lips, then drew his hand away to look at the dark blood that stained his fingertips.

"Oh," he murmured, and placed a kiss on the corner of Natan's mouth where it had been cut from Gavin's blow. Heat licked through Natan but he turned his face away.

"Don't," he pleaded, but his voice broke as easily as Kavi shattered his will. Triumph gleamed in Kavi's eyes.

"Hush." Kavi brushed their lips together. He let the flame he held go out, leaving only the glimmer of light from the camp, and slipped onto Natan's lap.

"Fool," Natan's heart told him, but he didn't care. At that moment Kavi was life to him, his familiar weight pushing the pain and fear to one side. Only this moment mattered, Kavi in his arms, Kavi's lips inches from his own. He leaned up and Kavi pressed their lips together. He outlined Natan's mouth with his tongue, slid it inside. *Oh gods!*

Natan crushed the pliant body to him and devoured Kavi's sweet mouth, kissing him back with equal force. It took only moments to bare Kavi's chest to his urgent touch, his mind plunging into chaos as Kavi shifted his hips, grinding them together.

He teased the small buds on Kavi's chest between his fingers, drinking in Kavi's breathy moans. He wanted to suckle them, biting gently until Kavi sobbed his pleasure. Natan hardened with the thought, but Kavi suddenly pushed off him, rising to his feet. Natan blinked in the flickering light of their refuge as Kavi stripped out of his clothes. What did he mean to do? Voices from the others reached them, quiet talk as the camp settled for sleep. Surely Kavi wouldn't…

Heat tore through him when Kavi nudged his legs apart and knelt between his thighs, but he put a cautioning hand over Kavi's when his lover untied the laces of his pants. "I don't—"

"Hush, love," Kavi said, voice thick with need. Natan watched his dark head lower, and pleasure exploded through him when he was engulfed in the warmth of Kavi's mouth. He leaned back helplessly, but after a few hard sucks Kavi released him, leaving Natan as wet as possible. He quickly climbed onto Natan's lap, and Natan couldn't control his groan as Kavi lowered onto his cock, pushing down, enveloping him in heat. *So tight!* Kavi moved, rocking, and pleasure soon flushed his cheeks, matching Natan's own. A mad lust took over Natan. He grabbed Kavi's hips hard enough to bruise, urging Kavi on, wanting to share the glorious bliss. *So good.*

Kavi groaned, body shaking as he collapsed against Natan's chest in surrender. With a shout, Natan brought them both to shuddering completion. His head swam in ecstasy, and he came slowly back to himself to find Kavi panting in his arms. His capricious lover laughed softly, clearly happy, as Natan slipped out, and Natan pulled Kavi's cloak over them both, holding Kavi tightly.

Power thrummed in the close chamber from the Karthagan people, filling Natan with fear. He knew it tugged at Kavi, alluring, seducing him from Natan and any ties he might have with others. Kavi would leave him soon, wanting his freedom, but for the moment he was Natan's, and that was everything. Natan closed his eyes as Kavi nuzzled his neck and settled into his arms, then allowed sleep to claim his sated, weary body.

NATAN AWOKE LATER to pitch darkness and silence. Had the others left him? He stood, swallowing his panic, then started walking, careful to keep his left hand on the cavern wall. He remembered the tunnel they had been traversing continued on the other side of the basin, so if he just made his way along the perimeter…

He came unexpectedly to an opening and almost stumbled into it. This wasn't right. He tried to picture where he stood in connection to the main tunnel. No, he still wasn't far enough around the basin. Dangerous to let go of the wall and cross the opening. What if he missed the wall on the other side? He took a deep breath, having no choice but to go on.

He swore with relief when his fingers caught the opposite wall. Fifty paces farther brought him to the tunnel he sought. Turning into it, Natan shuffled forward for what seemed an eternity, his only company the beating of his heart and his muffled footsteps.

Screams roused him from his walking stupor in that endless darkness. Natan raised his head and saw a dim light some distance ahead. Hurrying forward, he crouched at the cavern's mouth, blinking as sunlight stabbed his eyes. The wind on his face was a rare pleasure, but the things he saw when his sight cleared drove all joy from his heart.

A gentle slope of ancient trees glimmered in the early morning sunlight, as did the mangled lumps of flesh and bone spread out before him. Fifteen bodies at least he counted at the cave's entrance, others farther down. Screams arose from somewhere to his right.

Natan hesitated to leave the cave and then shrugged. If the Red Twins were still close, he could do nothing to evade them. He crossed the slope and found a woman kneeling beside what had once been her child. The small body seemed to have been torn in two as if struck by lightning without heat. At Natan's sharp breath the woman looked up. Terror twisted her features and she scrambled back.

Natan held out his hand. "Please."

The woman rose to her feet, screamed uncontrollably, then stopped abruptly. Her eyes grew wide. Shrill laughter escaped her, and with a wild shout she ran off into the forest as if her mind had broken. Natan watched her go and wondered why he felt nothing at all. He turned back to the boy, then looked at the carnage on the slope. Well, he'd been on a battlefield before. His first concern now was survival. He'd worry about his empty heart later.

He walked among the dead to search their packs. Someone had been there before him, so he couldn't find much left in the way of food except some hard bread and nuts. Making his way down the slope into the forest, he headed north toward the sea. He refused to look at any of the faces of the dead caught in the Red Twins' trap. Kavi wasn't there, his spark of life still bright in Natan's mind.

As he neared the sea, a longing to be back in Amara seized him. He wanted to go home. He wondered if anyone in Belega gave him a fleeting thought. Bryon, maybe. Hearing shouts, he hurried forward, pausing at the tree line. Kayden's people stood on the edge of the beach, Gavin's company somewhere in the trees across the sand, drawing near.

Natan suddenly looked to his left, and his heart thudded painfully. Kavi jumped from the nearby rock where he'd been watching the scene unfold on the beach. Natan could feel the power surging through him, finally unveiled, matching that of the Red Twins. With the power he held, Kavi could command the world. Natan had to stop him.

Kavi seemed unaware of him, so Natan slipped into the trees, coming up behind Kavi, who was focused on the others. Springing up, he captured Kavi in his arms and wrested him to the ground. Kavi struggled to rise, but Natan set his full weight on him, pinning him down.

"You!" Kavi shrieked, then fought wildly to be free. Natan held on and Kavi drew his head back to glare at him. Fury distorted his face.

"You can't do this," Natan urged, shocked by the madness in Kavi's eyes.

"I *will* do it," Kavi snarled. A sly expression touched his face. Natan screamed as the Karthagan violently entered his mind.

"What if I catch your breath?" Kavi murmured, his voice a caress as he tightened the muscles of Natan's throat. He smiled cruelly at the rasp of Natan's desperately indrawn breath. Fear tore along Natan's nerves as Kavi's thoughts focused on his heart.

"Don't," he begged as his lover captured his wildly beating heart, but Kavi willed it to slow, grow calm. It missed a beat, filling Natan with agony. Kavi lifted a hand to push the damp hair from Natan's forehead, holding his gaze.

Thump. Natan's heart skipped again and his body contorted with blinding pain, his breath a shuddering gasp. An overwhelming sadness flooded him, a longing for a life that would never be. "Kavi," he whispered, anguish shredding the last of his strength.

Panic swept Kavi's face, his eyes clearing. Natan heard his desperate plea through the haze of pain closing his mind. "I'm here! Help me, Mage, please…" Kavi's voice trailed off in despair.

Natan clutched at the gossamer threads of his life. "Let the energy go," he breathed the words, praying Kavi would hear him. "Darling, be free of it."

Kavi cried out as one awakening from a dream. "Breathe!" he urged and placed his hands over Natan's heart. Natan screamed again as Kavi poured every ounce of power he had into Natan's dying body. Natan's heart stumbled, then renewed its strong beat. He drew a full breath, and Kavi pressed Natan's face to his chest, trembling violently. Natan put an arm around him, stroked Kavi's hair while black exhaustion claimed his last thoughts.

Chapter Fourteen

GAVIN THREW HIMSELF behind a tree, crouching as he caught his breath. Alek came up and sprawled against the tree beside him, and they exchanged a grim smile. The Red Twins had harried them for the last two days. Not anymore. This was where they made their stand.

Giving a sharp nod, Gavin flung from the tree and raced across a stretch of beach, Alek on his heels. At fifty paces from the farthest tree line they halted. His remaining people straggled out of the forest in twos and threes to range themselves behind them, some twenty strong. Now, if they held fast, perhaps they could…

Fear struck every heart as the Red Twins emerged from the trees opposite.

"Hello, cousins." The boys waved. Clasping hands, they walked a few paces onto the sand.

"Courage!" Gavin cried and opened his arms for life's energy. It flowed into him from the earth and from the tangy sea air, filling him until it pulsed in his body. Vibrating with power, he felt nothing could stop him. He took a shaky step forward and flung his arms out toward the boys. Energy rushed from him in a crushing wave that struck the twins. Trees toppled behind the boys in a roar of wind and sand.

The Red Twins stood still, a smile twisted on their faces as they took in the incredible power to feed on it. Gavin fell to his knees in disbelief as the boys continued to pull the energy from him, draining his life along with it, as he was unable to stop them. Seeing this, Alek cried out in alarm and dropped beside him, wrapping him in his arms. In a desperate attempt, his people linked hands, giving their strength to him as well. The Red Twins continued to smile.

BRYON STOOD AT the prow of the small boat they'd procured in Amara, his gaze straining to glimpse the shoreline on the horizon. After days at sea they'd soon be at the Isle of Wind. What would they find? His nightmare of Kavi had been terrible. He thought of Kirstin and smiled despite his worry. The girl was so strong in herself, her spirit so full of life that even though she should have died in that cell under Siagan, she'd merely slept, believing only her father could release her. Power over death? No, he didn't believe that. Only postponement. He prayed her strength would be enough to keep her safe.

He glanced at the Nagal officer coming up beside him. They'd both been at it for hours, working the sails to catch what wind they could, watching the fog, waiting for the isle to come into view. There was a strange tension in the air that made sleep impossible.

"How are you holding up?" Bryon interjected into the heavy silence.

Jaden gave him a curious look. "I'm well enough." He slid a look at Kirstin taking her turn at the tiller. "Still trying to wrap my head around what you told me about her. The Karthagans are an unusual people." Bryon scowled and he hurried to add, "Forgive me. I meant no offense." He made Bryon a formal bow, concern on his pleasant features. "Sometimes my tongue gets carried away."

"Sometimes?" Bryon allowed a grin. "It's of no consequence. I'm feeling jumpy this morning." The sky had begun to clear, and as he glanced to the east, he let out a sharp cry.

"What is it?"

Bryon shook his head. "I don't know. Everything seems wrong."

He wasn't surprised when Kirstin joined them, the boat rocking slightly. A gray mist slowly burned off the water, a dark smudge in the distance showing them the isle. The sight of the shoreline smote Bryon a physical blow, and he clenched his hands. Horrible images crowded into his mind, one on top of the other, until he grabbed his head with a tortured cry. What was happening? Soft hands touched his face. Heart pounding with fear, he glanced into calm amber eyes, and he focused on them as a lifeline in the black chaos waiting to claim him.

"Bryon." Kirstin's voice threaded through the clamor in his head. "It's only a dream. Let it go."

Her voice continued with words of encouragement, so Bryon fought to control his breathing. The images slowed, pictures of fire and blood and twisted bodies and screaming madness…

"Bryon, let go." Kirstin's voice was the merest whisper that Bryon strained to hear. The visions snapped, and he pushed them back into a small corner of his mind where they might visit him in nightmares. For now, his mind was clear.

He turned to the isle. "You'll need to be strong, Kirstin. As strong as life itself. That wasn't a dream," he warned, having no doubt she'd seen the same images. Kirstin nodded, her own face pale. Dread wound itself into Bryon's heart as they drew closer to the isle.

"Kirstin, will you tend the tiller? Jaden, tack the sails."

Bryon judged the breakers while Kirstin angled the boat toward land, the wind ruffling their hair. "Now, Kirstin!" he called. She steered the boat into the wind while he and Jaden dropped the sails and rode a swell inland to beach the craft on the sandy shore. Bryon leaped out, he and Jaden pulling the boat out of reach of the tide.

They hadn't taken more than a dozen steps across the sand before Bryon grabbed his head as daggers of pain pierced his eyes. He heard the laughter of children in his mind, and it took a moment for him to regain control of himself.

"Now for it," he gasped, looking at the tree line.

"I'm ready."

Bryon turned a startled face to Kirstin. She had spoken with arrogance, the light of battle shining in her amber eyes.

"Come on," she said almost merrily. "I have a surprise for my dear family." She strode confidently up the beach. Bryon exchanged a grim look with Jaden as they followed her. In a moment, two groups of Karthagans came into view on the sand, facing each other. The nearest, with their backs to them, seemed to be in distress, while the other stood still as stone.

Kirstin walked through the people fainting on the beach as if she didn't see them, intent on the twin boys standing there. She stopped beside one man who knelt in the sand holding another man in his arms, tears on his face.

"Hello, nephews," she called across the short distance between them. The boys looked at her with suspicion.

"Who are you? How do you know us?"

"Why, Aiden, I'm your father's sister. I'm your Aunt Kirstin. I sensed the Red Twins long ago, as I perceive all of our people."

"Kirstin's dead. Father told me so," Aiden sneered. The other remained silent, alert.

"Nevertheless, here I am. What game are you playing? Ethan?"

"Do you want to play?" Aiden asked in sudden doubt.

"I think she means to punish us," Ethan said, narrowing his eyes. "Isn't that what you've come for, auntie? To punish us for killing Father?"

"That, and other things." Kirstin's voice had grown cold, so the twins quickly stood close together, tightly linking their hands. Bryon braced, not sure what would follow. The twins seemed to gather their strength. The earth trembled as they drew more and more upon the essence of life, making Bryon's scalp prickle. They flung out their arms and hurled the energy at the woman who'd come from death to meet them.

Kirstin laughed as the power struck her, yet tears wet her fair skin while she wept, rapture in her expression. Still the Red Twins sent their strength against her, and she pulled in more. Bryon saw the bewilderment on their young faces as they tried to withdraw, sever the bond between them, but they couldn't escape. Kirstin drank them in until Aiden threw Ethan's hand from him, and they fell to the sand, seemingly emptied. Kirstin turned to the others, wild-eyed, and Bryon watched as she wrenched the power from them one by one as well, with such brutality they staggered, lost in confusion.

Kirstin seemed to glory in the power, and Bryon gripped her arm. Distracted, she turned to him in surprise as if she'd forgotten his presence. She gave him a brilliant smile, and he touched her shining face.

"It's time to let it go, Kirstin," he said with quiet certainty. She looked at him, perplexed. He waited patiently as she lifted a fist in sudden anger, then paused.

"Let it go, my dear, as we discussed," he said softly. "It's of no use to you. It will only hurt you."

Kirstin held his gaze while he watched her internal struggle: pride and doubt, and—he hoped—with some concern for him.

"Come back to me," he said after a moment, not sure she even cared. In a heartbeat she nodded, then closed her eyes. He heard her sigh, and then her vibrant body slumped as she allowed the energy to flow from her back to the earth and air.

Bryon helped her to a stump of driftwood, where he held her against him while she shivered, half blind with reaction and grief.

"My brave girl." He stroked her hair then leaned closer to whisper, "I'm proud of you. Terrified, but proud."

She giggled reflexively.

The Karthagan people began to stir. Many wept openly. But a few, though dazed by events, set about finding wood for a fire while others gave thought to food. In the madness of the last few days, they'd neglected to eat, and hunger soon overcame all other thoughts for the moment.

Kirstin watched them with pity. "So few children," she murmured.

Bryon nodded. They were a beaten people by their own hands. He brushed the fair hair from Kirstin's face. "Shall we help them?"

Kirstin looked at her empty hands. "How?" she asked, forlorn. "I no longer have the power I've felt to my fingertips since childhood." She glanced at the people milling around them, moving in slow motion, exhausted. "It was taken from me, as it has been from all Karthagans, when I sent it back to the earth. How can I help anyone now?"

"Well, we could tend to the injured. I also may have some dried fruit in my pack, to start with."

Kirstin looked at him in wonder. "Aid and comfort? Is life so simple for you? But then you haven't lost anything," she observed in bitterness.

Bryon drew away from her and looked at his boots, troubled and unsure of his next move.

Kirstin rose to her feet. "I may have some fruit as well and perhaps a bit of cheese. Come on." She held out her hand. Bryon took it in relief.

SENSING A SHIFT in the world, Natan forced his heavy eyes open and wished he hadn't. He felt as if his ribs were smashed, and every breath he drew brought pain. Sitting up proved a monumental struggle, and he leaned weakly against a rock when upright. While he caught his breath, he recalled Kavi's face twisted in hatred, the man wanting him dead. But then Kavi had saved him. Where was his lover now?

He took another deep breath, feeling as if he'd been caught in a jelly press. An unusual quiet lay on the air. What had happened? Noticing the Karthagans setting up camp on the beach, Natan presently climbed to his feet, needing answers. Glancing at the sun, he realized it was only midmorning, although it seemed an age had passed since he'd left the caves. Pressing an arm tightly against his aching ribs, he stumbled across the sand and sprawled beside the first fire he came to. Out of breath, his chest burned.

Bryon appeared suddenly before him. "Natan?" He squatted across the fire. "Are you in pain?"

"I feel bruised inside," he admitted.

"Let me ask Kirstin to brew you up some tea for that. The girl's finding out she has more gifts than just calling up the wind."

"Kirstin?"

"She's the one who called me to Siagan. The one who defeated the Red Twins."

Bryon described their journey and the battle he'd witnessed. As he listened, Natan filled with both wonder and concern for Kirstin's bravery and the Karthagans loss of power. When finished, Bryon glanced around. "I'd like to see everyone settled, but I'll return shortly."

He gave Natan's shoulder a reassuring squeeze before setting off across the camp, stopping a moment to say something to Lieutenant Jaden. Then they both looked at him. Natan raised his head to catch the cooling breeze off the ocean and realized something he hadn't noticed in his pain. The air felt clean, clear, as did his mind. The dread and black madness that had tormented him for days had gone.

He closed his eyes and drew in a lungful of air, wincing at a slice of agony. Once he could breathe again, he looked over the camp. He spotted Kavi on the beach and dragged himself up. Shoving the pain to a corner of his mind, he joined the small group hovering over Gavin's prone body.

"How is he?" he asked, kneeling with concern beside the unconscious man as Alek made room for him.

"I don't know," Kavi answered tersely. "We can't wake him."

"I'm afraid he used all his strength in the battle," Alek put in, sadness in his voice.

Natan set his hands on Gavin's chest, feeling it rise and fall with each shallow breath he drew. Alek stirred in resentment but Natan glanced at him, steadily meeting his accusing gaze. After a moment, Alek lowered his eyes, which glistened with tears.

Natan touched his arm. "Your power's not gone forever."

Alek looked ashamed, yet sudden hope flared in his eyes at the reassuring words.

Natan placed his hands on Gavin's forehead, calming his racing thoughts to look for the man's spirit. The current of life flowed into him, and his skin prickled, a joy bordering on pain flooding through him. Those closest to him looked up with a futile longing, perhaps feeling the draw of power as Natan sent his thoughts out. He took a deep breath, returned to himself, and with a quiet word let the energy dissipate.

He turned to Kavi with sorrow. "He's far away, dear. I perceived him for a moment, but he's content on his journey. It's not my place to call him back."

"He's dead, then?" Alek looked at Gavin's body with apprehension, watching the rise and fall of his chest.

"His spirit is fleeing. He won't last much longer."

Kavi hid his face in his hands, but even as Natan reached for him, Alek rose and moved to his side, drawing Kavi against his shoulder. Natan watched the cousins a moment, then climbed to his feet and silently left them, feeling like an intruder on their grief.

He joined Bryon where he sat in the sand with the Red Twins and a pretty woman. Bryon smiled, though his eyes were weary. "Natan, I'd like you to meet Lady Kirstin."

Natan inclined his head, searching her face, then fell at once into her bright amber gaze. Images of the cold lake under Siagan and the young woman's imprisonment rose in his mind. He swallowed a sudden lump of pity. So much horror…and loneliness. He understood that all too well.

"They seem to have taken to you," he said, nodding to the boys sitting cross-legged on the sand.

"I see their mother in them," Kirstin explained. Aiden had been holding an animated conversation with her, but Ethan lay quietly, his head in his brother's lap while Aiden played idly with his hair. Natan frowned, realizing Ethan's mind had been shattered on the battlefield.

Aiden wrapped his arms protectively around his brother. "I'm going to take care of him."

"Of course," Natan assured him. "Shall we find you some dinner?"

Aiden nodded, and they rose to their feet. Ethan took his brother's hand and walked with them to the central fire where shellfish were being steamed. Aiden politely thanked Lieutenant Jaden when he was handed a bowl of mussels. When they returned to their seats, Ethan babbled merrily while Aiden fed them to him one by one.

There was a pensive look on Kirstin's face as she watched the children, and Natan asked with concern, "What is it?"

"I'm not sure what's wrong with Ethan." Kirstin tilted her head. "Maybe Aiden will allow me to examine him in a little while. In the meantime, I could make him an herbal tea to help him sleep. Maybe his shocked mind simply needs to rest."

Natan gave her a smile. "Bryon thinks we'll make a healer of you yet. I'm inclined to agree."

She tapped a finger to her lips. "I think I'd like that." She frowned suddenly. "I wish I had my powers."

"It's not magic, Kirstin."

"It felt like magic. It was so effortless, but now it just brings pain when I reach for it."

Natan searched her face. "Kirstin," he began quietly. "You have the ability to call up the energy again. Just start with very small things. And my dear, be very careful. The desire for more power can be irresistible, as well you know."

He bit his lip when Alek approached them. "My uncle has passed on, Mage," he said in a tired voice.

Natan embraced him. "I'm truly sorry." He turned to Kirstin. "Will you excuse me?"

They walked through the camp, Natan helping Alek impart the news to his people. Gavin's death had been expected, but that made it no easier to bear. They buried the Karthagan leader as twilight descended and the first faint stars appeared in the violet sky. They removed stone from the old manor house to build his cairn, and Alek commended his body back to the earth.

Kavi wept freely as he stood by his father's grave. Natan made a move toward him, but Alek took his hand first, and Kavi leaned against him. After the ceremony, they sat quietly around the fire while the Karthagan people settled in their blankets to sleep. A few of Kayden's company had joined them during the day, led by Camron, and Alek had sent a party out to gather the rest.

"What shall I do with them?" Alek indicated the camp. Upon his uncle's death, he'd become the leader of his people, and Natan could see the responsibility already weighed heavily on him.

"You could bring them back to Belega," he offered cautiously.

Kavi raised his head with the first sign of interest Natan had seen in him. Alek looked startled. "Would we be welcome?"

"Would that matter?" Lieutenant Jaden asked with quick anger, jabbing a stick into the fire. "I'm sorry, but Nagal opposed Barkuit's removal of your people to this isle. It never should have been done."

Bryon nodded agreement. "Come back to Belega where you belong."

Alek rubbed his face. "I can't think straight. I'm sure you're right, but let me sleep now, and we'll speak of it in the morning."

"Of course. You're not alone, Alek," Natan assured him as Alek rose to his feet to gather a couple of blankets.

"I'm for bed too." Kavi stumbled up.

"Goodnight," Natan uttered bleakly, wanting to say something to comfort him, but Kavi moved a few paces from the fire and lay down, throwing his cloak over his head.

NATAN SLEPT FITFULLY, the pain in his chest not lessening until the sky grew light with the rising sun. With a sigh, he rolled to his side and at last fell into a deep slumber, not opening his eyes again until midmorning. Alek crouched beside him and helped him sit up, handing him a cup of tea.

"I think we should start for Belega this afternoon when the tide changes." Alek shrugged when Natan raised his brows in question. "I've had my fill of this isle."

"As have I," Natan agreed. "The pain your people endured on this tortured land is becoming more than I can bear. Let's take them home and start over."

He finished his tea in one swallow, then propped his shoulder against a stone, his mind racing. "I'll send Lieutenant Jaden to Nagal as soon as we land and arrange to meet with Governor Basal and the Regent Syros. Here." Natan drew a rough map in the sand, indicating the Lake of Glass. "I'll advise them to let you have the old city of Karthag that had once belonged to your people. Not many live there, and it will lend you a bit of isolation."

"Very well." Alek ran a hand through his dark hair. "Thank you, Mage."

Natan looked idly at the map he'd drawn as Alek excused himself. He'd need to convince the southern leader to give up one of his cities. Not an easy task since he didn't know Syros well. How he longed to be home! He glanced up and climbed to his feet as Kavi and Kirstin approached.

"Kavi," he said tentatively. "May I speak with you?" The Karthagan gave him a frightened look, and Natan's temper stirred.

"Now," he growled and took hold of his arm, then pulled him into the nearby trees. He turned on Kavi in hurt and anger, then bit his tongue at his downcast eyes.

"Won't you look at me, dear?" he asked quietly. "Kavi?" He gently raised his chin.

"You should hate me!" Kavi cried with an anguish that twisted Natan's heart.

He touched Kavi's face. "That person wasn't you," he whispered, lowering his head to kiss his lips. The kiss deepened, and he pulled Kavi close against him, desperate to have him in his arms. But he felt the sadness of Kavi's recent loss, his uncertainty, so eased his hold.

"Friends?" he asked, touching Kavi's mouth with a finger.

"Of course," Kavi said with a hint of his old sarcasm.

Natan shook his head, his smile wry. He never should have allowed himself to fall in love with the sardonic man, his sharp wit a dangerous attraction to Natan's unworldliness.

"I wish things had gone differently here," he began, struggling to find words to express his grief, not only at Gavin's loss, but for the pain of all the Karthagan people. A shutter seemed to close in Kavi's expressive eyes. His cool appraisal stabbed Natan to the heart.

"You have nothing to say on the matter." Anger tightened Kavi's lips. "You kept your powers. Shall we join the others?"

Natan bit his tongue on an angry retort. "After you," he motioned and followed Kavi onto the beach. It was a long walk to the harbor, and Natan's chest began to tighten with the exertion. It was a relief when they reached the coastline, and his heart lifted at the sight of the schooner anchored offshore.

"We built the ship last year," Kavi said with obvious pride. "The Mage showed us there was a better way to live, a way of peace. We'd meant to follow his teachings. The boat was supposed to unite the two families by a common goal. Trade with Belega." He shook his head. "Things must have broken down when Gregor and I left the isle. Perhaps if I had stayed…"

"You can't know what would have happened. Your people might have been lost all the sooner. We can only move forward now." Natan held out his hand. "Come, Kavi. Let's meet your future." Kavi linked their fingers without hesitation, making Natan's heart thump.

Kavi kept hold of his hand as they crossed the sand to the waiting dory, climbed in, and were rowed to the schooner preparing to sail with the tide.

Chapter Fifteen

ALEK WATCHED THE shore of Belega draw closer with a rising panic. The three days at sea had passed peacefully, but what was he to do with his people? He glanced over the deck of the schooner. Only fourscore of Karthagans remained. They had never been large in number, and too many had been lost to war. And without their power over nature, they were completely at the mercy of the Belegan countrymen.

His gaze found Natan standing at the prow of the ship, face lifted to the wind, a slight smile playing on his youthful face. The Mage was on their side. Natan had assured him of that, and Alek believed him, sensing his pure, true heart. But would the others trust him? Alek knew the Karthagans were jealous of his remaining gifts when they'd lost their own. Alek shook his head. He could only hope Natan was strong enough to lead them to safety.

The sound of waves recalled him, and he turned his attention once again to the beach and small harbor coming into view. Firming his lips, he crossed the deck, shouting orders to the men to be sharp about the sails and bring the ship safely into port. The bay was calm, so they anchored near shore, then took the dories through the mild waves to the warm sand.

Alek was in one of the last boats, leaving a handful of sailors with the ship. After landing, he quickly crossed the beach to join Natan, where he stood with Kavi and Kavi's cousin, Kirstin, at the tree line.

"We're here, Mage. What can we expect next?"

Natan turned a serious face to him. "Bryon and Lieutenant Jaden have left for Amara to retrieve horses. From there, they'll ride to Nagal and speak with Basal, then on to the border to send for Syros. We'll make camp at the Lake of Glass and wait. The governors should be with us in less than a week."

"Very well." Alek glanced at Kavi who stood impassively by. "Thank you, Mage. It may not seem like it, but we're very grateful for your help."

"It's my pleasure." Natan looked at Kavi as well.

Kirstin had also remained silent, so Alek nudged her. She roused from her thoughts and glanced from Alek to Natan.

"How long will we have to wait for their return?" she asked, a hint of worry in her bright eyes.

"Five to six days," Natan assured her. He turned back to Alek. "But it's a fair march to the lake. Perhaps we should start?"

"As you wish." Alek made him a slight bow. Shouldering the responsibility he never wanted, Alek beckoned those closest and requested they start gathering their meager supplies. In moments, the group was ready, and they followed Natan on the narrow trail into the forest.

THEY'D BEEN AT the lake for six days, living on supplies sent by the city of Amara, a boon Alek hadn't expected, and he took a moment on the shore of the Lake of Glass to watch the ripples caused by a slight breeze. The Mage's influence was already spreading. Runners had come in bearing the news that Governor Basal would be with them shortly. Syros had arrived that morning with his shadow, Lieutenant Davis, tasked with his safety. Alek ran a hand over his face, not sure what the day would bring for his people.

"Lord Alek."

He glanced up to see Natan standing beside him and rose to his feet as Lieutenant Jaden and another man approached. The Mage motioned to the stranger. "Governor Basal, this is Lord Alek."

Basal inclined his dark head, and Alek made a short bow. "Governor. Shall we go to the tents?"

"If you don't mind, since it's a beautiful day, may we speak here?"

"Of course."

"I'll retrieve Syros," Jaden offered and trotted off. They took seats on the soft sand, and Basal made an appreciative sound as his glance skimmed the shining lake. "How are your people this morning?"

Alek gave him a close look. The governor returned his gaze with intelligent, earnest eyes, and Alek let out a breath he hadn't been aware of holding.

"We're well, my lord," he answered. "Although there seems to be a lethargy clinging to us, a slight confusion of the mind. The Mage says it will pass."

Natan nodded in assent. Kirstin and Kavi arrived with Bryon, and Alek was relieved to see the interest in Kavi's face as he settled beside him. His cousin had kept to himself this past week, Alek beginning to worry what might be going on in his sharp mind.

Once Jaden returned with Syros and Lieutenant Davis, Alek wasted no time. "I don't mean to rush you, lords, but will you send us to the city of Karthag as the Mage suggests? My people need to be settled."

Syros nodded thoughtfully as all eyes focused on him. "Natan informed me of what had transpired on the isle, and I agree this would be ideal. You'd have a stronghold for your people and the isolation to keep your own culture. On the other hand…" He gave Natan a sharp look. "The Northern Province will lose a city. Who's to pay for that?"

"Isn't the city abandoned, my lord?" Kirstin put in sweetly, then folded her hands in her lap at Bryon's scowl.

Syros tightened his lips, saying curtly, "There are a few families there along with a troop of soldiers. But perhaps something could be arranged…"

"Perhaps," Natan put in before Alek could comment. "It will be some time before Karthag can make a payment of any kind." He paused, holding Syros's gaze. "I have a different proposal."

"Natan, no," Alek interjected, not liking the glint that had entered Syros's gray eyes.

Basal stirred. "Perhaps the south could—"

"No!" Syros interrupted him. "The north has no need of your money. I'd like to hear the Mage's offer."

Natan shook his head. "I make no offer. But I would be in your debt."

"Natan," Alek cautioned, dismayed, sensing the deceptive nature of the regent.

Syros rose to his feet, Lieutenant Davis quick to follow, standing slightly behind and to his left. "Done. But Mage, be aware, I *will* collect."

"I have no doubt," Natan said dryly, then clasped the regent's hand. "Done."

"Someone's coming," Jaden cautioned, and a man strode up to them. Alek cursed under his breath, knowing this wouldn't be pleasant.

Camron stood over them, hands on hips. "I heard you were making plans for the Karthagan people this morning. How remiss not to invite me." His raspy whisper sent a shiver through Alek. Jaden dropped a hand to the knife at his belt, and Camron gave him a cool stare.

Basal looked the Karthagan over. "You are?"

Camron turned his mocking, light-brown eyes to him. "Camron, my lord. Didn't Alek speak of me? How negligent."

Kavi rose to face him. "I know him, my lord. This is Kayden's nephew." His eyes narrowed. "Not to be trusted."

"Did you need something?" Syros asked suavely.

Camron sat, making himself comfortable. "I'm here on behalf of Kayden's people, to make sure they're remembered in your negotiations."

"That's why Kirstin is here. As Kayden's sister, she's the rightful leader of his people," Kavi stated.

"I believe Kirstin has other interests now?" Camron raised his brows at Bryon who sat close beside her. Bryon's face was stone as he returned the man's stare. Camron grinned broadly in return.

"Please allow him to remain, my lords," Kirstin said, though she glared at Camron. "I want to see what he has in mind."

Camron inclined his head to her and turned to Syros. "As I was saying, my lord, what of my people? Karthag is not our home. We're from Siagan. When can we return there?"

Syros looked at him in astonishment. "Don't be absurd. Siagan has belonged to the Northern Territory far longer than you've been alive, and the people living there have a far greater claim on the land. You'll find Council Leader Mandel a dangerous foe if you have designs on his city."

Camron drew a breath, but Alek scrambled to his feet before he could protest. "Forgive me, Regent. Camron speaks out of turn. We're very grateful for your thoughtfulness in giving us Karthag. It seems my cousin has forgotten that it's only by your generosity that we have a home at all."

"Of course." Camron stood up beside Alek. "Pay no attention to me. My mind must still be a bit muddled." He bowed to both Syros and Basal, then gave Alek a mocking salute before he sauntered away. Alek watched his retreating figure in dismay.

"Take great care, Alek. I believe he means to stir up trouble," Basal warned as Camron disappeared into the woods.

"That has always been his way." Alek wondered if the old strife between the families would ever come to an end.

Syros seemed to reach a decision. "Lord Alek, I think it's best if we leave for Karthag immediately and help your people settle in."

"Thank you, lord," Alek said, giving him a curt bow. The others rose to their feet and parted. At Alek's word, the Karthagans hastened to break camp. When ready to leave, Alek stood by the horses as he watched, bemused, while Bryon paced restlessly beside him. What was troubling the soldier?

"Why don't you ride with us? Natan would like the company," he offered and could see Bryon was tempted. But then the man tensed. Alek followed his gaze to where Camron leaned against a tree speaking with Kirstin, Kavi beside them.

"No," Bryon said, clearly distracted, then he roused. "Basal wishes me on the ship with your men when they sail into the harbor at Karthag. Syros has already dispatched a runner to the city—" Laughter from the group at the tree snagged his attention. Bryon started toward them, but Natan came up at that moment.

"Is everything in order?" Natan glanced at the trio across the way and seemed disquieted but said nothing. Alek sighed. Had Camron already started a rift between them? He swung into the saddle, with the rest of the camp following, as Bryon took his leave to join the others on the ship.

They traveled the coastline for eight uneventful days, Alek taking in the beauty of the land while he watched the haunted look leave the eyes of his people, replaced by one of hope. They came to their city on a warm summer's morning, and he drew his horse to a standstill on the edge of the mountain path. Karthag lay below them in a small vale, its walls shining in the sunlight.

"It's like a dream," he murmured.

Unlike the other cities of Belega, there were no gates barring access through the tall stone walls of Karthag. They descended, and Kavi stopped his mount just inside the walls as the others continued on to the stables. Alek gave him a questioning glance when he slid from the saddle, but followed suit, handing the reins to a passing rider.

Natan rode up beside them, then dismounted. "Kavi?"

"In the Karthagans' last battle here, my great-uncle's army had gathered outside the walls of the city," Kavi began in a troubled voice, facing the large opening. "Grandfather stood here, inside the walls, knowing his brother Rodrik waited outside, but he was beyond caring. He called the winds from the sky, but the winds came too close. They swept my uncle's people away, but they also struck the gates and almost took Grandfather with them."

Kavi fell silent, and Alek took his arm as they started up the city streets, Natan beside them. He smiled slightly, relieved, when Kavi threw off his somber mood and admired the beautiful figures sculpted into the stonework of the old buildings. They rounded a corner and stopped at the sight of an ancient redwood tree growing in the center of the city. A small stone wall surrounded the tree with a few benches set outside the circle.

Alek drew a shaky breath, his eyes stinging with unexpected tears. "I never thought I'd see this."

Kavi turned to Natan. "This is a sacred place to my people. The tree roots grow toward the heart of the earth. My grandfather used to climb this tree when he was a boy," he confided. "He would use a rope to reach the lower branches. Strictly forbidden, of course, but even then Grandfather made his own rules."

They parted at the rose garden, the other two going their own way while Alek continued his inspection of the city, then met with Syros to discuss the best way to house everyone. Several Barkuit families had moved out of Karthag the day before, but those remaining were curious about their new neighbors, and anxious to make them feel welcome.

Chapter Sixteen

SYROS REMAINED IN Karthag a month to help Alek settle his people and learn the economic and social structure of Belega. Natan sat in on the meetings but felt he had next to nothing to contribute. To his dismay, he discovered he had little aptitude or interest in politics. And he'd been dreaming of Gregor again, reliving his loneliness, his deep longing to return home. Did Gregor's family miss him? Natan felt sure they did.

The need to make the voyage to Sennia grew in him as his dreams intensified. Gregor urged him to return to his homeland, with Natan coming to realize he owed the man that much. He'd speak to Syros about it. And Kavi would need to be told. Natan's face darkened. If the man cared anymore. Kavi had avoided him since they'd landed on Belega.

"Have you given any thought to the council leader's seat in Amara?" Kirstin asked Bryon one evening as they sat on the wall of Karthag with Alek and watched the sun lower in the sky. Natan waited curiously for his friend's reply.

"Not since Governor Basal mentioned it," Bryon admitted. "What do you think?"

Kirstin leaned her head against his knee. "I think Amara would be honored to have you," she replied, and Bryon flushed from the sincerity of her words.

Natan lost the thread of the conversation as Kavi emerged from the forest, walking down the trail toward the city with his cousin. He frowned, not liking the intent way Kavi listened to Camron's words.

Alek followed his gaze. "Trouble?"

"I'm not sure." He rose self-consciously. "I think I'll join them."

He hurried down the stairway to the cobbled street and followed it outside the city walls, stopping when he came face-to-face with Kavi. Camron had disappeared.

"Camron says you're leaving," Kavi stated abruptly, and Natan flinched at his accusing tone. How had Camron known? He'd only confided his dreams to Bryon. Had he been listening in?

"Soon." Natan hesitated, then added, "Gregor's family should be told of his death. But also, Alek must be given the chance to establish his leadership. He turns to me on every question and needs time to find his own strengths."

Kavi shrugged. "You brought us to this strange land, and now you'll abandon us with people who hate and fear us. Was your offer of friendship a lie, Mage?"

"No!" Heart thumping, Natan took a step closer to Kavi. "I'll always come if you need me. You have only to call." He pulled Kavi tentatively to him. "Come with me," he urged, pressing his lips to Kavi's warm neck, breathing him in, achingly. "I need your strength." It stung when Kavi hastily withdrew from his arms and left him without a word, entering Karthag ahead of him. Why wouldn't he speak to him? Natan widened his eyes on a sudden thought. Was Camron influencing him in some inimical manner? A concern to investigate once Natan returned from Sennia.

He passed through the gate opening and returned to the group on the breezeway, where he motioned to Bryon. "May I speak with you?"

Bryon nodded, following Natan some distance from the others. Natan ran a hand through his unruly curls, frustrated and hurt by Kavi's behavior.

"Can Kirstin spare you a day or two?" he asked. "I'm leaving for the harbor as soon as I'm packed and would like the company." He smiled crookedly. "You could also bring my horse back after I sail."

Bryon's forehead creased. "There's a ship coming? From where?"

Natan shrugged. "I'm being called home. That is, the part of Gregor that is in me compels me to return. I can't explain it, but it can't be ignored either."

"I'll go with you—"

"No." He paused at the flash of anger in Bryon's eyes and touched his arm. "I'm not being stubborn. Only I won't endanger anyone else until I know what's going on."

"You expect me to let you go alone?"

"I do."

Bryon blinked at his tone, commanding, brooking no argument. Then he gave Natan a deep bow, disconcerting him. "As you wish, Mage. I'll see to the horses."

In dismay, Natan watched him walk away, wondering if he'd have any friends left when all was said and done. He bid a quiet farewell to Alek, who urged him to stay. But Natan couldn't be dissuaded. Kavi was nowhere to be seen, so Natan mounted the horse Bryon held for him and followed the man from the city, heart heavy with sorrow and fear.

It proved an easy enough ride to the harbor following the old road from Karthag to the eastern coast, the dense forest crowding close. They arrived late in the night and made camp without a fire, simply staking the horses, then rolling out their blankets in the darkness.

Natan moaned in the night, struggling through layers of sleep. He dreamed of a black ship coming to take him home. He came awake with a jolt, knowing it was true. It was time. He blinked the images from his eyes and sat up. There were tears on his face. An hour of darkness remained before sunrise, but he climbed to his feet anyway.

"Bryon, wake up." He shook his friend's shoulder. The soldier grumbled and rolled away from him. "Bryon," he urged. "They're coming. Wake up."

Bryon opened his eyes. "What?"

"The ship's come in. I have to go." He gripped Bryon's hand and helped him to his feet.

Bryon rubbed his eyes, yawning. "Are you sure, lad?"

"Yes. It's the one that's come for Gregor. I'm afraid all they'll find is me." Natan looked at his friend in sudden panic. "I don't know if I can do this."

The moon was on the point of setting but glimmered enough to show his face. Bryon frowned. "Then don't go, lad," he urged. "You don't owe them anything."

A tremor passed over Natan and he clenched his hands to keep them from shaking. "I don't have a choice," he said softly. "The Mage died in my arms. With his last breath he passed his secrets to me." His voice shook as he continued, "Gregor's in my head. His final desire was to see his mother. He keeps at me. I have to find her and tell her what happened, if only to find peace."

He bit his lip when Bryon looked doubtful and shoved his hands into his pockets. "It doesn't matter," he said unhappily as he walked toward the shoreline.

Bryon followed him, offering his help. "I could still come with you."

For a second a wild hope sprang into Natan's heart, but then he shook his head. "They'll only allow me passage, for Gregor's sake." He took Bryon's hand in a firm grip. "Thank you for seeing me off."

"Take care, lad," Bryon returned awkwardly.

They could hear the oars of the dory that would take Natan out to the ship. He picked up his pack and met the two oarsmen on the shore, tall men enveloped in gray slickers against the ocean spray, hoods pulled low over their dark faces. If they were surprised to see a boy instead of Gregor, they gave no sign and helped him into the waiting boat.

Natan gave a last look at the man who'd been a father to him as they rowed into the waves, then turned his face from his homeland. He wondered if he'd have to wander in solitude as the Mage had done. How soon would he see his home again? He forced the painful thoughts of Kavi from his mind. Natan loved him, but that seemed to bring more hurt than joy these days. Maybe distance would help…but he doubted it.

The black ship waited off shore, looming dark on the horizon. A rope ladder descended and Natan climbed to the deck of the schooner, to face a silent crew, as dark-skinned as Gregor. A young man stepped from the group to sweep him a bow. "If you come with me, Mage, I'll show you to your quarters."

Natan followed him, conscious of eyes on his back as he crossed the deck. He heard the dory being raised behind him and the clank of the anchor. The boat shifted with the tide. The two of them made their way down a short flight of stairs to a narrow hallway, Natan relieved when the youth opened a door halfway along into a small private room.

The young man flashed him a grin from the doorway as Natan entered the tight quarters. "I'm Daran. Holler if you need anything. And don't mind the crew. They'll grow accustomed to your presence soon enough. It's only that we rarely have guests on board, and even rarer, ones with such fair skin." Daran drew a breath. "Oh, and the captain sends his regards and will see you shortly."

"Thank you," Natan said, feeling lost, and grateful for his friendliness. Daran nodded as he closed the door. Natan drew a deep breath. He was committed now.

NATAN SAT AT the prow of the schooner with a racing heart, eyes wide. So much had happened to him in the last fortnight. He felt young, excited, and scared, the boy Bryon always called him. The coastline of Sennia came into view with the ship dropping anchor as the sun rose over the green hills. The town of Gahva sprawled down to the sea and fishing boats were leaving the harbor for deeper water. He'd wondered why they hadn't taken him to the harbor at Mennon, Gregor's home, but Daran replied there were items on board for the Vice-King in Sambola, and Gahva was the shorter distance.

Natan took a breath of the salty air and laughed aloud in the pure joy of adventure. Daran, who'd taken him under his wing, waved him off, wishing him well. They rowed him ashore with the cargo and the men bid him a cheery farewell. They'd grown fond of the quiet lad who lent a hand wherever needed, whether on the deck or in the galley. Natan gave them a flamboyant bow, then made his way up the cool beach to the town.

He spotted a cloaked figure in the middle of the roadway and eyed him curiously as he approached. The young man raised a solemn face. "Why have you come to Sennia?"

The challenge dismayed him. Natan knew he carried grievous news, but he hadn't expected animosity. He was baffled when the grim lips curled into a grin.

"Sorry," the man said, failing to sound contrite. "Aunt Aubre told me to be kind to you, which always makes me want to do the opposite. But truly, I meant no offense. I'm Niko, by the way."

"Natan." Natan sketched a bow.

Niko gave him a close look, then linked their arms and drew him down the street. "Come on, let's get some breakfast, and then we'll be on our way."

Natan held back. "Wait," he said. "Who are you and where are we going?"

Niko glanced at him in mock surprise, then stepped closer to search his eyes. "You truly don't know, do you?" he whispered after a moment. Natan was stung at the hint of contempt in his voice, feeling he had failed some test. The two men stared at each other until Niko gave a sudden shrug and a laugh.

"No matter." He took Natan's arm again. "My aunt, or rather my great-aunt, Lady Aubre, dreamt that her son yearned to come home and had the ship sent." He gave Natan a sidelong look. "Her next dream revealed that there would be another man coming in his stead. I was sent to meet you, and since you're here as Gregor's representative, I just assumed you'd be as strong as he. I see I was mistaken."

Natan shook off his arm. "Perhaps."

He walked through the town, head lowered, his heart growing heavier with each step. He knew the curious townsmen watched him, but he couldn't bring himself to speak to them of the Mage's death. And what of Gregor's mother? She knew he was coming. Did she know of Gregor's death as well, or would he have to be the one to break her heart? He heard Niko fall into step behind him, but he ignored the brash young man. Any more chinks in his self-confidence, he'd be fleeing for home.

They spent the morning in silence as Natan trudged doggedly up the dusty road. Niko followed, humming snatches of songs as he tossed pebbles into the tall grass. He just as often pulled something out of his pack to eat, which Natan found extremely irritating. His own provisions were limited, and he had no idea when they might reach another village.

At noon the grasslands gave way to a large oak grove. Natan halted, sitting cross-legged to rest on the thick moss beside a clear spring. The weather proved warmer on Sennia than in his own country, and he removed his cloak and sweater, folding them into his pack. After a short debate with himself, he took out a packet of dried fruit and nuts. He felt Niko's eyes on him so impatiently rolled to his stomach to eat his meager lunch while he watched the sunlight play on the water.

Niko shrugged and sat with his back to a wide tree, playing with the dagger he kept in a sheath up his sleeve. Seeming bored, he returned the blade to its hiding place, then held out his hand. Natan watched as sweat burst out on his face. His breathing grew labored. Suddenly, a tiny glow appeared in his palm and sprang into a flame. It disappeared instantly, but Niko leaned back against the oak, looking satisfied.

"How did you do that?" Natan asked, impressed. He'd seen the Karthagans do the same and wondered if everyone on Sennia had the gift. Flattered, Niko moved beside him.

"It's very difficult," Niko warned. "Open your hand." He continued when Natan complied, "Now, command the flame to appear, and it will."

Natan frowned at his palm. "Command?"

"Yes," Niko said impatiently.

Natan concentrated and a flame burst to life in his hand, bright but without heat. He watched it a moment, then asked it to leave. It made him uneasy to demand anything of nature. Flashing Niko an apologetic glance, he surprised a look of intense jealousy on his face. Natan scrambled to his feet, slinging his pack on his shoulder, before taking to the road again without a word. Niko trailed behind.

They hadn't gone far when Natan stopped and held his hands away from his body.

"Why, Niko?" he asked softly as hooded men stepped out of the trees, several with notched arrows.

"Because, my dear friend," Niko stepped behind him and pulled a leather strap from a pocket. "The people in your country may honor an enchanter, but here in Sennia we know how to deal with the like." He tugged Natan's hands together at his back and tied them tightly. "Why do you think my precious cousin fled all those years ago?" He gave a vicious tug on the leather so that it bit into Natan's wrists.

"You don't have to do this."

A man strode out of the group and struck him across the mouth. "None of that. You'll be putting a spell on us next. That, we can't allow."

Natan held himself still, tasting blood, as he caught a strange gleam in the man's dark eyes. He could feel the malice in him, the delight he took in another's pain.

The man stared him in the face as he played with another strip of leather. "Smart boy."

He lunged suddenly and jabbed Natan in the stomach. As he doubled over in agony, the man thrust the leather between his teeth, quickly tying it behind his head. Natan grew dizzy as he fought for air. The leather chewed into the corners of his mouth and forced his tongue back. He gagged several times before he could work his tongue around the leather to open his airway.

"Bring him, Danul," The man turned on his heels and strode into the forest. Rough hands took hold of Natan, but he ignored the laughter as he stumbled. Niko's shocked breath at the needless brutality gave him hope.

They traveled at a quick pace for the afternoon, though it grew stifling under the trees. Thirst became a separate enemy to Natan. They made a brief pause as evening drew on, and Niko managed to give him a few drops of water before a glare from the grim leader stopped him. The group made camp just as night settled in.

Natan lay on his side outside the fire's glow, shivering without his cloak. He could also have done with a swallow of precious water, but that was hardly likely. It puzzled him why Gregor had sent him to that place, not sure what he could learn from these angry men. There were four others, besides Niko and the tall man, whom he'd heard called Mazzo. Despite hunger and thirst, he found himself nodding off.

Gregor's mother waited in his mind, worried, a well of sadness on her face.

"I'm coming home, Mother, as soon as I may," he whispered in Gregor's voice. The woman nodded gently, her touch on his cheek sending him to happier dreams.

Morning brought the misery of numb arms and the trial of breathing. Natan's throat burned with thirst. They continued traveling the extensive forest, a man ready with a push and jeer if he faltered. They reached a glen in the early afternoon. Through the blur of exhaustion, Natan saw a rough-hewn cabin as he dropped to his knees. He could hear the murmur of water close by. As soon as the dizziness passed, he meant to have a drink, one way or another.

Too soon someone gripped his arm and jerked him to his feet.

"Tired?" Mazzo asked. Natan kept quiet as icy fear touched his heart. "Come. I have the perfect place for you to rest."

Natan kept his head bowed as they led him across the clearing to a spot behind the cabin. The cruelty in the man beside him was a living presence he didn't want to stir. They came to a halt and he raised his eyes. A black hole gaped open in the hillside, an iron grate across the entrance.

He took an involuntary step back as horror and decay boiled out of the shallow cave. With a guttural cry, he threw himself to the ground, breaking their hold on him, then rolled desperately to the side, needing to get away from that place. Gaining his feet, he stumbled blindly toward the forest. Angry shouts rose around him, and he was knocked to the ground, Danul's heavy body driving the breath from his lungs. Natan twisted from under the man, only to be kicked savagely by another. Then they had him, and he was swept up in their arms. He fought, dry sobs catching in his throat as they forced him back to the cave. He saw Mazzo's wild eyes as the man gripped his hair.

"Sweet dreams," Mazzo snarled and kissed his forehead. With a cold laugh, he motioned, and they threw him bodily into the hole. Natan landed hard, then heard the clank of metal as they set the grate into place. The resonance of the bolt being drawn echoed in the blackness long after the men had departed.

Natan couldn't raise his face from the damp, rich soil, and then panic sent him scrambling to his knees, wondering if they meant to bury him alive. No, the iron grate let in air and the sound of voices moving away. He huddled against the earthen wall, shivering as the cold seeped into his tired body. The shallow cave closed in on him, terrifying as he sensed the despair hanging in the blackness. He whimpered a little at the cloying smell of decay and slipped to the ground as nightmares chased him into exhausted sleep.

A sharp jab in the ribs woke Natan later; then someone helped him sit up. A knife flashed in the darkness, and he drew back, but an impatient breath halted him. The man slashed the cords from his wrists, then set the blade against his cheek. He found himself staring into Niko's dark eyes in the flickering light from the cave's entrance.

"You mustn't say a word," Niko whispered. Natan nodded, sensing his fear. Niko cut the tight cord at his mouth. Natan choked down a cry at the sudden ache of jaw and ruined lips. Niko held a flask to his mouth but pulled it away after a few swallows.

"Wait a moment," he insisted, so Natan clung desperately to his self-control until Niko let him drink again.

"We must go before Mazzo becomes impatient," Niko warned him, and Natan struggled to a crouch. He motioned to the strange red glow at the mouth of the cave and gave Niko a questioning look.

Niko hung his head. "He's gone too far."

The muttered words filled Natan with dread. He feared he'd soon learn what had caused the aura of despair that lingered in the grave. For grave it was. He could smell the bodies under the loose soil.

Niko led him outside. Night had fallen, and Natan stood blinking at the scene that met his eyes, not sure what it meant. A huge bonfire had been lit in the center of the clearing, the men gathered in a circle around it. Mazzo stood close to the fire in robes of silver and black. Natan faltered, but the prick of Niko's blade at his throat told him he'd find no help there. Niko shoved him, and he walked with leaden feet toward the fire.

"Have you come to repent?" Mazzo asked in sonorous tones.

Natan looked at him in confusion. "I don't understand."

Niko's sharp hiss reminded him too late not to speak. With an angry roar, Mazzo stepped closer. Excitement glittered in his eyes.

"Silence," he spat out. "The sorcerer is not to speak. Or should I call you Mage?" His voice turned deadly. "Are you our teacher then? A wise one? Arrogance! No matter. We'll soon cure you of that." He turned to the others and opened his arms. "Behold the transgressor, the perverter of nature." He nodded sharply as men grabbed Natan. "Take him."

Natan struggled violently, but the men merely laughed and painfully twisted his arms, while Danul replaced Niko with a knife to his throat. They dragged him close to the rushing flames. Stripping his shirt, they then tied him between two saplings by the wrists. He stood too close to the fire. Heat poured from the flames and reddened his skin. Sweat broke out on his face, and he grew faint as he breathed in the searing air. Mazzo approached him, and Natan couldn't take his eyes off the iron tongs the man held in his trembling hands.

"Don't worry, my boy," the man crooned and caressed Natan's hot face. "We shall save you. Those others—" He nodded toward the open grave. "—were weak. They died in sin. But I can feel the strength in you." He placed an open palm on Natan's chest. "I can also sense the dark magic in you."

He turned from Natan and removed a burning stick from the bonfire with the tongs. He blew lightly on the end, watching the black smoke curl into the air.

"Never fear." He moved closer. "We shall burn it out of you."

Natan couldn't prevent the screams that burst from his lips as the man placed the smoldering tip of the wood against his chest over his heart. Lost in agony, he embraced the darkness that claimed him as he swooned.

He awoke to a pain that tore at him with each indrawn breath. Someone touched the agony on his chest, and he flinched away with a shuddering sob. Did they mean to drive him mad?

"Silence," a voice warned. Natan shut his mouth with a hard click of teeth. Through a haze of pain, he saw the night was giving way to day. The fire had burned low, so he felt cold to his very bones. Niko touched him again to apply a salve on his burns, and he swallowed the groan that shook his body.

Niko muttered under his breath, glancing around them. Drawing his knife, he quickly cut the bonds holding Natan to the trees. Natan dropped heavily, his exhausted muscles unable to support him.

Uttering a dark oath, Niko slipped an arm around his trembling body and helped him rise, supporting him as they made their way into the forest.

They came to Niko's horse staked in the trees, where Natan managed to haul himself painfully into the saddle. Niko swung up behind him, and they rode swiftly in the direction of the road. The jolting horse became an agony, so with a slurred apology, Natan slipped into unconsciousness.

Chapter Seventeen

NATAN PRESSED HIS forehead against his knees as he listened to the waves crashing on the shore. After two days of traveling, he needed to replace the dressing on his wound. But he didn't know if he had the strength to do it when the slightest touch brought agony. Gritting his teeth, he gripped an edge of the soft cloth, tugged, and bit back a cry as it tore the skin as it peeled away. He wrapped trembling arms around his knees and rocked until the worst of the pain receded.

Hearing a step beside him, Natan raised a face slick with sweat and tears. "Nothing like a little pain to remind one they're alive."

Niko grunted as he threw down the wood he'd gathered for a fire. "Let me see."

Natan sat cross-legged and raised his chin, remembering how he'd done the same for Bryon when he'd gotten hurt as a child. The burns were raw and ugly with bloody patches where the knitting skin had been torn, but there was no sign of infection.

Niko started suddenly, looked closer at the burn, then turned a shocked face to Natan.

"What is it?" Natan glanced down in alarm. He winced at the ravaged skin but he didn't see… But then he understood and his blood turned to ice. He hung his head, thankful for the first time since meeting him he didn't have Kavi with him, finding the thought of his lover's fingers on his burned chest unbearable. In his hatred, Mazzo had traced into his skin an arrow's tip run through with a horizontal line, the symbol for madness.

Niko watched him with pity, then set about building a fire. Its cheery crackle drew Natan from his dark thoughts, and he wearily dug in his pack for the salve and clean cloth. He winced as he pulled his shirt back over his head when he'd finished.

He glanced over at Niko as he rubbed the excess paste into his wrists. The man was busy whittling a long stick. "What are you doing?"

Niko merely raised his eyebrows and grinned, ignoring Natan's question. When he had a sharp point, he laughed as he jumped to his feet.

"Fish for lunch," he promised and waded out into the breakers.

Natan watched his antics with amusement, but when after a time Niko's attempts seemed destined to fail, he dug out his camping pot. He fetched water from a nearby spring, set it on the coals to boil, then climbed out on the rocks of a tide pool. Taking a calming breath, he lay perfectly still, hand in the water, and sent his thoughts out. Soon two crabs climbed out of their holes and sidestepped over to his fingers.

Natan lifted them gently from the water. "Thank you, little ones," he said to them.

Niko joined him as he slipped them into the pot. The man scowled, then shrugged and sat down to eat his share.

"We should make our way a little farther up the shore before we stop for the night," Niko advised between mouthfuls. "We're still several days from the town of Cahna, and then Mennon where Lady Aubre waits, and I can't guarantee Mazzo will stick to the road, even though we sent the horse that way. He may remember I spent my childhood here on the coast."

Natan nodded absently. Something had begun to niggle in his mind, but he couldn't place it. He put a hand on Niko's arm when they rose.

"Thank you," he said simply, encompassing everything the man had done for him. Niko gave his characteristic shrug.

"I don't have you safe yet, Mage," he grinned and strode off over the sand.

Natan pensively followed him, startled by his use of the title. He hadn't done very well up to this moment, but he would do his best to earn the name.

Day turned to night as they traveled, with enough moonlight to guide their steps. As they walked along the shoreline, the vague intrusion in Natan's mind turned to an urgent need. He stopped to listen, hearing the crashing of the waves. He felt the wind on his face. There was something… He tilted his head as he tried to catch it.

Niko looked questioningly at him but remained silent at his intent pose.

"I'm being called," he said, surprised at being drawn so insistently toward some unknown purpose. He took a few hesitant steps in the direction of the road still several leagues away. He quickened his pace, ignoring Niko's mumbled protest.

They reached the tree line before Niko caught his arm to gain his attention. "Have you thought it might be Mazzo?"

Natan blinked, caught in the flow of energy that pulled at him.

"No, it's not him," he said with assurance after a moment, discerning no taint in the flow, only a clean brightness. "But there is fear, so Mazzo may be close," he added and moved off at a trot. Niko followed, shaking his head. They traveled for an hour through the forest before catching a glimmer of light ahead.

"We're there," Natan said and saw Niko shudder at his dreamlike tone. They crawled from tree to tree until they could see down into a small clearing. A fire burned in its center with several men sitting about warming their hands. Natan drew a quick breath on spying two children tied to a sapling a few paces from the fire. Mazzo stood over them.

Niko rose with a cry as the man lifted his fist and struck the smaller child, knocking her to the ground. Natan was up instantly, springing down the hillside. "Don't touch them again," he barked as he stepped into camp, his harsh command startling everyone to their feet.

Mazzo whirled to face him. "You," he snarled, then his stance relaxed. "I wondered how long before we netted you. Did you mean I shouldn't strike the children? But how else would I have gained your attention?" He viciously kicked the other child in the stomach.

Thunder roared suddenly in the sky, and a fierce breeze raced from nowhere. Mazzo glanced around, startled, his gaze returning to Natan with caution. Fury burned through Natan, causing Mazzo to take a step back from him. The men cried out in terror as the earth moved under them.

"Leave," Natan commanded.

Mazzo's eyes flashed in answer, but he gave Natan a stiff bow. "As you wish. I have a matter to attend to, and now would be fortuitous." His lips curled in a sneer and he said with cold assurance, "We will meet again soon."

He motioned his men to the horses. As they swept from camp, the stark hatred in his last glance at Natan made Niko gasp where he crouched by the children.

Energy pulsed in Natan. He gloried in it, knowing in that moment he could do anything he wished. He smiled before letting the power flow out of him in a gentle wave. He looked at the clear night sky, his heart full. The power had been in him but had not controlled him.

"Thank you for this gift, dear friend," he whispered to Gregor as tears ran down his face. He brushed at his eyes and hastened to help Niko untie the children and see to their hurts.

Niko watched him with awe, then went to his knees. "Forgive me, lord," he said and bowed his head.

Natan looked at him in surprise. "What are you doing?"

"I sold you to Mazzo out of jealousy. I knew he and his faction hunted men of power, and I thought it was an easy way to be rid of you. Only, I didn't realize… I've been a fool. I'm very sorry."

"Never mind that now. Can you see if there's food for the children?" Natan said gruffly, embarrassed.

"Of course." Niko stared at the young ones. "Aren't you Gregor's family?" he asked.

The youngest child looked shyly away, but the boy sat up. "Yes, I'm Kayle. This is my sister, Tillie."

Natan smiled slightly at the proud lift of the child's curly head. The way the boy put his arm protectively around his sister touched his heart, though he felt the loss of the Mage more than ever. "Peace, Kayle." He held out his open hands. "Let me help you."

Kayle saw the abrasions on his wrists, looked at the similar marks on his own skin, and gave a small nod.

"Thank you. Where do you come from?"

"We have a house in the forest now. Mother moved us after the bad men came to our old home." The boy frowned. "I guess they found us anyway."

A knot settled in Natan's stomach. "And your mother?"

"She had gone to market when the men came. I hope she's home now."

"Can you show me where?" Natan asked. Recalling Mazzo's last words, he felt ill with the urgency to be there.

The boy puffed up. "Of course. I'm eight, after all."

Natan rubbed the boy's springy hair. "You are indeed." He smiled, hiding his fear, and stood as Niko approached with bread and a bit of stew abandoned by the fleeing men. "Eat now, and then we'll go."

As if sensing his mood, the children ate quickly, and they were soon on their way, Natan and Niko carrying the children on their backs. They jogged as swiftly as they could through the forest, but the sun rose before they reached the cabin. Exhausted, they put the children down to walk the last league, seeing the smoke of the fire long before they reached it. Natan knew with dread that they'd come too late. He gripped the children's hands to keep them from running ahead as they approached the smoldering cabin.

"Where's Mother?"

"Wait a moment, Kayle," Natan said gently, his voice heavy with sorrow. The boy looked at him as if to rebel, but seeing Natan's expression, covered his face with his little hands. Not a sound escaped him. Tillie looked at her brother and took his hand. They leaned together for comfort.

Natan turned from them in pain. "Will you stay with them?" he asked Niko who nodded, his face reflecting the horror Natan felt. Natan touched his clenched hand. "This is not your doing," he said earnestly. "Many others have been deceived by Mazzo's cunning. You're not to blame here."

Niko nodded and squatted beside the children, looking unconvinced.

Natan made a wide circle around the cabin, the timbers of which looked ready to collapse. A darkness crept into his heart as he approached the garden in the back, Gregor's grief and rage rising to the surface inside him. The Mage found her there, his lovely wife, staked out in the mud with the last spike through her heart.

He dropped to his knees beside her and touched her face with a shaking hand. "Heart's dearest. Elsa, be at peace."

Natan choked on the sobs that escaped him, then in sudden fury, tore at the leather strips that bound her hands and feet. Placing his coat over her, he rose unsteadily. He'd need Niko's help to bury her.

"I knew you'd come."

Natan whirled at the voice and saw Mazzo standing outside the garden, a fierce, exalted expression on his face. He did nothing to conceal the madness within.

"Why?" Natan begged, trapped between Gregor's grief and his own.

Mazzo smiled coldly. "To snare you, of course, my dear sorcerer. You see, you're not the only man with power here. A lesson I'm obliged to demonstrate."

Natan held himself still as Mazzo reached for the energy of life, his blood tingling as the man lifted his hands to the sky and drew the power into himself.

"Understand, my boy," Mazzo said, his voice thick with pride. "I'm not against the use of power. I just claim it for myself."

"Nature doesn't answer to your will, Mazzo. Let it go before it consumes you."

"Ha!" With a look of triumph, Mazzo stretched his hands out toward him. Natan emptied his mind as the wave of energy struck him. Pure light surged through him in a measure that could have destroyed him had he sought to hold it. Instead, he simply let it flow through him and back into the earth.

"No, it can't be." Mazzo's voice held fury and disbelief.

Startled, Natan opened his eyes as Mazzo drew a long knife from his belt. He waved it at Natan, then with a wild laugh of despair put it against his own abdomen.

"Don't, Mazzo. Wait!" Natan raced for him.

"It's too late. You've come, just as I foresaw. The world's ending, and I can't stop it!" With a last cry, he plunged the blade of the knife into his body just as Natan reached him, Mazzo curled over the wound, falling to the ground. Natan knelt beside him, went to roll him over to get at his injury, and stopped. There was no helping him. Mazzo still clutched the knife handle, gasping, hands covered with blood as his life poured steadily from him.

"Mazzo," Natan mourned as he raised Mazzo's anguished face. Blood flecked his white lips. At his gentle touch, Mazzo's eyes cleared, and for an instant he looked at Natan with wonder. Then life left him and his body slumped in a heap. Natan bowed over him, letting the tears slide down his face as he grieved for all the lives taken, and those yet to be lost, in the treacherous pursuit of power.

NATAN ROUSED FROM his grief, remembering the children waiting for news of their mother. He walked with dragging feet to the front of the house, steadying his features as Kayle ran to meet him.

The boy stopped a few paces from him and took Tillie's hand when she came up beside him. "Can we say goodbye?"

Natan swallowed, remembering the pain etched on their mother's face. "No. She wouldn't want you to see her right now. Can you and Tillie sit on the steps here while Niko and I find her a beautiful spot to lie in? You can say your goodbyes then."

Kayle set his lips, but his face crumpled at the small sob from Tillie. "We will," he promised, and pulled his sister to the porch, putting his arms around her as the little girl began to cry.

Natan watched them, then turned away, his face working. Niko picked up a shovel from the nearby shed and followed him around the house. They carried her up a nearby hill, burying her in the sun. When they'd finished the sorrowful task, they called the children.

Tillie dropped a flower on her mother's grave then stepped back to take Natan's hand. Kayle slipped his small hand into Natan's free one as they stood quietly on the hillside.

Niko came up behind them and grimaced slightly. "Mazzo's taken care of."

"Thank you, Niko." He looked at the children. "Shall we go?"

Kayle gave a loud sniff and nodded his curly head. Tillie made a tiny cry as they turned away, so Natan gently squeezed her hand, suffering Gregor's anguish for his orphaned girl.

Niko fell into step beside them. "We should reach Cahna by evening."

"Uncle Tolban has a house there with Mirah," Kayle volunteered.

"He has no magic, so the bad men leave him alone."

Niko laughed at the boy's careless dismissal of the powerless uncle.

"Do you have magic, Kayle?" Natan asked as they walked through the forest.

"Mother did," the boy answered with a kick at a stone. "Sometimes me and Tillie can do things together. Mother taught us."

Natan nodded, curious if the ability was inherent in certain people or if it could be taught to anyone. He grew eager to learn the answer, though it might take a lifetime.

He scooped little Tillie up into his arms and carried the sleepy girl the last hour into Cahna, shifting her from one arm to the other until his arms grew numb, then throwing her over a shoulder. She giggled and Kayle made a face at her. Niko refused to carry him one step.

They entered the town at dusk, where many people watched the small parade with interest. Very few travelers came that way, so when they saw the children with a pale stranger, they became anxious, and followed. A boy ran ahead and presently a man came striding down the road to meet them.

"Uncle Tolban!" Kayle cried and ran to jump into the man's arms.

"What's this?" Tolban's grave, intelligent face looked very much like his sister Elsa's, the children's mother. He glanced from Natan, who couldn't hide his pain, to the crowd gathering around them.

"Let's not talk here," he decided. With a reassuring farewell to the townsmen, he led them to his house on the end of the street. His daughter, Mirah, met them at the door and took the children into the kitchen while he showed them to comfortable chairs by the fire in a nearby room.

Natan settled into the cushions and closed his eyes. Gregor's grief inside him was hard to bear.

Tolban cleared his throat. "Will you tell me what happened?"

When Natan remained silent, unable to speak, Niko began the story leading to Elsa's death, not sparing himself in the gruesome tale.

They stayed by the hearth as night set in. Natan couldn't remember ever being so tired. Witnessing Tolban's distress and sorrow at the news of his sister's death and bearing Gregor's grief had drained the last of his strength. He wanted to go home. He wanted to see his friends. But more than anything else, he wanted Kavi to hold him and tell him everything would be all right. Natan missed him, ached for the comfort of his arms. Loneliness ate into his soul.

Tolban showed him to the couch. Natan stumbled in his weariness, and Tolban helped him gently down, throwing a heavy blanket over him. He tried to thank him but fell asleep before he could form the words.

In his dream, Kavi waited for him at his home near Amara, and Natan rushed to him with a broken sob. Kavi took him in his arms, holding him close. They walked along the shore and sat beside the glimmering water, watching the first stars appear overhead.

"This was our favorite time of the day, wasn't it?" Natan murmured and looked into Kavi's face. Kavi smiled at him, then took his hand. They sat quietly for many moments as they listened to the water lap on the sand. Birds whistled their last trill of song for the evening. Crickets began to chirp, and even a few bats came out.

Natan took a deep breath as the moon began to shimmer on the ocean, his heart swelling with pain. "Is this a dream?" he asked, full of sorrow.

"You know it is."

"No." Natan's arms convulsed around Kavi, his body aching. Hot tears stung his eyes. He at last raised his head and kissed Kavi, tasting his sweet warmth. This had to be real! But the vibrant body in his arms became a mist and slipped from his grasp. Loneliness filled the hole in his heart where Kavi had been. Natan awoke in tears, sleep eluding him for a long time after that.

NATAN SAT ON the porch steps the next morning, absently rubbing the sleep from his eyes while Niko and Tolban tended to the horses. After a moment, he rose to stomp around the small yard to loosen stiff muscles. The front door flung open and he braced as the children ran out. Tillie jumped into his arms, and he lifted her up with a broad grin. He winced as she rubbed against the scabs on his chest, but the bright smile on her face made the pain worthwhile.

Kayle hung back with Mirah, so Natan set Tillie down and resumed his seat on the steps. Tillie instantly took a spot beside him, and he beckoned Kayle over. After a brief hesitation, the boy sat on his other side.

Mirah leaned against the railing. She was a quiet girl of sixteen with lovely features and dark-brown eyes. Her black hair curled in soft tendrils around her face. She smiled at him, and Natan gave her a good morning.

"You're leaving us, aren't you?" Kayle said but wouldn't look at him.

"Yes. A dear friend of mine has died and I have to go to Mennon to tell his mother. I promised that I would." Natan bit his lip, unable to bring himself to tell the children of their father's death. Maybe Aubre would share that burden with him.

The boy looked solemnly at him. "Will you come back?"

Natan took his hand. "I will, if it's in my power to do so."

The boy nodded. "Good." He jumped to his feet when his uncle and Niko led the horses into the yard. "Guess what," he cried when Tolban swung him into his arms.

"What?" He tickled the boy.

"Natan said he'd come back."

Natan stood and gave a deep bow. "If I would be welcome."

Tolban smiled. "You'd be more than welcome, Mage. The children need you. In fact, from what Niko has told me of you, there are many people here who could use your guidance in the use of their powers. Please come back."

Natan glanced at the sunlight in the forest, at the snow-capped peaks of the mountains far to the east. He looked at the children and suddenly felt as if he belonged. "Thank you," he said, and bowed low once again. He kissed Tillie's forehead then shook hands with Kayle. Mirah gave him a shy embrace before Natan mounted his horse with tears in his eyes for the coming separation.

"Goodbye," Niko waved from his saddle.

Tolban went to him and gripped his arm. "Give my best to your aunt. And Niko," he continued with his eyes on Natan's profile. "Take care of him."

"That's my intention." Niko nodded, then his irrepressible grin leaped to his face. "Although it's more than likely he'll be doing the protecting. Goodbye."

After warning Tolban once again of Mazzo's men, who were still in the forest and quite capable of going on with their violence without their leader, they started their journey, making good time on the road to Mennon.

Natan grew quieter as the day lengthened and they drew near to

Gregor's home.

"Are you well, Mage?" Niko asked him in concern. Natan nodded, though sorrow had tears in his eyes again, so Niko left him alone.

Natan ran a hand through his hair, discouraged. He couldn't think of the words to tell the little mother of her son's death. In the end he didn't have to say anything. They entered the bustling city of Mennon in the late afternoon, and Niko showed him the small house that had been Gregor's home.

Natan stopped at the fence to stare at a house so familiar it could have been his own. He dismounted and pushed open the gate, following the path through the garden as if in a dream. The door of the house opened, and he roused suddenly at the sight of the beloved woman.

"Mother," he whispered in Gregor's voice.

Grief flooded the woman's face. She drew him inside the house without a word and took his face in her hands. Natan could feel her gentle touch enter his mind. With surety she walked the halls of his memory until she came to where Gregor dwelt. In what seemed an eternity and merely seconds, he relived his time with her son. She withdrew her hands, and he found that his memories from Gregor were still intact, but the man's lingering presence had returned to the mother he loved.

"Thank you," she whispered.

Natan couldn't answer except to put his arms around her, sharing her deep sorrow and joy for having known such a man.

Niko coughed slightly, breaking them apart. "Auntie." Niko kissed her cheek with a glance at Natan.

Aubre followed his eyes. "Thank you for bringing him to me safely."

Niko flushed but then laughed and took her in his arms, swirling her around.

"Stop, you bad boy!" she said through her laughter.

They shared a pleasant meal, with Niko keeping them laughing with his foolish jests and stories, then they spent the warm evening in the front garden. Natan went to bed that night with a smile playing on his lips. He thought of Tolban and the children and gave a contented sigh. He'd be returning to them soon. With a whispered goodnight to Kavi, hoping he was safe, he closed his eyes and slept.

Chapter Eighteen

KAVI LAY PRONE in the soft dirt under the ancient redwood tree with his face pressed against its trunk. Alek watched him dispassionately from a bench outside the wall. There was power there, where the roots sank deep into the earth. It rose into the branches until the very air shimmered with it. Kavi was a fool to…

Suddenly a scream of agony burst from Kavi, and he rolled away from the tree, coming to a hard stop against the low stone wall. He struggled to his knees, panting against the stonework.

Alek frowned. Every few days Kavi would come to the redwood, and though at first Alek had been stirred to pity, now Kavi's stubbornness began to irritate him. They all desired to have their powers back. Did his cousin mean to kill himself in trying?

The boy Aiden raced by, his laughter floating on the air. Alek waited. Sure enough his shadow, Ethan, burst into the courtyard and chased him around the tree. After a moment, Aiden threw himself on the bench beside Alek.

"Hello, Uncle," the boy chimed, his face wreathed in smiles. Panting, Ethan sat at Aiden's feet with a vague smile of his own. Alek had quit trying to reach the boy. No one could, except maybe Aiden, and that only in a limited way. Ethan wouldn't let anyone near him or touch him, and he would only speak in soft hisses to his brother. Alek frowned. If the boy should ever regain his power… He shied away from the thought and turned his attention to Aiden.

"What are you doing today?" he asked kindly.

"We're going to go watch the soldiers. Brendan said we may."

Alek sighed. Commander Brendan had taken over the garrison of southern soldiers Governor Basal had sent out to compliment the Barkuit presence. That had been a week ago, along with his right hand, Lieutenant Jaden. Aiden had attached himself to the man. Brendan tolerated him with good humor. Alek supposed it was nice for the boy to be friends with an outsider. Goodness knew his own people weren't so willing. Not that he could blame them. The boys had done terrible things.

He touched Aiden's bright face. "Just don't get in the way."

"We won't, Uncle." Aiden jumped from the bench and ran down the cobbled street, his voice lifted in some little song as he went. Ethan followed silently at his heels.

Kavi had recovered his breath, and Alek slanted him a look as he took Aiden's place on the bench.

"Do you find it worthwhile?" he asked dryly and motioned to the redwood tree.

Kavi's lips thinned. "Of course. Anything is worth it."

Alek watched him thoughtfully. "Why not wait until the Mage returns? He's sure to help us."

"Natan?" Kavi's voice was so full of scorn that Alek sat up in concern.

"Yes. He promised to come back."

"So he did, but when? He abandoned us quickly enough. And he was very careful to keep his own powers intact, I might add. No, my dear cousin, I don't think I need wait on him."

"Kavi, you shouldn't speak thus," Alek admonished. "The Mage helped save our people. He's a great man."

"Surely? Then why did he let my father die?"

Alek thinned his lips at the bitterness in his cousin's voice but turned his eyes to the blessed tree. Kavi's words were a dismaying echo of Camron's.

"I don't believe the Mage has power over life and death," he began to explain, but Kavi's expression went cold. Alek sighed. There was no reasoning with the man in this mood. When Kavi remained silent, he stood, frowning down at him.

"Be careful of your thoughts, cousin," he warned. "They may betray you." Kavi ignored him so Alek turned on his heel and left before anger got the better of him.

WHEN ALEK HAD gone, Kavi returned to the tree. A cold anger burned in him for the death of his father and the loss of his abilities, but most of all at Natan for leaving him alone when Kavi needed his friendship the most.

He pounded his fist against the redwood tree in hopeless frustration. No one could help him, Alek least of all. Alek wouldn't even try to regain his powers. And the Red Twins were just as useless.

"Any progress, Cousin?" a husky voice inquired.

Kavi sent an impatient glance over his shoulder. "What do you want, Camron?"

His cousin was a slim man with a hint of his Belegan heritage showing in the lightness of his olive complexion. He'd breathed in searing air during the firestorm at the Iron Hills, and his voice had been left a not unpleasant rasp. Kavi didn't trust him.

"My dear, don't be so rude. Sit down. I've something I'd like to discuss with you, about your, hmm…preoccupation."

Kavi eyed him with distaste, but his allusion was irresistible. He returned to the bench Alek had vacated and sat beside him.

Camron drew closer than Kavi liked. "What if I told you I've seen the Red Twins call up the wind?"

Kavi thrilled at his words even as Camron's voice rustled down his spine. "Is this true?" He dared the man to lie.

Camron's laugh was a rustle of parchment. "Darling, have some faith. I may have teased you when we were children. I would never dream of doing so now."

"I only saw you once when we were children, and I believe Father gave you a bloody head with a rock as you were fleeing with your uncle Kayden."

"Now, let's not dig up unpleasant memories. I choose to remember that we were friends. It was our parents who were at war, not us."

Kavi shook his head. He would never forgive the people who'd killed his father.

Seeing his set face, Camron tried a different tack. "Shall I tell you about the Red Twins? I truly did see them blowing leaves around with the wind."

His light brown eyes appeared guileless but there always seemed to be a hidden motive behind his actions. "Why are you telling me this?"

"I'd like to have the twins touch the tree."

Kavi stood up in horror. "Alek would never allow it, and neither would I. If the boys should regain their powers…" A shiver of apprehension ran through him. "You're mad, Camron."

"Not anymore, dear Cousin. Auntie Kirstin saw to that." Camron remained seated and watched him with speculative eyes. Voices approached, so he moved suddenly to snatch Kavi's hands, pulling him down to his side again. "I think we can regain our abilities and the children are the key. Think on it."

"What possible good could it do for them to regain their abilities?" Kavi countered.

"Come now. I know you're intelligent enough to work it out." He leaned against Kavi and spoke in his ear. "If the children can regain their powers, that would prove that the rest of us can too, and dear cousin Alek would have to quit dragging his feet."

Kavi searched for the trick. "And what do you need from me?"

"Come, dear." Camron was suddenly irritated. "Do you think Alek would let me go anywhere alone with the boys? He has eyes on me every second of the day."

Kavi nodded. He'd seen it and approved of Alek's caution with their ambitious cousin. "What do you want me to do?"

Camron's eyes glinted. "Bring them to the tree."

Kavi drew away. His whole being screamed against the idea, and yet… His eyes stung with tears of frustration. He'd give almost anything to have the energy of life flow through his veins once again, feel the tingle of it in his fingertips, hear the pulse of it in his ears.

He sensed Camron's gaze as he spoke, "Don't answer me now, cousin. I have to meet with some friends tomorrow, and on the day after that I'll be at the tree at first light. Bring the boys then. You won't regret it."

Kavi looked into the intense brown eyes, listened to the pleasant murmur of Camron's voice. It slid along his senses, removing every caution Natan had left with him.

Chapter Nineteen

NATAN CROUCHED IN the scrub brush on the edge of the clearing. Niko and he had only been in Mennon two days when rumors of a man who'd been dragged from his home for using the powers of the earth reached them. That the man had rescued a child lost in an old cave seemed to be of little concern to the men who'd taken him. Natan could see the young man now, strapped between two trees by his wrists.

"It's Mika. A close friend," Niko whispered angrily. They'd stripped the man to the waist, his dark chest glistening with sweat and blood in the merciless sun. Several men stood around him, Danul, who'd been Mazzo's second in command, at the front. A shudder ran through Natan at the wild glee burning in his eyes.

"Where is your strength now?" Danul sneered. Anger suffused his face at the prisoner's silence, and he raised a whip and struck. Natan sickened with the satisfaction on the men's faces at Mika's grunt of pain.

Without thought of the danger, he rose to his feet and strode into the clearing.

Danul quickly recovered from his surprise on seeing him.

"My lord Mage." He sketched a mocking bow. Danul stood as slim and wiry as Natan, although a few inches taller and broader of chest. When Natan didn't slow, Danul's eyes widened at the knife that appeared in his hand and quickly pressed to his throat.

"Let him go," Natan growled in his ear.

"Yes, please do," Niko added, his own knife out. He gave a sudden cry of alarm, as a heavy blow landed on the back of Natan's head from a man he hadn't seen. Natan fell hard and watched with blurry eyes as his attacker went down with Niko's knife through his throat. Danul's men fled. With another mocking bow to Natan, who was sprawled at his feet, Danul slipped after them.

Natan struggled to stand as Niko stormed up to him. The disgust on his friend's face confused him, so he was unprepared when Niko struck him in the face with enough force to drop him to a knee. He rose in bewilderment only to have Niko kick his legs out from under him. Controlling a flair of anger, he climbed once again to his feet. "Niko?"

"I've had enough of this. That man," Niko pointed to the body, "could have easily killed you a moment ago. You go charging into these situations without any thought to your safety, or ours." Niko's anger dropped from him as quickly as it had sprung up. "Do you wish to die?" His eyes narrowed as Natan hesitated to answer.

"I'm not afraid to die," Natan admitted. "Though I can't believe death is the end of everything. And in a situation like this," he waved to the tortured man, "I don't think. I'm driven to action. But don't worry, Niko. I don't want to die. Life is glorious and awful, and I have no wish to leave it anytime soon."

Niko grunted, then retrieved his knife and cut Mika down, helping him to a low boulder. He handed him a water skin. Natan approached them. The man appeared to be not much older than Niko, tall and muscular, his hair in a loose braid at his neck.

"Thank you, Mage," Mika inclined his head, wincing as he did so. Welts ran across the top of his shoulders as well as his back and Natan could see that every movement brought pain.

"Do you know me?" he asked.

"Aubre is my neighbor as well as my friend, and I am often at her house. She helps us understand our…gifts."

"Are there many with your talent?"

Natan saw him hesitate and flushed hotly under the man's scrutiny. He was so anxious to help he'd forgotten the people of Sennia would need time to learn to trust him, a stranger. It seemed he could add patience to the list of things he lacked.

Mika seemed to reach a decision. "There are many of us, lord, from Mennon and Cahna and the surrounding countryside who meet at Aubre's house. There may be others in hiding. The Vice-King, Jacom, tolerates us, but Danul's faction has his ear, and Jacom tends to overlook actions such as this." He waved toward the saplings to which he'd been bound.

Natan stared at his boots. How could he help these people? He'd never felt so lacking, still not sure what Gregor had planned for him to do when he'd given him his gifts. A pebble struck his boot, and he looked up to catch the flash of Niko's white teeth.

"Can we go home now?" Niko asked.

Natan rose. "I'm sorry." He turned to Mika. "Do you have someplace safe to go? You're welcome to come with us. I'd like to speak with you further."

Mika smiled. "Gladly. My wife and child should be at Aubre's waiting for me. It's our safe house." He climbed carefully to his feet. Natan gave him his horse and swung up behind Niko.

"Will you tell me of this group that meets at Lady Aubre's?" he asked, his gaze on the surrounding forest.

"What would you like to know, Mage?"

Natan smiled, relieved at the man's willingness to help him. "Tell me everything."

"There's a lot to tell. Where to begin?" Mika looked at the shadows in the trees. "Many of my people have the ability to use nature's gifts. We thought nothing of it until Mazzo began his persecutions." Natan shuddered and he broke off. "You met him?"

"Yes."

Mika nodded. "Mazzo is Jacom's cousin, and a little over six years ago, he became the Vice-King's chancellor, and our foe. To this day I don't understand the man's motivation. He hated those of us with power, and people began to disappear. We grew afraid and concealed our gifts. Only Gregor opposed him, and for that he was hunted by the Vice-King's armies until he was forced to flee Sennia."

"And die far from home," Natan murmured.

"I'm afraid the Vice-King is a rather weak man. Aubre encourages us to meet at her house to share our knowledge, and to keep one another informed of the political movements of the Vice-King and Mazzo. And now of Danul. We can also go there for protection, as I believe my family has been protected in my absence."

"Is there a king?" Natan asked in growing distress for the Sennian people.

"Yes, Piter Allon, but so far he gives the Vice-King free range."

"I'd like to attend your next meeting, if I may."

"As you wish, Mage."

The road to Mennon was well kept, so the travelers made good time, speeded perhaps by Mika's desire to see his family and make sure all was well with them. Natan grew eager to see his little mother. She always had a warm smile and embrace for him, making him feel welcomed and loved. And he loved her in return, Gregor's emotions so jumbled up with his own that he had finally quit trying to separate them and just took her into his heart.

They arrived in Mennon in the early evening and Natan led the way up the path to the familiar house. He had a warm embrace for the woman waiting on the doorstep.

"Good evening, Mother." He kissed the top of her graying head.

"Hello, dear." She touched his face. "You look tired. Come in, all of you." Aubre held the door open. "Niko, how are you, my child?"

"I'm well, Auntie." Niko kissed her gnarled hands. She patted his cheek, then turned and embraced Mika. "I'm glad to see you are safe. Your family is out back."

With a joyous smile the young man raced around to the garden.

"Come into the kitchen. There's tea and some little cakes. Niko! Please wait for us, naughty child." She playfully slapped at his hand as he grinned, then ate a cake in one bite.

Mika joined them presently and introduced his wife, Kendra, and his little boy, Kam. Kendra smiled warmly at the strangers while Kam hid behind her. After a brief moment of greetings, Mika begged to be excused to take them home.

"I can never repay you, Aubre." Mika's tears fell unashamedly on the old hands as he kissed them. "I'll return for the meeting tomorrow."

"Goodnight, my son. Keep your doors locked." She walked them to the front steps. While she was gone, Niko led Natan to the back garden where they began to idly argue over who would have the couch and who the floor.

Aubre tutted when she joined them. "Why don't you take Natan to your house tomorrow after the gathering, Niko? I'm sure he'd be more comfortable."

"You have a house close by?" Natan asked him curiously.

"Yes, on the beach. Or rather, it's my parents' house, but they've loaned it to me. They live in Sambola and I rarely see them. We've had a falling-out."

"Over what?" Natan asked quietly. He wouldn't have asked at all, except Niko looked so uncomfortable and Aubre's eyes were anxious.

Niko shot him a pleading look, hesitated, then hung his head. "Mazzo is my uncle, my mother's brother."

Shock flushed in an icy wave through Natan, and he shivered in the warm air. He pushed the feeling down to go to his friend. "Why didn't you tell me?" he asked, knowing what a burden it must have been to him.

"I thought you would hate me."

"I would never judge you."

Niko bowed gravely, then his irrepressible grin touched his face. "Just for that, you can have the bedroom with the windows facing the sea."

Natan spent the evening talking with Aubre while Niko went into town. He'd urged Natan mercilessly to join him, but a vague uneasiness kept him close to Gregor's mother. Night fell as he settled on a bench in the far corner of the back porch. The house went dark, and Natan put his feet up on the railing, willing himself to relax.

The moon rose, illuminating the yard, and his thoughts strayed to his own porch on the little cabin in Amara, near the sea. He'd spent many nights on that porch, at first sneaking out as a child, later fleeing the silence of empty rooms. He wondered how Bryon was doing. A smile lifted his lips as he thought of Kirstin and the happiness they'd found together. Warmth touched his heart, knowing his friend's loneliness had ended.

A soft step in the garden brought him to his feet. Natan slipped his knife into his hand as he waited in the darkness. Five forms scurried across the lawn and paused at the steps to the porch. Natan recognized Danul among them. The man motioned and two of the hooded figures started up the steps. The rest moved to the front of the house.

The two on the porch proved easy kills, though Natan felt sick at heart for the necessity. He waited as one crept to the window nearest him, and silently slit his throat. The other turned, startled, but Natan's thrown knife pierced his heart before he could utter a sound. Natan wrenched the blade free, then hurried around the building to the front. Danul and another man crouched under the closest window while a third tried the door. Natan's thoughts raced. He could take a man out, but that would leave him weaponless, and the little mother would still be in danger. No, best to lure them away from the house.

He stood from his crouch and sauntered into the middle of the pathway, smiled grimly when they failed to notice him. "Hello, Danul."

Danul swore, his knife glittering in the moonlight as the three left the front step and approached him. Natan backed toward the gate. If he could keep them entertained long enough, maybe Niko would come home before they finished him. He bumped into the gate, but unlatching it took a moment too long, and they caught him as he ran into the street.

Danul threw his knife, then the fight turned swift and dirty with many a savage kick or blow dealt on either side. In a wild fury, Danul flung himself at Natan's legs and they went down hard. Fingers sought Natan's throat. Though he managed a wicked kick to the man holding his legs, it was the shouting in the distance that finally drove them away.

Natan struggled to prop himself up on an elbow, trying to ignore the pain thundering in his head while Niko chased after the disappearing men. There were several deep slashes on his forearms and a burning spot on his thigh where Danul's thrown knife had skimmed him. He sat up gingerly, pressing a hand to the ribs bruised by someone's heavy boots. His head swam, so he closed his eyes. Footsteps returned and he could only hope it was his friend. He felt too ill to put up much of a fight.

"Mage," Niko mourned as he dropped beside him. Cool hands touched his face. Natan opened his eyes with care, thankful he wasn't going to be sick and embarrass himself.

"Hello," he said thickly. "Help me up, please."

Niko's strong arms went around him as Natan rose unsteadily, letting out a relieved breath as the dizziness passed. They just needed to stop the bleeding, and he'd be all right. He said as much to Niko as he helped him to the house, Niko swearing long and eloquently.

Aubre had met them at the door and clicked her tongue, then set to work, having more than her share of experience with wounded men. Natan sat on a stool in the kitchen as he was washed and bandaged, growing sleepy in the warm room. Niko jumped and fortunately caught him as he slipped off the stool.

THEY LET NATAN sleep, making him almost late for the weekly gathering the next morning. A dozen men and women were sitting on the grass in Aubre's garden when Natan joined them. He took a seat on the bottom step of the porch, so he could lean against the post, and listened intently to the discussion. Apparently, Niko had told them of the attack in the night since they were discussing means of protection and how best to make the Vice-King listen to their grievances. Much to his chagrin, Natan's mind wandered, yet he couldn't believe that solving the political unrest on Sennia was the reason Gregor had sent him there.

Mika entered the yard with his family. "Sorry to be late."

Natan noted the bow and quiver of arrows at his back. A wise precaution, all told.

Kam raced into the garden but halted midstride on catching sight of Natan on the steps. The boy hesitated, then carefully walked up to him and touched his face. Natan grinned. Kam smiled broadly in return.

"Do you remember me from yesterday?" Natan asked, and the boy nodded solemnly.

"Kam, we need to go," Kendra called to her son.

"Will you come too?" Kam held out his hand. Natan raised questioning brows, and at Kendra's nod, took the small fingers in his. He noticed Niko detach himself from the group to follow.

They strolled along a path through the trees to a park with a tiny brook meandering through the flowers. Natan's injured leg ached, and he began to limp even after such a short distance, so he sat gratefully on a stone bench beside the water to catch his breath. Niko settled a little distance away.

Kendra hurried to a young woman surrounded by half a dozen children. "I'm sorry I'm late, Mirah."

"No matter. The children are full of energy this morning." Mirah smiled at Natan. "Hello again." Her expressive face turned troubled. "Are you well?"

Natan inclined his head. "Yes. Thank you. Is Tolban at the house? I didn't see him."

"Father sends his regrets. We discovered a leak in the barn roof this morning. But he hopes to see you again soon. As it is, I need to be at the meeting in his stead." She said goodbye to the others, then hurried down the path to join the adults. The children had grown silent and now stood in a semicircle in front of Natan.

"What is it?" he asked Kendra, thoroughly embarrassed by their intent stares.

Kendra laughed softly as she sat beside him on the bench. "They don't mean to be rude. We've just never seen a man with such pale skin before, or with your unique eyes."

"Does everyone in your country look like you?" a tall boy asked.

"They may have my skin coloring," Natan answered. "Though, for the most part, the men are taller and broader."

"Does everyone have powers like yours in your country?" Kam asked. "Father thinks they do."

The children sat in the grass at his feet to hear his answer. Natan's heart warmed.

"Not at all. In fact, only the Karthagan people had any practical abilities, but they lost them through their abuse of them." He went on to tell them how the Karthagan ruling houses went to war and of their consequent banishment from Belega.

In time, a silver bell rang in the distance. Kendra gathered the children to take them back to Aubre's house. Natan promised to continue the story during the next meeting. It was an excited group that joined their parents, and Natan wondered if he shouldn't have shared his stories. Kendra assured him that the lessons had been good for them to hear.

"Some of the children are already showing signs of having the gift. They should hear that it's not something to use lightly."

Natan thanked her as they entered the house.

"Niko tells me you'll be staying the night at his house on the beach?" Mika queried as Natan walked to the front gate with them.

"Oh, you have to!" Kam's eyes shown. "You'll be right next door. Can you come now? I can show you my turtle."

Natan held up his hands, laughing. "Let me see what Niko wants to do."

"That would be fine," Niko agreed when Kam excitedly asked him. They gathered their packs.

Aubre hugged him and gave him fresh bandages for the morning. Natan frowned, uncertain. "Should you stay with a neighbor, Mother?"

"Don't fear, Son." She patted his cheek. "I'll lock the doors and windows, and I'm a light sleeper."

"I don't want to leave you alone."

"And I won't be driven from my home," Aubre said firmly. Natan almost offered to stay with her, but temper flashed in her eyes and Natan knew that was the end of it.

The merry group walked across town to the sea with Kam skipping beside his new friend, chattering nonstop. The turtle was duly admired, but Natan had to apologize as weariness came over him. The two men crossed the sand to Niko's bungalow. A slow smile crept over Natan's face.

"This is beautiful," he enthused on seeing the faded blue-and-white structure with its wide porch facing the sea. Niko grinned and showed him around.

He threw open the door to a small chamber with a large corner window. "And this is your room, as promised. This was my brother Toma's room." He paused, then continued in a quiet voice, "Toma died when we were children. A squall had sprung up while Toma was in the rowboat. Instead of coming in, the little fool thought he could calm the sea with his abilities. The first wave capsized the boat, and Toma never resurfaced."

"I'm sorry," Natan began, but Niko shrugged it off and paced the room as if he had something on his mind. Natan put a hand on his shoulder as he passed him. "Talk to me."

Niko shifted uncomfortably, averting his face. "I'm restless and angry and afraid. Danul's attacks on my people have increased. We're being taken from our homes, and it's killing me to sit idly by and do nothing."

"Niko, have you thought of going to the Vice-King and pleading for his intervention?"

Niko snorted. "I'm sorry, Mage, but Jacom won't listen to me." He ran a hand in frustration over his curls, swearing as his fingers caught in a tangle at his neck. "How can I explain?" He frowned at the dark sea outside the window as he absently worked on the snarl.

"After Toma's accident, Mother couldn't bear the sight of the ocean. She and Father moved to their house in Sambola. There, they quickly came under Mazzo's influence. He was a passionate and hypnotic speaker, and they already had cause to hate the ability many of us possess."

Niko swallowed. "Mazzo worked on their pain and that of the Vice-King's family, most especially Jacom's daughter, Corha. We grew up together, and Toma was a favorite to all of us. It was easy for Mazzo to build up a prejudice against those who use their powers. It's a prejudice I carried myself until just recently."

He rose to his feet. "Mage, why won't you stop this? Why won't you find this Danul who's taken Mazzo's place and stop him before he hurts anyone else? Are you waiting for him to take Aubre, or Mika, or any of our friends? You have the power to end this. You can silence them all!"

Natan looked in Niko's impassioned face and a nightmare vision of blood and broken bodies and twisted trees and scorched earth screamed in his head. He buried his face in his hands with an anguished cry. "I can't!"

"Of course not." Niko's sharp words stabbed him as did the slammed door as he left the room. Natan choked and pressed his face tighter into his hands, tortured by his own inadequacy.

Kendra sent them some smoked fish for dinner. After they'd eaten, Natan made himself comfortable against a pile of driftwood while Niko took a hike along the shore. Niko had wanted to stay with him, but Natan laughed and said he didn't need a nursemaid. Niko scowled, muttered something about fools, and stomped away.

Natan closed his eyes to listen to the waves break on the sand. He breathed deeply of the tangy air. The cry of a gull pierced his heart. Opening his eyes, he watched the sun set in glorious reds and oranges that glowed on a low bank of clouds. He smiled at the beauty of it, but then grew wistful. It struck him that he never had anyone to share such wonders with.

He climbed to his feet and strode along the shoreline, but the ceaseless tide that had so often calmed him only stirred restlessness. He stopped with a pounding heart and stared desperately across the water. Waves of longing and loneliness crashed into him. Just for a moment, he allowed the carefully constructed walls around his heart to drop. The love he kept trapped there surged to life and set his pulses hammering.

He thought of Kavi across the sea who held his heart with such careless hands. Did the man ever think of him, there behind the safe walls of Karthag? Natan lived a moment of joy and anguish, then sank to his knees, covered his face, and began to build the walls of his heart over again. Such thick walls were needed to keep it from breaking.

Chapter Twenty

ALEK WATCHED THE glittering fountain, breathed the rose-scented air, and swore when it failed to calm him. Camron had approached him earlier in the day with an ultimatum from Kayden's people: either help them regain Siagan or they would do it themselves.

He realized that laughing at the man hadn't been the wisest of moves. But thinking that a handful of people could take one of the Northern Territory's largest cities was ludicrous. Camron replied with his infuriating grin and left the hall. Alek could wish he'd leave the city as well, but he couldn't ignore the uneasiness that crept relentlessly over him. He'd thought Kirstin had burned the insanity from them when she'd stripped away their powers on the Isle of Wind, but he had his doubts with Camron.

Folding his arms on his chest, he stared at the cascading water of the fountain, wondering what his next step to protect his people should be. He was still there when Kavi wandered into the garden sometime later and sank on the bench beside him.

"What are we doing here, Alek? Wouldn't it have been better to stay on the isle?"

Alek didn't answer immediately, gathering his thoughts.

"Kavi," he began. "I have a plan, and please don't laugh until I've finished. You're always laughing at my ideas."

"Not the good ones," he answered, and Alek's heart lightened at his smile.

"As you know, the Regent and Governor Basal will be here in a few weeks to check on our progress. I want to propose they allow us to expand the harbor. The Dakon Forest has the best hardwoods in the country, which we could harvest and export to the cities along the coastline. And now that there is a treaty between the Northern and Southern Territories, we can trade with Barkuit and Nagal both. It would make us financially independent and give our people a position in Belega."

Kavi brightened. "Alek, that would be wonderful. Father was right in choosing you to lead us. You give me hope."

"I'd like you to help me."

"What is it you need?"

"As Gavin's son, the people naturally look to you for guidance. I hope you will help me persuade them this is for the best."

A soft voice spoke behind them, startling them. "Quite a touching scene, cousins. Am I interrupting?"

Alek didn't hide his irritation. "What do you want, Camron?"

"Nothing, dear cousin. I saw you sitting so intimately and wondered what it was all about."

Alek stood abruptly. "You're no kin of mine. And remember, Gavin chose *me* as leader."

"Threats, Alek? I wouldn't have imagined it."

"Just stay out of my way." Alek glowered and stalked off, his hands clenched as he fought to control his rage. He would need to do something about the man, sooner rather than later.

"WHAT A BORE." Camron slid beside Kavi before he could make his escape. "Now tell me, what were you two so serious about? Not our little chat from the other day, I trust?"

Kavi shivered at the dangerous note in his voice. "No, Camron."

"Good."

Kavi turned his face away from the man's stare, knowing Camron could read too much of his expression, his restlessness. Loneliness.

"Oh no. You can't still be pining for that pasty-skinned Belegan of yours?"

"You're not one to throw stones, Camron."

"True. My mother was as much of a fool as you, dear." Camron ran a finger over the smooth skin of Kavi's arm. "Though I must admit Belegan men can be handsome. My father was one such as Natan. You must miss him. Does it still hurt, Kavi, late in the night?"

His whispery voice ran along Kavi's nerves. What was the man doing to him? Alek had spoken the truth when he said they weren't blood relatives, but he shuddered as Camron's voice lightly caressed his ears. It wound its way inside his mind and along his spine in exquisite pain and soft pleasure, the raspy voice working like heady wine on his senses.

"You miss Natan, don't you?" Camron pressed against him, the rustle of his voice in Kavi's ear making him shiver. "My poor boy, you've lost so much. And it was a Belegan who stole it from you, never forget that." His voice dropped lower, and Kavi strained to hear. "It was the Mage who killed your family. It was the Mage who stole your powers. Say it!"

"The Mage," Kavi gasped, and though his heart screamed in denial, the voice droned in his ear until his mind swam in a sea of doubt.

"I can help you regain your abilities, darling."

Kavi whimpered as the words throbbed along sensitive nerves.

"Would you like that?"

"Yes," Kavi breathed raggedly and Camron pushed closer and kissed his mouth.

"Good." Camron stood, his mocking laughter floating back as he left.

KAVI STARTED FROM the bench as if awakening from a nightmare. Heart pounding, he fought to catch his breath. What had just happened? He'd been speaking with Alek, but now he was suddenly alone. He looked around the sunny garden and gave a short laugh. He must have fallen asleep. Sitting down again, he pressed his fingers to his throbbing head.

The vague feeling of uneasiness persisted in him throughout the day carrying into the evening, as did his headache, and at last Kavi fled to his bedroom and the comfort of his blankets. The pain was similar to what he experienced while trying to call up life's energies, but he hadn't done that in days. Kavi rolled over in irritation, buried his head under his pillow, and willed sleep to come.

Nightmares chased through his dreams, following him into wakefulness in the morning. In his mind a rasping voice called and Kavi rose, dressing without thought. Creeping from the castle, he went to the Red Twins' window and tossed pebbles until Aiden's tousled head poked out. "Cousin?"

"Do you want to play a game with me?" Kavi asked.

Aiden's golden eyes lit with anticipation. In a moment, he and Ethan joined him and Kavi led them to the center of town. They stopped at the tall redwood tree, a shiver of expectation running over Kavi.

"You came," Camron's voice rustled in his ear, and the man's slender body pressed against Kavi's back. Camron placed his hands on his shoulders, but Kavi shrugged him off, going to the tree with the boys.

"What game are we playing?" Aiden hopped from one foot to the other, and Ethan laughed as he did the same.

"Ask Camron." Kavi felt uneasy and irritated. The vague sense of fear from the previous evening had become a creeping dread as he stood by the ancient tree.

Camron joined them and sat cross-legged at the foot of the tree with a motion for the boys to do the same.

"Come, Kavi." He held out his hand, and Kavi sat on his other side.

"What do we do?" Aiden asked suspiciously.

"Put your hands on the tree, like this." Camron placed his hands with fingers spread on the rough bark. "Now close your eyes. I'll do the rest."

The Red Twins copied his example, though Aiden looked skeptical. Kavi put his hands on the tree as well. Instantly, energy surged up from the deep roots and crashed into his mind until he screamed with the agony in his head. He almost pulled away but Camron clamped his hands over Kavi's, and he couldn't move. The pain seared through him as if his mind would burst. And then it seemed as if it did burst, and he floated in a red haze.

Aiden took his hands off the tree and nudged Ethan. "This is a stupid game. I have a headache."

Ethan skipped as he followed his brother away from the tree.

A long moment passed before Camron took his hands from Kavi's and pulled him into his arms. Kavi's hands dropped limply to his sides as he floated in a sea of pain. As Camron ran his fingers gently over his temple, the pain receded somewhat. He fluttered his eyes open and blinked at Camron.

"Come on." Camron helped him stand, keeping an arm around him for support. His cousin turned for an instant to the ancient tree, and Kavi saw his face glow with fierce exaltation. Then he glanced at Kavi, frowned, and gave his cheek a stinging slap. Kavi roused at that, enough to walk on his own as Camron led him from the city and up the trail into the woods.

They hadn't traveled long, less than an hour, before Kavi stumbled with exhaustion. A rough hand gripped his arm, pushing him onto a fallen log. He ate the food that was handed to him, drank when water was pressed to his lips, but he felt no emotion and had no sight beyond the red blur in his eyes. The only sound he heard was the blood pounding in his ears.

A hand struck his face, struck again, and he felt a faint sting on his skin. He opened his eyes. Dark shapes gathered around him, screaming words he couldn't understand. Exhaustion settled its warm blanket over him, but he clung to the pain in his cheek as a lifeline in the red swirling chaos of his mind.

Harsh laughter grated on his sensitive ears. "What did you do to him?" Kavi felt a finger jab his shoulder. "Is he poisoned?"

"Oh, I hope so," another voice lisped, and trembling fingers touched Kavi's lips.

"Step back, Jan," came a command from the first speaker, none too gently. "Fredrik won't pay a copper if the Karthagan is…damaged."

"Speaking of payment, Grant, I believe you have some silver for me?"

Kavi knew that rasping voice and struggled to rise, to be instantly pulled to his feet and seized in a tight embrace. "Be good, cousin, and maybe they won't kill you." Hard lips were pressed on his, before Camron pushed him away. "Goodbye, dear." Kavi could see a vague shadow climb on a larger silhouette, and then hoofbeats faded into the hazy distance.

Someone grabbed him. "Yes, be good." A breath touched his throat as hands fumbled at his coat until he was pulled violently from the stranger's arms. Unbalanced, he fell hard against a log across the path.

"Touch him again, Jan, and I will certainly kill you. Now, get the horses."

"Yes, Captain."

"Get up, boy."

There was no kindness in Grant's voice, and Kavi scrambled to his feet. The man helped him into the saddle, then swung up behind him. "Try anything, and you'll pay. I know many ways to hurt you that Fredrik would never detect." He whispered the details in Kavi's ear as they rode. Kavi believed every twisted, cruel word he spoke.

After a time, his sight began to clear, and he wondered if Camron had caused his blindness, though he didn't know how his cousin had done it. The gloom of evening was gathering on the countryside; he didn't recognize any of the landmarks. Kavi could vaguely make out the figure of the man riding ahead of them. The soldier turned his head, and his glittering gaze pierced Kavi. He shivered when the captain chuckled unpleasantly at his back.

"Can't we make for Lord Fredrik's hall now, Captain? This route will take us two days out of our way," Jan asked after a period of silence.

"Don't be a fool," Grant sneered. "Syros expects us in Barkuit tomorrow. We'll just have to hide the Karthagan somewhere for a day or two until we can throw the regent off our track."

Jan grumbled a reply and turned away, but his eyes kept straying to them. They made a brief stop during the night, then pressed on the next day. Evening found them within a few hours of Barkuit.

"We're here, sweetheart." Grant pinched Kavi's cheek to wake him and dumped him unceremoniously from the saddle. Kavi landed hard on the ground, where he lay in a daze, tasting blood. They hadn't fed him much, and the earth swayed beneath him. He became aware of a pungent odor. His eyes cleared to a decomposing corpse a few inches from his face. He drew back in horror.

"Don't mind Travis. He won't bother you, much." Laughing heartily at his own joke, Grant proceeded to bind him hand to foot, his head pressed to his knees. The captain propped him against a tree and squatted in front of him. "Now, if you promise not to squeal, I won't stuff a gag in that lovely mouth. Promise?"

Kavi nodded, keeping his head bowed so Grant wouldn't see the anger in his eyes.

"Good boy. Keep still and the rodents shouldn't bother you either. They have plenty to eat as it is." Grant rose with a grim snicker, and Kavi heard him call to Jan as he moved off.

All was quiet after he'd gone. Kavi closed his eyes but cringed when someone knelt in front of him again. Hands gripped his hair and yanked his head up. Jan's eyes burned as he stared into Kavi's. He ran rough fingers over Kavi's face and stroked his neck.

"Captain Grant is on duty in the morning, so I'll come early to check on you. And don't worry." He leaned closer. "I also know many things to do to you that won't leave a mark for that fat lord to see." He touched the blood on Kavi's mouth and his eyes gleamed.

The two rode away, leaving Kavi alone on the battlefield. He knew the Nagal soldiers had removed their dead on Basal's orders, but Barkuit men lay where they'd fallen. Kavi couldn't help glancing at the body close to him, relieved that he lay with his face turned away. Grant had called him Travis. Had he no family to grieve for him and take his body home?

He thought of Gregor lying somewhere close by in the tall cairn they'd built for him.

"Mage, are you here?" he whispered. Something scurried in the brush, and Kavi closed his mouth with a click of teeth. He thought of Natan but turned his mind from him, disturbed. Natan could no longer be trusted. Hurt and sad, exhaustion finally overcame him, and Kavi tumbled to the ground and slept.

A touch on his arm startled him awake some time later. Kavi tried to scramble away only to have the cords binding his hands and feet bite into his skin.

"Peace," a somehow familiar voice said at his side. Kavi blinked several times in the predawn light to bring him into focus. The soldier sat cross-legged, and Kavi watched warily as he removed a slim knife from his boot and cut the leather at Kavi's wrists and ankles. He helped him to sit up and they stared curiously at each other.

A slight smile touched the man's lean face. "This is awkward," he admitted. "By my own law I should have you imprisoned in the dungeons of Barkuit. And yet I'm curious to know how a Karthagan came to be here. This is very strange. And you seem familiar to me. Who are you?"

"My name is Kavi, my lord."

"Ah, the Mage's friend. Now I recall you. And I am Syros, the Regent of Barkuit. What happened to you?"

Kavi smiled bitterly. "My dear cousin sold me to some Barkuit soldiers, who in turn wish to sell me to Lord Fredrik."

"Which soldiers?" Syros bit out. Kavi straightened, realizing the man could be dangerous if crossed. "Captain Grant and Lieutenant Jan."

Syros rose to his feet with an oath. They both heard voices approaching. "It's my men. Come." The regent held out his hand, his voice urgent. "We have to go before they see you."

"Why?"

Syros frowned and swung into the saddle of his waiting horse. "Because, my dear Karthagan," he growled as he pulled Kavi up behind him, "an old hatred has been roused in my people not even I can protect you from. Now, hold tight."

He kicked the horse and they broke into a dead run. Syros leaned along the horse's neck and Kavi lay against him as they urged every bit of speed from their mount. Syros glanced over his shoulder, baring his teeth in a fierce grin that boded ill for anyone who tried to stop them.

They rested the horse as often as they dared, but still the animal was lathered with sweat and blood when they at long last reached the harbor city of Kangar, beyond Barkuit. They slid from the horse's trembling back, and Syros removed a cloak from the saddlebags. Kavi hid in its folds, drawing the hood low over his face while Syros unsaddled the shaking animal and led him to the stables to be cared for.

"What are we doing here?" Kavi asked when Syros returned and they approached the harbor.

"I dare not take you south, and there's no safe place for a Karthagan in the north outside of your city. But too many soldiers lie between us and Karthag to return you there. I'm afraid you must flee Belega for a time. Now, if I can just find the captain… Ah."

Kavi trailed the regent in a daze. Leave Belega? To go where? Sennia? As the name entered his thoughts, Kavi had a sudden overwhelming desire to see Natan again. There was something he must do, something he must tell the Mage. But as he tried to recall what it was a blinding pain struck behind his eyes and he stumbled.

"Careful." Syros took his arm and the memory fled. Never mind. He would have three days on the ship to recall it. Syros left him on the dock to speak with the captain of the waiting schooner. At first, the sailor made animated gestures of refusal until with what seemed a great reluctance, the regent took some silver coins from his pocket. A broad grin spread over the captain's face as he beckoned Kavi over with a hearty shout. Syros winced at the display.

"Stay out of sight on the ship as much as possible," Syros told Kavi and gripped his hand. "And if you would, please tell the Mage that I beg him to return home. Belega is becoming dangerous, and I fear we'll have desperate need of him soon." He removed his hand and Kavi looked at the few pieces of silver he'd given him. "Just in case."

Kavi took a step back to sweep him a low bow. "Thank you for this, and for my life. I hope I can repay you one day."

Syros flashed a rare smile. "Never mind that. Natan is a good man, and I'm honored to help his friend."

Kavi nodded, then followed the sea captain to his ship.

Chapter Twenty-One

SYROS WATCHED THE Karthagan board the vessel to Sennia, already regretting the impulse that had led him to give away the last of his silver. He chose a fresh horse from the stable, then paused. He should pay his respects to Council Leader Ardan. Maybe see Sharana… But there was no time. Jumping to saddle, he raced the animal on the return journey to Barkuit. He'd been on his way to the border when he'd found Kavi. Rumors of a Karthagan uprising were rampant in the Northern Territory, and he'd been checking their veracity, leaving Lieutenant Davis guarding the infant governor despite his vehement protests. But these were dangerous times. The actions of Captain Grant troubled him as well. Lord Fredrik's hall was a formidable stronghold in the south. What did the man want with a Karthagan prisoner? Torture and murder? Or did he want to learn the secrets of their power? Either way, the man would bear watching.

The streets of Barkuit were quiet as he entered the city, sidestepping the men repairing the gates, and he hastened to the castle. Striding through the echoing hallways, he stopped a moment at the governor's rooms. He tapped gently on the door lest the baby slept, being well acquainted with the loud protestations of the boy when he was awakened early from his nap. There was movement inside before the door opened a crack.

"My lord Syros." Marda's small face lost its worried lines as she opened the door with a shy smile.

"How is Willum today?" Syros walked cautiously to the crib and looked at the sleeping child. He searched the tiny face with its fringe of light hair. "He looks well, Marda. You're taking excellent care of him."

"He's easy to care for, my lord."

Syros could see the girl's fondness for the child. He nodded. At least one thing went smoothly for him. His face turned to stone as he thought of his next task. Leaving the child, he sent a runner for Lieutenant Davis to meet him as he made his way to the council chamber.

Crossing the room, he looked out a high window while he rubbed a hand over his face. He was coming to love the city with its beautifully sculpted buildings and winding streets, the new gates almost completed. He would like to bring peace to her, but change took time, and the people had long ago learned to mistrust their leaders.

Lieutenant Davis entered the long room followed by the council leader, Caleb. Syros crossed the stone floor to greet them.

"Davis, is Captain Grant still in the city?"

"No, sir. He left yesterday at noon with Lieutenant Jan. They failed to report for duty this morning."

Syros swore. "Gather your men, Lieutenant, and meet me at the gates. We're going after them. Caleb, come with me."

He left the chamber with quick strides, addressing the man at his side as they walked. "Caleb, I can't say how long I'll be gone. Please continue the repairs on the city." He stopped. "I have to say you're doing an excellent job. Thank you for your care."

Caleb smiled at the praise. "Remember, I was born here. It's a pleasure to restore the city. And the villa you've given my parents…"

"Take care of the governor." Syros knitted his brows. "I hear that Landlan has been voted into the council. Keep an eye on him."

"I do. An ambitious person, my lord. The council is thinking of making him our next council leader."

"Landlan is a manipulative bastard. Keep two eyes on him. At least with him in the city we can keep track of his activities."

Caleb nodded and Syros left, walking once more through the city. He met Davis at the gate with several of his soldiers already mounted. Swinging into his own saddle, he motioned, and they rode out at a swift pace.

JADEN FROWNED AT the hoofprints in the dust. The horse no longer carried double. Alek had come to him and Commander Brendan at their outpost near Karthag three days ago, something he'd never done before, the strain showing on his face bringing them to their feet.

"Kavi has disappeared, and the fact that Camron is missing as well has me worried," he'd confessed. "I can't bring myself to trust Camron, and the Red Twins claim they saw them together earlier this morning."

They left on Camron's trail immediately, but although they pushed the horses, they hadn't been able to overtake the Karthagan and failed to make his rendezvous with the two mysterious riders. The riders had obviously met with Camron, then returned the way they'd come, one of their horses carrying double. He glanced up. "Which way, Commander?"

"We follow that rat, Camron, as ordered," Brendan stated, although his eyes continued to follow the second trail out of sight.

"But what of Kavi?"

Brendan glowered. "Come on, Lieutenant." He nudged his horse, leaning low to follow Camron's tracks south and east. They pressed on now, but stopped at dusk lest they miss the route in the dark.

First light found them once again in the saddle, and they entered the Dakon Forest at noon. Jaden grew uneasy as the day wore on and they drew closer to Siagan. Council Leader Mandel was no friend of theirs. The trail of single hoofprints they followed met with at least six riders from the southeast. Brendan pulled rein.

"I think we'll walk from here," he said with a frown. They picketed the horses and Jaden loosened his sword. There hadn't been much cover on the plains, but in the forest they could slip soundlessly through the trees.

Voices ahead slowed them. They crawled into a clump of scrub brush overlooking a camp of men. Jaden drew a sharp breath when he saw they were Karthagans. Brendan touched his arm and pointed to the center of the group. Camron stood over two bound soldiers who knelt in the dirt. The Karthagan seemed fascinated by the glittering blade he held up to the sunlight. "What have you done with Kavi? You had the simple task to deliver him, and Fredrik is growing impatient. As am I."

His raspy voice sent a shiver through Jaden, and he saw the Barkuit prisoners shudder as well. The larger of the two turned to his confederate. "Well, Jan, you got to him first this morning. What did you do with him?"

"I never touched him," Jan swore before his voice rose to a shriek, betraying his fear. "He was gone when I got there! You know that, Grant."

"Easy, Jan." Camron continued to study his knife.

"Come now, Camron," Grant put in plaintively. "We promised to help you with your campaign to retake Siagan and you're treating us as enemies. So what if Kavi escaped? There's others Lord Fredrik would pay just as well for."

"Good riddance," Jan added vehemently.

Camron moved, the knife flashing in his hand as he swung it in an arc across Jan's throat. Blood spurted from the gaping wound as the soldier toppled over.

"What were we saying?" he asked as he wiped his knife on the dead man's cloak. He turned to Grant, who dropped his head to his chest and kept silent. "Very good." Camron slit the leather binding his hands and helped him to his feet.

"Now tell us of Siagan's defenses," he drawled as the soldier rubbed his wrists. Grant's eyes darted around the alien faces of his Karthagan captors. Trapped, he gave a quick nod of acquiescence.

Jaden felt his anger gaining the upper hand, and he ground his teeth against the emotion as the Barkuit captain betrayed his people to Camron, identifying the number of soldiers in Siagan, guard posts, shift rotations. By Brendan's sour look, he knew the commander wasn't any happier. At last Captain Grant fell silent, and Camron walked thoughtfully over to the brush where they lay concealed.

"You may as well come out," he said as if he could see them. Brendan muttered an oath and they stood. Camron laughed with the sound of rustling parchment. They walked into the midst of the Karthagans, hands open before them, and Jaden looked with disdain at the Barkuit captain standing with his head hanging. The man glowered back.

"Bind them," Camron rasped. "And Jaden." He walked right up to him and ran his fingers along his hot cheek, stroked the pulse racing at his neck with his thumb. "Don't resist. I'm afraid we have little use for Belegans at the moment, love."

Jaden jerked his head away, though Camron's amused laughter slithered down his spine and left him feeling sick.

Chapter Twenty-Two

THE SALTY SPRAY of the ocean stung Natan's cheeks, hands, and gave his skin a rosy glow. Mika taught him a nonsense song as they pulled in the net full of fish, his laughter ringing in the morning air, filling Natan's heart with joy.

They rowed to shore and Mika whooped to announce their arrival as they dragged the boat onto the sand. Kendra met them with reed baskets and they hauled the fish to the shed, debating the best ways to bake them. A loud knock on the shed door made them look up.

Niko stuck his head around the corner, wrinkled his nose, and hastily withdrew. "My dear Mage," he called from outside, "are you planning to go to the meeting this afternoon? Tolban and Mirah have already taken the children up."

Natan frowned in dismay. "I didn't realize it was so late." He rose to his feet, reluctant to burden the couple with all the work. "I could stay and help finish," he offered, but Kendra shook her head.

"No, but you could take Kam with you, if you don't mind. He misses his friends on the days we have a good catch. Let Mirah know I'll be there soon."

"Certainly." Natan left them to their work. Niko was nowhere in sight, and he whistled the nonsense song on the way to their house to change. When he returned to Mika's, he found Kam on the back porch with Niko feeding the turtle pieces of fruit.

"Your parents said I can take you to the meeting with me, if you'd like," he said, with a chuckle for the boy's bright smile.

"Let's go!" Kam grabbed his hand, and Niko laughed, probably at the sight of the small boy dragging the Mage up the beach as he trailed behind them into the city.

Natan had hardly closed the gate to Aubre's front yard when Tillie raced off the porch. "Papa!"

He swung her into his arms. "How's my girl?"

"I'm happy." She hugged his neck tightly and gave him sweet little kisses as proof. He shifted her to his shoulder, then held his hand out to Kayle, who waited on the steps while Niko went inside. The boy took his hand solemnly, but then a small sob escaped him, and he buried his face against Natan's side.

Natan set the girl down to put an arm around the trembling boy. "Tillie, will you tell your grandmother I'll be in soon?"

"Yes, Papa. Come with me, Kam," she ordered. "Kayle wants to talk to Papa alone." The children ran into the house and Tillie's voice was heard crying for her grandmother.

Natan sat on the steps and beckoned Kayle to him. "What is it?"

The boy pressed his thin little body against him, bravely swallowing his tears. "You're so late. I thought you weren't coming back."

Natan's heart ached for him. "My darling boy," he murmured and put an arm around him. He searched for the right words. "I can't promise you I'll always return," he said as he tilted Kayle's face to look into his dark eyes. "Life doesn't work like that. But I can promise to come back as long as it is in my power to do so."

Kayle nodded but sighed. "Father made me the same promise."

Natan searched his face. "Kayle, I'd like to give you a gift, but it will feel very strange in your head at first. You won't be afraid?"

Kayle's face wrinkled in thought. "No, Papa."

Natan pressed his forehead to Kayle's and smiled. "Close your eyes," he whispered gently and followed suit. The air crackled around them. Natan felt life as a pulse of energy that hummed in the air and earth. Then suddenly he became part of that flowing force. It gathered speed as it raced through his blood and hammered in his ears. He drew a breath at the power and joy that filled him.

He bent to Kayle's ear. "I love you," he said, such simple words, spoken quietly, but they entered Kayle's ear and slid into his mind. He felt Kayle squirm at the strange crawling sensation Natan knew he experienced. Then the boy grew still as the words crept into his thoughts, finally settling into a little spot toward the back of his mind.

Natan rose to his feet and breathed deeply in the glory of life, then let the energy go. He ran his hand over Kayle's springy hair. The boy looked at him with his large brown eyes.

"Think of me," he asked. Kayle blinked, and a slow happy smile crossed his face at the feeling of warmth, security, and love Natan knew vibrated through his memory.

"Is it magic, Papa?" he breathed in wonder.

"No, dear." Natan touched his face. "I've just left a bit of my life's energy with you."

"Did it hurt?"

"No, and what's more, I have a bit of you with me now, so if you ever need me, call and I'll hear you."

The door burst open, startling them. "Grandmother says to come in right now," Tillie told them in a perfect imitation of Aubre at her most severe. They found the others in the garden, and Natan realized that Mirah had already left with the children for the park. Kam pulled on his arm.

"Come with us. You promised to finish the story of the Karthagans."

Aubre nodded at his questioning look, and he swung Tillie onto his shoulder, starting after the boys.

Mirah took his hand as he joined the group of children at the park. "It's nice to see you again."

"Hello. Kendra sends her apologies and says that she'll come as soon as she can."

The children heard his familiar voice and quickly left their games.

"Have you come to finish the story, Mage?" a boy named Andri asked and blushed at his own boldness.

"Indeed I have," Natan answered with a smile and sat on the grass with the children around him. "But first I want to show you something. Take a deep breath," he instructed them, and they followed his example with excitement for the new game. "Did you feel the air enter your mouth and go down into your chest?" He continued at their exuberant nods. "Good. Now I want you to do something for me. Don't be afraid."

Kayle sat up straighter. Natan gave him a smile as he leaned toward the children. "Hold your hand out and close your eyes. Feel the air on your skin?" He waited for their silent nods.

"There's an energy in the air, and that energy is also in the earth, and in the trees and rocks and animals, and in us. It is the energy that makes up life, and it's in constant motion. Just as we can breathe in the air and make it a part of us, we can take in this energy from the earth and make it our own. And also, like a spent breath, we can let this life force pass from us to others.

"Open your eyes."

Natan kept his hand out, palm up, vaguely aware of the adults joining them.

"Feel the air again," he whispered. "Wiggle your fingers." The children complied. "Now think of the bits of energy that are racing around in the air. Can you feel them?"

Suddenly the air was charged, tingling on his fingers. It made the children giggle as their hair stood on end. "And now I will ask the energy to do something for me. I will ask it to bring light."

The children gasped at the tiny flames that sprang to life in their hands, bright and wonderful.

"It doesn't hurt!" Tillie chirped.

"No, dear. I could make it burn, but I wouldn't do that. I would never want to do anything dangerous with the energy."

"Make it do something else, Mage." Andri rose to his knees with a fire kindled in his eyes. Natan closed his hand and the flames were gone.

"No, Andri," he said solemnly. "Life is not mine to control. I may ask it for help in need, but there is something you must understand." The children were silent, breath held. "There's a great danger in using your ability to call up these powers. The danger of becoming greedy and wanting more than you need. When life's energy fills you, it makes you very happy. But you have to let it go, give it back. You only borrow it, you see. If you hold on to it and try to take more and more, it begins to hurt you, and to hurt the people you love. Don't do that! It leads to madness."

The last words were a whisper of anguish. A hateful voice shattered the silence. "Quite touching, Natan."

Natan reacted, surging to his feet, his only thought to protect the children as he bounded across the grass, drawing his knife as he came to a halt in front of Danul, where he stood by his horse. He made note of others still mounted, swords in hand.

"What do you want?" he asked with ice in his tone.

"Why, to hear you prattle, friend. My dear Natan, are those tears?" Danul touched Natan's face and clicked his tongue as his fingers came away wet. There was derisive laughter from the horsemen behind him. Natan heard a sharp breath as Niko stepped up, his knife held low.

"Come, come," Danul swore impatiently. "I just want a little chat. Or do your dogs always do your fighting, Natan?"

Natan gave a sudden laugh and stepped closer to Danul, who jumped back, startled. "If you've come to take me Danul, do so. If you can." He opened his arms, but a dangerous note sparked in his voice. The breeze stirred his unruly hair.

The creaking of a bow being drawn broke the tension. "I would just as soon you didn't, Danul, if you don't mind."

Mika was on a boulder to the left of them, the arrow unmistakably trained on Danul's heart.

"Another time then, Mage," Danul sneered with a mocking bow to the group. He swung into the saddle, and the men's harsh laughter filled the air as they galloped away.

Natan watched them go, strangely disappointed. With Danul out of the way, he felt certain the others would disband. That he was a match for the man he had no doubt. A coldness touched his heart as he looked at his knife. He'd had plenty of empty nights recently in which to practice. He slipped the knife into his belt, and with a sudden stifled feeling, walked into the woods.

He was drawn to the harbor. There was a bustle of activity on the wharf, though the schooner that had arrived remained a faint dot on the horizon. He found a comfortable section of driftwood on the beach to lean against and closed his eyes, letting his thoughts drift into sleep.

The clang of a bell roused him. He watched as the ship unfurled its sails in preparation to depart. Had he really slept that long? A lone figure approached him from the dock, and an unexpected joy flooded his heart. He was on his feet, running, before he realized it, then stopped with a sheepish smile. He struggled to catch his breath. *And stop grinning*, he mocked. He'd nearly given himself away. Kavi drew closer while Natan's pulse thundered in his ears.

"Kavi," he breathed as the Karthagan came up to him. He doubted his senses as he took Kavi's hands. "I can't believe this. What are you doing here?"

"Natan." Kavi's smile dazzled him. "I missed you. I wanted to see you again."

"You came to see me?" Natan did nothing to hide his delight, but then he recovered and sobered. "What is it, Kavi? What's wrong?"

When Kavi dropped his gaze, Natan noticed the dark smudges under his eyes. "Things are…disturbing, back home. But I am weary, Natan. Can we speak of this after I've slept?"

"Of course." Concern overrode his pleasure. Kavi's beloved face was pale in the sunlight. "My house is this way."

He took Kavi's hand and led him up the beach. As they passed Mika's house, Kendra came off the porch to meet them.

"Kendra, this is my friend Kavi," Natan introduced them. "He arrived unexpectedly on the last ship."

"Welcome," Kendra said warmly, holding out her hand. Her gaze grew concerned. "Why don't you come up to the house and refresh yourself? The voyage from Belega can be grueling."

Kavi inclined his head. "Thank you. That would be welcome." He turned his tired gaze on Natan. "We'll talk tomorrow, when I'm more rested?"

"As you wish." Natan watched them enter the house, feeling dismissed. He looked at his own empty house farther up the beach, and with a sudden violent movement strode in the opposite direction.

What had he expected? That once Kavi saw him again Kavi would realize how much he needed him? That every moment apart was its own separate agony? Natan laughed harshly, then in desperation plunged into the surf and swam until his body screamed in protest. Only Mika's shout from the beach recalled him, so he paddled back and threw himself on the sand, exhausted.

Mika gave him an intent look. "I'm taking the dory out in the morning, if you'd care to come with me again."

"Wonderful," Natan panted, catching his breath. He avoided Mika's eyes as they made their way home.

"The others have gone up to Aubre's for the rest of the day," Mika informed him. "Will you join us?"

Natan shook his head. "I'll see you in the morning," he said and entered his empty house, neglecting to open the curtains against the gloom inside. As much as he longed to see Kavi, he needed to get his heart under control first.

NATAN CAST HIS snag line over the side of the dory the next morning and sat with his chin in his hand, idly watching the small circles that spread out from the string. Had Kavi thought of him last night? Natan had lain awake until early morning, knowing he'd been childish and a fool not to have spent the evening with him and the others. He looked up, startled, as an oar clattered at his feet, a blush stinging his cheeks when Mika gave him a wide grin.

"Sorry," he stammered and sat up, pulling the line in to cast it farther. "Daydreaming."

Mika watched him a moment. "My friend Gabral has a dory he wishes to sell," Mika began tentatively, continuing when Natan nodded. "What I'd like to do is buy it from him and take on a partner. Trade has increased with Belega, and I think we could make a good living at this." He indicated the fish in the bottom of the boat. "Do you think you'd be interested?"

Natan opened his mouth but closed it again. He looked at the sea. "I would like nothing better," he said gravely and reached across to take Mika's hand in a firm grip. They rowed ashore soon afterwards where Kendra met them with the baskets. They transferred the fish to the work shed and began scaling and gutting the large catch.

"I think we'll smoke them all," Mika decided, surveying the lot. "We didn't have enough at the last market."

Natan looked up from his task when he heard footsteps outside the shed, and his breath caught when Kavi looked in at them. "Hello."

"Come in." Mika waved his scaling knife.

"Aubre asked me to invite you to lunch."

"Is it that late already?" Kendra put down the knife she was using to slice open the bellies and wiped her hands on a nearby cloth. "I'd better see if I can help."

"Niko brought Kayle and Tillie down. They are at your house with Kam," Kavi informed her after a quick embrace.

"Then I'd better go with you, dear." Mika hurried to Kendra's side. "Kam bothers Niko to distraction with his unending questions. I'd better rescue the man."

"You made a nice catch this morning," Kavi noted as he picked up Kendra's knife and expertly sliced open a fish. He tossed it in the basket at Natan's feet. Natan smiled at him while he continued to cut off heads and tails and remove the guts.

"Are you feeling better today?" he asked with a keen look at the Karthagan. Kavi appeared a trifle pale, but the deep weariness had gone.

"Yes. I slept well. Lady Aubre is kindness itself."

"And you met the children?"

A delighted smile crossed Kavi's face. "Tillie is adorable, isn't she? Kayle shook my hand quite seriously and asked me why I hadn't brought you home with me."

"I don't see them as much as I'd like to," Natan confessed. "I'd have them here with me, but I fear it's still not safe to do so."

"I thought Mazzo was gone?"

"He is, but his lieutenant took over and nothing has changed." Natan fought down his frustration. "What of you? Can you tell me what drove you here?"

Kavi quietly began to describe the growing tension between the Karthagans and the Barkuit people, and the widening rift between Alek and Camron.

"There's something wrong, Natan. Something about Camron…"

As his voice trailed off, Natan felt a shiver of dread run down his spine.

"What is it?" He put his knife down and went to him. Kavi stared at him, bewilderment in his dark eyes.

"I don't know." A shudder passed through Kavi's slim body. "He sold me to Lord Fredrik, who seems to have a hatred for my people." He shook his head a little as if he still couldn't believe it had actually happened. "Regent Syros found me before the Barkuit traitors could hand me over to him. Syros sent me here."

"Kavi, look at me," Natan spoke quietly, but Kavi raised his head, startled. "Tell me what's wrong."

"I don't know." Kavi's voice broke. "I met with Camron at the redwood tree early in the morning; then I suddenly woke up in the hands of the Barkuits. I can't recall anything in between." Hope sprang into his eyes. "Natan, can you help me remember?"

"I would have to enter your thoughts."

"I don't mind. You've done it before," Kavi reminded him. He laughed as Natan's face flushed with heat, and Kavi touched his cheek. "I don't have anything to hide from you, dear friend."

Natan took a steadying breath. "Close your eyes," he requested and did likewise. Energy burst to life inside him, which he gathered for his task. Cupping Kavi's face in his hands, he became part of the energy and sent a tendril of thought out to Kavi. He found him instantly and slipped into his mind.

Being so close to him was wonderful. Kavi tempted him with all the bright paths and secret doorways and unexpected turns in his mind. Natan felt a sudden great desire to know all about his lover, down to his very last thought.

Instead, he took a firm grip on himself and started down a path darker than the others. He knew the answer lay at its end, but as he walked, a red mist formed at his feet which began to climb the walls until Natan found himself in an increasingly narrow tunnel.

"Kavi?" he called. He'd never encountered the mist before. Hearing a faint cry, he hastened forward. The mist rose as a red barrier between them. Natan could see Kavi's agonized face on the other side, but though he tried to push through, it only became more substantial. Tears streamed down Kavi's face, and he begged Natan to help him. In desperation, Natan pitched every ounce of strength he had against the barrier. Kavi started to scream.

Natan fell back into himself with a violence that almost dropped him to his knees.

"Kavi!" He tried to take his hands, but Kavi batted them away.

"Don't touch me!" Kavi shrieked and clutched his head.

"Let me help you," Natan begged, but Kavi threw him a venomous look and fled outside. Natan watched him go, stricken. It took a moment before he felt composed enough to trail him to the house. Niko had waited on the porch for him with Kayle and Tillie, and after a cheery greeting, they began the hike up the beach toward Aubre's house. It troubled him that Kavi wouldn't look at him, choosing to walk with Niko instead.

"So, my little girl, have you been good for your grandmother?" he asked Tillie as she skipped beside him into the trees bordering the beach as the others strolled ahead of them.

"So good!" she piped and leaned against him with a contented sigh. "Grandmother only had to remind me once not to jump on Kayle when he's asleep."

Natan stifled a laugh as he bent to kiss the top of her curly head. As he straightened, a knife grazed his shoulder, and he stumbled into the little girl. At his cry, Niko swirled toward him, drawing his own blade. Natan blindly handed Tillie to someone and strode with Niko to where horsemen waited in a row between the trees.

"What is it now, Danul?" he asked with barely concealed anger.

Danul sputtered in outrage as he motioned to Kavi. "You know damned well, sorcerer. You insist on using your powers, and now you've brought one of your depraved followers amongst us. You have to be stopped."

Natan wondered if the man was going to ride him down. He put his hands up, palms out. "Wait, Danul. I refuse to fight you with the children present."

"What?" Danul was beside himself, incredulous.

Natan's face turned to stone. "I won't fight you today."

"Then what's to stop me from killing you this moment?"

Natan stepped up to Danul's stirrup. "I wouldn't advise trying it. I wouldn't fight fair." Energy filled the air, and the hair on Danul's head rose on end. His men felt it too, murmuring nervously.

Natan continued, "I'll return here tomorrow. We can settle matters between us then."

"What, so you can set a trap for me? Use your magic on me?"

Natan gave him a look of contempt. "I won't need to."

Danul swore angrily and would have jumped from his saddle if one of his men hadn't grabbed his arm, urging, "One day, Danul. Surely we can wait that long?"

Danul tightened his lips at his follower's obvious fear of the Mage, but gave a curt nod. "Be here," he muttered. He turned his horse and disappeared into the forest.

"Let's get the children home," Natan said in clipped tones. He rubbed absently at his shoulder, wincing. He'd forgotten the knife injury.

Blood soaked the front of his tunic and Niko pushed him toward an old stump. "We can at least take a moment to look at that wound." He reached for the wet fabric but Natan pushed his hand away.

"You'll rip it." He untied the knot at his neck and pulled the tunic over his head. Kavi brought up a water skin and Niko poured the liquid over his shoulder to reveal a thin slash in the muscle.

Natan looked up at Kavi's quickly drawn breath. He was staring intently at the brand on Natan's chest and hesitantly began to trace the image with unsteady fingers. Hot blood flooded Natan's face. He felt sure Kavi could feel his heart pounding beneath his touch.

"Who did this?" Kavi asked in a strangled whisper.

"Mazzo," he said just as quietly.

"But why?"

"He found pleasure in it." Natan pulled his shirt back over his head. The cut on his shoulder had already begun to congeal. Kavi gave him a strange look. He stared into Natan's eyes as if searching for something hidden. Natan's heart lurched at a growing wariness in Kavi's gaze and rose quickly to his feet.

"We should go," he murmured and swung Tillie up on his back. Niko took up Kayle, and he and Kavi followed Natan's swift steps. It didn't take long to reach Aubre's house, where Natan set Tillie on the porch, kissing her cheek. He ran a hand over Kayle's soft curls.

"I'll see you soon," he whispered to the little man. Mirah opened the front door and smiled on seeing them. He heard pleasant conversation in the background.

Niko raised his brows. "You're not coming in?"

"No. I need to think," he said, hoping his friend wouldn't push. Niko thinned his lips but nodded, letting Natan go without argument. Kavi looked aside when Natan tried to catch his gaze.

Natan returned to the beach and walked along the shoreline, his mind racing. He would need to kill a man on the morrow. His nature screamed in horror with the thought, a knot of dread tangling in his gut. There had to be another way, but he couldn't see it.

As the sun began to set, he threw himself on the sand and rolled to his back, then fell to dreaming about Kavi. He knew he shouldn't, but the sun shone warmly on his face, and the ceaseless waves were making him drowsy. Wistfully, he wondered if Kavi could marry a fisherman. He didn't think he would mind. After all, Kavi's family had fished the sea. And it would be easy enough to put in a raised bed in the back of the house for a vegetable garden, if Kavi wished...

He pictured Kavi in his mind, and faint heat rose in his face. Of course, Kavi was lovely, all his people were handsome, but Natan remembered the sparkle in his dark eyes when they'd first met, reflecting the joyous spirit within. Natan would give anything to see happiness in Kavi's face again. Anything to be the one to put it there.

Someone sat beside him. Natan peered through his lashes, wondering if he should feign sleep. His breath caught at the sight of Kavi so close. Natan was reaching for him before he recalled himself and scrambled to sit up.

"Hello," he stammered, then cleared his throat.

"Did I wake you?" Kavi asked as he wrapped his arms around his knees. "I hope you don't mind that I came looking for you."

"You didn't wake me." Natan turned his gaze to the sea. Kavi had caught him off guard, and his love was pounding through his body as relentless as the tide. How was he to keep it from him? But then, why should he? He believed he could make Kavi happy. In time maybe Kavi could learn to love him in return.

His breath quickened. He'd do better not to think of that. If Kavi could only care for him a little, the heavens knew he had enough love for both of them. Natan leaned toward him, the confession trembling on his tongue.

But Kavi began to speak, and Natan's words turned to ash in his mouth.

Kavi's accusations battered at him. "I understand why you did it, Natan. Why you took our power from us and kept it for yourself. But did you have to let my father die as well? Were you that threatened by him?"

"What?" Natan faltered, dazed by the cruel attack. "Do you truly believe me capable of that?"

Triumph gleamed in Kavi's eyes. "Yes I do, though it's not your fault. The madness had us all at one time, dear. I'm sure Kirstin can help you, as well."

Natan rose to his feet, his heart leaden. "I'm sorry if…" He couldn't continue and gave Kavi a deep bow, acknowledging all that he had said. Unable to raise his eyes, he walked away, heading toward home.

NIGHTMARES CAME TO Natan that night, but no one was there to comfort him. Mother and Father were buried deep in the ground. He crept out to the porch and sat on the steps with Mother's blanket around his thin shoulders. Covering his face, he gave in to the lonely ache in his heart. The days weren't so bad, but the emptiness of the cabin at night was unbearable. He wanted them back! Why had they left him alone? Natan thought of Bryon only a few leagues away. He'd go see his friend. The man always had a kind word for him.

Natan had taken a few steps into the dark yard before he came fully awake. A desperate laugh escaped him when he realized he'd been walking in his sleep. Returning to the porch, he wrapped again in the blanket, hoping he hadn't woken Niko, asleep inside. The moonlight on the ocean soothed his hot eyes, but it couldn't ease his heart. He didn't know what to do, wasn't sure how to get through the next day, or hour, or the next moment. Kavi had no faith in him, believing Natan's mind had fallen under the same madness that had touched his people. Natan rested his head on his knees and suffered.

He raised a tired face in the morning when Mika approached him, then leaped to his feet on seeing his expression. "What?"

"It's Aubre—" His friend choked on a sob and covered his face.

Natan bounded away, racing through the empty streets to her home with a hard knot of fear in his chest. He could see the door had been forced open and stopped on the threshold. Signs of a struggle were evident in broken glass and toppled chairs and in the agony on grieving faces. A crumpled figure lay on the floor covered in a blanket. Natan went to her, then sinking to his knees, he gathered the dear woman to him.

"Mother?" he whispered in fear. He searched with his mind as well as his eyes, but not even a flicker of life remained in the shattered body for him to focus on. *Have I killed you?*

"Mother?" he called again, a small boy standing on the beach where his parents' bodies lapped against the sand. His fault. Father had told him to be at the shore early to help with the nets. He knew Mother was ill. But there were mushrooms along the path and robin eggs to see hatch. They'd sailed without him, and then the storm had taken them. If his hands had been on the tiller…

It had taken him all morning to pull and drag their bodies up the beach to the small hollow where he hid his treasures. Tears at last touched his eyes when he had to let them fall so heavily into the dark earth. He could hardly see to drop stones on top of them.

"Mother," he whispered one last time and buried his face in Aubre's hair as he wept.

"Natan?" He felt hands on his shoulders. He struggled to focus on Niko's words, the man out of breath. Mika must have fetched him as well.

"It was Danul. He's taken Mirah and the children. Mage, he also has Kavi." Niko paused as a shudder ran through Natan, then continued, "Tolban found their trail. We should go. Tolban wants his daughter back and is holding horses outside. He won't wait for us long."

"I'll take care of Aubre, Mage." Kendra's voice reached him, and he looked into her sad eyes. "Go with Niko. I won't leave her."

Natan touched Aubre's battered face. It was his fault. Lurching to his feet, he dashed away his tears with a rough hand. Without a backward glance, he strode outside and flung himself onto the horse Tolban was holding for him. He spent a fleeting thought for the people in Belega. He'd promised to return after finding Gregor's mother. Governor Basal and the new regent of Barkuit, Syros, expected him to help maintain the peace between the north and south. He couldn't even help those closest to him. Natan shook his head, despairing that they'd placed their hopes in a fool like him. Gregor should never have made him Mage.

Mika joined them, and with grim faces they raced from the yard.

Chapter Twenty-Three

SYROS RODE SWIFTLY east with his men toward Siagan. The trail seemed endless, so he allowed his thoughts to wander as the afternoon progressed. A mocking smile touched his face. That he'd become Regent in the first place seemed ridiculous, and that he now rode after two Barkuit traitors and the Karthagan rebel, Camron, was something he could never have imagined.

His horse snorted and sidestepped, or he would have ridden over the men sprawled in the glen. He jumped from the saddle and threw the reins to Lieutenant Davis, biting out an oath as he recognized the southern soldiers, Commander Brendan and Lieutenant Jaden. It was obvious they'd been tortured. Contusions and burns covered chest, shoulders, and back. Their faces were hideous to see. Syros pressed fingers to each neck in turn.

"They live, but these blows to the head are dangerous."

Davis's face darkened. "It appears they were left here for us to find.

What kind of a madman are we following that he would do this?"

Syros shrugged. "The Karthagan goes too far. To think he can take Siagan from us…" He sighed. "Doesn't matter. Lieutenant, leave at once for the city of Karthag and let them know about this. Alek will want to be informed. Also, have them send their healer. We'll have need of her."

"At once, lord." Davis made a short bow and swung into his saddle, disappearing into the trees.

Syros looked at the bloody soldiers, then began to gather wood for a fire. First things first. The men needed warmth and shelter before he could see to their wounds.

JADEN STIFLED A groan and cautiously opened an eye. The tent confused him, and he wondered if he were still in a dream.

"How are you feeling?"

"Bryon." Jaden struggled to sit up on the cot, and Bryon lent him a hand. "How long have I been asleep?"

"Hard to say, lad. You were unconscious when Syros found you yesterday afternoon. It's nearly daylight again. I've brought Kirstin. What have you gotten yourself into this time?"

Jaden shrugged his shoulders, groaning at the renewal of pain. He waved off Bryon's concern. "How is the commander?" Anguish touched his face. "Camron was terrible—"

"Brendan's a strong man and Kristin has hope. Don't give up on him." Bryon rubbed his chin, scowling. "Can you tell me what happened?"

Jaden leaned back on the cot. "The man's insane," he said hoarsely. "He laughed as he broke Brendan's arm, and we hadn't resisted up to that point. Most of what you see on us Camron inflicted himself and took pleasure in it. His men held us, and I think even they were afraid of him at the end, when he took up a stone and started smashing Brendan's head."

He fell silent and stared at the floor, holding back tears.

"He'll survive. Kirstin's very good. Why did Camron become so violent, if neither of you put up a fight?"

Jaden's voice was a ragged whisper. "Brendan laughed at him."

"Why?"

"To distract him from…me."

"Bastard!" Fury flashed in Bryon's eyes, but he controlled it. "Did you learn what Camron means to do at Siagan?"

"He means to take it," Jaden said abruptly. "He bragged that he would walk up to its gates and demand that Councel Leader Mandel let him in, and he seems to believe that he would."

"Jaden," Bryon hesitated as if fearing the answer. "Does Camron have his abilities back?"

Jaden shook his head, wincing as pain shot through his skull. "I don't believe so. Base greed and passion rule him. I saw no indication of stronger powers at work."

Kirstin called softly from outside the tent, and Jaden eagerly invited her in.

"You should be resting." She pushed him back until he was lying on the cot.

"But what of Commander Brendan? What can you tell me?"

"I believe his skull has a minute fracture over the left ear, but if I can keep the swelling down, he'll make it."

Bryon agreed. "He's strong, Jaden, and I've never met a man with a stouter heart. He won't give in easily."

Jaden glanced away to hide his worry. Bryon gripped his arm. "We leave for Siagan in the morning, but if you'd rather go to Barkuit with Brendan…"

"No, sir," Jaden said heatedly. "I'd like to meet up with Camron again and thank him personally for his kindness." He relaxed back on the cot as Kirstin felt his forehead, willing himself well so he could fight.

CAMRON SURVEYED SIAGAN'S walls with a derisive smile. It was mid-morning, and he knew that the inconvenience he'd left on his trail in the way of the southern soldiers would prevent his pursuers from arriving before evening. Surely enough time.

He strode impudently into the clearing before the gates with a white cloth in his hands, a trick he'd learned from his Uncle Kayden. He waved it over his head and waited. A brief moment later, the gates swung open and out strode a dozen northern soldiers with bright swords and shining black-and-silver jerkins, black helmets clamped tightly on their heads.

The troop of men stopped ten paces from him. Camron bowed. "Gentlemen."

A broad man stepped forward, probably the leader of the little band. "Who are you?"

"Camron of Karthag, my lord." Camron bowed again. "And you?"

The man flushed darkly at the sneer evident in Camron's whispery voice.

"Council Leader Mandel," he ground out. "What do you want?"

"I have one of your soldiers. A traitor, I feel obliged to tell you."

Camron motioned toward the trees, and his men stepped into the clearing. One of them pushed a bound man to Camron's side. The man staggered and would have fallen if Camron hadn't taken his arm to gently hold him upright. "I expect you know Captain Grant?"

"I do." Mandel's voice was stone. The smashed features and slumped body of the broken man were unrecognizable. "A traitor, you say?"

"He told me all about your defenses, sir. He even drew me a map."

Mandel looked at the captain again. Grant's eyes were glazed and dull, his face, what was left of it, gray with pain. Mandel stepped back with a cry of alarm. The man's hands had been severed at the wrists and fresh blood dripped onto the dirt.

"What's the matter, Mandel? Oh, you want me to finish the job? Very well." With a swift movement Camron slit the prisoner's throat. He laughed at the look of horror on the council leader's face and lunged toward him, knife flashing in the sunlight. It was only a feint. As the northern soldiers surged forward, he dodged to the side, the two groups colliding with a clash of weapons.

Camron sprinted for the gates. The guards on duty had come out, drawing their swords. One stood steadfast in his path while the others swept around him to join the fray. Camron threw his knife at the remaining soldier and sidestepped around his falling body, dodging through the gates into Siagan. He crouched against the wall in the confusion as more soldiers ran past, then slipped down a back alley. Camron heard his men shouting and shrugged. His fellow Karthagans had served their purpose. They were forgotten as he crept along the shadows to the castle, flushed with anticipation for what he would find there.

COMMANDER BRENDAN WOKE briefly in the morning, much to everyone's relief. They made a litter for him between two horses, and Kirstin rode at his side as they started for Barkuit.

Syros led the remaining men at a quick pace through the thinning forest, coming within sight of Siagan by late afternoon. An acrid smoke filled the air as they approached the city's gates, and he slid off his horse. Flanked by Bryon and Lieutenant Davis, he left the horses with Jaden and went to the burn pile watched by several Barkuit soldiers.

"My lord Regent!" A rotund man detached himself from the group around the fire.

"Mandel, what's happened here?" There were more than a dozen bodies in the mound, and they stepped back a pace as the flames roared higher.

"We were attacked by Karthagans, my lord. There were only a handful of them, but they fought fiercely."

Bryon shifted on his feet, his impassive gaze on the fire. "Did any survive?"

Mandel shot him a look and shook his head. "None," he said curtly, then spun on his heel to lead them into the city.

"You checked the tunnels?" Bryon persisted as they passed through the gates.

Irritation crossed Mandel's face. "Of course."

Syros watched Mandel closely, sensing his evasiveness. He pulled the council leader aside while the others went on ahead, Jaden leading the horses to the stable.

"What aren't you saying?"

Mandel pressed his lips into an angry line. "We think one Karthagan escaped, but we searched the city. There's no trace of him. He probably fled to the forest."

"And the tunnels—"

"Sealed weeks ago and undisturbed."

Syros nodded, remaining in the courtyard while Mandel followed the others inside the castle. He breathed deeply of the warm air and rubbed his tired face. Maybe the man they searched for had escaped the city as Mandel suggested. The way his skin crawled told him otherwise.

Syros glanced around the courtyard with a grimace. What a dismal, squalid place Siagan had become. He'd been there only once before, years ago, but didn't remember this feeling of decay. As he walked along the ugly streets his depression grew. Entering an overgrown park, he dropped on a stone bench and put his face in his hands. For two silver pieces he'd throw the whole ludicrous affair over. He felt control slipping from his grasp. Maybe it was time he packed his things and left the Northern Territory to its fate.

He raised a troubled face to the sky. He'd run once before, to lose the love of his lady. The look of betrayal in her soft blue eyes as she turned her face from him still cut him to the heart. She hadn't spoken a word to him since, and he couldn't believe how much it continued to hurt.

Syros stood and stretched. After the business with the Karthagans was finished, he'd return to Siagan and set the city to rights. He sighed. The problem was there were few men he could trust. Davis's name came to mind. He smiled as the lieutenant appeared in the road as if conjured. He went to meet him.

Davis gave a quick bow and answered Syros's unspoken question. "No sign, my lord." He looked into the park and scowled at the rank growth. "Something's not right here. Have you noticed how oddly some of the men are acting? And the air has a strange feel to it." Davis broke off with a quick laugh. "Forgive me. I'm probably overreacting."

"Perhaps." Syros kicked at the weeds under his boot. He came to a decision. "Davis, I'm going to remove Mandel as council leader and put you in his place, which will give you a dangerous enemy from the start. And the council will probably be against you as well." His eyes flashed a challenge. "Do you accept?"

Davis glanced at the dirty streets and crumbling buildings of Siagan. "As you wish." He saluted smartly, but they exchanged a grin. Both were lowborn soldiers and the irony of the situation was not lost on either of them.

Syros returned to the castle and found Bryon and Lieutenant Jaden in the courtyard. He joined them at the cracked and dripping fountain. "No sign of the Karthagan," he said in answer to Bryon's look. "And by Mandel's description of him, my guess is that it's Camron who's escaped."

"That is also my belief," Bryon said. He turned his gaze to Jaden prowling the yard.

Syros watched the soldier as well. "We'll start for Barkuit in the morning. I'll leave several of my men to keep up the search, but you shouldn't be here. Tempers are short, and it wouldn't take much to ignite an incident between our two territories."

Bryon inclined his head in agreement.

The travelers spent the night in comfortable rooms, then morning found them waiting at the city's gates while Syros spoke to his new council leader. Mandel had been dismissed from his duties the night before and the man had stormed out of the room with several councilmen at his heels.

"Keep your eyes open," Syros warned now. "Mandel can be a dangerous adversary. We haven't seen the last of that Karthagan either. I'll send help as soon as I can."

"Don't worry, my lord. I'll have fun," Davis assured him, though his lips settled in a grim line.

CAMRON WATCHED THE company ride into the forest from the tower room, and his laugher bordered on mania. On catching a hesitant knock, he stifled his glee as he crossed to the heavy door. "Come in." He drew the latch as he spoke, and a soldier scurried in with a fearful look over his shoulder.

Camron laughed again, witnessing the young man shudder at the whispery sound and avert his face. He'd forced the youth into hiding him and the lad had chosen the tower. It had been easy for Camron to see the shadows in his gray eyes and the nightmare visions scurrying in his mind. The young man confessed to being one of the soldiers in the tunnel with Kavi when he'd released the spirits from the lake.

There were others like him, soldiers lost to nightmare, and Camron had begun to gather them to himself by promising release from their madness, gaining their trust by bestowing moments of peace with the slightest touch on their minds. They never realized that the small suggestions he left behind were not their own.

At the moment, Cecil was his favorite, with his fair hair curling around his face and the fear in his wide haunted eyes. Camron grinned at the lad as he softly closed the door behind him. A disturbed mind was so easy to manipulate. He beckoned, and Cecil went to him, diffidently taking his hand, obediently raising his face for Camron's kiss.

"Are you ready, my dear?"

"Yes, sir," Cecil murmured, his pale cheeks flushed by Camron's attention. "The others are waiting."

He motioned and Cecil led him with caution through a deserted section of the castle to the cellar rooms. Camron leaned against a wall as he watched the men remove the boards and debris that had been used to seal the underground tunnels. The four worked in silence while Camron coiled his little spell of contentment and peace around them, keeping the nightmares at bay. It would be an easy matter to drive the dreams away forever, but he might need the men at some future date. The door gaped open at last and he waved the soldiers away.

"Stay a moment, Cecil." He touched his arm. Cecil blinked his troubled eyes and Camron swept the light hair from his face. "Are the visions worse?"

Cecil nodded and would have looked away if Camron hadn't gripped his chin. He liked to keep the young soldier on the edge of a nightmare. He was much more pliable that way. But perhaps the lad deserved a little peace. He brushed his hand over his fluttering lids and watched the shadows leave his eyes. Cecil drew a ragged breath.

"Would you like to go to the lake with me?" Cecil pulled away from him, the terror on his face delighting Camron. "No? Perhaps you'll remain on the stairs and keep an eye out?"

Cecil looked at the floor, shame darkening his eyes. "You won't be long?" he whispered.

"Not very, dear. Now, go and sit down." He watched Cecil settle on the bottom step with his arms wrapped tightly around his knees and his head turned from the tunnel. Camron wondered how long it would be before he'd have to kill him.

With a shrug, Camron entered the tunnels, unerringly following the pull of energy to the underground lake. He hurried down the last passageway, unable to control the wild excitement surging through him. At last! After hearing Kavi's stories of the place, he was anxious to see it for himself. He laughed, wondering where his dear, deluded cousin found himself at the moment. Hopefully with that fool, Natan.

His torch sent shadows chasing across the still water of the lake and up the sides of the cavern. Camron moved to the right along the shore where he found the splintered doorway of Kirstin's cell. He dropped the torch outside the room, and trembling, stepped into the darkness.

Chapter Twenty-Four

NATAN RODE IN icy silence, the pulse of life thrumming through his body, his ears, pounding with the hoof beats of his horse. *Move, move, move.* Morning came and they rushed on, Niko riding low in the saddle to read the trail that led slightly north of the road toward Cahna and Sambola.

He followed where Niko led them, berating himself. He'd been too slow to act. They'd warned him. Everyone had warned him. Yet he'd hesitated, and because of his timidity, Aubre was dead and Danul had the children and sweet Mirah. And his Kavi. Iciness spread throughout his body. He would hesitate no longer.

They found Mirah at noon. Tolban pulled rein on his horse with a sharp cry as they rode into a small clearing. Sliding from his saddle, he hastened to his daughter's side before the others could dismount. "Mirah?" he called in fear. There was no response in her pasty face.

Natan knelt beside her and stroked her forehead and cheek. Sweat had long since dried on her skin, her breathing slow and labored. He bowed his head, emptying himself of all thoughts and feelings, to be instantly filled with the power of life.

"Mirah?" he called and sent his spirit out. It was gray and insubstantial where she waited. Natan grew nauseated as the walls and floor and the very air undulated in sickening waves. Mirah huddled with her arms pressed to her belly, her face lined with pain.

"What is it, Mirah?"

"I don't feel well," she managed to say. Natan put his hands on her abdomen, and a tiny grateful smile touched her face as the pain receded. She sighed deeply. "I could sleep now."

"No, dear." Natan touched her face to catch her wandering attention. "You've been poisoned, and you need to stay with me."

"Very well," she murmured, her tone docile. Natan cradled her as if she were a child, talking of inconsequential things to make her smile. Often, she would close her eyes sleepily, and he would rouse her with a sharp command or entreaty. When her breathing slowed even further, he held her tightly and kept her with him by sheer force of will.

Suddenly his eyes snapped open, startling the others. "Mirah, wake up!" If anything, the girl seemed to lose what little strength she had left.

"Mirah, awake!" he shouted, and the power and command in his voice sent the others to their feet in bewilderment. Mirah gasped and drew a deep breath and then another.

"She'll be fine now," Natan whispered, his words slurred with exhaustion. "She's merely sleeping." He crumpled to the dirt, utterly spent in mind and body. But he started up from his swoon almost immediately, with Kayle's cries ringing in his ears, his poor child, scared and hurt. Struggling to his feet, he swayed.

Niko put a hand on his shoulder. "You should rest."

"No," he answered. "Get to the horses."

He looked with pity at Tolban who sat beside Mirah and held her hands. His daughter still slept. "I'm sorry, Tolban. We have to go, but I think she will be well."

"I understand, Mage. Find your children."

Natan watched them a moment, heart heavy, and sighed as he swung onto the horse Mika held for him. "Find them for me, Niko," he asked, holding off his exhaustion.

Though they raced the horses, Natan fought a rising panic as they fell farther behind Danul. They flew past Cahna in the evening and took the road east toward Sambola. Midnight came before Mika insisted they rest the horses. Niko slipped from his horse and caught Natan as he fell from the saddle.

"Here." Mika tossed him a blanket. Niko set it over Natan's trembling body, so Natan pulled it over a shoulder, falling asleep where he lay.

Natan became frantic. He couldn't find him. Kavi wasn't anywhere. Then he stumbled on him in the forest. Kavi hadn't left the children. Natan strode up to him where he sat on the ground and pulled Kavi roughly into his arms. Such was his relief that he forgot himself. Soft endearments slipped between the kisses he pressed on his lover's face and eyes. He found Kavi's lips and his heart overflowed with the love and quiet despair he'd tried so hard to bury. He delighted in his sweetness. Kavi's soft kiss in return shattered him...

Natan awoke and blinked at the flames of a campfire. Was he too late? He climbed to his feet to scatter the fire, rousing the others.

"I've found them," he said, his voice ragged. He turned his face from their searching eyes.

They followed him into the night. Morning came and still they rode on. Natan felt trapped in a nightmare. Once again, they rested the horses while he paced, then rode onward. As morning passed into afternoon, they rounded a corner in the road and burst into Danul's camp.

Natan threw himself from the still moving horse and strode into the midst of the company without a thought to the men there or their swords. His eyes were fixed on the man tied to the tree and the prone child beside him.

"Well, if it isn't the Mage," Danul sneered, stepping toward him. He held a knife. Natan lifted his hand, and Danul stopped as if he'd been struck. A look of agony crossed his face as he crumbled to the ground.

One of his followers sprang to his side. "He barely breathes!" He raised a shocked face. "What power is this?" His companions shared a panicked look, then threw down their weapons as they fled, disappearing into the trees while the other lifted Danul in his arms and followed. Natan motioned, and Mika turned his horse to race after them.

Niko dropped to a knee beside Kavi, slipping his knife through the leather strips binding his hands and feet then gently removing the gag from his bloody mouth. Much to Natan's relief, Kavi took several deep breaths, seeming unhurt. Natan turned to the child.

"No," he mourned and touched Kayle's cold face. Dark blood matted the child's hair, his breathing a faint whisper on Natan's cheek. His quick search revealed no other injuries as he spoke soft words into the boy's ear.

"Can nothing be done?" Kavi asked brokenly. Niko remained silent, though his eyes pleaded.

"I can find his spirit, but… I'm not a healer!" Natan's breath caught on a sob as he stared at his bloody hands. "Oh, my little child." He brushed his tears aside and began to probe the wound on the boy's forehead with gentle fingers. A blow from a mailed fist had left an ugly bruise and swelling. He could feel the boy's spirit, sleeping soundly, warm and safe. But he wouldn't wake him to a body Natan couldn't mend. He swore bitterly at his own helplessness.

A horse returned. Mika dismounted and crouched beside them. "They travel north, with several taking Tillie on to Sambola."

Natan lunged to his feet in a violence of action, kindled with fury and apprehension, but he hesitated, shaken with indecision.

"Go!" Mika told him. "I'll look after them."

Natan nodded. With a last desperate look at Kayle and then Kavi, he rushed to the horses with Niko and sprang into the saddle. They took the road at a dead run.

KAVI LISTENED TO their retreating hoofbeats, pain squeezing his heart for his mage, while Mika built up the abandoned fire and placed Kayle's limp body on a blanket close to it. His breathing was still shallow. Kavi carefully bathed his face and the wound on his forehead. As he settled on the blanket to watch over the boy, he sent his thoughts out in search of Natan. He'd believed without a doubt that Natan had let his father die, even though he'd had the power to save him. Now, recalling the anguish in Natan's voice when he admitted he couldn't help Kayle, he knew better.

He let out a cry, alarmed, as his spirit came upon Natan's wild, anxious soul. Natan became aware of his presence in his mind and ran up to him, a desperate fear in his eyes. "You mustn't be here!" he cried with a quick look over his shoulder. "Go, now!" He pushed Kavi in his distress, and Kavi flung back into himself.

The fire blurred across from him, and Kavi rapidly blinked at his tears. What had he done? A voice suddenly rustled in his mind, whispers of doubt and hatred. Camron! Kavi clenched his hands. *Never again, cousin.* Not one more minute would he listen to the treacherous man. Kavi had seen what Natan feared. A black madness had coiled up behind him even as he'd pushed Kavi away. But it wasn't real. It was the seeds of self-doubt Kavi had sown in his mind taking root. What could he do? Natan would need help soon.

The answer came to him. Kavi cleared his mind with a plea for life's energy to fill him. Pain struck him instantly, and he clutched his head in a silent scream. But he would fight through. His body twisted in agony as he embraced the pain. If this was the price to save Natan, he would gladly pay it. Then suddenly his spirit broke free into the night sky.

"Kirstin!" he called and prayed that his kin would hear him. She had the power of healing, stronger than his people had known in his lifetime. Could she heal a broken mind as well? He prayed so, repeating his cry until Mika's hand on his shoulder recalled him.

"Kayle's awake," he said. Kavi looked anxiously at the boy. His dark eyes were open, but they appeared glazed and unfocused.

"Kayle?" Kavi knelt, taking his little hands. They were hot and dry. "Can we move him?" he asked.

"If we're very careful. Do you wish to take him to Tolban and Mirah?"

"No! We need to get to Natan. The Mage will need all of us."

Mika gave him a puzzled look but asked no more questions as they prepared the boy for travel.

Chapter Twenty-Five

NIKO LED THE Mage into Sambola in the late afternoon, allowed to pass through the gates only because Niko had been recognized. They galloped the horses over the city streets to the castle, and when they entered the courtyard, Natan leaped off his horse, ignoring the guards as if they had no substance as he passed inside the castle. Niko nudged his horse into the doorway, watching from the saddle.

Natan stormed into the audience chamber with the force of his anger sweeping before him. It burst against the walls with a clap of thunder that sent the occupants to their knees, covering their heads as glass shattered around them. Without pause, Natan strode to Tillie, on the dais beside the Vice-King and Danul, and swung her from the chair into his arms while they cowered. Danul recovered first, yelling for the guards. Soldiers roused themselves and leaped after Natan as he dashed back across the room.

"Here." He lifted Tillie to Niko, who reached for her. "Go!" he shouted as soldiers rushed him. They seized Natan, throwing him roughly to the ground.

An arrow whistled past Niko's ear, and he cried out, kicking his horse into a run, Natan's mount following. Swallowing his fury, Niko clung to Tillie as he fled the city, though his heart burned as he left Natan behind.

He rode through the evening holding the sobbing child close to his heart and swore in frustration as he recalled his last sight of Natan. The Mage had looked defeated, his head lowered as if he no longer cared what became of him.

The flicker of a campfire some hours later roused him from a half sleep. Thankfully, the horses had kept to the road and the firelight glowed only a short distance through the trees. He could hear the rush of a water-fall. As Niko walked the horses into camp, Mika hailed him from atop a nearby rock. The Karthagan, Kavi, rose from the fire, and Niko lowered Tillie into his waiting arms, then wearily fell from the saddle.

"Let me take the horses," Mika told him. He gladly relinquished the reins, swaying on his feet. Kavi put a cup of sweet tea in his hands, which he drank, then stretched out on a blanket by the fire and closed his tired eyes. He would rest, just for a moment…

He woke at first light and struggled to his feet with a cry. He hadn't meant to sleep, wanting to return directly for the Mage. It made him shudder to think of what his friend had endured in the night while he slept in comfort. Kavi woke as Niko stirred up the fire, and seeing his face, he put water on to boil, then began to gather their packs. Mika blinked at them from his blankets and sat up.

"I have to go back for him." Niko wouldn't look at them as guilt ate away at his heart.

"We will."

The surety of Kavi's voice calmed him, and Niko rubbed his weary face.

Mika touched his arm. "Think, my friend. Will the Vice-King help us?"

"No." He shook his head slowly while his thoughts raced. "But perhaps Corha…"

"Corha?"

"The Vice-King's daughter. We were friends once. Perhaps she'll help me convince him."

"Niko," Tillie's voice reached them, bewildered, and they went to her where she lay by her brother.

"What is it, darling?" Niko brushed the hair from her little face.

"Kayle's thirsty."

Niko looked quickly at the boy to find his eyes wide and alert.

"Water, please," he whispered hoarsely. Kavi knelt beside him and held his hand while Niko fetched the water skin.

When he returned, Tillie scrambled onto Niko's lap. "Where's Papa?"

Niko's arms convulsed around her. "Kavi and I will bring him back, dear."

Mika helped them saddle the horses. Niko could see it fairly killed him to remain behind, but someone had to stay with the children, and judging by Kavi's set face, it wouldn't be him.

"We'll get him back," Niko assured Mika, who gave a sharp nod in agreement.

They mounted the restive horses and Niko sped with Kavi back to Sambola, pausing only once to breathe the horses. The streets were quiet as they rode in, and although they were watched closely, no one approached. They left the horses at the stable, then made their way to the castle at the heart of town. They'd arrived at the noon hour and the large courtyard was deserted, except for a lone figure in its center chained to a stake in the unforgiving sunlight.

Kavi drew a sharp breath when he caught sight of Natan. Niko refused to look again and shook his head slightly to keep Kavi silent, needing to retain his focus if he wished to help the Mage. He knocked firmly on the hall door, and though the guard showed surprise, he let them in without a word. The audience chamber stood empty but Niko knew where to find them.

"May I speak with you, my lord?" he asked from the open doorway of the dining hall. The family was assembled, as he knew they would be, but it rattled him to find his parents present also.

"Niko, my boy. Come in." The Vice-King waved from his cushioned seat and Niko entered the room with a grim smile, Kavi at his side. Jacom, at his kindest, was also the most irrational. He glanced at Corha where she sat beside her father, and his smile turned genuine. She had always enchanted him, and he reddened slightly as she watched him advance.

He put a hand on Kavi's shoulder when they stopped before the Vice-King's chair. "My lord, may I present Kavi, our Karthagan visitor?"

A grunt from the end of the table stiffened his back, but he decided to ignore Danul, for the moment.

"My lord, I am honored," Kavi swept him a bow.

Jacom's eyes widened and he sat up, giving Kavi an appreciative look. "Please, join us."

"I protest!" Danul shouted from his place at the table as if he could no longer contain himself, red in the face. "The Karthagan is a sorcerer and Niko is obviously in league with the Mage. They should be seized immediately."

"Must I answer to him?" Niko asked, his voice dripping contempt.

"Niko's right, Father," Corha unexpectedly put in. "What is that man to us?" She leaned toward the Vice-King, a charming pout slipping on her face. Niko held his breath, wondering if her plea would work. "I should like him removed from our table."

Jacom cast a perplexed glance at Danul, then looked at his daughter's beguiling expression and nodded indulgently. "Very well, Corha, if that is your wish."

Jacom waved a hand and guards stepped to either side of Danul. He sputtered a protest, but Jacom turned his face away, would no longer see him or listen to his words. Danul sent Niko a venomous look as he was led from the room.

Niko turned gratefully to Corha and caught his breath as she gave him a radiant smile. He glanced away before his face betrayed him.

"Will you sit with us?" Jacom invited.

Niko bowed low. "No, my lord, although I thank you. I've come to beg for the Mage."

"What, that hound that attacked me yesterday?"

"Father, he didn't attack you," Corha said patiently, as if addressing a child. "I think he came for the girl."

"For his daughter," Kavi put in quietly.

The Vice-King looked at Kavi, his face softening. He leaned toward the Karthagan as if he were a novelty. "Tell me, my dear."

Niko saw his parents stir and he shot them a warning glance. They knew him in that mood so kept silent, but the mockery and disappointment in their faces still had the power to wound him.

Kavi knelt at the Vice-King's feet and Jacom touched his long silken hair as if intrigued.

"The Mage means no harm to your people, my lord. He merely wanted to save his child from that monster, Danul," Kavi told him in gentle tones.

Jacom bowed his head in thought. "Corha, what do you think?"

Niko watched her, knowing the influence she had with her father.

"Niko, does the Mage mean so much to you?"

He held her eyes. "Corha." He stopped and let his pain show. "Corha, he's taken Toma's place in my heart. He's become my brother."

"Oh." Corha's sweet face reflected Niko's sorrow. The three of them had been children together.

"Father, please let the Mage go, if it matters so much to Niko. I think we have done wrong to listen to Mazzo and this man Danul." She spat the names as if they were distasteful.

Niko's mother gasped in outrage, but an irritated glance from the Vice-King silenced her.

"As you wish, my love." He turned to Kavi and took his hand. "You may have him."

Kavi didn't speak, but his bow from the waist was deep and formal, and the tears glistening on his face were answer enough. Jacom smiled, seaming pleased to have made him happy.

Niko hesitated, then abruptly moved to Corha's side to kneel at her chair. He bowed over her hands and began to kiss them over and over. She gently removed them from his clasp, ran a hand through his crisp hair, then raised his face.

"Is he very like Toma?" she asked.

He nodded. "The very same, in his kindness, courage, and gentle spirit. Corha, will you come to us soon and meet him?"

Niko let his love show in his eyes, and she nodded, touching his cheek, her smile shy.

THE SUN GLARED off the white bricks of the courtyard and sent stabs of pain through Natan's closed lids. He found himself alone, although occasionally the murmur of voices would reach him then fade into the distance. Not like yesterday, when there were voices all around him and unkind hands when someone would brave to touch him.

They had dragged him across the courtyard, stripped him to the waist, then shackled him to a stake with his arms stretched above his head. Soldiers had beaten him, and he supposed they would have killed him outright for being a sorcerer, if superstition raised by the scar on his chest hadn't kept them from it. Bad luck to kill a man with a diseased mind.

Natan's laugh was a croak in his parched throat. They intended to let the elements do the job for them. He'd shivered in the freezing cold during the night and now the sun seemed determined to bake the life from him. He winced at a pang of hunger, but that pain he could ignore. He'd been hungry before. It was the desperate thirst that could drive a man insane. A grim smile split his cracked lips.

His mind wandered in the afternoon heat, and he went over his every decision since leaving Belega, quickly determining he'd made many mistakes. But he could find no trace of madness in his actions. Would he, though, if he looked deeper? His thoughts kept returning to the suspicion in Kavi's eyes when he'd looked at him, and at last he hung his head in defeat. If Kavi believed him mad then surely he must be.

His eyes filled with tears. "I'm sorry, Gregor," he whispered as sorrow touched his soul. He'd failed his mentor. He thought of Bryon and knew how disappointed he'd also be. "I'm sorry, Father." Dry sobs wracked him. He could no longer feel the hurt of his tortured body from the anguish in his heart.

Natan flinched when fingers brushed his face, and he stiffened for the blow. Instead, a flask was pressed to his lips and drops of glorious water trickled on his swollen tongue. When the flask was withdrawn, he threw his head back against the stake and fought to slow his hard breathing. He knew he had to wait a moment for more of the life-giving liquid, but every second brought agony. At last, he was allowed a few more swallows.

The chain rattled above his head, and suddenly his arms were free. He fell heavily to the ground, jarring his knees, but strong arms went around him as he was helped to his feet. Someone muttered in his ear, but he still felt dazed and couldn't make out the words. He tried to open his eyes, but the fierce light stabbed at him again. He was guided to a horse, helped to mount, so he lay along the horse's neck and threaded fingers through its mane. His rescuer climbed behind him, and they began to move at a fast trot.

Natan gave himself to the motion of the horse, having no fear of falling. In fact, he had no fear of anything. He felt numb and confused. No doubt he should know the people with him, but he couldn't think clearly. Unable to catch his breath, he panted against the hot pelt of the animal under him.

Hours passed, or maybe an eternity. Natan sat up suddenly, thinking he heard water, and the person with him caught him as his head swam dizzily. He swallowed a ragged breath when the horse turned toward the sound.

A river and waterfall appeared through the trees. Natan slipped from the animal before it had completely halted. He staggered to the sandy bank and watched the beautiful water fall from a high cliff into a pool far below his feet. The water shone clear and clean in the bright sun. With sudden loathing he stripped the filthy garments from his body and leaped, plunging feet first into the icy pool, the cold rush of water sharp knives along his skin.

Surfacing, he swam to the bank and sat in the shallow water lapping the shore. Scooping up the fine sand, he scrubbed his body free of the dirt, blood, and filth clinging to it. He worked the sand through his lank hair and continued over as much of his back as he could reach, unmindful of the fresh blood he drew from the welts. When satisfied, he dove once again into the pool, then dragged his shivering body onto a low rock overhanging the river. He wrapped his arms around his knees, content to let the sun begin to warm him.

"Thank you," he chattered through blue lips when Niko appeared and placed a blanket around his shoulders.

Niko sat on the rock beside him and opened his pack. "Can you eat?"

"Yes," he said with surprise as he took the offered bread and cheese in his shaking hands. He managed a few mouthfuls, then turned his head until the sharp pains in his stomach subsided.

Niko passed him the water skin, then opened the pack again and drew out clean pants and a tunic. "Put these on and come to the fire," he commanded, his voice rough.

"As you wish." Natan looked at him but then quickly averted his face, not wanting Niko to see the madness lurking in his gaze and become afraid. He avoided Kavi as much as possible when he joined them at the fire. Shame burned in him, and he couldn't bring himself to speak to him, much as he longed to. He couldn't bear to see contempt in Kavi's eyes. Fear would be worse.

If they would only let him be. They were kind and gentle with him. It warmed his heart to see the children safe by the fire. But they didn't know to fear him. The madness was growing. He could feel it. Visions of pain and blood and death were coming with more frequency. A voice began to mutter in his thoughts, a whispery voice that spoke of insanity, despair, and the suffering and death of his friends. Deaths he would be responsible for.

They began the journey home in the morning, while the voice became a rustle along Natan's spine until he clutched his head and buried his face in his horse's mane. He trembled as the voice plucked at his nerves. He wanted to go home, back to Belega and his little cabin where he could be alone. His friends watched him anxiously, quickened their pace, but Mennon was a two days' ride, and an empty house and Aubre's burial awaited him.

Chapter Twenty-Six

SYROS LET OUT a relieved breath when they arrived safely in Barkuit on their second day after departing Siagan. They quitted the horses at the stable and Jaden and Bryon wearily followed him through the city. Tables were set in the sun where they ate a much-needed meal in near silence. Afterward, they gathered in Commander Brendan's room.

Syros bent over the prostrate man. "How are you, sir?"

Brendan's eyelids flickered open, and though his body remained emaciated with suffering, there was a glitter in the depths of his eyes that spoke of resolution. Jaden put a hand on his arm while Syros glanced a question at Kirstin across the bed, tucked against Bryon's side.

"He'll live, but it will take time for his body to heal," she told them.

Jaden cleared his rough throat. "That's good to hear." He tightened a fist. "Wish we'd found Camron."

"We will," Bryon muttered, anger in his voice. He gripped his commander's hand, his face working. They stayed only a moment so as not to exhaust Brendan further and were returning to the courtyard when Kirstin suddenly stumbled.

Bryon helped her to a bench and took her shaking hands. "What is it?"

Her face had grown white, an unfocused look entering her eyes. She tilted her head, listening.

"Kavi?" she whispered. "I thought I heard him the other day, but this is much clearer." She scrambled to her feet with a soft cry. "It's the Mage! He needs me, now." She looked around in a panic as if she meant to start for him that instant.

Syros touched her hand. "A moment, my lady. Let me see when our next ship sails for Sennia. Is Natan injured?"

"Yes…no. I'm not sure. Kavi's thoughts are a jumble of confusion and a terrible fear for the Mage." She looked at Bryon with stricken eyes. "We may lose him."

"We won't," Syros put in, refusing to believe it.

While Kirstin packed, Syros met with his council leader. He frowned as he listened to Caleb's report, glancing up as Kirstin entered the council chamber with Bryon. He finished his softly spoken instructions and Caleb bowed, then exited the room. Syros beckoned the couple over.

"There's a schooner leaving from Kangar's harbor tomorrow at noon," he told them. "We'll have to do some hard riding to catch it."

"Thank you." Kirstin placed a hand on his arm. "I sense it's hard for you to return there."

His mood darkened at her words, but he gave her a slight bow. "Some painful memories I need to put aside. Shall we leave?"

As they rode swiftly, Syros developed a grudging admiration for Bryon and his lady. He'd always considered Nagal soldiers to be weak and the Karthagans soft. But they kept up, despite the hard pace, with one short rest for the horses. He would have to change his views. They arrived in Kangar on time for the ship, though thoroughly exhausted. Bryon held Kirstin close to his heart and kissed her with passion before he let her go.

"Bryon, I'll be all right." She caressed his troubled face. "I love you."

"Do you want me to go with you?"

"No." She traced his lips with her fingers. "You're too distracting. Besides, Kavi's there to meet me."

"Take care of yourself." They embraced then Bryon helped her into the waiting dory. She was rowed to the schooner, and he had tears in his eyes as the ship took sail, headed for the horizon.

Syros watched him from where he perched on a piling on the edge of the dock and jumped restlessly to his feet. He hadn't been to Kangar for over a year, not counting his brief halt to see Kavi on his way. It was past time for a tour of inspection.

The city gleamed. The council leader had to be commended. Syros went up the white steps of the manor house, knowing Ardan preferred to work in his courtyard instead of the council rooms near the center of town. He followed the porch to the right, then hesitated at the courtyard's gate. His face settled into a cold mask, and he entered the yard with a sharp knock.

Ardan sat at a long table perusing several city maps. A scowl crossed his face on seeing him.

"Regent." Ardan rose and bowed, his mocking glance burning Syros's heart.

"I wanted to pay my respects, Ardan, while I'm in the city. Kangar is as beautiful as ever."

"Thank you. Was there anything else?"

Anger flicked through Syros. He almost spoke, but the door to the house opened and Sharana walked into the sunlight. He couldn't recall his words. He'd forgotten how lovely she was. Her dark hair hung loosely around her rosy face. She stopped dead at the sight of him, but he turned away before the contempt reached her blue eyes.

"I didn't know you had company, Father." Her low voice thrummed through Syros's body. "I'll come back later."

"No need, my lady. I was just going." Syros bowed stiffly and moved toward the gate.

"I'm surprised you came back at all, Syros."

He halted at her words. Ardan looked from him to his daughter's fuming expression and excused himself. Syros unclenched his hands, then with a sudden swift movement, went to her side. His heart raced as he looked down at her flushed face. "You'll never forgive me, will you?"

She jumped at his harsh voice. "Syros, you stole money from my father and let another man take the blame for it."

"I owned up to it, didn't I?" He knew he'd made a mistake when her face hardened.

"After he'd been imprisoned for two weeks. You'd better go, Syros. Don't come back."

"Wait, please," he asked softly, taking her hands when she paused. He leaned his forehead on hers but didn't dare look in her eyes. "I loved you, Sharana. I still do. How long will you make me suffer for a mistake I've regretted every day we've been apart?"

"I don't know." She pulled her hands from his shaking ones. "I loved you too, but I can't give my heart without trust."

"I suppose not." His laugh was bitter. He gave her a low bow and walked away. With his thoughts turned inward, it hardly registered that he passed Bryon on the street. Then he sighed, wrenching his mind to the problems at hand. First Kavi had gone to Sennia and now Kirstin, two Karthagans of power. And the third, Camron, was lost somewhere in Siagan. The Mage needed to come home to help set things right.

Chapter Twenty-Seven

DARK SPOTS SWAM in Cecil's eyes as the council leader's hold on his throat tightened. He'd been watching on the stairs for Camron, but must have dozed off, allowing Mandel to catch him where he didn't belong. Afraid, he fought off the blackness swallowing his mind as his lungs screamed for air, not knowing what Mandel might do to him if he passed out.

"Really, Mandel," a voice lisped somewhere in the haze. "Let the boy breathe."

"He and a handful of others are the only ones who know you're in the city, Camron. You should let me kill him."

"Perhaps later. Leave him with me for now."

Mandel struck Cecil viciously in the face so his head snapped back and hit the wall. He sank to his knees, his skull ringing with pain.

Camron's fingers slipped through his hair while Mandel tied his hands behind his back. Camron's raspy voice slithered into Cecil's thoughts. "So pretty." He winced as the Karthagan's thumb stroked his bruised throat. *What did he want?*

"Camron, you shouldn't…"

"Enough, Mandel! I got what I wanted from the lake. It had been too easy. The Mage, so in love he can't think straight, with Kavi dripping just the right amount of self-doubt into that troubled mind. It had been nothing to slip in, confuse Natan, and plant the phantoms I borrowed from our Cecil here."

Cecil shivered and Camron's gaze heated. "Delicious. And if Natan is my strongest enemy, I'll soon have the world, or at least the parts of it that interest me. All that's left for me to do now is take care of a small matter in Karthag, then disappear into the wilderness. No doubt Alek will come after me himself, and I can take care of that problem as well." He gripped Cecil's chin, raising his face. "It might be good to have a hostage…"

He put a hand under Cecil's arm, helping him to stand. Cecil swayed on his feet, dizzy, hardly aware of the cord biting into his wrists. Camron touched his cheek and Cecil stared into his handsome face, caught in the glitter of black, cold eyes.

"Yes, you'll do nicely," Camron purred, then leaned forward to kiss him full on the mouth. Cecil jerked back but the Karthagan stepped with him, pushing him against the cellar wall, plundering his mouth with a darting tongue and hard, cruel lips. Cecil panicked as Mandel bit out a dark oath and left the room with a bang of the door, then choked out a cry as Camron dropped a hand to his groin, rubbing him through his breeches. Surely he wouldn't…

Camron chuckled, tightening his hold, stroking him up and down. Pain and pleasure slammed through Cecil's body. He desperately shoved against Camron, trying to throw him off. He screamed as the man bit his lip, simultaneously crushing his balls in his hand, and grew faint from the pain, sobbing in a lungful of air.

Camron eased his grip. "Let go," he murmured against Cecil's ear, his breath cool on his sweating skin. "No one here will help you. And you may find pleasures with me you've never experienced. Fight me, and I'll kill you where you stand."

Cecil hung his head as Camron slipped his hand inside his clothing. He closed his mind to what he did, shivering as Camron brought him to that exquisite pinnacle of orgasm. Cecil hovered on the edge, thrusting unconsciously into Camron's hand. And then he was over, and soaring…and cried out in agony as a nightmare burst into his mind, bodies floating in an icy lake, mutilated, staring at him with horrible eyes as they shrieked his name with bloodied lips.

With a moan, he slipped to his knees, bewildered, lost. Camron would call up Cecil's nightmares again and again until there was nothing else. He jumped when Camron touched his shoulder, urging him up. "Time to go, love. Mandel has horses at the gate, but I don't trust him to wait forever."

Cecil hesitated. Camron's hand dropped to his belt knife, and alone and friendless, Cecil followed him from the room. Siagan's streets were nearly deserted in the evening hours. Although a few citizens watched them curiously, they knew Cecil and let them be. Camron secured the horses from Mandel and walked unmolested out of the gates, crossing the clearing to the forest.

"Come." He disappeared into the trees without a backward glance. A shudder ran through Cecil's slim body. Flushed with shame, he followed. Once under the fragrant branches, Camron had Cecil mount, then tied his wrists to the saddle horn.

"Can't have you running off," Camron murmured and gave Cecil's thigh a squeeze before climbing into his own saddle. He guided them to a narrow trail, then laid heels to his mount. The horses sprang forward, the path leading them deeper into the forest. All too soon, the journey became one long torment for Cecil, bound as he was to the saddle. He was unable to rest for fear of slipping off the moving animal and being crushed under its pounding hooves.

The days slipped one into another, unending pain. Yet as bad as the days became, he dreaded the nights more, filled with Camron's lust and nightmares. Time and again Camron would bring him to sobbing orgasm, only to send visions of mutilation and death at the peak. The act that had once brought him such pleasure now left him in anguish, despairing.

They spent a final long day in travel, with Camron laughing mockingly as he pulled his horse to a stop on the hill overlooking Karthag. Cecil shivered at the rustling sound as he drew rein beside him. There remained an hour until dusk, and Camron smiled in the crooked way that made Cecil feel cold. "Are you ready?"

"Yes, sir." Cecil dismounted and picketed the horses, not sure why he was there. He should have stayed in Siagan. He should have stayed at home! He'd left Kangar in anger for service in Siagan, and he'd give his life to see his mother again, beg his father's forgiveness. It was unlikely now. The nightmares were growing worse, and he felt lost and bewildered, following the cruel Karthagan.

Camron was watching him and Cecil started as Camron touched his face, placing his fingers beside his eyes. "Peace," Camron whispered, and the phantoms gathered in a gray mist and dissipated from Cecil's mind. His thoughts were clear for the first time in days. The coil of fear unwound from his spine to slither out his mouth in a harsh breath. He gripped Camron's hands and kissed them, his tears falling on the olive skin.

"It's time to go."

Cecil nodded and hurried from him.

Darkness was creeping into Karthag's streets as he carefully made his way to the redwood at the heart of the city. Camron had told him the children would be waiting, but his heart faltered at every stray sound. Pausing at the low wall encircling the tree, he peered into the gloom. He drew back at the sight of the boys, then laughed shakily. They were only children, after all. But one stood proud and the other…his golden eyes…

A sob caught in Cecil's throat. His nightmares had become real. "The Red Twins," he moaned and didn't know he spoke aloud.

"Is our cousin Camron with you?" the proud one asked, his voice merely curious.

Cecil let out his breath. They were only children. "Yes. Will you come?" He held out his hand. The boy came close and took it.

"I'm Aiden," he confided as he pulled his brother beside him. "This is Ethan."

Cecil looked into Ethan's vague eyes and shuddered. Is that what he would become, a hollow shell behind which he hid from the frightening world? He thought it very likely.

"Tell me, Aiden," Cecil asked as they walked into the night. "How did you know to meet me?"

"Ethan knew," Aiden said, and Cecil feared to ask anything more. He found it easy to leave the city. The few soldiers on the wall glanced at them, their eyes blank.

Deep in the night, Cecil sat on the soft moss of the forest floor against a rock near where Camron slept and sucked absently at a cut on his lip. The forest was quiet, Camron's soft breathing and that of the boys nearby somehow soothed his taught nerves. He despaired suddenly of ever escaping from the Karthagan. He'd slipped from him twice since his capture, only to have Camron track him through the endless forest and beat him senseless, nearly killing him the last time.

Exhausted, he laid his head back against the hard stone, dozing, then suddenly he jerked awake, staring into the dark night. "Hello?"

"Don't be afraid," a gentle voice uttered, bringing peace, though Cecil knew the words were in his head. The image of a beautiful man, a Karthagan, filled his sight, tall, his dark hair gleaming in the moonlight. The apparition knelt beside him. "I'm Alek. Don't despair. I won't give up on you."

Camron stirred at that moment, and Cecil stifled his distress as the vision left him even as Camron reached for him in the dark.

"What are you doing?" Camron asked with suspicion.

"I didn't want to disturb you."

Camron smiled in the soft light and pulled Cecil's head against his shoulder. "I wouldn't have minded," he murmured then lifted Cecil's hair, watching in obvious delight as the moonlight glinted off the fair strands. Cecil made no answer and Camron lowered his head. "You're so lovely," he whispered in Cecil's ear with possessive pride.

Cecil held himself ready as Camron shifted position, pressed his mouth to his, and ran his hands over Cecil's bruised and hurting body. Then the Karthagan's touch became cruel once more. Cecil's heart broke as he endured the dark time while Camron used his body. Pain and pleasure and horrific visions were a jumbled chaos in his mind, leaving him spent and weeping when Camron finally turned from him. Cecil sat numbly in the dirt as he felt his mind going…

He startled awake. He must have dozed again, but it was morning and he had to see to the horses. It was a hard climb to his feet, a struggle with the saddle straps, leaving his hands shaking with his exhaustion. Camron soon joined him, mounting his horse and taking Ethan in front of him without a glance at Cecil. Cecil pulled himself onto the back of his roan, lifted Aiden, and followed Camron along the obscure trail. Camron had won. He wouldn't try to escape again.

Chapter Twenty-Eight

THE WIND BLEW in Kirstin's face, her silken hair streaming in the sunshine. Breathing in the tangy sea air, for one brief moment she felt as she were flying as the schooner crested the high waves and came into Mennon's harbor. She understood completely Natan's love of the sea.

She scanned the dock. There he was, Kavi's tired face standing out in the crowd of bustling men. Kavi embraced her as she came up to him.

"It's good to have you here," he murmured but was obviously distracted, his thoughts elsewhere. "How's Bryon?" he asked politely as they walked into the city.

"Probably getting himself into trouble." Kirstin shook off her stray concerns. "Where's our Mage?"

"Natan's—" Kavi's voice broke.

Kirstin glanced around and pulled her cousin to a secluded bench under towering maple trees. "Tell me."

Kavi began haltingly, confessing how he'd deceived Natan, tricked him into believing the madness of the Karthagans had overcome him. A strange vagueness came into his voice as he spoke and Kirstin searched his eyes.

"May I?" she asked as she touched his temple.

Kavi looked startled but then nodded. Kirstin closed her eyes, gathering her strength. Intense pain flashed through her, but then she was in Kavi's mind and swiftly found the cause of his conflicted thoughts.

She rose to her feet in horror. "Camron!"

Kavi stood swiftly, and they stared at each other. Kavi swore as fury overcame him. "He used me," he said and paced rapidly.

"Yes, he did." A shiver ran through Kirstin. "Kavi, where's Natan?"

Kavi's face blanched. "He's on the beach," he whispered.

Kirstin hurried along the shore and found the Mage watching the waves break on the sand. He made no move as she sat down beside him. Her heart grieved. Where was her merry friend, the young man who'd given her a shy kiss and teasingly called her Mother when she promised to marry Bryon? This man crouched listlessly on the sand with his unruly chestnut hair hiding his eyes from the world. She brushed the hair from Natan's face and turned him to her. The bleakness in his eyes unnerved her.

She leaned her forehead against his. "Will you let me in?"

"Aren't you afraid?" He laughed harshly but didn't resist as her thoughts entered his mind. He shuddered and Kirstin sympathized with him, remembering the crawling sensation of the contact. She drew a quick breath at the brilliance of his spirit. The wonder and awe and joy in which Natan held life was that of a child, and his compassion burned. Yet even as she watched, Natan's light dimmed to a dark shadow that fled before her own light. She followed. The paths of his mind were many and intricate. She could feel the extremes of happiness and great sadness in the various branches. The shadow led her to a doorway opening onto blackness. She hesitated a moment. Despair was in there. She plunged in.

The smell of earth and damp decay closed around her, the cry of her dying people echoing in the cavern on the far side of the cell door. Death was with her. She felt thirst and hunger and fear. Despair and insanity lurked on the edge of her mind.

But no, Bryon had come and released her with his courage, humor, and gentleness. His love had kept her from madness. Kirstin laughed in the sudden joy of that love, and the cell dissolved. She stood alone with Natan in an empty room. His head was bowed. She raised his face with gentle hands and his eyes were coals. Kirstin pushed deeper into his mind. There it was, the rustle of a voice, dry leaves whispering the twisted words of madness and pain, fear and blood.

"These are Camron's words, Natan," Kirstin told him. "Thoughts from his dark mind. His own phantoms, borrowed from others. They were never yours."

"Look," she whispered, and in her hand appeared a flame as clear as crystal. "This is your spirit. See how pure and bright it burns? There is no taint in it, no madness. Be free, Natan!"

She watched his face with tentative hope.

NATAN LOOKED AT the white flame of his life and a strange awe filled him. He felt humbled, knowing he could be more than he was. With that acceptance, Camron's hold on him broke. Tears stung his eyes, and he lifted

Kirstin's hand to his lips, finding words inadequate. She smiled through her own tears, and they were sitting once again on the beach.

Kirstin leaned and kissed the corner of his mouth. "Be at peace," she told him.

Natan gave her a crooked smile, the warmth of a blush in his face.

"Should Bryon be worried?" Kavi asked as he came up and settled comfortably on the sand across from them. Mirah was with him and sat cross-legged beside Natan.

Natan looked at her closely for any signs of lingering poison. "How are you feeling?" he queried, realizing he should have asked the question days ago.

"I'm well, Mage." She squeezed his hand. "Father sent me to bring you to dinner. We're at Aunt Aubre's tonight."

"Thank you," Natan said gratefully, knowing she and her father had remained in Mennon to be close by, in case...in case he broke down completely. He hated that Camron's hold over him had been so strong. They walked as a group to the house, with Natan's heart skipping when Kavi kept close to his side. Tolban had the children there, and their joy at being with their Papa again tore Natan's heart. He must have been mad indeed to stay away from them.

Niko and Mika joined them as the sun was setting, and they sat on the back porch long into the night, Niko keeping them laughing with his absurd stories. Kavi nestled in Natan's arms, though they hadn't talked like they needed to. One by one the company trailed into the house and sought their beds, until Natan was left alone under the stars. He'd touched Kavi's hand when Kavi had bidden him goodnight, but Kavi had turned away, not ready to speak of what had happened between them. Natan wanted to reassure him that all was well, but Kavi's very silence made him shy from it.

He felt lonely so rose and went inside. No one lingered in the kitchen as he passed through it on his way to check on the children, and he told himself he was glad. The children slept, their faces beautiful in the candlelight, but instead of the quiet happiness he usually felt on seeing them, the sadness of loss touched him. He hurried from them to Aubre's room, which he was using for the night. Lighting a candle on a low table, he flung into a chair by the window and pressed his forehead to the cold glass.

He was overtired, he knew, but grief flowed through him for the life he might never have. He'd dreamed of Kavi living with him, of Kavi and the children being his family. That joy seemed as far away as ever. Natan ached, closing his burning eyes as the long night began and the empty years stretched before him.

The urgent knocking on his door had been going on for some time before he roused enough to respond. "Kavi?" He rubbed at his gritty eyes.

"Will you come?"

The anxiety in Kavi's voice woke him fully, and he followed without a word. Kavi had lit several candles in the room he led Natan to, where Natan found Kirstin tossing restlessly as if with a fever, muttering unintelligible words, bathed in sweat. He knelt by the bed and touched her face. To his relief it felt cool. He leaned closer and called her name. She grew still at his voice, but then shied away from him with a pitiable cry. Natan saw the dark paths of her dreams. They filled him with sorrow.

"Wake up, dearest." He brushed the wet hair from her face and stroked her cheek with a trembling hand as his spirit reached for hers. She drew a deep breath, stirring from sleep, and he moved from the bed to stare out the window as he waited for her to wake completely. He pushed the shutter open a little farther. The cold mist felt good on his face.

Kavi knelt by the bed and took Kirstin's hands. She drew another quick breath, then her eyes fluttered open. With a cry she scrambled from the blankets to join Natan by the window.

She gripped his arm. "You saw?"

He glanced at her unwillingly and nodded, a nightmare moving behind his eyes, of violence and death.

"What is it?" Kavi asked. Kirstin waited, but Natan turned back to the window, losing himself in the darkness outside to escape the black turmoil within.

"Camron calls us," Kirstin said with dread.

"We leave for Belega in the morning," Natan added through gritted teeth.

NATAN STOOD ON the foredeck of the schooner and let the ocean spray cool his hot face. They'd been at sea four days while the driving compulsion within him brought tears of impatience to his eyes. He needed to be in Belega, now! He'd dreamed of Camron again as he slept on the deck last night under the stars. The man's dark hair streamed in a wild wind as he gathered all the forces of nature to him. Camron took them in, and the madness within him spread out to Belega and Sennia, and on, until all the world was engulfed in chaos, war, and death. Even now in the bright sunlight Natan felt sick with dread. He didn't know where the man was, let alone how to stop him.

"You're awake," Niko observed as he joined him at the rail, putting a hand on his shoulder. "Doesn't matter that your moaning and tossing in the night kept the rest of us up. As long as *you* slept."

Natan shook off his dark mood, grateful for Niko's teasing in an effort to cheer him. "You insisted on coming with us," he reminded his friend with a smile.

Niko shrugged. "Tolban, not to mention Mirah and the children, would have had my head if I hadn't."

Natan sobered and looked at the gray rolling waves of the sea. It had been hard to say goodbye to Kayle and Tillie at the harbor when Gregor's memories of farewell had mixed with his own.

"Still, you didn't need to come," he repeated. "I go because I'm called. And I'm going home. You should return with the ship."

Niko gave him a close look. "You know, friend, that power of yours is turning out to be quite tiresome. Sending you here and there without a thought of the inconvenience to your friends." He watched the sea and Natan smiled fondly as Niko began humming a familiar song.

Hearing him, a nearby sailor took up the words and soon others joined in. They'd taken at once to the merry young man but sensed a dark turmoil in Natan that kept them at a polite distance with him. He missed the easy comradeship he'd shared with the sailors on his first voyage, but he didn't begrudge the men their wariness of him. Men feared what they didn't understand. Perhaps that's why he carried so much fear inside himself.

A cry went up. Belega had been sighted. They would reach the continent within hours, and unexpected excitement filled Natan on seeing his homeland. He was anxious to see his friends as well. Footsteps sounded behind him, causing a tremor to run through him. He'd know that sure tread anywhere.

"Good morning," he said, and cleared the gruffness from his voice, his focus on Kavi's slim fingers as Kavi gripped the rail beside him.

"Did you sleep?"

He turned and Kavi captured his gaze, the concern in his dark eyes shaking Natan to his core. Did Kavi care? His heart squeezed. How could he love Kavi so deeply if Kavi wasn't meant to be his? Doubt flooded him while he looked back at the sea before he gave himself away.

"A little," he answered dismissively, then went on, "It will be dangerous for you and Kirstin in Belega. Promise me you'll walk carefully. Stay safe."

"And you, Nattie?"

Warmth flooded Natan at the intimacy in Kavi's voice, calling up moments of shared fondness and pleasure. He drew a deep breath, trying to calm his racing heart, then widened his eyes as a sudden clarity of thought came to him, and his role as the Mage settled firmly on his shoulders. He stepped into the role meant for him.

"They can no longer hurt me," he said. He felt Kavi's startled gaze but refused to look at him. Kavi had no need to witness his despair. He'd never wanted this responsibility.

The afternoon passed with him, Niko, and Kavi working alongside the sailors to bring the ship safely into Kangar's harbor. Kirstin joined them once the schooner landed, having spent the time on board with the ship's doctor. Natan bowed in his grave way to the captain and thanked him for a safe voyage. The captain nodded, but Natan saw him make the sign to avert evil as they left the ship.

The quay was unusually quiet, but then Natan looked up from his preoccupation in alarm as soldiers approached. Niko moved in front of him, hand on his knife, but Natan shook his head. It was too late for that. Any move on their part would only bring danger to the Karthagans with them.

The soldiers halted and the nearest one addressed Natan. "You're to come with us."

"Why are you detaining us? We're simply travelers on our way home," Natan queried, knowing it would make no difference.

The guard looked at Kavi and Kirstin and narrowed his eyes. "Given a choice… But your companions weren't mentioned and can go. You are to be brought before Council Leader Ardan immediately."

"As you wish." Natan sketched a bow. Niko swore, clearly wanting to try his blade against theirs. Natan touched his arm. "Please see Kavi and Kirstin safely to Barkuit. I'll find out what Ardan wants and meet you there."

The Karthagans remained silent, though Natan saw the glitter in their eyes. Fear shook him for what they might do, especially when the northern soldiers dropped a hand to their weapons. "Kirstin, please go. Tell Syros what is happening here."

Kavi stepped up to him. "We'll leave." His eyes flashed when he looked at the guard. "See that I needn't return for him."

"I'll keep him safe," Niko promised Kavi, ignoring Natan's frown and his demand that Niko go with the others. Kirstin inclined her head.

Kavi touched Natan's face, startling him. "We'll do this your way, for now. But if any harm comes to you…" His words trailed off, but Natan saw the soldiers shiver once again at his fierce glance in their direction. Kavi picked up Natan's hand, kissing his knuckles. "Goodbye," he murmured, and he and Kirstin started for the stables. Natan's heart ached as he watched them, then turned reluctantly to follow Niko and the guardsmen to the council chambers.

Council Leader Ardan strode up and down the long room when they arrived, his anger growing with every step. Finally, Ardan stopped in front of him, a scowl on his handsome face.

"I'm sorry, my lord Mage," he said with a low bow, much to Natan's surprise. "I have my orders from Landlan, a leading councilman in Barkuit. He's demanded that if you were ever to come to Kangar, I was to send you to him, no delay." Arden rifled some papers on his desk and pulled a missive out of the stack.

"His exact words: Bind his hands so he can't weave a spell. Stop his mouth so he can speak no evil. Blind his eyes so he can't kill with a look." Ardan gave him a doubtful glance. Natan had gone cold at the word blind.

"Well enough." The council leader threw down the paper with disgust and beckoned the guards. "Bind and gag the prisoner and throw a sack over his head. That's as close to blinding a man as I'll ever come."

Natan submitted quietly as his wrists were restrained at his back with a leather cord and a thick strap was shoved in his mouth. He winced as it opened old sores from his time as the Vice-King's prisoner.

The rough sack went over his head and Ardan swore violently. "Forgive me, but that jackal Landlan has my daughter, Sharana."

Niko shifted impatiently. "What do you intend to do now?" he sneered.

"I'll send him to Barkuit, of course. What else? Then my daughter will be returned safely to me. I must do this. You, on the other hand,

Landlan made no mention of. You may go."

"I go with the Mage," Niko said stubbornly.

"As you wish," Ardan said. "Let Landlan choke on that."

Rough hands gripped Natan as he was led once again outside. They lifted him to a saddle and the horse moved at a pull on its lead rope. Natan clung desperately with his knees, at last lying against the animal's neck to keep from falling. He gave himself up to the motion of the horse and managed to gather snatches of sleep as the day proceeded into an interminable night.

He lost track of time, finally jolting awake with a cry as he felt himself falling, landing with a thud on the hard ground.

A harsh voice laughed. "Morning."

"Leave off." He heard Niko threaten, then caring hands helped him sit up.

"Close your eyes," Niko warned and gently lifted the sack off his head. Blinking several times, Natan slowly opened his eyes then drew a sharp breath. The forest appeared incredibly beautiful in the dim morning light with the first rays of the sun touching high in the treetops.

Niko scowled with impatience. "How can you bear this?" He motioned to the rough soldiers and the sack at his feet. "Why don't you call the lightning from the sky or have the earth open up and take these filthy men? You said they couldn't hurt you."

Natan looked at him, for an instant his anger kindling at the abuse from the Barkuit soldiers. Then he shrugged and drew up his knees, resting his forehead against them. His life wasn't in danger. He wished he could tell Nico that.

Niko swore under his breath and got out his water flask. It was hard for Natan to swallow the blessed liquid with the leather strap in his mouth, but Niko was patient and let the water trickle onto his tongue until he had his fill. Dust and blood dripped off his chin into the dirt. Niko moistened a strip of cloth and wiped his face.

"Remind me to never have children," Niko said, and Natan choked on an involuntary laugh. He gave Niko a grateful look then motioned to the sack. The Barkuit soldiers had shown more patience than he'd have thought, but he didn't want to test their limits.

At that moment, a large man strode up and hauled Natan to his feet. He jerked the sack back over his head and flung him into his saddle.

The day passed in long hours of weariness and pain for Natan. The sun grew hot as the afternoon advanced, and the sack began to stifle him. The air became thick, difficult to draw in, until he longed for just a hint of breeze on his face. Sweat stung his eyes. He grew faint as his thirst increased, but he finally gave it all up and went to sleep.

All too soon, someone shook him awake and seized his arms, pulling him from the saddle. Hearing voices around him, Natan panicked, thinking he was back with Mazzo and they were leading him to the fire. A hard blow to his face staggered him and he fell to his knees, tasting blood. He tried to stand on legs grown numb. A knee in his side sent him sprawling in the dirt, and he choked on the dust that filled the air. What did they want him to do?

Their harsh laughter reached his ears and he took a calming breath, willing his heart to slow. They were making sport of the prisoner. He dragged himself to his feet and stood swaying in the blackness of the sack, awaiting their pleasure. It wasn't long in coming. A fierce jab in the ribs stole his breath, and he dropped to a knee, fighting for consciousness as he struggled for breath. He feared what they might do to his unconscious body.

They'd yanked him to his feet again when a cold voice intruded. "What goes on here?"

The men fell silent and Natan could hear them move back to let the person through. The icy voice spoke from his side, familiar. The regent, Syros. "Who is this?"

"We're bringing him to the council chamber. Landlan wants him," an insolent voice answered from the crowd.

Natan jumped as a hand touched his arm. "Come with me. I'll find out what this is about."

He heard the anger simmering in Syros's low tones, boding ill for the soldiers around them. The regent led him into the coolness of a building and down so many passages and stairways that Natan's aching head lost all sense of direction. They suddenly halted. Syros spoke to a guard, a door opened, and Syros took Natan's arm once more, leading him through the doorway.

"Regent Syros with a prisoner," the guardsman announced. A curious murmur rose from what sounded like a crowd to Natan.

Syros swore violently and called the council leader to his side. "Caleb, what is that fool Landlan up to?" Natan heard his controlled fury and appreciated he wasn't the target of his anger.

"I'm not sure," a troubled voice answered. "Landlan called us to assemble, as is any council member's prerogative, but he gave no reason for it."

Rough hands suddenly seized Natan and dragged him farther into the room.

"What do we have here?" a hated voice drawled before the sack was ripped off Natan's head. Intense sunlight struck his eyes, for a moment making him feel truly blind.

"Natan, my lad. How good of you to visit," Landlan taunted. Natan blinked rapidly to clear his eyes, then glared at the familiar figure.

Landlan mocked him. "There, there. I missed you too." He patted Natan's cheek. A sly smile touched his face at a commotion in the hallway. Natan took advantage of his distraction to look over the room. Barkuit soldiers and civilians ranged the long hall. He chewed his lips, dismayed, when he caught sight of Kirstin's indignant face in the crowd. Kavi stood by her side, his beautiful eyes shooting daggers at Landlan's tall frame.

A hiss drew Natan's attention, and he found Niko standing several steps away. An ugly gash bloodied his friend's forehead, but otherwise he appeared unharmed. Natan tried to smile but the cord at his mouth bit into his flesh.

"Out of the way!" a voice shouted in the doorway. Natan turned in disbelief as Captain Bryon stormed into the room.

Landlan drew a satisfied breath. "Ah, Bryon, my friend. Welcome. I was just about to question the prisoner. Your arrival is excellent."

"Natan." Bryon leaped forward.

Landlan lifted a hand and a soldier drew his sword to place it against Natan's back, effectively halting Bryon midstep.

"Good." Landlan smiled. He turned and struck Natan savagely across the face. He struck him twice more, laughing when the guards had to restrain Bryon.

Natan's head rang. He knew Landlan was speaking, but he couldn't seem to focus on the words. The hand that struck him gently touched his face, confusing him further.

"Don't cry, my lad." Landlan wiped Natan's tears with his thumb. "I haven't even begun to hurt you." He leaned close so only Natan could hear him. "You've interfered with me for the last time." Natan followed his look across the room, fear stabbing his heart when he met Kavi's intent gaze on them.

"Yes, I see him too," Landlan whispered in his ear, sending a shiver through him. "When I'm done with you, I'll take him to Lord Fredrik. Never fear! He'll spill his secrets as easily as his blood before we're through with him." Landlan trailed his hand down Natan's neck and along the collar of his torn shirt. His fingers skimmed the puckered skin of his scar. "What's this?"

Natan jerked back, but with a cry of triumph Landlan tore his shirt to reveal the brand. A breath of surprise escaped him and then a raucous laugh.

"Look, gentlemen!" he roared. "The perfect emblem. I always thought the boy was slightly mad."

Natan hung his head in the complete silence of the room. Shame burned through him. He wished himself anywhere but there. It hurt to know Kavi witnessed his humiliation.

"Ah, Natan, simply perfect." Landlan patted his hot cheek almost fondly. Niko stirred and Landlan turned to the Sennian. "And you? Are you also insane?"

Niko stared at him. "Perhaps," he murmured. A knife suddenly appeared in his hand. Landlan took a step back, but before Natan could say anything, Niko lunged and with a quick slash of the knife, he neatly sliced open Landlan's bare throat. The man fell to the floor, and Natan watched in shock as bright blood spread across the white marble.

"Hold." Syros raised his hand, stopping the guards who were on the point of slaying the prisoner. He stood thoughtfully over Landlan's body.

"Go." He motioned to the guards. "Protect the Governor. The rest of you." He turned to the room. "Go home. It seems we'll have to choose another councilman in the morning."

Nervous laughter answered him as the room slowly emptied.

Niko jumped to Natan's side, slit the bonds on his hands and mouth, then hid the knife back up his sleeve.

Syros turned to them. "Come with me." He led them to a small sitting room off the audience chamber. Niko helped Natan to a low couch as he began to tremble in reaction.

"Could I have some water?" he managed to say. His tongue felt thick while his throat burned.

"Of course. Caleb," Syros motioned to the council leader waiting in the doorway and gave hasty instructions for some food to be brought as well. Spotting Bryon rocking on his heels outside the door, he called him in.

Bryon hurried to join Natan, where he sat limply on the couch.

Natan smiled slightly. "Hello. What are you doing here?"

"I'm with Commander Brendan. Never mind that," Bryon said impatiently, voice thick with concern. "The question is, what are you doing here? Oh lad, what have they done to you?"

"I'm all right now, Father," Natan leaned into his friend's hard embrace. "Did Kirstin find you?"

"She and Kavi are anxious about you."

Natan shook his head, shivering, grateful when Syros draped a blanket over his cold shoulders. "I don't want to see them. I can't face—" Natan stopped, scrambling to collect his scattering thoughts. "I'm sorry. It's been a difficult couple of days."

Syros dropped a hand on his shoulder. "I think our Mage needs to rest, Bryon. Please make his excuses to the others. He'll eat a little then we'll find a quiet room where he can sleep."

"Of course." Bryon squeezed Natan's hand. "We'll see you in the morning."

Natan rubbed his tired eyes. Caleb returned and they ate the spare meal, then he and Niko followed Syros to a room down the hallway where beds had been prepared. Natan tumbled onto his with a mumbled word of thanks to Syros, then fell into a dreamless sleep.

Chapter Twenty-Nine

NIKO KICKED HIS heels on the flour barrel he sat on in the kitchen of the Barkuit castle the next morning and stifled a yawn.

"Rough night?" Kavi inquired dryly from the stove, where he sliced potatoes into a sizzling pan, his gaze straying now and again to Natan, bright with fondness and concern.

"The worst," Niko acknowledged. "First I had this crazy dream that an exotic woman came into my room…"

"As if that would happen," Kavi snorted.

"No, truly. And then I was kept awake by this horrendous snoring. You'd think with all his power, he'd be able to do something about it."

Natan grunted from where he sprawled on a bench in the corner. As much as his body ached, his head felt worse. A messenger had arrived from Karthag during the night with the news that the Red Twins had disappeared the previous week, and Alek had gone after them. Syros swore with heat for the Karthagan's secrecy—they needed to work together, dammit!—and left immediately on their trail, but pleaded for the Mage to follow. Natan winced when Niko jumped off the barrel with a thump and started cracking eggs into the pan Kavi tended on the stovetop.

"So, when do we leave?" he asked the room in general.

"As soon as we've eaten." Niko glanced up at the sound of approaching footsteps. Natan smiled as Bryon and Kirstin entered the room.

Bryon crossed to Niko and gripped his hand. "Sorry I didn't get a chance to speak with you last evening. Thank you for the care you took of the Mage," he said gruffly, then nodded to Kavi. "It's good to see you safe."

Kirstin went to Natan on the bench, and he sat up, stifling a groan.

"Let me see your face," she said matter-of-factly. Natan reluctantly turned to her. Kirstin gently ran her fingers over the bones and swollen features until Natan was thoroughly discomfited.

"You're very lucky nothing is broken," Kirstin assured him. "Landlan didn't hold back. Now let me see your chest." Natan's eyes widened as she began to unlace his tunic. "Don't be silly, boy," she chided, and Natan blushed scarlet. Kirstin carefully examined the puckered tissue of the scar until she finally let out a cautious breath.

"Wonderful. I've seen burns like these fester under the skin, sometimes bringing death."

She glanced at Niko, by the stove. "I believe we have you to thank for the excellent care of our Mage. We're in your debt." She rose and gave Niko a deep curtsy. Niko sputtered and made her an awkward bow in return, reddening under Kavi's chuckle.

The group ate hurriedly, with appetite, Kavi making sure Natan finished his plate. Natan wished they were alone so he could steal a kiss, but it was enough for the moment to have his lover pressed against his side. The council leader joined them presently, Caleb apologizing for the rush. "Camron's been spotted at the border in the Dakon Forest crossing into the far north. Syros plans to join Alek as soon as he can and wants the Mage with them at once, before they come upon Camron, if possible."

On reaching the stables, they found a Nagal soldier holding the horses for them. Natan smiled with pleasure. "Jaden."

"Nattie. I was hoping to see you."

Natan embraced him. "It's good to see you, cousin. I thought you'd be with Governor Basal."

"I've been traveling with Commander Brendan, and the governor now wishes me to accompany you and the others. He would have dispatched an army but feels haste is the better strategy here."

Urged by Bryon, they mounted the horses and rode swiftly over the plains toward the border. They made a short stop at noon to rest the horses and eat. Natan couldn't sit still. He felt that time was running in a tightening spiral toward some horrible end with him helpless to stop it. Waking nightmares formed behind his eyes as the group took to the saddle once more. Camron had grown stronger.

They came to the border the following night, where the commander of the Nagal patrol on duty informed them that Alek had waited for Syros there, and they'd gone in a northeastern direction, following fresh tracks. "Also, Governor Basal has gone to Karthag with a troop to help secure the city until Alek returns. He says you are to ask for anything you may need from him, Mage," the man informed Natan.

Bryon insisted they get some sleep, though the others were for pushing ahead. "You'll be of no use if you're half dead." Natan saw the worry under his scowl. "Now get off those horses. We'll leave at first light."

Natan slid from his horse and fumbled with the girth of his saddle, despairing as phantoms chased through his mind. He jumped at a hand placed on his shoulder.

"Let me do that," Niko told him. He nodded and turned blind eyes to the border camp. Kavi guided him to a small fire where the others had dropped in exhaustion and drew him down on the blankets laid out for them.

"What is it?" Kirstin leaned forward to look into his haunted eyes. She touched his drawn face.

"No." Natan jerked back. "You don't want to see," he assured her. The rotting face rose to the surface of the lake in his mind until it filled all of his vision. No matter how many times he willed it gone, others followed until he feared he'd go mad. He pulled away from Kavi's touch, but Kavi wrapped a blanket around him and pulled him into his arms.

Natan lay stiff against him at first, then with a shuddering breath, relaxed into his embrace as Kavi's fingers soothed his forehead and stroked his damp hair.

"Rest, darling," Kavi murmured, then bent to his ear to whisper sweet words of love and hope. Natan's breathing calmed as he drifted into sleep, although his body twitched as the nightmares chased into his dreams.

He awoke almost immediately, then realized he must have slept longer than the short moment it seemed so sat up, blinking in the early morning sunlight. Someone had replenished the fire, and he stared groggily at the cheery blaze. As the camp bustled around him, he wondered vaguely why no one had roused him.

Gruff laughter caught his attention and he glanced to where Bryon and Jaden jostled each other for the coffeepot at another fire. Apparently, they'd set snares earlier in the morning and had returned with the small game. Natan struggled stiffly to his feet to help with the skinning.

The company ate in relative silence, then once again climbed into the saddle, Jaden leading them on Syros's trail. They crossed into the Northern Territory at its easternmost point, passing Siagan before noon. The trail took them into an area of Belega none of them had seen before, and the beauty of the untouched forest caught Natan's breath. They rode with only short breaks thereafter and came upon Syros's camp in the late evening.

As Natan dismounted, Syros rose from the fire where he'd been sitting with Alek. His greeting was warm but Natan could see a grimness around his mouth and eyes.

Natan bowed to him. "Tell me what has happened."

"Of course, but come and sit down. You're exhausted."

The others dismounted, and then while Niko and Jaden saw to the horses, they moved to the comfort of the fire. Alek stood as they approached, going directly to Kavi. They embraced, though Natan noticed Alek's restless, troubled eyes.

Kavi searched his cousin's face. "What is it?" he asked in concern.

Alek shrugged. "I'm not sleeping well."

"Nightmares?"

Alek startled at Kavi's sharp tone and shifted uncomfortably under their combined gaze.

"The visions aren't mine," he hastened to explain. "But they're always the same. I see a young man, no older than our Mage." He smiled at Natan, whose face heated as all eyes swiveled to him.

"Phantoms move in the lad's eyes," Alek continued. "I try to reassure him we're coming, then suddenly the specters are in my eyes, dead faces rising from a cold lake and screaming into the blackness around me."

He stopped at Kirstin's indrawn breath. "I know that lake," she whispered painfully.

"As do I." Bryon pulled her close. "That's the lake beneath Siagan," he explained. "I was there when Kavi released the entrapped spirits. They rushed over my head with terrible shrieks. I often hear them in my dreams." His voice dropped low on the last words.

"But why would this man have such visions?" Kavi asked in distress. "Unless," he paused. "Unless he was there when it happened."

"I've seen the phantoms," Natan confessed. "Do you know who the man is, Alek?"

Syros stirred, looking uncomfortable with the talk of magic and visions. "We've tracked Camron and the Red Twins to the valley beyond this one," he told them, adding dryly, "We could have caught him sooner if Alek had informed me as soon as the Red Twins had been taken."

Alek gave him a cool look. "I did what I thought safest for the boys. Camron is unstable at best and may have harmed them if feeling cornered. When I realized he travels slowly, more than likely setting a trap for me, I asked for aid." He turned back to Natan, his expression thawing. "Another person travels with them. We believe he is the one I've been seeing. Perhaps he's calling out for help."

The group fell silent as they considered the possibility. Syros frowned. "Are the Karthagans regaining their powers?"

"They never lost them," Natan said quietly. Kavi met his eyes and turned back to the fire. He opened his hand. Pain flashed across his face and then a small flame came to life in his palm.

"Kavi!" Natan leaned toward him in utter delight. He knew what it meant to him, even such a small accomplishment. Kavi blushed, looking pleased.

"That was nothing. Let's see you turn these rocks to water," Jaden said, making them laugh.

"That's next," Kavi promised with a hint of his old arrogance.

Natan dropped his eyes to the ground, heart pounding. The company fell silent, lost in their own thoughts. When darkness settled around them, Natan slipped into the forest and walked until the stars came out. The beauty of the night eased the vise gripping his chest. Hearing a longed-for step, he turned and was pulled into Kavi's embrace.

"I wasn't sure—"

Kavi's mouth covered his, silencing his words, and he opened readily to the sweet tongue demanding entrance. *Oh gods!* Natan had begun to fear he'd never taste Kavi's kisses again, never have that virile body against his own. His head reeled with how quickly the walls around his heart crumpled, leaving it throbbing, vulnerable, aching for this man he belonged to.

Kavi's lips were warm, soft, curving into a slight smile as his wicked tongue slid along Natan's mouth, teasing, drawing soft moans from him. Unable to resist, Natan surrendered, lacing his fingers behind Kavi's neck and holding on while Kavi's hands slid down his back to pull him tight against him. Natan tilted his head back and Kavi's teeth grazed down his throat, sending shivers through him. Natan shifted, seeking friction.

Kavi raised a face flushed with passion. "I'm so sorry—"

Natan nipped at his lips—they could talk later—and Kavi groaned, crushing their mouths together.

"Tell me what you need," Kavi pleaded when he broke off the kiss, his voice thick with desire. But fondness and joy were there also and the last of Natan's reserve dissolved in his chest. Kavi wanted him. That was enough.

He hid his face on his lover's neck. "I want to feel you, Kavi. Need that closeness with you," he whispered, pulse rushing with the thought of the man buried inside him. Kavi's low moan caught him on fire. He pushed a hand between them, quickly loosening Kavi's pants, startled when Kavi suddenly gripped his wrist.

He looked up and caught his breath. Kavi was beautiful, framed in the light from the rising moon. His eyes danced with mischief. Natan could swear his gaze was tender, loving.

"You'll not go on your knees to me, Mage," Kavi chided, though his impish smile belied his stern tone. "Turn and brace yourself against that tree."

Heat scorched along Natan's nerves, leaving him tingling with anticipation. He glanced at the large pine, then went over and rested his forehead on his arms against its rough bark. His heart lurched when Kavi's breath hitched behind him.

"Are you ready?" Kavi asked as he lifted Natan's hair and kissed his neck, sending shivers through him. Kavi's fingers feathered over him, under his shirt, tugging his pants. Natan whimpered as yearning spiraled inside. Kavi knelt and a warm breath ghosted across his bared skin. Natan's pulse ran riot with exquisite expectancy. Not even in his wildest fantasies had he thought… He cried out, not caring who heard, when that roguish tongue flicked against him, prelude to the pleasures to come.

Chapter Thirty

JADEN WAITED PATIENTLY in the brush before the sun rose, stifling a yawn at the early hour, while Bryon circled around, supposedly to flush the quail in his direction. So far, they'd simply scattered. The predawn light made the covey difficult to see as well. A slight movement to his right caught his attention. Two boys stood on the trail, their golden gaze fixed on him. Jaden rose unsteadily, drawn to them against his will. "Hello?"

A voice spoke behind him, startling him. "Natan."

He hadn't seen the man, and as he turned toward him a heavy weight struck his head, dropping him to his knees. He moaned at the flashing pain in his skull as he struggled to rise, striking out blindly with his fists. But the rock smashed against his temple, and he slumped into blackness, taking the boys' frightened faces with him.

He awoke sometime later, pain throbbing in his head and in his bound arms and legs. Face in the dirt, he could see the sticky pool of blood that had formed against his cheek. Carefully raising his head, he saw the edge of a green meadow. The merry sound of a nearby stream made him desperate to be free. He struggled fiercely against his bindings.

"You shouldn't do that."

The subdued voice made him jump, and Jaden twisted to see a pale Barkuit soldier sitting on the grass beside him.

"Hello?" He wondered if this was the soldier appearing in Alek's dreams. The young man had his face pressed to his drawn-up knees, and his light hair veiled his features.

The soldier drew a shaky breath. "Camron will return soon. You shouldn't anger him."

Jaden was struck by the hopelessness in the man's voice, as if his mind were trapped in some dark labyrinth from which he couldn't escape.

"Why are you with him?"

The soldier flinched at the question and pressed his face all the harder into his knees.

Jaden shifted his stiff body and found fresh sources of pain. "You can leave him, you know."

The lad gave no answer, but Jaden knew he was listening. His whole body had tensed.

"My friends are in the next valley over. Go to Natan. He can protect you."

The soldier raised his head, revealing a face pinched with suffering, but at the moment covered in bewilderment. "Aren't you Natan?"

"No." Jaden understood at last. He wasn't the one Camron wanted.

The soldier struggled to his feet, obviously stricken with fear for him. Suddenly his gaze darted across the clearing. "He comes!" he cried, the terror in his voice shaking Jaden to his core.

"Run," he urged the lad. "Run, now. Find Natan. Go!"

The young man sent one last desperate look at the approaching Karthagan and fled into the forest. Jaden braced himself. Footsteps drew near and the slim man with piercing black eyes crouched at his side. Camron seemed startled when he saw his captive in the morning light and his face mottled with temper. He leaned closer.

"I know you," he hissed. The cold tones rasped along Jaden's nerves and touched his soul, bringing fear.

LOW VOICES SPOKE close by, and Alek opened his eyes to see Syros and Niko by the fire sharpening their knives. He groaned, wanting to sleep, but the sun rose and the coffee did smell good. He reluctantly climbed from his blankets.

"Good morning," he said as he joined them. He reached for the pot simmering in the embers.

"Morning," Niko answered pleasantly. Syros nodded, but his eyes were on the Mage as he approached them, the smile leaving his face.

"What is it?" Natan asked and took the mug of coffee Alek offered, his attention on Syros.

"You left the fire last night and went into the forest alone." Syros stopped but swore with frustration. "Mage, why do you put yourself in such obvious danger? We know Camron is close."

Natan flushed. "You're right. I apologize. I wasn't thinking."

Alek snorted softly. He'd seen Kavi follow Natan into the trees. He enjoyed watching the Mage's blush deepen as Kavi and Kirstin walked by arm in arm, Kavi giving Natan a wide grin. Syros scowled and moved off to join them at the forest's edge, beginning an animated conversation with the Karthagans.

Niko fingered his knife. "Shall I dissuade him from interfering, Mage?"

"Niko!" Natan laughed, but then his laughter died while his face turned to stone. Alek followed his gaze and his heart jumped. A young man stood beneath the trees, his pale hair hanging limply over a face twisted with wretchedness and fear. He took a few hesitant steps toward them, but then he stumbled and covered his face, trembling.

"Cecil." Alek recognized the man from his dreams and walked carefully to him, taking his hands. The stranger's name had leaped into his mind, as did the horrible visions. He brushed the images from the soldier's thoughts as he pushed the hair from his eyes. "Tell me," he demanded, though he kept his voice low.

"Camron has your friend," Cecil choked out. At his words, Syros strode over with the others.

"Are you sure?" Syros asked roughly and Cecil shrank from him. At that moment, Bryon stumbled into camp. Blood streamed from a gash on his forehead, and he impatiently wiped at it. He stopped dead at the sight of the Barkuit soldier.

"You!" He would have grabbed the youth if Niko hadn't stepped between them. "What have you done with him?" he asked around Niko's sturdy frame.

Cecil closed his eyes and once again hid his face in his hands. Soft moans escaped him with each hard breath. Syros turned away in disgust. Impatient, he made for the horses. Bryon had a quick conversation with

Kirstin and followed him.

"Hurry. Camron can't be far," Bryon urged.

Kavi glanced at Natan. At Natan's nod, he ran for the horses with Niko, looking back with pity in his eyes. Alek hesitated by the soldier. "I'd like to stay with him," he said, strangely drawn to the youth. He'd seen Cecil so many times in his dreams. He couldn't leave the lad to suffer alone.

Natan gave him a tiny smile. "Be careful," he warned.

Alek touched his arm in sudden affection. "Use great care, Mage. We don't want to lose you." He continued fiercely, "We need you."

"I can stay," Kirstin hesitated, though Alek knew she wanted to be with Bryon.

"We'll be fine," Alek assured her.

Natan took her hand as they hurried after the others. Alek watched them go and his heart lurched. There would be pain and death that day. Where would it end? He turned to the young man.

"Cecil?" He kept his voice soft. The soldier gave no reply, so Alek touched his hand. "Come to the fire."

He led him to the warm blaze. Cecil knelt and held out his hands to the flames while Alek sat cross-legged beside him. He studied Cecil's pretty face. The risk was great but he had to try. Closing his eyes, Alek opened his mind. A thousand knives stabbed into his brain, and he almost swooned with the exquisite pain of it.

Then his mind broke free. Perhaps the pain was merely a reminder to use care. No need for that. He'd been mad once before and had no desire to return to that hopeless and chaotic state.

He touched Cecil's white face. The lad flinched but opened eyes bleak with horror and lurking nightmares. Alek hesitated, then gathered his strength. The lake was there in the man's mind, the dead faces and terrible screams, with always the rustle of a voice that promised salvation, yet only brought more pain.

"My poor child," Alek murmured. "Look."

He crushed the visions in his hands and withdrew them from Cecil's mind. So easy! He wondered why Camron had never done so before. He looked again at the soldier's delicate features and knew why. Camron wouldn't have resisted the sweet allure of the man. The thought made him ill that such a gentle soul could have been used so cruelly.

"Cecil." He drew the lad's wandering gaze to his hands. The gray mists of the broken nightmares swirled in his cupped palms. He blew lightly, sending them floating into the air, to disappear into nothing. Cecil blinked several times before a smile spread across his face.

"They're gone," he breathed in wonder. He took Alek's hand, awkwardly kissing it as if he couldn't find the words to thank him. Alek's hand shook as he gently withdrew it. He pulled a blanket from the pile and wrapped it around Cecil's shoulders.

"You should try to sleep," he urged, rising to his feet. "I'm going to take a short walk."

Cecil nodded and obediently stretched out on the ground with his face turned to the fire. Alek walked under the trees, gazing in awe at the bright sky. His heart had been stirred by Cecil's trusting touch, leaving him bewildered and excited and fearful. He sent out a quiet prayer that they would survive the day, for the future which had always appeared dim and empty had suddenly brightened. He didn't want to lose it to a madman.

SOMETHING WASN'T RIGHT. They rode close on Bryon's heels as the soldier unerringly followed Camron's trail, but Natan felt an urgent pull toward the east, as if the earth itself called to him in anguish. He slowed his horse, listening, then called out to the others before turning into the forest. He needed to see what Camron had done.

Dread and anger crept into his heart as he rode between the trees. He knew what he would find over the ridge. He'd dreamed of it many times, the torn earth, twisted trees, and bloody ground. Fury blinded him, so he drew his horse to a walk, fighting the desire to chase Camron to the ground. He could easily rip the world apart in that instant if it would give him Camron. How he would make the Karthagan suffer!

His horse snorted and came to a stop. A shudder passed through its large frame. Natan slid from the saddle, holding onto the pommel to steady his shaking body. He was vaguely aware of Kavi slipping from his horse and stumbling to his side as he entered the horror waiting in the glen.

It was as if a child in the throes of temper had been there. The green earth was heaved into rocky mounds. Deep pits of bubbling tar rose to the surface. A hundred trees had been snapped at the trunk and hurled in all directions. Small animals lay where they'd burst apart from an intense pressure on their tender bodies.

Natan grew ill as the nightmare overwhelmed his senses. He wanted nothing more than to crush Camron in his hands, make him feel the pain of the poor creatures dead on the bloody soil.

He fought a rising panic in his breast that seemed to snatch at his breath. He couldn't fight that way. He mustn't fight that way! Sobs choked in his throat. He didn't know what to do. Kavi's whimper at his side broke him. He moved to take him in his arms in a sudden desperate need for human contact. He was in agony.

"Don't," Kavi moaned, horror in his gaze, and pulled from Natan's clasp. Natan dropped his arms instantly. He couldn't take on Kavi's pain as well. He turned from him and lurched across the broken earth, brushing into Kirstin.

"Kavi needs you," he managed to say, and would have passed her, but she touched his face. He cried out as her fingers burned his skin. "No!" He jerked his head away. The fierceness of his voice brought Bryon to their side.

"Natan!" Kirstin cried in pity as he fled from her. "Bryon, go with him. He mustn't be alone when he finds…no!"

Kavi ran to her and, together with Bryon, followed Natan to the edge of the field. Jaden lay bound in a shallow ditch, his body a lump of dark bruises and dangerous contusions.

"Why?" Kavi whispered.

Desolate, Natan climbed down and held his cousin's battered face gently in his hands, saying in a hollow voice, "Cecil mistook him for me. Camron was…angry at the error." He motioned for Kirstin, who helped him cut the bonds from Jaden's ankles and wrists. They laid the tortured body out with great care, and Kirstin began instantly on his wounds while Natan, with bowed head and aching heart, went in search of his cousin's soul.

He found Jaden on the edge of a lush forest. Filling his lungs with the warm pine-scented air, Natan gazed at the ocean glittering below, delighted to be home.

He turned to the man beside him. "Jaden."

"Hello, cousin. It's nice here, isn't it?"

"Yes, it is."

They stood in easy silence while they drank in the peace and beauty of the world. Jaden gave a sudden laugh.

"I have to go, Nattie," he said, and the joy in his voice broke Natan's heart. His face kindled at some vision out of Natan's sight.

Natan shook his head, touching Jaden's arm. "No, Jaden. This is an illusion planted by Camron. He wants you dead to make me suffer. But I sense the life still in you. You're not as injured as he would have you think. Come back! We need you. Please, cousin, stay with us."

Uncertainty crossed Jaden's face. "Must I, Mage?" He looked toward the horizon. "There is peace waiting for me, something lovely, just out of reach…"

Natan's lips firmed. "Come back," he commanded. He'd be damned if Camron took a man before his time. Jaden still had a future, one filled with laughter and friends.

A shudder ran through Jaden, and Natan blinked, returning to himself while Jaden slipped into his tortured body. He looked at Jaden's battered face, unconscious still, when a small moan of anguish escaped him, knowing the pain Jaden would endure before he recovered. He slowly became aware of voices and movement around him, and a hand dropped on his hunched shoulder—Kavi, lending him comfort.

"Natan, we have to go." Niko's voice was raw above him.

He looked beseechingly at his friends. Bryon helped him to his feet as Kirstin approached with a blanket for Jaden's broken body. Kavi drew him away toward Syros and the horses.

"We'll come back. I swear," Niko said, his eyes glittering with anger and grief as he walked beside them.

Bryon called to him from Jaden's side. "Kirstin and I will watch over him, lad. Go. Do what needs to be done."

Natan couldn't answer. He numbly swung into the saddle alongside the others.

They rode until late evening, Syros assuring them their quarry remained only a step ahead. A strange sleepiness crept over Natan as the sun lowered in the sky. He seemed to be falling behind the others as well, but when he tried to call out to them, he found he had no voice. A shiver of dread passed through him, feeling Camron's touch on his mind. He realized the man blocked the others from seeing his plight, and he raged at his helplessness.

Startled suddenly from sleep, he found himself alone in the dim twilight, his horse walking without guidance under towering trees. A faint cry echoed in the air and he drew rein, climbing wearily from the saddle. He followed a deer trail into the thick brush. The Red Twins huddled by a fallen log. Natan approached them cautiously, and seeing their plight, he sat cross-legged on the cold earth.

"What is it, Aiden?" he asked. The boy held Ethan in his arms, his golden eyes full of worry.

"I don't know," Aiden's young voice trembled on the edge of tears. "He won't wake up."

Natan placed his hands on Ethan's waxen face and carefully entered the boy's mind. He came upon Ethan on the Isle of Wind dangling his feet off a bridge over a sparkling stream.

The boy looked at him in dismay. "You shouldn't be here."

Natan shrugged and sat beside him, watching the water flow beneath their feet.

"I remember you."

"And I, you," Natan assured him. "Why do you hide here?"

Ethan cocked his head in thought. Uncertainty crossed his face. "It's very…hard, out there."

"You've left Aiden alone," Natan said quietly. "Come back with me."

Ethan raised his head, alert. "It's too late. Camron comes."

Natan started. He'd been a fool. He tried to pull from the boy's mind, but a clinging lethargy weighted his spirit. Too late, he realized the boy had been poisoned, and he was enmeshed in his sluggish dream. Peering through dreamy eyes, he saw Camron bend over his sprawled body, a heavy club in his hands.

He struggled to free his mind from Ethan's, but the club swung and caught the back of his head with a sickening thump. In desperation, he flung himself from the boy and crashed into his own mind. Blinding pain engulfed him even as he saw Camron raise the club once more. The Karthagan hesitated as shouts rang in the distance. Muttering a furious oath, he kicked Natan in the ribs and fled into the forest.

Natan's head reeled on the edge of unconsciousness. *No!* Camron had to be stopped now, or all would be lost. Gentle hands were suddenly on him. "Niko," he breathed, and the Sennian bent closer to hear. Desperate, Natan reached out and pulled his friend into his arms. Niko struggled, panicked, but Natan's grip was unbreakable.

"No, Mage! Don't do this," Niko begged, frightened as the energy built in Natan.

"It's all right," Natan soothed. "I think this is how it was meant to be all along. Gregor sent me to Sennia to find you. You're so much stronger than I." A sense of peace and rightness filled him even as his gift of energy and power from Gregor poured into his friend. He ran a hand through Niko's springy curls as Niko sobbed on his chest, while his own eyes filled. The engulfing darkness on the edge of his mind reached out and drew him in, and he knew nothing more for a while.

The piping of two small voices brought him back.

"See, Ethan. I told you he was just sleeping."

"Maybe."

Natan opened bleary eyes to see the Red Twins on the ground beside him. He lay on a blanket, trembling to his fingertips. The pain had left him, but the empty numbness that took its place was frightening. He felt a pressure at the back of his head and turned to see Syros's worried gaze on him as he tied off a strip of cloth against his forehead. Kavi knelt at his elbow.

"Hello," Kavi said gently. "How do you feel?"

The tender concern in his voice bothered Natan. He blinked several times but had no answer to give him. He glanced back at the boys.

"Now that he's awake, let's go after Niko," Ethan told his brother, and they jumped to their feet.

"No," Natan whispered, then cleared his throat. The horrors of the isle were still fresh in his mind, and he didn't want the boys anywhere near Niko and Camron. "Will you stay here? We will need your help if Niko…fails."

Ethan looked at him curiously.

"All right." Aiden plopped back down.

"If that's what you want, Mage." Ethan added. Natan winced at his use of the title and turned his face into the blanket, welcoming the darkness waiting for him. He heard the boys speaking as he drifted off.

"Is he dying?" Aiden asked, puzzled.

"No, only sleeping. Let's play," Ethan answered. Natan opened an eye and watched him run off into the forest, his brother at his heels.

Chapter Thirty-One

NIKO STRODE THROUGH the forest as twilight deepened and laughed aloud with the sheer joy of the power that pulsed in his blood and hammered in his heart. It tingled in every cell. He gloried in it, half embarrassed by his inane attempts to create a flame in his hand just weeks before.

He walked with purpose, sensing Camron ahead of him. Once he reached him, there would be no escape for the Karthagan. Natan had been a good teacher, but he was timid. Aubre had died because Natan hesitated to use his gifts against Danul. Niko felt no such compunction with Camron.

His prey darted behind a tree. *Run, little rabbit.* Niko broke into a trot and almost stepped into the hole Camron had set in his path, full of bubbling tar. Leaping over it, Niko's thoughts turned to a cold resolve. He focused his gaze across the treetops and wind tore through the branches. Smaller trees toppled. He heard Camron's yelp of surprise as he was nearly crushed by several.

"Come out, little one," Niko invited mockingly.

Fire roared over the broken timber toward Niko, and he called to the sky. Clouds formed, and in an instant rain poured in torrents from the thundering firmament. Camron appeared across the clearing from Niko, his face livid with fury.

"So, the Mage sent you to die in his stead?" the Karthagan snarled. "So be it."

He glanced up and Niko's hair rose on end as a sizzling bolt of lightning stuck the earth between them. The percussion knocked both men to the ground, their nerves shattered by the deafening boom.

Niko scrambled to his feet in the slippery mud, rushing toward his fallen enemy. A blackened trench ran the field where the bolt had plowed the soil, and he dodged around it. Camron regained his feet. A strange crawling sensation entered Niko's head as Camron threw up his hands.

He knew that game. Niko concentrated, sending his thoughts back at Camron. For an instant they were held suspended, their powers equal. Then the Karthagan's body jolted. Niko firmed his thoughts, and Camron screamed, then began to tear at his hair. His body jerked again, and he clutched at his chest, his face white with agony as he dropped to his knees. A look of utter disbelief crossed his tortured features as, with one last sharp cry, he slumped to the earth.

Niko stared at the twitching body at his feet. A slow frown replaced his triumphant smile. He nudged the body with his boot but there was no response. Stepping closer, he stared in shock. Blood poured from Camron's nose, ears, and eyes as if the pressure in his head had burst out. Unexpectedly, Camron blinked, and Niko knelt at his side.

Bewilderment crossed the Karthagan's face. "Father?" he asked, his voice that of a child. Niko drew a quick breath as he realized Camron had fallen into his past. He sat in the mud and pulled the shaking body into his arms.

"My head hurts," Camron lisped.

"I know it does." Niko soothed the lines of pain from his sweat-drenched brow. "Try to sleep."

"Daddy, I'm afraid!" Camron cried out. His body arched as a tremor tore through him, and then he fell back into Niko's arms.

Niko held him, numb, as Camron died. Was this the person he'd hated moments ago? Looking at the bloody face, he realized he hadn't known him at all. He had no knowledge of Camron's past nor his father nor what madness had brought him to this point. Niko took in the torn earth and shuddered. His thoughts turned to Natan, who'd always been careful with the use of his power.

In his frustration, Niko had often thought his friend cowardly, but Natan had been exactly right in his fear. Niko had taken a life that all the energy of the earth couldn't restore. He wondered if there had been a way to rescue Camron from his madness. Natan and Kirstin had done it for others. Now it was too late.

He picked Camron up with care and laid him in the shallow trench torn by the lightning, folding the earth over him.

On his way back to the others, he passed a small stream, plunging in to wash Camron's blood from his hands and garments. Niko shivered in his wet clothing but gave no further thought to it as he joined his companions in the clearing. Syros left the fire and strode over to him.

"Is it done?" Syros asked, his expression troubled. Niko gave him a sharp nod and would have moved on, but Kavi came up and put a restraining hand on his arm.

"I felt the moment Camron died. You did the right thing, Niko," Kavi said urgently, and Niko felt himself crumble inside. He closed his eyes and fought the sobs that rose in his throat. Kavi put an arm around his shaking shoulders, holding him close. Niko withdrew from him after a moment and gripped his hand. The desperate knot in his chest had been loosened by the contact, so he could think clearly again.

"Thank you," he said. Kavi nodded.

He went to Natan's prone body by the fire and knelt, touching his friend's white face. So much of the Mage had passed to him along with Gregor's knowledge. Natan's pure spirit filled him with awe.

"How is he?"

"He woke for a short time but has been sleeping heavily since." Kavi offered. "The Red Twins assure me he's well." He motioned to the children playing nearby and they ran up.

"Boys," Niko said in greeting. They looked at him gravely.

Ethan reached up and touched Niko's cheek as he obligingly bent down. "You have Natan's powers now, don't you?"

Niko nodded.

"Good. They made him sad." Ethan jerked his thumb at Natan. Aiden pulled on his arm and they ran off. Niko frowned. The boys had power, and combined, they could be dangerous. They would need looking after.

He turned back to the others. "We should move Natan from here," he told them.

Syros agreed with a shudder. "We can go back to camp. Alek will be wanting news, and Natan may need Kirstin's help."

"And you need dry clothes," Kavi said firmly as Niko began to shake. Niko smiled at him, his first step toward normalcy. They gathered the horses and Syros carefully lifted Natan into Kavi's arms as he reached from the saddle. He still slept, so Kavi held the trembling body close to his chest. Syros and Niko took the twins on their horses, and they thankfully left the clearing.

Niko set a slow pace, not wanting to jar Natan any more than necessary. After a time, Syros trotted ahead, probably to warn the camp of their approach. It was early morning before Niko spotted the fire. Alek stopped his pacing as they rode in, and Cecil scrambled to his feet to help with the horses.

Kavi handed Natan down to Syros, then dismounted and hurried to the fire, taking his slumbering lover back into his arms on a quickly thrown blanket. Niko shook his head at Alek's concerned look. "The Red Twins promise he's only sleeping."

"Yes." Aiden jumped into Alek's arms as Alek settled at the fire, pulling Ethan down with them. He tousled their black hair and smiled with pleasure when Ethan said a quiet hello to him.

"What happened?" he asked the boy.

Ethan shrugged with a tinge of arrogance. "I followed Natan out of my dreams."

Niko looked to where Kirstin sat with Jaden a few steps from the fire, Bryon standing over them. "How is he?"

Kirstin glanced up. "He weathered the trip here well enough, though he's badly bruised and will be stiff with pain for many days. I found no internal injuries, which is a blessing. We'll take him home in the morning."

After a necessary meal provided by Cecil, Syros recommended that everyone get some sleep and moved a few paces away, unrolling his blankets. Natan moaned softly in his dreams, so Kavi stroked his cheek, then played idly with the chestnut hair escaping the cloth binding his damaged head. He looked beseechingly at Niko across the fire. "Will he be well?"

Niko shrugged, not wanting to face the terrible possibility. "Gregor died while passing his gifts on to him. Let us hope Natan proves stronger."

Alek gave Niko a keen look from where he sat by Cecil and the sleeping children, then took a deep breath. "May I?" he asked, motioning to Natan. "I'd like to seek for any break in the hard bone."

Niko watched closely as Alek put his hands on Natan's face, feeling the prickle of energy in the air. Alek moved his fingers over the wounds, searching. Blood stained the bandages. "The tissue has swollen, but there are no fissures," he said at last.

Niko let out a held breath, then found himself caught in the gaze of hazel eyes dark with pain.

"Niko?" Natan's voice was a soft whisper. Niko murmured in assent. Distress touched Natan's white face, his eyes wide and tormented. "I feel like a part of me has died!" He turned his face into the blanket and wept brokenly. Kavi leaned into him and gripped his hands while Niko bent close to his ear.

"I know it does, Natan. I know," he soothed while tears blurred his eyes. He recalled the exquisite joy he felt as the energies of life surged through him. He couldn't conceive of giving them up willingly, as Natan had done. He whispered comforting words in Natan's ear and sent his soft voice into Natan's thoughts, calming his distress.

Chapter Thirty-Two

NATAN BLINKED IN the bright morning sunlight and sat up, then immediately regretted the movement, and Kavi had to hold him while he was violently ill.

"Thank you," he murmured, embarrassed, after the world stopped spinning and the nausea passed.

"Go slowly, love. You need time to heal."

Natan grunted. He glanced across the camp at Jaden, who was sitting up as well, but leaning heavily against Kirstin while she held a water flask to his lips.

"Bryon, I think it's time you took your people home," Syros commented from where he stood by the fire.

Bryon added more wood to the flames. "I was thinking the same. Basal will need to be told what has happened. I'll take Alek and the boys to Karthag, along with Kirstin and the injured men. Niko can take the ship to

Sennia from there, and we'll go on to Nagal."

"I hope you'll allow me to escort you," Syros said, grimly watching the fire. He stated after a moment, "The Karthagans are regaining their abilities."

"It appears so."

Natan watched the two soldiers scrutinize each other.

"Be on your guard," Syros said.

Bryon nodded curtly. "And we may have trouble with Lord Fredrik as well. Remember the plot against Kavi and his hatred of all Karthagans?"

Syros agreed. "It will be an interesting year."

Alek and Cecil joined them, and Syros outlined their plans. Cecil stood in the background, uncertain.

"What of me, sir?" he asked when Syros finished.

The regent gave him a brief glance. "I assume you'll return to Siagan. I have a message for Lieutenant Davis."

"Yes, sir." Cecil bowed, but Natan saw his face blanch.

Kirstin hurried over. "My lord regent."

"My lady?"

"Forgive me, but I don't believe Cecil is ready to return to Siagan. He suffered at Camron's hands as much, or more, than any of us."

"As you think best." Syros inclined his head, then gave the young soldier a perplexed look.

Alek regarded Cecil as well. "You could come with us," he offered diffidently. "Karthag is near the sea, and I'm planning to expand the harbor and construct a small outpost there. I should like a man I could trust to oversee the project for me."

"You're redoing the harbor?" Bryon asked curiously.

"Yes. And building several more schooners, with Nagal and Barkuit's permission. My idea is to harvest the part of the Dakon Forest belonging to Karthag for its hardwood and export it to Sennia. And to the Northern Territory, of course, if you're interested."

"Indeed we are," Syros told him. "As you know, our only hardwood is here in the east, and this land has hardly been explored. Let me know when your ships are ready, and we'll gladly do business."

"I know several excellent shipwrights that could use the work," Niko put in. "They've assisted in the building of all Sennia's cargo vessels."

"I think that settles everything." Bryon shook Alek's hand. "Well done, sir. I'll inform Basal of your plans."

Cecil watched the exchange and seemed to catch something of the excitement in the air. He stepped forward. "I should like to help you, my lord Alek, if you could use me."

"It's done, then." Alek smiled at Cecil and shook his hand.

Natan noticed the glad look in his eyes, and it warmed his heart. He cleared his throat, coming to a decision. "I'm going home with Niko to Sennia. My children are waiting for me."

Syros raised his brows but said nothing. Bryon looked troubled. "Are you sure, Natan? We miss you here."

Natan nodded, hiding a wince at a stab of pain. "I'd like to spend a little time with you before I go, of course, but it's where I'm needed," he said, hoping with all his heart it was true. It was where he was happiest, anyway. Kavi studied him and Natan sighed when he made no comment. Damn, Natan should have talked his plans over with him first. This would be the second time he left without considering his lover's needs. Maybe he deserved to be alone. Though part of him had hoped Kavi would ask him to stay.

They soon had the camp packed and were on their way. Every hour of the three days ride to Karthag became a nightmare to Natan. His head alternately throbbed, then burned, and he couldn't sleep from the relentless pain in his body. Kirstin watched him closely, in time making him share a horse with Kavi or one of the others, as he would often grow disoriented or his mind would wander.

He was with Niko the evening they arrived at Karthag. He'd been in and out of consciousness the last hour and opened bleary eyes as Niko handed his exhausted body down to Kavi. Alek led them directly to his own room.

"It's coolest here," he explained at their questioning look. Kavi tucked Natan in the bed with an intense care that would have embarrassed him if he hadn't been so tired.

Kavi bent to his ear. "Kirstin is settling Jaden in the infirmary and promised to come check on you shortly."

Natan nodded, letting the relentless waves of sleep wash over him. Nightmares haunted his dreams, an endless chase of some dark shadow through the forest, and the morning came all too soon.

Everyone rode to the harbor to see him and Niko off. Syros came up to him as the dory was readied to take them to the ship and gravely shook his hand.

"We'll miss you, Natan. Please come visit us often," the regent told him earnestly.

Natan gave him a rueful smile. "I'm sorry, my lord. It seems I can no longer fulfill my debt to you."

Syros's expression altered, sorrow mellowing his piercing gaze.

"There was never any debt between us, Mage. Only friendship and respect. Go with my good wishes, Natan."

Natan inclined his head, his heart warming. "What will you do now, Syros?"

Syros gave a painful laugh. "Try to be a good leader to my people. I will go to Kangar and beg my lady's forgiveness. I can see no happiness in my future without her."

"Go with all luck, Syros. You are a good man." Natan flicked a glance at Bryon standing near. "Bryon, make sure Sharana knows I've said that, please."

Kavi shifted at Natan's side, his mouth set in a stubborn line. "You didn't ask, but I'm going with you, at least to see you settled happily before I trust you with these strangers."

Niko snorted at his words, but Natan noticed he was smiling with suppressed excitement. "It's Corha, isn't it? You want to see her again. Show off your new talents," he teased.

Niko blustered but Kavi laughed outright. Natan startled at the delightful sound, wishing he was the one to make Kavi laugh. He looked at his shaking hands and gripped them tightly, moving toward the dory. What did he have to offer him? How could he convince Kavi to stay with him?

It was a struggle to cross the sand to the waiting boat when every step brought pain. Niko helped him climb over the side of the dory, and he leaned his weary body against Kavi as Niko sat opposite. It shocked him when Jaden climbed into the boat as well.

Sitting beside him, Niko raised a brow and Jaden winked. The bruising on his face was turning yellowish, though his lips were still slightly swollen.

"Why are you…?" Natan began.

"Surprise, cousin." Jaden gave him a smile, but grimaced as it pulled his lips. "Syros asked me to join you. He and Bryon both want to come but are needed here. They agreed a Belegan should be with you, as a representative of our country, and since I'm known to all…"

Niko snorted. "More likely you pestered them until they gladly agreed to let you come with us." He picked up the oar beside him and nodded with his chin to the one on Jaden's side. "Make yourself useful," he grumbled, though a teasing light was in his eyes.

Jaden inclined his head. Natan drew a contented breath, happy to have his cousin with them as they were rowed to the ship. It was nice to be at sea again, but it wasn't until the second day of the voyage that he recovered his spirits. He couldn't help it. It was a glorious day with a steady breeze speeding him home. Kavi stood by his side, his face raised to the tangy sea air. His hair danced around his head and occasionally brushed Natan's lips. Natan's heart filled. He decided to make the most of the short time he might have with him. He stepped closer and thrilled as Kavi leaned back against him.

"You were right, Natan. There's nothing more wonderful than the sea," Kavi murmured.

There was an exaggerated groan beside them. "I think I'm feeling ill," Niko said, and rolled his eyes at them, leaning far over the railing.

Jaden threw several damp rags at him. "You may as well help me clean the deck while you're here."

As usual, the young men worked alongside the sailors on the voyage. Natan gave Kavi a playful shove away and continued with his chore of polishing the brass work.

Niko tossed Kavi a rag. "You may help," he said, laughing aloud as Kavi made him a bow and complied. The friends worked in amiable silence for a time.

Niko rose and stretched from the deck he'd been scrubbing and smiled as the sun and wind kissed his cheeks. Natan saw the intense joy that lit his face, and knew he felt the stirring of power inside him. Pain fierce as a knife's thrust stabbed his heart. Kavi heard his indrawn breath, but Natan turned from him in shame, unable to hide his jealousy.

"Natan?" Kavi put a hand on his arm as Natan hung his head.

"It hurts, Kavi, not to have my powers," he confessed a grief never far from the surface. He straightened and took a steadying breath.

"Well, I can no longer fly," he admitted. "But I can come close."

He felt Kavi's gaze as he sought out the deck officer. At first the man refused, clearly not wanting to risk his safety.

"I know what I'm doing," Natan assured him.

"I'll take him," Daran spoke from where he worked close by. Natan's smile broadened. Daran was the young sailor he'd met on his first voyage to Sennia.

"It's your neck," the officer said, and the limber youth scrambled up the rigging with a whoop. Natan followed more slowly, ignoring a hitch of pain, as they climbed to the crow's nest. He swung himself into the basket and spread his arms wide as the sea unfolded below him, laughing in sheer joy as the ship rode a deep swell.

The sailor looked at him with approval. "It's as if we're part of the sky."

"Thank you, Daran."

"I'm at your disposal, Mage," the young man bowed, and Natan found that the title didn't sting so badly on top of the world.

Chapter Thirty-Three

THE EVENING OF the sixth day brought them into Mennon's large harbor. Natan drew a deep breath, excited to be home. A messenger handed him a note on the dock from Mirah, and he insisted they go at once to Aubre's house where his children were waiting.

"Papa!" Kayle and Tillie flew off the porch into Natan's eager arms, and they fell in a heap on the long grass. He tickled them mercilessly, even submitted to Tillie's wet kisses on his cheeks. His friends watched in amusement as he climbed to his feet with the children clinging around his legs, and he motioned them to the comfort waiting inside.

Mirah and her father, Tolban, had prepared a meal for them, so the travelers sat eagerly around the table exchanging news. While they talked, Natan noticed Jaden's gaze slipping to Mirah time and again and witnessed her soft blushes in return.

"What of you, Mirah?" Jaden asked during a pause in the conversation. "I know next to nothing about you. Who are you, girl?"

Mirah laughed softly. "Let me think. My mother died of fever when I was a small child, and I've helped Father keep house ever since. And I take care of Gregor and Elsa's children when Natan is gone, and…

"No." Jaden cocked his head, studying her. "Not that. There's something more to you." He looked closely at her flushing face. "What do you like most to do?"

Mirah shrugged. "I paint a little."

"Of course, you do," Jaden nodded, an admiring grin spreading over his face. Mirah looked shyly away, and Natan smiled to himself, happy for them.

It was the beginning of a pleasant week for Natan, either fishing with Mika or just pottering around the house as the weakness from his injuries slowly left him. Niko had gone on to Sambola to pay his respects to the Vice-King and to see Corha. Natan wondered if his friend would reveal to them he now carried Gregor's powers.

Mika and he had brought in a large catch of fish at the end of the week and decided to do some much-needed repairs in lieu of fishing the next day. Natan drew in a deep breath of the fresh sea air, enjoying the morning sunlight as he sat on the beach in the midst of the net he was mending. He hadn't seen much of Kavi, as the Karthagan was exploring the surrounding countryside, but he always had a smile for Natan these days. Natan could get used to seeing them, but hoarded them away in his memory, in case his lover didn't stay. He soon grew tired of being guarded, though, and returned Kavi's smiles with brilliant ones of his own.

The sun grew hot as the morning advanced, and Natan finally had to strip down to the short pants he wore on his dory. Intent on a stubborn knot in the netting, he didn't realize anyone approached him until Tillie jumped into his lap.

"Hi, Papa," she chirped.

"Hello, darling. What are you doing here?" He rose and swung the tiny girl onto his shoulder. Kavi waited as he stepped carefully over the netting, ignoring the tangles Tillie's small feet had made in the fine mesh. Natan's heart pounded inconveniently as he drew near to Kavi.

Kavi returned his smile. "Good morning." Natan was growing brown and strong in the sea air and sunshine, and Kavi gave him an approving look, his gaze kindling. Natan's face warmed as he retrieved his tunic from the sand where he'd thrown it.

"What's this, Papa?" Tillie touched the scar on his chest as he set her down.

"Nothing, dear," he said as he pulled the shirt over his mop of curls. "It doesn't even hurt anymore."

"Good." Tillie ran off at the sound of voices and joined her brother. Natan watched, puzzled, as a group of people walked toward him.

"Kendra? What's going on?" he asked when they reached him.

"The children wanted to see you. As did we." She motioned to the members of the company who still gathered at Aubre's house once a week.

"You haven't finished your story, Mage." Kam pulled at his hands. Natan shot a startled look at Kendra. She wouldn't purposely hurt him, would she?

She touched his arm. "You still have a lot to teach us, Natan. And with or without Gregor's powers, we still love you. Now come and greet your friends."

Deeply moved, he joined the group, their faces brightening as he spoke to each in turn. He caught Kavi's gaze on him and arched a brow in question, but Kavi merely smiled, though Natan caught the look of pride on his face. Natan turned back to sit among the children he loved. "Now, where was I?" he began.

He spent the afternoon in their company, then took a long walk along the shore, happy to have kept his place with the Sennian people. Mika met him on the way back with the news that Niko had returned and invited them all to dinner. "A ship is sailing to Belega in the morning. Apparently, your friend Kavi is taking it home, so it's a farewell party as well."

They continued up the beach, Natan fighting a rising panic in his breast. It was too soon. He wasn't ready to say goodbye. But then he hadn't asked Kavi to stay either.

He took a deep breath as he looked at the house he shared with Niko, though Niko now owned Aubre's house as well and spent his time between the two places. A bleakness swept him when he thought of the coming separation he might have with Kavi. The days would be utterly lonely if he was by himself. But he wouldn't let that happen. Firming his lips, he climbed the stairs, only to stop in the doorway.

Sunlight flooded into the kitchen, shining on the faces of his friends gathered at the table. They were laughing at some remark Niko had made, and Natan imprinted the happy scene in his mind. His gaze unerringly found Kavi across the room. Tillie had placed herself on his knee and was playing with his dark hair. Kavi gave him an uncertain smile, seeming troubled.

Natan closed his eyes in pain.

"There you are, Papa."

Natan reached down and scooped Kayle up in his arms.

"Stop, that tickles." Kayle squirmed as Natan hid his face in the boy's hair. Kayle jumped down. "Come on. Mirah made a cake, and Tillie won't let us have any until you're there."

"By all means, lead the way," Mika said. Natan was greeted warmly on all sides as Kayle dragged him to the head of the table and sat him down.

"You're here, Papa," Tillie said. "I made them wait for you, even though he wanted to begin without you." She sent a fierce glare at Jaden.

"Ah, yes." Natan pulled the little girl into the crook of his arm. "Jaden's always been greedy of his cake." The cousins grinned at each other amidst the general laughter. Natan searched for Mirah. She sat halfway down the table. "The cake looks delicious. Thank you."

Mirah gave him a friendly nod. They had a merry dinner, then exited to the beach afterward, Niko and Jaden gathering driftwood for a fire. Natan waylaid Kavi as he came out onto the porch, smiling up at him from the bottom of the steps. "Will you walk with me?"

"Of course." Kavi trotted down the stairs and gave him his hand. It was a beautiful evening, so they strolled along the white sand in companionable silence, watching the waves break on the shore. The sun had begun to set behind them and their long shadows marched into the sea.

"Will you be happy?" Kavi asked unexpectedly.

The question caught Natan off guard. He couldn't look at him. After tomorrow, if Kavi left, he didn't think he'd ever be happy again.

"I'm content," he managed. They sat in the sand, Natan laying back with his hands behind his head, intensely aware of the man beside him. Kavi moved restlessly, and Natan rolled to his side, propped on an elbow.

His friend's expression looked pensive as he gazed at the sea. Without thought, Natan picked up his hand.

Kavi turned to him, a tentative smile curling his lips as he ran his fingers through Natan's wavy hair. "I've been waiting all week for you to talk to me. Isn't there something you wish to ask?"

His touch set Natan on fire. He wondered if Kavi would let him kiss him. Recalling the last time they were together, he risked a look into Kavi's eyes, which shone bright with anticipation, and was lost. He pulled Kavi to him, trapping him beneath his body. Natan kissed him in growing desperation, unable to hide his love and his need for him. Kavi's sweet kiss in return broke his heart.

"Kavi," he choked out and buried his face in his silken hair. "Darling, I know I'm not…" He tried again. "I think we could be happy together. Kavi, I'd give my life to make you happy! If you would stay with me."

Kavi raised Natan's face and Natan's heart lurched at the hope in his expression. "After the way I betrayed you, you still want me? Be sure, Natan. Once I give my heart, it's for always."

"Camron is the only one I hold accountable. Kavi, you know you hold my own heart." Natan lowered his head, murmured against his soft lips. "If you give me a little time, maybe you could learn to care—"

Kavi put a finger on Natan's mouth, stopping his words. "It's too late for that. You claimed my attention from the moment I first saw you, as lovely and pure as the forest you lived in. In fact," he paused to twine his arms around Natan. "I've fallen in love with you. If you give *me* time, I'll prove to you that you've stolen my heart."

"All the time you need," Natan whispered as he touched the velvet skin of Kavi's cheek, afraid to even breathe. "Are you certain?" he asked, but without waiting for a reply, sought his lips. The fervor of Kavi's response was all he could wish for, and Natan drew an elated breath and kissed him again, his beautiful Karthagan, knowing he'd found his home.

Acknowledgements

Thank you, NineStar Press, for giving my magical world a home, and also a special thank you to my amazing editor, BJ Toth, for her knowledge and expertise, and the insightful suggestions that helped me dig deeper.

About the Author

Dianne is the author of paranormal/suspense, fantasy adventure, m/m romance, the occasional thriller, and anything else that comes to mind. She lives in the beautiful Willamette Valley of Oregon with her incredibly patient husband, who puts up with the endless hours she spends hunched over the keyboard letting her characters play. She says Oregon's raindrops are the perfect setting in which to write. There's something about being cooped up in the house with a fire crackling on the hearth and a cup of hot coffee warming her hands, which kindles her imagination.

Currently, Dianne works as a floral designer in a locally owned gift shop. Which is the perfect job for her. When not writing, she can express herself through the rich colors and textures of flowers and foliage.

Email

diannewrites2@hotmail.com

Facebook

www.facebook.com/diannehartsock

Instagram

www.instagram.com/diannehartsock

Website

www.diannehartsock.wordpress.com

Other NineStar books by this author

Shelton in Love

Birthday Presents

Luka

Little Match Girl

The Mirror Maze

Callum's Fate

Sweet William

Coming Soon from Dianne Hartsock

The Red Twins

The Karthagans, Book Two

There was a commotion on the street leading from the castle, and silver bells chimed on the air as the procession approached the tree.

Tessa came first in the black and silver livery of her grandfather Kayden's house, and the people clapped and cheered for her youth and prettiness. Little bells adorned her ankles and wrists and twined in her hair, and she laughed gaily at the bright day and the happy crowd.

Kavi and Kirstin walked arm in arm in the respective colors of their houses with smiles on their faces. Kirstin's fair hair streamed behind her and caught the sun like a maiden's, the black and silver of her dress hugging her slim form.

Natan's heart rushed at the sight of Kavi, handsome in the black and crimson of his father's house. Every inch a Karthagan lord, from his proud bearing to the slight arrogance on his face, the amused lift of his full lips. He bent to whisper something to Kirstin, who covered her mouth on a wide smile. Natan assumed he'd said something biting about the crowd, and though he shouldn't admire Kavi for it, it was this very confidence and wicked humor he found dangerously attractive. He wanted to kiss that sarcastic mouth into submission.

Silence suddenly fell. The Red Twins were there, and their black and silver livery gleamed, their eyes bright golden disks in the sunlight. A ripple of apprehension passed through the people. Natan knew they had not forgotten the devastation on the Isle of Wind, and these proud lords filled all who saw them with foreboding. Ethan's head lifted in arrogance and a mocking smile twisted his lips.

Aiden strode in silence at his side, the leather showing his muscular body, his face somber and distant, the dark hair loose down his back. The Karthagan people fell grave. He appeared a warrior on his way to the battlefield.

A murmur rose as a last and lonely figure trailed the twins. Alek wore unrelieved black, his hands bound with silk at his back. A sheer scarf covered his eyes. His stride was loose and sure, his head tilted proudly as if daring them to do their worse. A shout went up at his boldness, and then cheers and affectionate cries filled the air for the well-loved man.

Alek paused, clearly startled, but Natan wasn't surprised by the crowd's reaction. The Karthagans knew who had saved them from the isle and brought them to their present home, giving them a new beginning. Alek's bow swept the ground, and he hurried on, tears glittering behind the silk.

www.ninestarpress.com

www.facebook.com/ninestarpress

www.facebook.com/groups/NineStarNiche

www.twitter.com/ninestarpress

www.instagram.com/ninestarpress

bsky.app/profile/ninestarpress.bsky.social

www.threads.net/@ninestarpress

www.ingramcontent.com/pod-product-compliance
Lightning Source LLC
Chambersburg PA
CBHW060616100726
47907CB00006B/1644